They discovered the impossible,

but the truth is harder to find.

Ordering Information: For quantity sales details and orders by U.S. trade bookstores and wholesalers, please contact Novabook Publishing at info@novabook.us or 323-871-0889.

First published in the United States by Novabook Publishing 2013.
10 9 8 7 6 5 4 3 2 1

Novabook Publishing
Los Angeles
www.novabook.us

ISBN 978-0-9894896-0-7

eXit PoiNt

A Novel by

Michael Jeffery Blair

NOVABOOK

Novabook Publishing

Exit Point

CONTENTS

†

A new God arose

His face electric with radiance

His eyes filled with sacred numbers

His voice flowing forth all the knowledge of the universe

His was a deafening roar that made men humble

And meek before Him

- I -

Mirage

"He's come up with something," the man sitting in the darkness said excitedly. His voice had a mature certainty that marked him as someone with a strong vested interest. His sweating hands gripped the cool arms of a buttery leather chair, "I don't know what it is yet...but it's something extraordinary."

Lights hovered with a dim glow down a long hallway. Cool, dry air hissed through ducts nearly silent. It was filled with deep greens; forest lush leaving the impression of nature...burnished brass and copper fixtures, amber glows, fine wood veneer beneath footsteps echoing from some unseen stranger passing. It was only one hallway in the Network's massive compound of structures that thrust up out of the city in sublime and muted brilliance. Inaccessible from the outside, its entrances and exits were guarded both electronically and by the only known predator vicious enough yet malleable and tractable enough to use for any purpose. Humans.

A woman spoke in a throaty voice halfway through the door, "What do you mean something?" She closed the door to the dim outside light and entered the plush, lightless room walking up to the glass looking intently at the huge control complex and the dark figure who presided over it.

They were in a room at the end of the hall beyond closed doors where huge, flat video screens bathed the darkness with flickering blue light and artificial, electronic colors. A frail, hunched figure sat at a vast quantum computer console, hands flying over the switches and keys in a euphoric dance he alone was witness to. He recalled great masters of lost centuries who themselves had sat at grander consoles of huge pipe organs and swept their fragile, mortal hands across the ebony and ivory eliciting god like crescendos that lifted all those within hearing on wings for an ascension into heaven prepared or not. The thought infused him with energy. Tiny lights from the switches and dials and liquid crystal displays reflected in the man's eyes as he knew he would soon affect people far more deeply.

Behind the glass in the darkened chamber beyond were other men. They were a different sort, another breed, more cunning, perhaps more adapted as if they were a species further on the evolutionary ladder who had not needed to pass through any perceivable strata on their sojourn to perfection but had arrived all at once in full possession of things that others sought in vain to hold. They had wealth and position and too many years of living well for good health. "It's happening... right now it's happening!" A younger man replied with a masked hostility. "God, it's so new... you'll see, just wait. It's like nothing you've ever known!"

"What the hell are you talking about?" Peering through the glass Roxanne was beginning to get curious, very curious. Whoever was at the console was oblivious to her, and so she pressed closer until her breath fogged the ice-like surface. The monitors flickered with rapidly changing images designed to grab attention and hold it with short vignettes never giving a full view, but leaving the completion of the scene to the viewer. "If I could hear it maybe..." wondering if she was missing the point or if they were just entertaining another anal management idea. The images that fled across the monitors were, she admitted to herself, striking, the colors saturated and lush, the pictures, mostly people, computer generated she knew but none the less beautiful and vital, yet nothing extraordinary, truly extraordinary like what they all wished for and worked for in programming to take the network into the next psychovideo level. It was the unknown she was after, and even if it were to present itself she wondered if she would know it or like other discoveries would it take a genius to see? She could picture herself in their place though, those electronic phantoms who flitted across the screen that were the result of computerized manipulations of 3D, holographic video that, despite her full knowledge of their creation, had begun to take on lives of their own often minimizing and dominating her own existence. Characters in the void that lived and breathed in the mind. This was normal. Expected. Everyone watched. It was as if she could feel the winds that brushed across the images, the wisp of electronic hair that she tried to brush away from her own face, as if it were real, as if she were…suddenly a violent embrace upon the screen as two virtual people grasped each other in passion. Roxanne felt uncomfortable and looked back into the darkness at the men who she knew, though nearly forgotten, were also witness.

Then it happened. The pressure of fingers on her arm that made her look to see who was there, the feeling of a kiss on her neck, the sudden blueness of the sky and a weightlessness, a sheer, frantic exuberance. Her knees nearly buckled the wave of sensation was so strong. A thick, sickly sweet feeling of desire that overcame her senses and knotted her stomach. And there were whispers, words, though she forgot them immediately and they passed like conversation among friends without consequence. Then she was staring into the darkness where the men were seated. Someone called her name.

"Roxanne?" he said distantly. "Did you see it? Did you feel it?"

"I don't know what I felt. Like I was hit by a car, I felt like I was…"

"…there, right? Transported…"

"More like I was experiencing it at the maximum, full blast. Everything was amplified. I've never had emotions that strong."

"That's it! I told you! Now you'll believe me. Some god dammed discovery huh?"

The mysterious figure on the other side of the glass looked down at the computer touchscreen into a familiar landscape. The function and purpose of each of the keys, switches and dials before him registered with symbolic meaning He thought of it all like a city. His city. It was the place he inhabited most, more than any place outside the control room; his home, the street, the sky, more than his own thought universe and memories. In fact, like most inhabitants of the Earth the virtual city was his home, yet with him it was more intimate, more essential as he was one of its creators. Its functions supplanted his own functions as a living being and gave him breadth and space and meaning where he perceived he had none before. Lent its color to a monochrome, its music to the silence of his heartbeats.

Once before the quantum computer had gone down, its digital images dissipated to the virtual ether while the photons and electrons slowly abandoned the printed circuits and optical fiber and cables bringing the entire system to complete blackness. For those few, brief minutes he ceased to exist. Darkness overtook him against his will, without any consent and simply erased his memory as finely as if it were the computer's own held in electronic equilibrium only mimicking the tension of a living being. The parameds had to revive him with a shock to the heart. This was the reason he was perfect for the job. Images came and went at his command, sounds were brought up and sweetened, universes were created with his every breath and transmitted to millions. He had finally devised a fail-safe back up mechanism in case the main quantum computer should go down again in the form of an independently powered, portable optical unit that automatically duplicated all files that raced through the central processor and would immediately switch on for his use within milliseconds of a blackout. This was a great comfort to him. He carried the portable unit with him everywhere and laid it beside him on the bed at night to console him for dreams that never came.

But of love, he knew nothing. It was a concept without meaning; not the bitterness of forsaken love, nor the cold remembrance of a love that was wrongly wasted, not the rage of betrayal nor the fond, fading, beautiful sadness of unrequited emotions. It was as a draft of smoke in a turbulent wind and perhaps only in a former lifetime might its embers be found coolly lying on burnt and salted ground.

"You felt it too?"

"Of course I felt it. You think I'm dead? Jesus!" Then the man grumbled as if apologizing for some imagined shortfall. "It's not complete yet, he's still working on it."

"What the hell is it?"

The man rose from his chair and walked forward to the glass looking into the control room where the strange figure was still furiously at work in total ignorance of the events taking place just behind him. "Photonics," he said.

A voice from the couch, "We really don't know yet. He's discovered something though, a new light particle he says. Over at R&D they say that's impossible. But still..."

"It can't be explained." The man at the glass spoke raising his fingers to the cold, smooth surface to touch the unnamed. "We wanted you to see this and perhaps toss a few ideas around as to how we might use it."

"It's incredible! It's unbelievable!!" she replied.

"You can see a slight burst of light if you look away you know," glancing at her with sly wonder from the corner of his eye, "that is if you're not looking directly at the screen. It's unusual, nearly outside the visual spectrum; it seems to have something to do with the new organic-iridium light emitting diodes, OILED carbon to you–only two millimeters thick, but the light radiation is intense. They were made in a complete vacuum so there is not even the slightest resistance inside and it seems to amplify the emissions somehow."

"But only at certain wavelengths. We have control, that's what's so exciting."

"Does anyone else know about this?" she asked keenly, suddenly, with full attention and a slightly malicious smile.

The man at the glass looked back at the older man in the chair, "No," he replied, "no one at all outside this room. Except him..." They all looked at the apparition seated at the control panel, hands still passing across the keys, still absorbed. "...and he's not talking to anyone."

"I hope not, we could lose millions, or even market share!"

The woman folded her arms tightly across her breast and rubbed the cobalt blue wool of her sleeves absently feeling a quick burst of energy as she began to realize the potentials of the phenomenon just witnessed. She surged to the center of the darkened room, animated. "I'd like to run this on some focus groups, hit the demographic spectrum and see where it falls." Her voice rich and dramatic punctuated by a lilt at the end of each major thought making the most innocent and capricious comment sound ominous in its final resolve. She appeared to know much more than she did with this illusion of certainty, and surely it was in part responsible for her promotion into management. "Have we got any cohesive product yet?"

"No. Just random visuals. Like I said, he's discovered something, we don't know what yet."

"Writers..." the older man interjected, tinged with disdain and a certain carelessness that was obviously being relished for some private reason, "and art directors - we've got them working with a team of sFx Technos to see what they'll come up with. We pulled some freelancers in from the outer networks just this morning so we should have concepts ready by the end of the week." He looked into the darkness and the other three people in the room could feel his attention on them like a chill. "I love the arts you know."

"What's he doing out there?"

All eyes went to the video monitors as a peculiar sequence of lights, colors and images raced by causing all of them to imagine they had skipped through time in brief segments like a strobe light missing every other interval and made their hearts race in anticipation of the power to come. "Jeeezus god! Did you feel that? I can hardly believe it? Can you imagine that with content, drama?"

"We've got the hook," the older man said.

"We've got the drug," the woman interjected with lights flickering, glimmering and shining in her eyes, dancing on the edge of brilliance, flirting with oblivion, wondering where the limits were. "The perfect drug."

Darkness and light intertwined and embraced, climbing the ladder between the fading sun and the glow that radiated from the city. Then twilight disappeared leaving a landscape orchestrated by night. The neon, halogen arc lights sang crescendos out across the tangled streets, tungsten glows in murky corners, sparks flying brilliant, deft blue and crimson. Nash buttoned the top button of his shirt and looked down from his window at the reflections of the traffic below. Millions of lights were coming to life and glittering with an incandescent seduction offering if not hope at least pleasure, or even reassurance that a faltering soul could reach out to and hold, or ride on the beam or the glow or the frosty edge of. The evening was ominous.

Sabiha had called. The message was still scrawled across the computer monitor next to the shimmering holographic recording that appeared on the screen as an iridescent silver dot in its compressed form. He hesitated to activate it. She always gave the impression of wanting something immoral yet couldn't quite bring herself to reach for it, and that disturbed him. Cursed with good and evil fighting for dominance he saw the battle that was completely beyond her. It would have been a mistake, he thought, a pity. She had an ethereal quality, and though she tried to fight it, there it was. The result was an ambiguity that disguised her true nature and gave only fleeting impressions of who she might be. Her face one day beautiful, the next plain, was about as close as anyone would ever get. Perhaps that was why he felt the strong attraction to her was a danger. "Nash," his right index finger had touched the cool glass and instantly Sabiha materialized in her sweeping silk scarf out of the scintillating silver dot, " I don't know how it happened," she said excitedly, breathlessly, searching, "last night, down in the Boyle Heights sector…" pausing, "they fused I think. That's not possible is it?" Her pale, blue eyes looked straight into the camera, "I think they fused. Nash, call me…" She vanished. He knew he should have left it until morning.

The old building was built before the Kaiein[1]* It was a relic that he had admired long before he took apartments there. Cold doorways where the wind seeped through spoke to him with clarity from the first moment. They had a history. Nash needed a history. He lit a cigarette. The last refuge. It was illegal to have them. The smoke mingled with the wood smell of the room, touched the walls where a thousand human fingers had left their oily mark and had moved on to no one knows what end. The war perhaps. He drank the aroma unconsciously letting its memories imbue him with humanness before he headed out into the congested distances of the Western Metropolis. Points of light were all that kept him rational. Mouths with voices, eyes that saw, grappling hands…moving from heartbeat to heartbeat never knowing when it would end.

The glare of the oncoming traffic caromed off the hood of his car and made it hard to see. His hand passed over a switch on the center consul and instantly the windshield polarized, tinting slightly warm gray, and filtered out the reflected light. A high thin whine of magnetic rotors drew taut in the purified air of the vehicle as it blended harmoniously with the sounds of all the other motors on the expressway. It was an old one, oxidized finish blushed under the lights with a silver-blue patina and the interior dark from years of use, but everything worked, almost everything except for the gyroscopic levelers, which acted as lateral shock absorbers. There was no need, he decided, to fix something he would never use since the roads never had a shock to absorb as long as the generators were functioning. He had heard an internal combustion engine once, been a listener to its voice and had felt it deep in his chest, even now its memory brought back a certain satisfaction, a certain desire, but that was from a time when men had a different relationship with machines.

1* **Kaiein** (Kã-ë´-ˇin) n.1. The state of a rapid, catastrophic collapse of a civilization. 2. An epoch in which previously known technology and amassed knowledge is lost due to natural or human cataclysm. 3. A dark age. 4. The reversion of a civilization to savage practices. (Old English hæthen-savage, heathen, one inhabiting uncultivated land + Latin cadere-to fall, from Greek kleiein to close.)

Over a rise ahead a glow became visible as he seared the wide thoroughfare relying on the accuracy of the particle beams upon which his vehicle raced. A glance at the screen confirmed the balance, a touch to a switch, a hand passed across an areorheostat, the silent adjustments of ultra-high technology mimicking the serene with an unobtrusive hiss of hydraulic barely heard, a momentary whir of an electric device, a complex system enveloping the living organism in its artificial womb not ever bothering to consult any intelligence or native ability simply seeing to all needs. It made him sweat, though he drove instinctively, gave him a knot in the stomach and an overwhelming urge to escape. At the top of the rise he suddenly cleared the cloistered tunnel of structures through which he had passed and bore witness to the magnificent, shimmering sea of the city. It stretched as far as eyes saw deep into the mythic distances where still there were more people and they in turn saw as far as their eyes could in any direction the spectacle of lights. It made him contemplate mortality and the meaning of life.

One frantic call had set him on this errand. "Mr. DeCoucy..." her voice, he remembered, a trembling whisper yet each word could be understood in its most subtle inflection, "we are losing him...they are here with their instruments..." the rush from outside the windscreen, the blur of lights, the scream of thousands of vehicles passed in silence, "we can't let him go like this, unprepared... hurry..." A thin whispering voice that he heard now in the stream of sound that rose up out of the expressway speaking in the old language. He chased after it for fear the illusion would dissipate and played the conversation over and over in his head listening to the music that he heard in that voice with its nut-like clarity and its desperate plea.

The multilevel interchange loomed ahead of him with twenty-seven layers of particle beam roadways and various lines of the Tunnel whose engines shot through the maze at over six hundred miles an hour, just below the speed of sound, except those that paused along the stations taking on passengers. Once an interchange had collapsed in an earthquake and thousands had lost their lives, but shortly thereafter legislation forced them to be more structurally sound, more "integral to the substructure" as it was stated in the statutes. Nash hated them. If anything symbolized the fall it was the junction of these arteries where millions of people passed within touching distance of each other at high speed never knowing one face from the next and having no need in a lifetime to ever speak to another in the process. Vendors clogged every available space like crustaceans vying for the attention of all those in transit who shoved and elbowed their way through the crowds to catch the next engine in the Tunnel or to make some other connection for leaving the interchange as quickly as possible. Everyone wanted out. He sunk down in his seat and pulled his collar up close to his neck peering intently out of squinted eyes as his vehicle raced into the oblivion of the interchange along with thousands of others, into the labyrinth as always wondering if he would make it out. The thin voice gave strength to his purpose.

He was absorbed by the gaping aperture through which the roadway spun in its crazy race. As he entered there was a great, unalterably deep moan, so deep it was barely audible, something that was felt, as an experience or a memory lingering in the neglected peripheral of ones self, or perhaps a chorus of spirits lamenting the loss of a more human existence as one would imagine they might sound...he always thought of it as the iron hand gripping the universe and molding it to needs it was never meant to fulfill.

At its furthest point this interchange was eleven miles from entrance to egress. Some were less, he had not heard of any that were longer. He had passed the electronic billboard over the access way on which were posted road conditions with his thoughts in flight and so missed any vital information that may have been waiting for him there. Lights raked his vision, clawed for attention in streaks of murky amber white flares accented with crimson, cyan blue and green. Signs at the turnouts were a blur. The cavernous passage was filled to its hundred foot ceilings with noxious gases, smog, exhaust, smoke and recycled air so that the powerful arc lights illuminating the interchange filtered down in a strange diffused glow radiating with an yellow-olive tint. Nash frowned. He could see the people waiting at the station stops as he coursed by at high speed, thousands of them, all waiting, prey to the petty criminals that infested the honeycombed structures and worse entombed, cut off from sun and sky and fresh air. All were desperate, those who were here by choice and others by circumstance...he thought of their voices raised up in the din growing hoarse trying to make meanings clear, or repressed, silenced by intimidation, certainly not filled with spiritual quality like the one which drew him through these iniquitous caverns like thread through the eye of a needle.

A shower of sparks glinted at the periphery of his vision, little blazing golden stars flickering in and out of his consciousness as he gripped the wheel. On the rear video screen he saw their source as a car flung loose from the particle beams and was sliding recklessly along the retaining wall sending rivers of flaming metal embers high into the air until it finally leapt the barrier and plowed into a turnout end over end. He did not see it come to rest, nor if any bystanders or stores were hit... it was only a brief flash, a slice of a moment that he reflected on only for an instant as it appeared and then was gone from the rear monitor. There was a cloud of blue smoke, then nothing as he made the bend of a slight curve in the interchange roadway and was now two then three and quickly five miles away. It did not occur to him the irony of his mission for one man when he had perhaps been witness to the tragic deaths of many, maybe even fifty, or a hundred. The war raged around him and those fallen were mourned but for an instant in the rush, the silent prayers wretched away from grieving mouths into the screaming distances until the soulless pursuit was the only thing anyone could think of. However it was all remembered, every last detail, and would lie waiting at the end of each day as soon as a man closed his eyes.

Nash finally broke free from the confines of the interconnecting chambers and with hundreds of others raced down the incline toward the Second City, which was the old section and had been the urban center long ago before the Western Metropolis existed, before the fall, the Kaiein and the subsequent reconstruction. The hand of the sun warmed the horizon with a muddy, ochre glow and the sky was shot with a breath of stars barely visible through the light reflecting haze that hung over the land in permanent repose.

He took an exit in the dark. Streets glistened and often as not in this sector were insufficiently marked, curbstones were chipped and great beams of diffused light shot up through huge gratings placed in the center of the old streets when the Tunnel was built beneath them at the end of the last century. The car traveled on its own wheels, and Nash was glad to have full control of it again. Finally he saw city cars and a Paramed van, all identical, with only one number on the license plate, black with thin red bar codes on the doors. He had arrived.

A small elderly woman whose short gray hair was growing thin met Nash at the door. She grabbed his arm and led him in. Her eyes spoke intensely crossing the barrier of lifetimes, of experience. "They want to put him on life support..." the woman said strongly in a crisp, military monotone, "or they want a signature for termination, the doctor wants power of attorney, he says I'm too involved, too emotional." She looked at Nash and pulled him up short by the arm. "God dammit! He's not prepared!"

Nash made his way into the other room where an old man was lying in bed. His cheeks flushed with irritation, but he suppressed it long enough to understand what was going on. Two parameds stood in the corner whispering to each other, one looking at his watch. A city doctor was sitting on the bed scanning the old man's chest with a diagnostic instrument. The nurse from the coroners office stood by, just in case.

He took his long coat off revealing the black and white clerical collar and threw it on the chair. "Alright!" he said roughly. "I need some space here..." throwing a hard glance at the two men in the corner, "You two will wait outside please." After a moment of trying to intimidate Nash with their solid, lifeless and startled eyes they mindlessly ambled out the door only slightly disturbed but taking it all in course as they were paid hourly and one hour was very much like the next, as long as they all added up in the end it would be alright.

The doctor was florid with the feeling that someone was doing something to him without his consent. "Who are you?" he asked indignantly, "...a relative? What? This is city business, department of health business and I'd..."

Nash leaned down and put his mouth to the man's ear with one hand on his chest and the other pressed to his shoulder, "Shhhhh, the

12

man is ill," he intoned, " you must keep quiet…" He forced the doctor to his feet, "just wait outside, there's plenty of time for your work, not much for mine." Both the doctor and the coroner's nurse were easy, they resisted, disgruntled, their resentment rising and Nash used the energy, simply directed it until they were out in the other room on the phones getting instructions or calling for assistance or whatever government people did on the phones. He closed the door

The room now suddenly quiet he stood over the man who was lying so detached from everything that had been taking place. Nash sat down. He watched the man's ashen face as he appeared to be drifting in and out of consciousness and noticed the breathing, like a shallow tide, the rhythms and streams of the body drawn inexorably to their destiny. He was calm and direct, questioning, each time waiting for the man to give a reply or in some way acknowledge that he heard. There were no thoughts in his mind while he did this, a complete silence invaded him as all his mental faculties were focused, by a prism, on this task. For hours the two men sat facing each other without an awareness between them until at last Nash began to feel a slight response in the hand he held. An imperceptible movement, a slight stirring, a motion easily overlooked yet it was with the rhythm of the questions. Soon the hand responded noticeably to each query, and then the old man opened his eyes. They were steel, almost chromium, luminous and though inexorably tired, alive. "Who are you?" he asked breathlessly.

"A friend." Nash replied as he placed the man's hand beside him on the bed and smiled.

"I'm confused, I think….a littler bit confused…

"My name is Nash…a minister"

"In the old way?"

"Yes."

"There's not many of you left is there?"

"Nor of you."

The distance in time closed in around them as the night formed a deep cocoon in which they could touch spirits. The old man struggled to raise himself up on his elbow. "I have much to tell you." He spoke with a hushed confidence, eyes wide and infinite and yet with desperation knowing there was little time left. "I'm listening."

- II -

Angel's Flight

Nash entered the Boyle Heights Sector on rain slick streets. The message from Sabiha lingered in his consciousness and he was drawn there to discover its meaning. He also needed to come to grips with what had just transpired between himself and the old man, which had left him shaken. Boyle Heights was in the Second City and wasn't serviced by the Tunnel or the magnetic beams so there were cars everywhere and he followed the heavy traffic to where sidewalks were alive with people walking in the night and brightly lit shop signs were everywhere. It never appealed to Nash before. The rush of people was a drug that one could never quite understand, but became addicted to by its promise and so he imagined the thousands of vacant eyes desperately searching for a feeling that long ago had ceased. He felt their hollowness and wanted to ease their longing.

The old man had slipped quietly into a realm somewhere between earth and sky. His life and his creations went with him. All that he had was riding on the wind now subject to its desires, its eddies and currents traveling from place to place touching down now and again in brief attempts at being settled and permanent only to become restless and move on. Time passes.

A child was born to an unwed mother somewhere else in the city tonight. She smiled, wistful, thinking of the future, excited and fearful. Her world is shaken by these comings and goings that have more effect than the marvelous engineering feats that employ thousands, or the computers and corporations and governments and blood letting wars...because these things too are riddled by the comings and goings. All are the servants of the cycle of change. Nash thought on these things reviewing events in his mind, hoping to find certainty that he had prepared the man well enough. It was all that he could do after a certain point, to make it easier, to help in the transition... or is it truly a transmigration of souls upon some brilliant celestial river that runs in rhythm to the rage of sin, the absolution of self forgiveness and the determination to survive? The wind knows.

Tonight though, he walked. He needed the drug. Pushing through the crowd on the sidewalks he felt a certain cool bite in the air that was unusual for the Western Metropolis. The climate was usually warm as the city originally, though forgotten now and only in memory, had been founded in a desert of scrub oaks, chaparral, wiry Palo Verde tree and Mesquite. More recently after a century of air pollution there was a permanent brown-gray pall that hung above the landscapes of the southern part of North America and acted as a layer of insulation trapping in the hot fumes of industry, combustion engines and millions upon millions of human bodies. Where once it was dry and hot, it was thick with moisture, not the kind that rolls across verdant forest canopies to the throaty whisper of the toucan, but the kind from an enclosure where too many had been for too long, or that of compost rotting in the sun. The people moved among the fibers, threaded their lives in the woof and warp.

Nash ducked into a cafe and pressed his card in the slot of a public telephone. Instantly a wall of glass surrounded him unfolding in overlapping petals automatically as soon as the legal tender had hit the sensors making the enclosure absolutely silent. He relished the moment watching the clash of bodies all around him in the small restaurant. The incalculable sea. He got Sabiha's voice mail, she was not at home. Walking again on the street in the damp embrace of people he wondered what it was that she had seen and where in this sector he might find a clue?

Music drifted from doorways. It hovered momentarily over the sidewalk until it was shot full of holes by the clamor of voices, by traffic noises and the cacophony of the busy street at night. Then it was replaced by more sounds, from the *videtel* arcades, shops and bars, lights and flashing images from the ubiquitous video monitors that occupied every vacant space. Crowds of people stood around them as they did at all hours, listening to the news, the metro-bulletins from the police and the public programming that was created especially for broadcast to the access monitors that were run by PIA, the Public Information Agency. He smelled the sweet fragrance of people mingling with that of food. Nash watched a group for a moment as they stood on the corner their eyes growing blank and a slack-jawed expression slowly stealing over their faces even as some, who scowled to show they were still in control of their mental processes, gave way to the hooded look of anonymity as they took in the tan young women and palm trees advertising a resort in Puerto Vallarta. Nash merged into the river and let it carry him up the avenue.

He was looking for something and when he found it he would know.

The waitress grabbed his elbow and moved with him as he walked in the assured manner of a woman who was used to men. "What can I get you?" She intoned, anxiously, yet still holding her eyes on his for a long instant, the way a hummingbird can hover motionless or a coyote can stalk a quarry with its head held completely still making him feel like she was interested even though he knew she wasn't.

"A water," he said, "a good one."

Since the end of the century drinking water had ceased to be something freely dispensed from a tap. The public water supply was mostly chemicals now, those that purified the reclaimed part of it, those that protected against several new strains of bacteria and of virus that had caused deaths of epidemic proportions after the year 2100 when the Colorado river had dried up as a result of a shift in the weather pattern leaving the Rocky Mountains without a snow pack for over seventy-five years. Reclaimed sea water supplied the needs of the western continent, and though it was palatable in a pinch, it did not taste good at all and it was considered coarse to actually drink it.

There were hundreds of well dressed people in the cavernous room, it was very upscale, a meeting place, but the roar of voices that always occurred when there was alcohol was missing. The ceiling was barely visible in the dim light and only steel girders could be seen crisscrossed beyond which was blackness. Along the far wall were the *videtel* booths filled with people. Vidtel were interactive, flat-screen, video computers tied to wireless networks and extremely popular in nearly all public places. The penultimate evolution of the multitrillion dollar computer gaming industry–now with total sensual immersion, but the full virtual environments were in the back in their own rooms where the devotes spent most of their time. The addicts. Nash always felt that was more his domain, where the truly lost dwelt.

With precious water in hand he made his way down the long line towards the rear of the room and perched on a stool at the bar. Over the tables he saw groups crowded into booths playing the *videtel*. Nash moved towards the arcade and stopped at a booth where several others lingered. On the screen were fleeting, colorful, sensuous images, shadow and light dancing in perfect counterpoint and as each person passed his hand over the controls the images changed to reflect new directions too fast for the casual observer... that was all one could tell without being in the booth wearing the virtual headset and having all the perceptions directed to the electronic receptors. It was silent to onlookers. Nash could only imagine what they might be feeling and hearing. He knew the path into self-annihilation and had stood guard his whole life against it, constantly vigilant, willing to fight, and he considered himself fortunate that he had not succumbed. All around him pleasures beckoned though he was driven by deeper requirements.

"They look sad don't they?"

Nash turned to a woman seated beside him. She held a drink in her hand. "Who does?" he smiled politely.

"The ones you were looking at." Nash looked around as she elocuted with lowered voice, "Those people."

"Oh," he uttered turning back to the room, "...those people."

"Sad," she said. "I look at them too."

"The name's Nash." he offered.

"Rose," she said smiling back at him disarmingly with an undercurrent in her eye revealing more than she might like. "No last names–I like strange men."

"Nash rejoined, "You've come to the right place."

"You drinking?"

"Water."

"Oh well," Rose purred with disappointment from deep in her chest, "...I don't mind." When she crossed her legs and shifted her weight on the stool to lean closer he suddenly felt in the presence of a large cat. She touched his arm with her fingertips. "You're not lost are you?"

"No... I'm looking for something."

"I figured. Don't see a minister in here every day."

He fingered the traditional cleric's collar that he insisted on wearing even though most had given it up before he was born and felt self-conscious. Perhaps it was the blatant sexuality she exuded without the slightest effort that unnerved him; spilling off her lips, from her voluptuous figure barely covered in a clinging dress and through her touch, though he was certain Rose would have been equally as sensual even if dressed in cold weather gear. It wasn't physical. The same as with Sabiha, whom he desired and rejected in the same breath, and though he tried to isolate himself from the feelings, there they were.

"Do you fuse?" Nash gestured toward the vidtel booths with his head watching for recognition.

"What?"

"Sorry... go virtual, get on the machines."

"Sometimes. I don't like it much."

"Why?"

"I'm too physical I guess. It makes me feel disconnected."

"Then why do you come here."

She shrugged, "People are here. I like people."

He surveyed the room where most were tucked away into booths immersed in the virtual reality they had come to experience. "Not very lively." It was quiet except for a low murmur of voices and soft background music kept low so as not to interfere with the headset audio. Though Nash had frequently visited these clubs, he could never get used to the perception that there was something inherently wrong with the virtual experience, something that violated natural law.

"I used to do it a lot," she continued.

"What happened?"

"I escaped."

Nash was intrigued by her use of the word. "What do you mean?"

"I got out. It's like living in a world that's too thin to experience. Everything's there, but you can't touch it..." She squeezed his arm. "I'm looking for the real."

Suddenly there was a nearly imperceptible flash from all the screens at once. It swept the room like a lightening power surge and startled everyone. Two young men threw off their goggles laughing hysterically and shaking their heads, then others did the same. One young woman fell out of a booth onto the floor at the feet of the crowd. Her long ashen hair spread out on the ground where she lay unconscious like white rose petals. Vomit trickled from her mouth. Nobody rushed to help her, instead they stepped back so as not to break her fall or in any way interfere with the flow of nature as if they were watching *videtel* and didn't want to lessen the full experience. There were snide comments about drunks behind cupped hands and raised glasses. Snickering. Compelled Nash appeared beside her, was drawn by her vulnerability and knelt down to the young woman who had very fair skin and whose cheek lay resting on the cool, dirty tile. "Help your friend!" he shot up angrily to the young men in the booth. "...just drunk..." was the belligerent reply and they could not stop laughing. He picked her up and brushed the hair out of her eyes and tried to talk her to consciousness.

Rose knelt beside him to support the girl's weight. "Let me help."

Her head rested against the crook of his arm and the flaxen hair spilled across his hand. There was no expression on the delicate features of her face. He noticed the breathing was normal, as if she were sleeping only deeper. They lifted her onto the chair in the booth then Nash put his arm around the quiet shoulders and spoke softly to her though she did not respond immediately. He stood by and watched.

'I'll call the Parameds," Rose offered.

"No!" Nash spit out hostilely, then realizing she was only trying to help added, "no... sorry, they can't do anything for this."

Then the young woman awoke with a start. "Watch out!!" she screamed suddenly agitated and tried to wrest away from the arm that held her steady and half rose pushing recklessly into Nash. "I have to get outta here!! Look out!! Watch out!!"

He spoke soothingly to her, gripped her shoulders and finally got her back down on the seat. Then as if realizing where she was for the first time she sucked in her breath, looked around as if for the hunter and was quiet. Gazing up at him were blank eyes, electric, agitated. There was an expression of complete spiritual chaos that swept across her as one who realizes they are not in control of themselves though up until that moment they were convinced they were. Confused she sank back into her chair.

"Hey buddy! What the hell do you think you're doing to her?!!" One of the men sitting at the booth rose up out of his chair at last coming to the realization of what was happening. He shoved Nash's shoulder sharply. Then tried it once again and his arm was pushed aside. "Pretty fast!" the young man said, "What the hell did you do?"

"What you should have if you hadn't thought it was so dammed funny."

The tall young man with short black hair turned to the flaxen haired girl. "Did he touch you? Did he do something to you?" She just shook her head no looking lost with her eyes.

Rose stepped in between them. "Come on, let's go."

Nash was furious. He felt the rage boil up inside and as he walked out the door, wanted to turn back and confront the black haired man. He wanted to do much more. He wanted to just walk up and smack him, but knew he wouldn't because he never did that. It was always a case of reason with him and after the fact he always thought of what he would like to have done. "What an asshole!"

"Yea." Rose agreed sweetly holding his arm and then kissed him on the cheek. "Well," she said good naturedly, "I'm glad you're human at least."

He glared at her still fuming, and then had to laugh despite himself. "Yea... me too."

She drew close to him. Close enough that he could smell her scent. Close enough that her breasts touched him and she placed one finger on his lower lip. "I want to take you home, you're sweet."

"No you don't," he said suddenly serious. "Not really."

"You mean I'd regret it in the morning?"

Nash gazed into her large brown eyes longingly for an instant letting the fullness of her sensuality enrapture him; the ripeness of her as if she were a melon too long in the sun wishing he could for once just let it go. Rose stood on one wide hip with her thin dress cascading down over breast and thigh and humid regions he could not let himself imagine.

"This is nowhere you should be," he replied, "you wouldn't like it here."

The nightsong raced through the streets oblivious to the drama. Always it had done this and its ritual was the stronger medicine between the technologies of men and the rhythms of nature. Its presence was felt in the deepest archive where there was no access to the outside and only an innate knowingness could account for its appearance. However, there were things, Nash knew, that had no reason and must by their nature remain unexplained. The appari-tion of the girl haunted him with her soulless eyes staring blankly as he thought open to any suggestion, a clean field, an empty sheet. An unfinished story not his place to complete, it was God's, if there indeed was any god, more rightfully the girl's herself. Looking back down the glittering incandescence of the street he savored Rose sauntering away and then slid into the driver's seat of the car and was gone.

The high walls soared. They rose above even the loftiest conversation that may have transpired in hurried whispers or disguised jingoism at its base through the years. For two hundred feet they rose finally meeting huge wooden beams that spanned the ceiling and reached down as flying buttresses against the walls giving the roof the illusion of being suspended by heaven and thus needing no further support to stabilize the rest of the structure. It was built by the Methodists in the last half of the twentieth century as a final resolute attempt to resurrect the failing congregations and recapture the grandeur that had lured the flock in earlier times. It was also a defense against the Baptist evangelists whose gospel of affluence and self redemption nearly eclipsed all other religious doctrines before the *Kaiein*.

The Cathedral smelled of dust and age. It was not a place frequented by many people, though once it had been and its floors bore the signs of their footpaths as they made sojourns on matters consequential; of baptisms and births, of weddings and confirmations, on matters grave; lost souls, lost loved ones and lost innocence. Sunlight bore through prominent sky lit windows that pierced the gabled roof letting in the breath, the essence, to a place of requiem, or remembrance of the once living who experienced existence with hands and hearts and all the emotion of life. All of them were gathered in one collective cauldron and any individual voice could be heard at a given instant speaking those words that needed to be spoken, that could not be suppressed, that lived in the mind even though the body had given way to dust, ashes, to the past where there are no rememberers. Perhaps this is the reason people did not come here often. There were ghosts in the walls, the ceiling, the floors, the pews, the pulpit, the vestibule, the old altar looming like a beached leviathan out of its element waiting eternal for the waters to resurrect its parched and dehydrated flesh. Incantations, chorales, the music of spirits lingered.

Nash wiped the rain from his shoes and placed them in the corner of an office to dry while slipping on an extra pair that he had at hand for just such purposes. It was a small office at the end of a long hall allotted to him because seniority dictated that more workable spaces be given to those whom the years had given more authority. He didn't mind. He had little use for an office feeling that his work lay somewhere in the realm between where sweaty hands grappled with life and the objects of their desire. In the fabric. There were just a few others around that evening, but they were busy doing things that only men of the cloth understood. Quiet things. He was alone in a house of spirits. Nash had tremendous respect for those who had spent their lives in service to a Church that had lost its place in the modern world and he too kept an inner burning that allowed him to continue, though not in the same sense as the others did. He embraced change. Welcomed its unknown name, its horizons. It was the difference between night and day, the others longing for what once was and he, (brother to the turmoil around him), rode the raw thrust of constant change, the stallion eternally bolting from the gate, enraged, infinite, relentless. There was no place for a man like him within the Church, the true Church, and he knew no matter how established life may seem he was just passing, a sojourner waiting for the epiphany that was up ahead...meanwhile he held fast as the typhoon drew him deeper in.

He had hung his long coat on a hook behind the door and it gave off the smell of damp wool. He sat by the altar on ancient spruce wood stairs. The shadow of the pulpit fell across his face leaving him bathed in half light and half darkness a reflection perhaps of who he might be. A quiet time was necessary and he sought it out as often as events would allow. The voices were always speaking around him, those in crisis, others lost and still others looking for answers from him. Then there were the black ones whose time in life was bitter and they spewed their venom quietly, surreptitiously. He lost the sound of his own personal voice often. It was not vanquished or overwhelmed so much as it was just indistinguishable in the cacophony of the city and his role in it. As he grew older he was finding it essential more often to listen for the quiet. At first it seemed to him that it was an escape from the rush of technology that raced inexorably through human existence confusing the values so delicately balanced that had been passed down by other voices in other times through thousands or even millions of years... lifetimes, only to be transmuted in the final instant that was the modern age. An attempt to make sense of it. This was, he knew, a justification for his own disability...there are no excuses in the end.

Still, he needed a perspective from which to view in order to grasp his surroundings, to comprehend his relationship. The regimentation of the order of the Church did not help him, though it gave some structure to an otherwise endless pursuit of a spiritual form and, at times, it gave refuge. Though not often did he turn to one of his fellows for help and had begun to wonder recently if he was, himself, a true believer.

The clatter and jolt of the entry door echoed through the cathedral and gave him a start. Footsteps followed. Sabiha appeared fleeting through the shadows of the antechamber the tails of her scarf and long coat flying like sheets before the wind. The thought suddenly occurred to Nash that she was frightened and he stood watching her angrily sweep between the pews her long brown fingers slicing the air in gestures of outraged resignation.

"Someone is following me!" she barked. "I think ..." looking back, "he's there... I saw him..." spitting the words to the back of the cathedral *"I see you!!"*

Nash rose to his feet straining his eyes for any hint of a shape, of movement in the shadows, and listening... quietly. The roar, breaths and whispers, ghosts... they were so quiet and he wondered if someone else was being equally so.

"There's no one there now," he said calmly hoping to reassure her. Sabiha was high strung. "It might have been someone coming in the side door... it's a busy place some nights." Though he knew it was too late for that.

She pulled her coat around her with a few bold steps forward, one glance back, a glint of fear overshadowed. "There was someone there."

"Well, come in then. What are you doing here?"

"Did you get my message?"

Nash thrust his hands in his pockets and regarded her for a moment. "A little cryptic?"

"Was it?" she stared down her straight nose at him exhibiting the intellectual aloofness that arose anytime someone did not completely understand what she said the first time. "I would have thought it was clear," she looked around, " but I was in a rush, and... somebody's following me, does that seem ordinary to you for some reason?" A curl of black hair stuck to her damp forehead. She was of distant Ethiopian lineage reaching far back before the Pharaohs and had the appearance of a sleek, black Abyssinian cat–lean and beautiful, elegant and earthy.

"I went down there you know."

"Where"

"Boyle Heights."

"Did you?" Impatient, still searching back into the shadows, alert.

"I don't know why. I should have talked to you first. I just can't stand mysteries" he shook his head, "I just can't.

When she moved it was like air through leaves. A rustling outside a window when it was still. He could never quite see the motion, the passage from one mood to the next. "The Chinese are here. I couldn't get out of conferences all day...I was very busy." She smiled suddenly feeling the warmth that always surfaced once she got into good communication with the enigmatic minister.

Nash felt it too. He was drawn emotionally and it made him uneasy, beckoning him to deeper waters. The smell of her was like bitter oak. "Let's go." He said nodding his head. "Let's get out of here." She looked relieved.

It was a short ride. The car was not like his. This one was beautiful, and so near new there remained in it the smell of the factory and comfortable enough to tempt almost anyone into a life of profiteering. Its lines swept down in graceful tangents appearing always in motion even at rest. Lights slipped by in a liquid stream.

"Are you in trouble?" Nash asked directly shooting a look at her aquiline profile against the fluid skyline.

"I don't know." The ambiguous reply answered nothing. It was obvious what the truth was. Her hands fidgeted on the wheel, dancing, while her eyes did not leave the road. She did not speak again.

He considered who might have been following her, if indeed anyone was, and for what reason. His feelings mostly having to do with her work as a translator for the United Nations. Perhaps she deciphered something she shouldn't have...politics was a dirty business. Though he tried not to, Nash kept looking over at her just for the pleasure it gave.

Up in the wind she was different. More relaxed and hungrily devouring the fast food they had brought. The sky was lit up with a rose glow painted in streaks along the bottoms of clouds while the indigo grew deeper, subtler and began to form a window into the universe. Nash drank steaming coffee and wrapped his hand around the cup to keep warm, took another bite of the hot sandwich they bought on the way to the roof of what once had been the tallest building in the old city, Los Angeles. Now it was just a nostalgic relic that had none of the features of contemporary skyscrapers like solar climate control, glass that automatically tinted when the light reached a certain intensity and biomechanical levels that were kept at optimum for human existence by optical quantum computers in the hermetically sealed environment. There were also no public monitors and no programming piped in by the PIA. The only reason it still remained standing was because of the Architectural Landmark Council who considered it art had been trying unsuccessfully to get it registered as an historical landmark, but were continuously thwarted by real estate tycoons. It was one of Nash's haunts. He sought out the places that used to be as if he were living a life continuum for someone from an earlier time who had wound up in this century desperately seeking a way back. The touch of the past propelled him into the future.

Sabiha Sahin stood near the edge of the railing that defined the perimeter of the observation deck. "I love this!" she said ecstatically her voice torn away by a powerful icy gust that was Los Angeles at its wintery best. "I was so hungry..." stuffing the last of the sandwich into her mouth, "this is good, really good... you've had these before. Do you come up here very often?"

"Yes. I do."

"Well," savoring the last few bites, "it's understandable."

"I like the view..." He just had to know, "Will you please tell me about that obscure message?'

"I was in a hurry."

"It was elliptical"

"You're here aren't you?"

Eyes trailed off into the distances with lights upon lights multiplied to the horizon beneath the San Bernardino Mountains where once the Angeles Forest stood and sheltered black bear, cougar and sometimes wolves. There was no living memory left of that, only lights. It was a heady feeling up in the wind with the cool air gripping the city and then racing away into the ether.

"I'm afraid of what you might tell me but not so much that I don't want to know."

"When I was at the language labs in the university we spent hours and hours on the computers with the interactive learning programs…" she started to draw pictures in the air with her hands gesturing as she talked. "They were extremely voice sensitive so that each improper inflection in response could be picked up and corrected. You couldn't so much as breathe without the machine responding to you." Her eyes sought him out, "It was supposed to be that way you see." She paused and watched his eyes for a moment and when certain he was fully listening continued. "It was very intimate." She said emphatically. "The programmers worked specifically on that so that the programs went right for your individual personality and gripped, parasitically, feeling almost like a mirror image of yourself, only smarter meant to correct and chastise mistakes. Twin sister, very intimate." Looking over the city she breathed deeply. "Occasionally students began to go into a sort of a trance. That was the problem."

"What do you mean *trance*?"

"It was the oddest thing. They'd lose control completely and end up staying on-line for days sometimes, without breaks or food just intently working away at the touchscreens and watching images flicker in front of them. It was an addiction. They invariably became agitated, a few incoherent. Not much attention was given to the phenomenon. The instructors just forbid them to use the labs until they got rested and began to eat regularly, some were barred permanently, but mostly it was ignored. The consensus was that certain types of mental states were most susceptible. One girl I remember who had been barred from the labs snuck back in late at night and logged onto a machine. They found her the next morning, conscious... but in a state...her memory was gone. I suppose that's what I meant by *fused*. I saw it again the other night. It bothered me. I called you. You're the spiritual one, not me..." She said while he watched her exquisite mouth, "I'm just a layman, but I saw it again, twice now, people fused and worse they seemed to like it. Isn't that your domain?"

"I saw it too." Rivers of air whispered around them and Nash felt the hair on his neck rise as he furled his brows with concern looming over him. "I think I did."

"That's not all."

"What do you mean?" He turned to her, breathing in the cold and letting it burn his lungs and confirm the fact that he was alive.

"I don't know for sure, it might not be anything... but something I was translating, I didn't get it all... bits of it...

"What was it?"

"Some new technology. I couldn't get much... I'm given this stuff all the time you know. East-West commerce is funneled through my department..."

"What made you take notice of this one?"

"It was encrypted, Mandarin, but encrypted."

"Is that unusual?"

"Very. But I've seen it before."

"What was it about...?"

"Electrically induced neurosynapse failure."

"What's that?"

"It used to be called Electronic Cybernetics, in a word...brainwashing."

"The Chinese?"

"No. Actually it's a Pan-Asian conglomerate of high tech hardware manufacturers. A trade group."

"Oh... then that's different," he frowned cynically.

"This was a trade paper, some type of prospectus for a new product."

"So... what?"

" I think it was industrial espionage."

"Because it was encrypted?"

In the silence a gust of wind brushed wisps of hair in front of her face and she pushed it from her eyes looking away. "No. Because I was followed."

Nash instinctively gazed behind them, into the shadows where shades of blackness played tricks and where anyone could be looking back in anonymity. He could hear sirens in the distance. Police hovercraft, hornets shaded by the night, poison, somewhere looking for someone. Ubiquitous lights arching down from heaven into the city streets flashing out of nowhere. He wanted to know more about this paper, but she had told him what little she could. They continued talking, however, into the night each a refuge for the other.

Nash liked being around Sabiha, he considered her a truly brilliant woman. It was the mystery of her, however, that captivated him. She was tall and always wore scarves that flew behind with the tangled mane of midnight black hair. He was not sure where her family had originated, in Ethiopia - somewhere near the Blue Nile; she had the look of ancient breeding. Her skin was black olive and cast deep shadows across her face while her large eyes were bright flickers above the prominent cheekbones. With a face exquisitely sculpted he had never seen her when she had not looked exotic and swept in a natural beauty. He did not come from good stock. If asked to define himself he would not give a physical description and might say that he could see things, small insignificant things that someone else may not notice. Points that defined his place in this world. Nash was thirty-seven years old, tall and angular and observant by nature. His face had that sharp definition of an overly bred aristocracy where each feature had become refined beyond perfection to nearing bizarre. The result was a strong mongrel character, pale skin, prominent bones and gray-green eyes. He was always trying to find something without any clear idea of what it was and so was never satisfied, never at peace. That characteristic bothered most people who longed for the luxury of complacency. Nash was impatient. Sabiha understood this. She was a perfectionist in a world defying perfection.

When she finally left him off in front of his old apartment building it was very early in the morning. She insisted she would be safe. He could not go to bed immediately with so many thoughts and so sat looking out over the metropolis and inhaled the aroma of a very old Claret. Dry and musty the breath of an earlier age. It was out of Bordeaux, beyond the *Kaiein*, from a time before Europe was absorbed into the Western Hemisphere. The glass touched his lips and he drank a toast to the city in the early hours seeing it shimmer from out his apartment window. Then he went to sleep, he had an appointment he'd nearly forgotten in just four hours. Nash dreamt of things to come, but with an urgency and a foreboding he had never felt before.

- III -

Silent Voices

He was tolerated because he was old. Or perhaps it was the fact of familiarity, or even nostalgia that allowed him to work past the retirement age of fifty. Strong enough, he thought, and he also liked to imagine that his wisdom gave him persistence and though there was so much precedence in education now that the young who flooded the job markets annually were expert beyond their years, there was still something in experience that could not be gleaned from a second hand source, could not be usurped from the living as the vital force siphoned from their spirits until they were derelict with self doubt. The life span had decreased ten years since mandatory retirement at age fifty was made universal law. It was only one reaction to the continuing explosion in population, reasoning that violent crime could be lessened if the young had more incentive, more share in the economy. There was less violent crime, nobody knew exactly why, so the retirement laws remained to the cheers of the naturally indolent. A man had twenty-five years to prove himself. *Hell*, he thought, *it takes twenty-five years just to find out what you don't know.*

The Sun had lost its meaning. It was a yellow star long on its journey into the season of a red dwarf after which, as every new child learned, was infamy for its light would no longer be a blessing to all living things across the planet. Radiant gods in the chariot who had spent so many eternities racing before the clouds, beating the stars to their resting places, and blending seamlessly into the shadows across the glistening seas as they too succumbed before the night, would for once be no more. The young easily understood this. Most were so caught up in the chaotic social change that the information, even if carefully explained to them, passed by as not of great importance in the drama of survival more real than the sunlight that poured through their windows as though it was never ending. Nothing lasts forever. Nothing lasts for long. When he thought of the Sun he thought of golden apples and the mask of Agamemnon of Mycenae whose brilliant courage was eclipsed by the hand of his wife. So have gone all luminous gods to which we, (men of the Earth, of soil, of salt, of wonder,) have followed unquestioningly in search of a more fundamental essence. So goes the Sun now in its tragi-comic exit leaving the bare ether to blankly greet us each morning ...whose eyes have seen the glorious splendor of your full radiance so intense as to cause men to drop to their knees in wonder and humility. He somehow felt betrayed, as if he'd been cheated of the grandeur his ancestors had possessed. He was bitter, and turned that bitterness into a cold sense of purpose. Like an animal who had been chased by civilization to the very limits of the earth and had nowhere left to go, but was unwilling to be tamed. Feral to the end. The Sun, he thought, was just a yellow star.

He burst through the double glass doors still wearing the dark glasses he wore at all times outside because of the ozone layer depletion and grasping an attaché, his palms sweating, fingers unfeeling. Today was the day he'd been waiting for. Though not the pinnacle of his career in public service, it was one of those milestones that made the long bitter stretches more easily endured and the object grasped just sweeter. Suddenly the huge lobby of the building enveloped him with its deafening panoply of sounds that lofted to the marble reaches of the ceiling, which hung suspended three stories above the crowd. He was swept up in the swiftness of the current and the sureness of the determinism that directed men and women around him to their destination no matter the obstacle. Usually he was numb to this story played out each morning leaving him senseless to its actual significance, but now, at the height of his energies with all his senses raw, drinking in sensations...the sweet smell of young women passing him, (which he had not noticed in such a long time that he had nearly forgotten), perfume in the air that hung like dust, virile voices that melded into the battles yet to be, the anticipated conflicts each young man sought out while the old ones avoided...here were the footsteps of armies tramping history each day across the lobbies of countless buildings as they manned the posts that bureaucracy demanded. It made him breathe a deep sigh of satisfaction despite himself that he was part of it all.

The elevator shot wildly upward while the force of two Gs was suspended by the artificial gravity devices that had been perfected on the first space stations of the late 90s. It seemed like no sooner had he stepped in than the doors parted to his own offices seventy-two stories from the street. He felt nothing, not a hair was out of place nor a bead of perspiration on any forehead as the workers poured out into their cubicles surrounded by the perfect environment controlled down to the last detail.

Cool blue light sprayed up the walls from the decorative holographic fountains in the reception area, although tinted warm by his dark glasses. He wanted to be incognito, anonymous, without name or shape and just let the power of his presence announce him. Hovering over the streets where the buyers and sellers wrestled, he knew he was better than they and enjoyed looking down from the windows just for that point of view and indeed took a moment each day to do it. Across rows of desks with computer monitors were faces, most looked up and smiled as he passed and some greeted him with the routine complacency that offices tended to breed in workers like a tenacious virus. Charles Iverson smiled back, beamed even as he popped off greetings and energetic rejoinders all the time keeping a brisk and steady pace, holding to the course as he believed a man should take broad strides and know where he is going, or at the very least give that impression, especially at his age. From the doorway of an office a voice, "Hi Chuck." The man engaged him, tried to bring him in to the circle. He nodded, keeping the smile, the pace, cringing at a private thought. "No... no coffee, I've got a meeting." He was always called *Chuck* when someone wanted to make less of him. Even *Charlie* he could accept, but *Chuck*...

it was dull with rough edges and no aesthetic senses, it was common, a workers name and he took great offense at its use. Each time he knew the person had a hidden agenda and from then on kept a guard up around them. Perhaps it was too personal, and he didn't want that closeness because it inhibited his effectiveness. Charles Iverson would rather be dead than ineffective, and by the time he reached the conference room he was frowning and clenching the attaché he carried in his hand with a sweating fist.

He pushed his way past some loose chairs trying to maintain an even keel, hoping his demeanor would not reveal the bitter taste he had allowed to develop over the use of the nickname. Most of the others had arrived and were already seated expectantly beneath the low, mottled ceiling lights that threw each one into shadows giving them a mysterious air that they did not possess.

"Sorry I'm a bit late." He smiled, a practiced gesture, expected, pronounced, perfected.

The comment was met with assurances, dignified support, friendly overtures and immediately gave him confidence that he was among peers who respected him, or at least his position. Even the thought that the politeness given him masked true hostility did not disturb the calm that now descended. It was too good a moment. Across the burnished Rosewood conference table sat the head of programming for the PIA. A man who Charles didn't like because he was too presumptuous. He had always considered the PIA a minor, rather liberal agency having evolved from the Public Broadcasting System who, having their funding withdrawn in the late 20th Century, nearly ceased to exist until they were resurrected as the Public Information Agency when some farsighted legislators saw the need for government presence in cyberspace. They were not affiliated with the Global Communications Commission of the United Nations, but were an agency of the Western Government. The man always addressed him as an equal much to his rancor. He nodded. There were also several people from the Cyberwks VT Network who he was expecting, and of course his team from the GCC. At the far end of the table, half in shadow, working on a thin notebook computer was an odd and disheveled looking young man who appeared out of place.

He pulled one of his aides aside, "Is that some tech person working on the network wiring?"

The answer was whispered, covertly. "He's with Cyberwks, a *special* guest for us... I can only imagine he's a programmer, or an sFx Techno."

This intrigued him, because he knew what the meeting was about, he knew more than any individual at the table and that was why he was not equal.

Just then the door opened at the far end of the room. All faces turned as one. A shaft of light tore into the subtle environment. A moment passed. Four men filed in with crisp, military correctness and lined up along one side of the table pausing before they sat while the one, the most senior member, laid his briefcase to rest on the cool rosewood surface and unclasped the fasteners in the silence that had impregnated the room with one resounding snap. He then looked at the other three who were standing straight up next to him and smiled in a relaxed manner telling them to sit with gestures of his hands. All four men sat down in the same moment, coincidentally but like a precision drill team. Now that the representatives from CommNet had arrived, they all thought, the *Trust* was complete.

There is chaos at the point on which centuries turn. It is inevitable. Perhaps it is the rising of youth's brash voice entreating and insisting in the same instant that the future is here to stay, and like the Sun, (of old not our dying new yellow star), who swept the chill mornings causing the winds to rise and the trees to dance and the birds to all embark as one great thrust of life force to live on the wing until the last moments of twilight. It was so as the 20th century began. The spectacle of the moment when nine kings rode in the funeral of Edward VII of England on that shrouded May morning in 1910, which was yet the last instant of events surrounding the change of those centuries. The workingman had committed to a new future, yet those in mourning formed a line five miles long for a last glimpse of their King and with him the 19th century passing. Here were two thousand years of emperors and monarchs fading away into the dust. They had arisen after all with the conquering of fear and insecurity leaving the new century now abandoned, however modern and self-reliant they might have been, without a sovereign, a law giver, an arbiter... into the chaos, the chasm of the unknown country. So they came. They may have spent the night in rousing socialist political or union meetings damning the classed, the bourgeois, the owners of the means of production, but in the morning they came and stood waiting five miles deep. There must be chaos, it is a part of the coming of age of the universe, and as the centuries turn we come face to face with the cauldron of universal law and bring down the wrath of heaven for our mistakes.

As the 20th century ended again all things familiar passed. Though in the ensuing chaos, even through economic disaster, technological advances continued due in large part to the global quantum computer networks that were already in place when the economic and social collapse occurred. The Internet and government networks of the last part of the century. This period, known as the Kaiein[2*], devastated the economic and sociopolitical structures of the planet and resulted in the forming of a world government at the United Nations and two central geographical regions, the Eastern Hemisphere and the Western Hemisphere. The network of computers, however, was spared destruction because it was non-centralized so even with huge segments and areas inoperable it still continued to function and stayed on-line based as it was in many different countries. A huge root system that supported many trees.

The most significant development by far of this era was the metamorphosis of the telecommunication companies into *Providers*. This was occasioned by the complete transformation of electronics from analog to digital-where quantum computer technology merged with video technology, which in turn became one with voice telephone and videophone and all other communications and media including the vanished print industry. Broadcasting, print publishing and traditional

---

2* **Kaiein** (Kā-ë´-ˇin) n.1. The state of a rapid, catastrophic collapse of a civilization. 2. An epoch in which previously known technology and amassed knowledge is lost due to natural or human cataclysm. 3. A dark age. 4. The reversion of a civilization to savage practices. (Old English hæthen-savage, heathen, one inhabiting uncultivated land + Latin cadere-to fall, from Greek kleiein to close.)

analog telecommunications quickly became obsolete and all extant systems evolved into digital signals which were transmitted wirelessly to provide voice communications, video programming and computer interactivity all on one device. *Videtel* it was called by the technicians and soon the word was coined and television was replaced by its progeny... *VT.*

The telephone companies had already begun to lay an optical cable infrastructure before the end of the 20th century. So, with the maturing of optical technology, all digital signals were now transmitted by photons over wireless networks supported by a vast array of satellites. Deregulation of the communications industry was already in effect prior to the Kaiein so at the outset of this new technological infrastructure there were many independent providers all competing for a share of the consumer business. This proved nonviable since it was found that the services could not be supported and black outs consistently occurred resulting in a chaotic reconstruction period. When the world government was formed from a coalition of major powers already in place as the United Nations, regulation of communications was reinstated in the form of the Global Communications Commission, which was formed on the model of the old FCC. The nationalization of the communications industry was accomplished for the public good.

In the end three major players were left. The holders of optical cable networks became the *Providers,* heavily regulated private owners of all the lines and communication exchanges across the planet each under a government charter. They were supposed to be competitive, but melded into a comfortable tacit financial agreement where each of the three had a relatively equal slice of the pie. Finally the *Providers,* CommNet the major of the three, became the most powerful economic force on earth having complete control of the world's communications. Not kings, nor workers nor democracies could match them.

The GCC was supposed to be the regulatory agency, but it proved too vulnerable to power and its individuals had rightly seen that it was better to be relegated slightly less than complete authority rather than none at all. As a result it was more of a partner with the Providers than a watchdog. It was a question of economics and survival. The PIA was one of the independent Networks that contracted with the Providers. It developed and transmitted government information and programming as a public service. This was a concession made as a good will gesture and was not charged for. Other networks, like Cyberwks VT, developed entertainment and after the Providers themselves the entertainment networks were the richest, most powerful social power the world had ever known.

Contracts were the essence of the business. Contracts were coveted. If one held a contract he could survive, if not... then he'd better find a new line of work because there was no other avenue. They were cloaked and guarded and protected with men's lives. They were handed down from the Providers arbitrarily and once obtained were a guarantee of financial success. After all, a network with twelve billion captive viewers generated fortunes that were unheard of in earlier times. The contracts were prized accomplishments of executive strategy and an obsession with all who ventured into the communications field. People would do anything for a contract. Murders were committed, extortion, betrayal, anything was fair. The pact that the Providers and their networks silently made one with the other no one would question if they in turn granted power to the GCC, and exclusive contracts to certain networks such as the PIA and other even more murky details that no one person knew all of or could even guess...this pact was known colloquially as the *Trust*.

Now that the *Trust*, (a word not breathed but only spoken in the mind), had come together there was business to attend to. Charles Iverson was certain he knew what it was and could barely contain his excitement for it would mean that, in his case at least, a step closer to his personal goal would be attained after all these years.

At the table serious concerns were slow in coming through the small talk, but the air was rarefied... electric, pungent with expectation. The discussion of business finally materialized as if they had been in conversation about it for hours.

"...a ten share on the eastern margin. We expect the ratings to rise as the new systems connect with more households...", One man was saying.

"Yes, yes we were pleased to see some of your daypart slots rising. Makes us look bright, good decisions..." another replied forcing an enthusiasm through his stodgy conservatism.

Charles watched his hands folded neatly on the table in front of him waiting for the right moment and then at last spoke.

"The Director sends his apologies but was unavoidably detained," he told them, "but here I am," he smiled and glanced over to his aide, "your servant." Then spoke quietly, but so the others could hear, "Is there any agenda for this meeting?" Knowing perfectly well there was not.

The aide fumbled through his briefcase, "I... don't see one," turning to a young woman on his right, "Was anything distributed?"

"Well!" Charles clapped his hands, as he was fond of doing at inopportune moments just for the effect, and for the reason that he had noticed the young didn't do it, they were adverse to loud outbursts and so it gave him a sort of place marker in time. "Lets get to it while we still have our attention focused. "

Hisham Mostafa 'Ali Fayed Al-Razio placed his fingertips on the table in quick anticipation having voraciously read the paper sent to him on the new technology developed at Cyberwrk VT. Known to acquaintances simply as Al-Razio he preferred to be addressed formally as Hisham Al-Razio knowing that a certain weight was lent him by reason of his position at CommNet and he desired to uphold it. He was not a casual person, nor was he ruled by conformity, he was high strung and over bred like a fine, lean Saluki his sculpted face as if the nose was of alabaster, brittle to the point of flaw and intellectually brilliant far beyond the capacity needed for any business undertaking. It appeared on his chiseled features as an austere mystery, which foiled some and struck fear into others by reason of his position on the command lines as Western Liaison for the provider CommNet. Whether or not he was irrational as some have suggested, or maybe even a little crazy could be chalked up to speculation by those to whom he was disastrous towards in their quest for a contract. The blood of the economy. In this age there were few opportunities by reason of the sheer numbers of people, and once missed...many lives lay drifting in the Great Mandala passed over for no good reason. Hisham Mostafa 'Ali Fayed Al-Razio was quick to point out however, that in the end there really are no mitigating circumstances. One simply succeeds or he fails.

"Roxanne," Charles continued, "we're ready now."

The woman rose with sublime poise and an air of suppressed sexual abandon that flushed her face with a blustering look of endless frustration. She carried herself in a state of grace, for she at this moment, in this room considered herself to be at the vortex of the social order; grace for the millions of people whose lives she would touch; grace for the sake of new technology and scientific advance; grace for those yet to be introduced into this world which she would leave a richer place than when she had entered it.

"We are at the point of embracing a whole new form of expression," she began, "and I am going to introduce you all to it today."

Roxanne continued and expanded her vision, taking the technical far into the realm of the metaphysical, indeed to the spiritual as she rode the Pegasus of her own lyric having become an evangelist for this new experience. Reasons were difficult to decipher in many phases of life, but for this… it may have been as obscure as the thoughts of the last snow leopard at the precise moment it was becoming extinct, ceasing to be as a species, a genus, for all time as it gazed a last time across the Himalayan foothills never to return again. Who could calculate such things? Or perhaps it was too obvious, too mundane, too commercial and could be categorized to the industrial arts where commerce, taken to such a high form, competes in the stratospheric realm with pieces of fine art, exquisite arias, and perfect narratives told in one breath without a pause.

"Here," she said, "is where the saints desired to be, but could not. It gives breadth and depth to the very way communication flows over the media…it's new, so new we could not even find a vehicle for its use within our existing frame of linear thought. And so we invented a new one… completely nonlinear yet cohesive… in a word, compelling." She placed her hand flat on the table top, "Gentlemen, I am going to show you the future."

It was then that it all became clear to her, and she would remember the instant long into her life as age advanced and many things took on new meanings and old values seemed complex and irretrievable... she held it in her hand, it was a tactile feeling of reaching the core of things, of feeling the actual heartbeat of the universe. Perhaps, she thought many times in later years, at that instant feeling that vibration like touching a raw hypo-electronic nerve she was being warned by providence, but if so it was of no use. Her basic knowingness was overruled by the headiness of the moment. Emotion carried her beyond common sense.

The room grew dim except for one light shining over the thin and intense man working with fervor on the small computer, his companion, his repository of souls. A large screen direct view *videtel* was revealed nearly covering the front wall of the conference room and for a moment the Cyberwks VT logo was emblazoned across the screen in an elaborate animation. The screen was, Roxanne reminded them, only two millimeters thick. Then the piece began. The short pilot drama, multi-tiered with parallel story lines seamlessly interfacing and fading back and forth between scenes and characters blending identities and emotions that was an exciting compilation of earlier works patched together to demonstrate the new technology. The flashes of light were not even seen, except by Roxanne who had averted her eyes to catch the screen in her peripheral vision, as that was the only way to note the pulses. For the others, they were transported each time a wave of the new light caught them, fused, and became one with the drama feeling all sensations and emotions as if they were living the story line, only amplified to a magnitude bigger than real life losing any sense of personal identity.

When it was over and the lights began to rise she noted their faces, all of them, and especially Hisham Al-Razio. He was the most illuminated. Though emotionally drained he was on fire and Roxanne could tell immediately thrilling with success at the prospect of a contract and even more at what would come in the future. For she was certain that they held in their hands a great social force by which one could mold men's minds, and even their most primal thoughts, into new realities.

At the chair of the table Charles felt the tremendous emotion too. A rage had built up inside him that he was barely able to control and he felt a strong, compelling desire to lash out in a destructive frenzy. His eyes were wild. After a moment it subsided a bit and he wanted a strong drink.

"Was everybody as impressed as I was? Powerful is the word that comes to mind. I hope we all realize the significance of this new technology and what Cyberwks has managed to achieve with it. I had a brief preview earlier, though nothing as complete as this, and can clearly see the implications for all of us. For myself, and the GCC, the question now becomes what do we do with what we have? It's clearly a new form of communication and like all new forms will be subject to speculative use in an effort to determine its long range viability." He paused and grinned wolfishly to himself, " I just can't get over the clever part about it."

Hisham Al-Razio sat upright and looked purposefully at Charles having had visions of his own regarding the revelations that just occurred and may have affected him more deeply than anyone at the table. "Which clever part?"

"That no one would ever know that it's happening, that this really is new technology, if they were not informed such as we were. Who would ever guess?" He smiled a crooked smile looking directly into Al-Razio's eyes.

"As you say the implications are quite significant and we at CommNet are prepared to do a feasibility study on the practical application of this new technology." Hisham replied shaking slightly with excitement. He had an imagination unique to a man in his position, a position only two other people on the planet could have simultaneously. Even those two were conceivably greater than the number allowed in the ambitions of one who, if the truth were known, still felt the drive for competition, the challenge, the adrenaline rush of crushing all opposition. "For now, let's make certain that news of this discovery does not leave this room for any reason." He furled his eyebrows to reinforce his intention. "Do you get my meaning?"

Charles relaxed as the honey of understanding flooded his senses. The sweetness of the moment filled him. "Who would ever guess?"

Nash held the child's head firmly in his hand. It was warm, almost hot to the touch with a vulnerable softness yet radiating life. He responded to the deep need for ritual almost without thinking, as if it were an axiomatic essence rising to the surface when all the living masks had been cleared away. He saw the desperate relief in peoples' eyes, a homecoming, no matter how far or how long they had been abroad on the errands that life had given them. Each a seeker denying his own salvation even when it was close enough to feel its breath.

A cry pierced the air of the neglected cathedral. New life, a torrent of life rushing headlong and embracing the future, whose voice rang off the walls which had not heard the sound of youth in many long years. The tiny child's mother doted over him as he squirmed and stretched and flexed his stocky little body in the man's hands while other relatives and friends of relatives stood around.

"We take a moment to connect the past with the future." Nash spoke the meaning plainly and watched the eyes knowing full well that it would be lost on most who were sailing this life oblivious to the reason; kind in thought, good in deed, but still not strong enough to bear witness to the fundamental responsibilities implicit in the act of being alive. But this was why he existed; *why else,* he thought, would one need another's help if not for the disabilities suffered by all in one form or another, to one degree or another. The voice was strong and resonant and rose up into the higher channels of the church where perhaps archangels dwelt or even the Methodists who had been here before. It disturbed no one. The loud, shrill cry. It was drunk like wine, like music as the child made his voice known among those of this generation where he now found himself, announcing his presence, trumpeting his arrival to all who should know. He would be recognized even without the naming ceremony. Eyes bright and clear, it was the future he was pursuing and all present wished him well and hoped he would avoid the mistakes that each perceived had brought them to their current circumstance. *He's an able one*, thought Nash, *a fortunate one*.

There was a chill hanging in the air that had persisted since the early hours when Nash had first entered the day. The child was bundled against the cold as they stood around the old Christian baptismal basin. There were few left now who had been active in that religion, once and always known by its practitioners as the *one true way*. Perhaps that was its downfall, but more likely was the rise of scientific method and its profound influence on intellectual thought and on the products of the mind. The twentieth century had proven to be the century of the observable, the tactile, the real and the illusion of the real which was about as spiritual as anyone cared to get. It was the age of technology where the truth had to be demonstrated as usable, workable, and viable in the economic scheme and was something held in the hand rather than in the mind. At its close was the cataclysmic conflict between the socialists' rush to salvage two hundred years of human progress and the fundamentalists' reaction to the chaos that is inherent in global expansion. Whether the *Kaiein* was a catharsis brought about by the mixture of these two volatile trains of thought or was simply an indicator of the deteriorating world economic state has never been defined properly. There are still too many points of view, too many authorities and too much that is unknown being still so close in time. Men rode the edge of disaster and at last turned to the unknown when they were desperate. Nash knew this. At first they fight until the institutions around them fail and then they are forced to new alternatives following the prime command, to survive.

"We all recognize your presence here," Nash concluded his voice blending with the child's in a spiritual affirmation, "and you are welcome."

He handed the child over to its mother. "This one will keep your hands full for a long time."

"I know he will. He's like his father... look at him, *so strong...*" she cooed in the high pitched voice used only to speak to babies, small animals and insects.

"That's right," Nash replied, "he almost jumped out of my arms."
"Just spirited."

"*Of course he did,*" she whimpered to the child. "He's alive and knows it." Speaking in a disjointed manner still smiling and cooing at the child "Harry doesn't pay any attention to him," as if he wouldn't know what she was saying, "except when he cries, and then it's only to tell me to quiet him. The other night he told him to shut up. A little baby! Can you imagine? Why do you suppose..."

"It's a man's way sometimes," he comforted her, "I wouldn't worry about it... babies are new things, they're not mechanical, not common in a man's life... give him time."

She smiled up at Nash. "Think so?"

"Surely."

"I dunno."

"He'll come around... Harry's good."

"I suppose."

The woman turned her face to Nash, there were lines drawn from her eyes and young as she was it foretold a future. What worries, he wondered, could mark a face like that, still with the grace of youth blooming across it, features that kept their evenness through dark times.

"Thank you so much for naming my child." Tears welled up quickly and glistened from the light of the high windows. " It's just... so much we wish..." The words hung suspended between them timeless. It was as if she were grasping at something that did not exist in this universe and could never be expressed, yet held her with the desire to speak.

"I know," he said and put his arm around her shoulder, "I know." And he did know as he walked away leaving her there in the yellow light that came rushing in from the morning sky cleansing them of all that may have happened previously. He knew it as well as he knew his own thoughts, but he could not speak it either because it was one of those nameless things that accompanied the ritual and that did not really exist except in the experience of people, in the interplay between the intellect and the emotion, in that place between where the hand grasps and where what motivates it lives. It was his domain and he knew its landscape, though he could not speak of it either.

He withdrew now having performed his trust with someone who had needed him and was thankful it was a life entering the stage and not leaving it. There was much about his calling that did not suit him. It was an ill fit, he and the clergy, though an essential and inevitable one which he had been driven to realize from early childhood. When he reached his office at the back of what was once a rectory he was reassured by the familiar scrape of the door, as he flung it open, across the wood flooring where it left ever increasing grooves the first of which happened long before he was born. It always smelled like dust. He fell backwards into a padded office chair and tapped his fingers nervously on the arms. The energy would not subside. He had tried to contain it for many years, and then having failed to do so tried to channel, to direct it in a smooth copacetic manner, but it was incorrigible. Relentless. Once he concluded that it was his basic nature revolting against what he had decided was important and was rising up in the form of a rage that slept lightly just below the surface. Waiting. It made some others ill at ease. He cared little for what effect he might have on them, but took it as an indicator that a man of the clergy must have a basic demeanor which he could never possess and it dogged him in every face he saw that disapproved of him. For years it had been his battle, as if with the containment of his life force into some disciplined vector it would bring him a sense of inner peace, but more importantly would make him more effective. For he did not just want to comfort people, but to change them.

In the corner on the top of an old desk sat a computer. It was used when he got it, and flickered too much at the wrong times and often could not make the network connection he needed to go on-line with, but it represented an essential element. No one else in the church had taken the interest he had in the technology that now enveloped the world in a tight wireless, borderless cocoon flooding every perception to the maximum, taking every nerve ending to its finite limit holding all the sensations that were possible and clouding the spirit in a cloak of virtual anonymity. He was frustrated by people's petty problems and longed to get on with it, to come to grips with the accomplishment he had envisioned in his youth. Because of this he sought to channel his energy, to apply himself to the problems that came before him in his work. But it wasn't working, he still had dreams.

An older man peered in the door from the hallway, just standing quietly gathering himself before he entered, looking preoccupied as if there were something else he should be doing but what that might be he did not know.

"So you've done the naming?" he spoke, and marched forward into the cramped office at the same time brushing wisps of gray hair away from his eyes and back across his balding head.

"Oh..." Nash was startled, "Anther," he sighed. "Yes, I've finished. A good strong boy. Did you see him?"

"No, missed it." He stood looking straight at Nash waiting for the connection. "I was at the High Advocator's, he wants a meeting again tomorrow... with all of us."

"Suppose I can't get out of it?"

"...with *all* of us."

"That's what I thought."

"It's not so bad is it?"

"No..."

"Well I don't like it either but these things have to be done if you're going to have a group that's worth a..."

"...not so bad if you like sitting there listening to a lot of tired rhetoric being rehashed. Anther, they just like to hear their own voices."

The man smiled and his broad face cracked in a hundred places, the ceiling light shining off his nose and forehead bringing out the redness in his skin. "Everyone's entitled."

"You can name a sow Marie and tie a ribbon in its hair, but its still a pig."

"You're not trying...?"

"If they'd just get out on the streets sometimes they'd get a better feel of things– can't tell anything from the media–they don't get that it's all made up. It's lies..."

"We should talk."

Nash grabbed his coat and stormed down the hallway raising a little wind like the one that stirs the ochre-yellow leaves crossing the seasons from the cool greens to the grays and white, the barren branches. "No. I have to go."

"You need to learn to relax," Anther said plaintively, "you're hyped up all the time, take it easy," following Nash down the hall, losing him, calling after, "you can't get anything done by yourself!"

Anther fumbled with the meanings. He tried hard to grasp the new realities that loomed with such sheer and monumental presence that he was washed and nearly invisible in their shadows. How could his values be so obscured he wondered? Old, but not so old as to see the fundamentals pass away before him in one lifetime...or perhaps it was just that with age he had come to view things differently, to see them in their more essential state, which had eluded him throughout his entire life until this last and sweetest moment.

Nash followed the light that came flowing through the open door. Oceans of light. Followed it until he was out under the sky and when he looked up it lifted him from the toil and he felt whole and integral and from far above the cool cirrus clouds blessed him. Stratospheric winds brushed his cheeks and gave him a bracing, wide-eyed look. He was glad to be out. He didn't like being confined in a building unless involved with someone, but was drawn to the cross thread fabric in the streets; of lives that brushed one another and overlapped unknown; where two men could be standing close enough to touch, maybe even look at each other, but of incidents and meanings they remain forever strangers. Yet there was an interchange, a granting of life, a secret knowingness which gave each license to exist and that each sought no matter how well hidden it had become. The symbiotic existence of things played upon Nash because in part he was acutely aware of all these elements by being removed from them, exterior to them, yet dealing with them as a trade like an explosives expert would with dynamite.

Reaching his car he drove off into the city. He lit a cigarette. The smoke curled in thin waves drifting up oblivious to the rush of wind outside. It was one of the few places he could have one without risking a citation...and trouble with the High Advocator again. If he saw someone looking he'd just incinerate the smoke in the electronic shredder. No evidence, no ticket. The last time he was caught he hadn't been paying attention. The cop was stopped in the middle of the street and though he should have suspected a ruse, Nash just slowed and drove by like honey making its way around the handle on a honey jar, but then riding behind him the officer could just make his hand out through the tinted window as he raised it to his mouth for a drag. He should have known. It cost him five hundred dollars, but even more painful was the loss of nearly a full package of black market cigarettes. The judge offered to give them back if he revealed where he got them. He couldn't of course, it was confidential, priest penitent privileged.

Policeman probably hadn't changed in centuries. They were an anachronism creating trouble to justify their position. But one cop he liked. One of his few friends who he had met accidentally some years ago at the suicide site of a young and gifted programmer and for no reason the chemistry or perhaps their similarity or even their differences formed a spiritual bridge between two worlds one ethereal and one brutal. It was an odd relationship. Neither could define it nor understand it, but each gained some unnamed thing missing in his own existence from it. For that reason Nash had come to see him now, because there was something missing that he was beginning to feel driven to discover.

McGilvery was in his office on the eighty-seventh floor. It had no windows and so he was deprived of possibly the one pleasure that could compensate for a living being so removed from the natural world. The only sound in the office was the hissing of air through the vents in the ceiling even though there were several people crammed around the equipment over which McGilvery hovered. Nash had ridden the elevator from the underground to the 87th in only a few heartbeats and after he passed through security at the divisional desk, placing his palm flat against a scanner that checked his prints against a global databank containing billions in less than twenty seconds, (there were iris checks for altered prints or when the computer spat out an alert), he found his way through the narrow corridors off which small, jumbled offices stood to Derek McGilvery's space. It was not unlike the other offices except that it was smaller and right now it was crowded. The recessed lights in the ceiling gave an indirect glow the color of cool daylight and dim, casting no shadows, while the floor was a mass of cables, some bunched into conduits and others simply a crisscross disheveled patchwork leading up to flat screen monitors and CPUs and all sorts of stacked peripheral equipment. Three people sat at different stations. The walls were all packed with built in electronic equipment that flickered now and again as a metaphor for the lives they represented.

Nash stood in the doorway watching the burly man punch in code on the touchscreen and leaning down over someone's shoulder to scrutinize the monitor barely a foot away. He had glasses, but refused to wear them most of the time convinced that they would make him lazy and infirm by offering a crutch and a reason not to try to focus on the fine print. McGilvery was the antithesis of the stereotype being sort of an intellectual virtual detective preferring to anthropomorphize bits of information, the zeros and the ones of computer languages, into personalities. Perhaps it made it easier for him to see the logic, to follow a purely human line of reasoning through the myriad of global networks on which almost all humanity was connected.

"They don't really think do they?" Nash asked calmly from the doorway.

"Of course they think," was the gruff reply without even bothering to look around, not moving a single muscle like a coyote homing in on a field mouse having learned the skill over the years of maintaining a complete concentration while at the same time carrying on a conversation competent enough to handle anyone who might wish to disturb him. "They think more clearly than you and I. Less distractions, no aches, no pains, no fears. Hey," he instructed a young woman at one station, "get through this protocol, I want that machine operating in the background"

"No dreams either. Or memories."

"Like I said..." he looked quickly at Nash and smiled, then was back at it.

Colloquially called Cybercops at the beginning of the twenty-first century when the law enforcement division dealing with the global computer networks first evolved now they were simply known as VOX, an acronym for *voice operated xmodem,* a once-special connection technology developed by the police to override the security of a terminal-to-terminal communication. In a few words, a digital listening protocol. Clearly VOX now comprised more than half of all the world's law enforcement personnel. The crimes they pursued were mostly financial either through electronic interceptions of fund transfers, hackers breaking account security codes and breaching firewalls to simply siphon off the money and place it in their own unknown account or industrial espionage–every business and personal computer terminal on the global networks was constantly under attack by hackers, amateur and professional–or terrorists. Security was the huge global business. After more than a century to mature it had become very effective. Unless the hacker was extremely sophisticated, more brilliant, more sublime, that's where VOX came in. The digital ecosystem of Earth was balanced on the razors edge in a dangerous and precarious way, more catastrophic in its consequences than anyone ever predicted, more dehumanizing than anyone ever imagined. As profession after profession had become automated with electronics there finally came an event horizon where the whole economic and social structure pivoted on computers. A point of no return. That was also the point they became the primary target of every ambitious criminal on Earth. VOX was the firewall between brilliance and oblivion.

Nash was silent, angry without knowing why. He watched McGilvery intensely working on a computer shoving his face up close to the flat screen and mumbling little epithets as if he could jump inside the virtual world any time leaving all earthly responsibilities without any trace or remorse at all. The light from the monitor glowed across his agitated features in fundamental rhythms that Nash recognized as not being part of the digital language, but rather a song that filtered through leaves and branches moved by moist jungle breaths to create a filigreed calliope of shadow and illumination. It spoke as plainly as it spoke to the last Pygmies who lived in the Ituri Forest over two hundred years ago as a harbinger of extinction. He absently raised his hand in the dim room and let the glow play upon it hoping perhaps to span the centuries and connect with a simpler time.

"I almost have you," the words rumbled up from McGilvery's throat in a raspy, determined, growl, "just keep on..."

"Is this a bad time?" Nash asked.

"Some little weasel no one's been able to catch because he's so *god dammed* smart but now, just now I got him on the line and he's going for it." Numbers flashed by on the screens, banks of numbers, columns, charts, all changing rapidly cycling though sequences as each of the three people on the terminals worked furiously at erudite passages of code that only a select few on the planet had taken the time to master. "He's trying to get in. I set up a site on the network with layers of firewalls and encrypted passwords just for him, the little *sonofabitch,* and now he's going for it! Once he's through? Pow! It's like a photograph, we'll get everything traced instantly and a team'll be on him in minutes." Derek slyly looked back over his shoulder. "This guy's been on line for five years and no one's got near him. Uses remote locations to log in, could never get a trace. He's nailed now."

"What do you mean?"

"He calls a mobile phone from the other side of the country and then logs onto the network from the second unit bouncing all over the place funneling through different sites so he always comes from a different location. He can break into anything. A god dammed criminal genius I guess! Been transferring money to offshore accounts carte blanche, then by the time someone finds it the cash is long gone. He's just generally raising havoc with corporate systems. But now..." leaning back in the chair watching the screen, "we'll see. Coffee's over there if you want it."

McGilvery fell silent and Nash couldn't tell if he was breathing or not. Outside in the hallway people shuffled by as if there was nothing going on under the pale lights that gave everyone a bluish pallor. The others in the room were motionless, waiting, the prey in sight, afraid to give him their scent. He understood the theory of what was happening, but not all the mechanics involved. Nash's comprehension of networks and their protocols was strictly from a users viewpoint. He pushed the button and expected it to work. After all it wasn't as if there was no tech help. It was so completely impersonal that he had a difficult time relating to it, but McGilvery didn't. To him it was just cops and robbers—he was chasing some sweaty little man down the street on a hot night through the soot covered walls with the sounds of traffic in the background and the streetlight marquees glaring off glistening brows and terrified faces.

"Yes! Yes!" With clenched fists Derek was sitting up in a chair holding on to its arms ready for flight. "Comon!" He was perspiring, though it was cool in the room for the computers and other equipment that had better care taken of them than most people. "Gotcha now!" He looked back at Nash as if he had just found the unifying equation for the universe. Standing, "He's in now, we got him. No sweat, we got him. Logged into Atlanta? Good. They got his stats… he's done. Yes!!!"

Twenty minutes later Nash and McGilvery sat in a small sterile conference room. The big man was hunched over a cup of coffee, which he clasped in two hands and cradled carefully between sips as if guarding it from a chilly wind. He was thinking about what Nash had asked him, about something that required him to gather all his attention in order to consider it properly and the effort caused him to scrunch up his brow and clench his jaw together with such a force as to make muscles flex in little spasms. "That's really the GCC's territory, we don't have jurisdiction on the Network lines." He spoke without looking up, "Or the PIA for that matter, though we've had plenty of reason to go in there…" Raising his eyes to face Nash, "we've been warned off on several occasions."

"Really?" Regarding his friend for a moment he felt a strange affinity, the source of which he couldn't determine since they existed in such different worlds. It was a harmonic existence, a coincidental meeting, chance pure and simple that balanced them in such a delicate way. McGilvery a man of Earth and physical sciences, while Nash dealt with the fading concept of souls. "You guys get wind of everything up here…must have heard something about it." There was no immediate reply. "Haven't you?"

"Yes and no."

"Meaning…?"

"Officially no, unofficially maybe."

Nash thought for a moment. "They call it *fusing*." He began. "I first noticed it maybe a year ago when some parishioners complained about their son becoming hooked on the network VT. I tried to talk to him about it, but he wouldn't–or couldn't. He's gone now, he left, they don't know where he is." Nash went on to explain everything he knew about the phenomenon. "There are others. It's the new techno-wonder-drug, without the drug. It's a legal way to lose oneself in a virtual world. I've seen people, even in public places on encrypted wireless circuits, completely gone. That's what made me think it was in the programming and not just an anomaly."

"Sounds like moral decay, more your business than mine."

"It's not that easy, there's something physical going on, something unholy. When I looked into that girl's eyes the other night, they were blank..." He studied the man, "You're the only one I know who can give me some information..." he said expectantly, "if you're willing..."

McGilvery laughed softly letting the sand run over his voice and the sea fog come in and cover the harshness of his eyes with a personal warmth he usually kept hidden, "Let's not get personal."

"You know what I mean."

"I'll look into it." He spat out half smiling.

Nash smiled and his eyes lit up. "You still in that antiseptic high-rise?" Referring to one of the apartment complexes McGilvery lived in that shot up out of the city like a huge blade slicing the sky with copper-mirrored glass reflecting the orange and olive sunsets of a pollution saturated atmosphere. Only on rare occasion did the winds rise up and clear the basin of its industrial clouds and it was not unusual for a person to live for a decade without having a glimpse of the mountains that ringed the city only a few miles away. Animal spirits lingered there, or so the Indians still said, waiting for the white man and all this to pass. But Nash knew they were here to stay. The newer buildings were completely self-sufficient. Hermetically sealed each with its own atmospheric generating station that purified all the air inside and maintained optimum barometric pressure, temperature and humidity. The artificial gravity devices that allowed for 4G elevators also maintained the structures during the frequent earthquakes, not levitating the buildings but steadying them much the way a gyroscope would so they rode out the tremors on huge concentric coils at their base giving them the appearance of rockets sitting on giant thrusters. The walls were honeycombed with fiber optic sensors and each living space was equipped with its own complex control panel that precisely monitored everything from climate to interactive communications. It was, in essence, like living inside a computerized womb, devices supposed to be the servomechanisms of men. The irony of it did not escape Nash.

"It's got a view."

"I always feel like it's been too long, but then... time just goes by doesn't it?"

"Little too fast for me."

"How have things been going?"

Derek McGilvery sat back in his chair and looked blankly ahead while he surveyed the internal carnage of his own life continually sorting out what was important from what was not. But he was never a casualty, never experienced the emotional turmoil most people were under or the economic crush. He had been drawn into the technical sciences early and suddenly was a young man thoroughly trained and working before he ever considered whether he had a purpose or not. "You know how it is. So much politics." He said reticently unable to form a cohesive statement from the many conflicting and turbulent situations he was concurrently involved in. "Sometimes I wonder if people ever change, they just seem to repeat themselves."

It was a sense of frustration that Nash could understand very well. "Has something happened?"

"Nothing unusual I don't think..."

"What is it?"

"You're walking on sensitive ground here... I shouldn't even be talking to you about this...how much do you need to know for God's sake?"

"It's confidential, privileged... I'm a minister."

"Maybe so, but this is agency business."

"Looks to me like it's your business."

"Yes..." McGilvery sat up close and leaned his elbows on the table taking a personal tone. "...that's right...I get warned off more times than I like to think about."

Nash's gray eyes were still. "So tell me." He was curious about answers he wanted for questions he wasn't sure of, but also felt a deeply personal concern for his friend and out of habit began to detach from his own needs and focused on those of the confessor.

"Like this guy we were nailing in there...he's not that bright, after all he's a criminal...so why has no one caught him before? I think they were warned off."

"Why were you allowed to continue?"

He considered this a moment, and spoke to himself while looking down. "I guess you might call me the last resort. I'm the guy they come to when all else fails. The thing is..." he glared suddenly, "the guy wasn't so difficult to catch, did nothing imaginative. I can see nothing new. It was just his time so they called me in as if someone had decided he wasn't useful anymore. Part of his activity involved breaking into research databases and stealing sensitive industrial secrets. He got into Bell Optics, The National Science Academy, Tectron Corporation, Cyberwk and other local independent production houses. Funny thing is, there were never any records of these crimes until far past the statute of limitations, and the real reason he was pursued only came up when he began to transfer funds. Oh! And he got arrogant, too confident... someone didn't like that."

"Then how did you find out about the other break-ins"

"They're all in the docket, peripheral data, background information. A lot of times a company won't press charges when their security has been breached because they're afraid it will call attention to the fact and will attract more hackers. There is a limit to encryption. With enough people working on it nothing is really secure. So, it's not that unusual. But this guy... these companies all did work for the network provider CommNet and I couldn't help seeing a pattern in the reports."

Nash listened silently nodding his head on occasion. "Who warned you off?" He asked.

"It's not that simple," McGilvery explained cautiously, "we get it in orders down normal command lines... or in a subtle hint from someone, a lack of funds maybe, an overload of work in another area, any number of ways. It all means the same thing. Get off the case, leave it alone.

"Do you think it relates to what I want to know?"

"I can't say, but something's wrong and it makes me furious... I hate being misled. I hate being lied to. I just hate it! If it's got something to do with your questions, I can't say... but something's going on. Something important. A storm is coming. Somewhere, far off. I know because birds are fleeing the wind.

- IV -

Epiphany

There have always been voices rising up in dissidence and harmonies, in crescendos of polyphonic reasoning mirroring the million eyes, each with a different point of view, trying to inhabit the confluence of humanity called The City. The ebb and the flow ride on the muscled backs that sweat out endless hours upon which lies the structures of daily lives. But someone had to pay the price of all the comfort, all the convenience, it didn't come easy. There were casualties. Here the moon peeked through the murky atmosphere a yellow cat's eye shedding pale light upon a dark errand.

The pungent smell of sweat hit his nostrils. It was unusually strong and gripped him with its fist, like an astringent causing him to gasp imperceptibly and hope that no one else smelled it and that it wouldn't betray their stealth. It was the smell of fear. He knew this, but would not admit it as he crawled through the air ducts on the ground floor of the network building sliding on his knees through the dust and neglect of the usually closed shaft after the other dark shapes. Being caught was something he had never thought of. He had no contingency plans for that occurrence. He looked at his companions, blackened faces hidden in the night only eyes emblazoned, he knew that they had no plans either. Each was on a mission that ran deeper than reason, one that transcended physical safety and indeed even at the cost of their lives. There has to be something one is willing to die for. It's fundamental.

He felt secure in the knowledge that God was with them. The innocent were blessed and immune from the mistakes of mercenaries and
professionals and so they proceeded without incident. They climbed the
dark stairs soundlessly, (he felt the cold bones of the building beneath
his fingers as if some slumbering giant lay waiting only for the light), all
seven of them, a holy number, a number as old as the ages.

The first steps had been easy. *I want six bold men,* he listened, and
I will make the sacred number to ensure our success. How his heart had
thrilled at the thought of it and he could not sleep for three nights, as
he lay awake feeling the rush of purpose, the glory of the moment that
denied him access to the nocturnal paths. Why sleep? He wished to
savor the moment, to relish it and loll in the magnificence it gave to his
otherwise uneventful existence. His hands felt the cool metal beneath
the dust and the only sounds were those of the others sliding along
as he was with their own thoughts as companions. (What might they
be?) It gave him strength to think that there were similar minds to his
and that others were filled with self-doubt and were struggling with
purpose and desires just as he was. (Who was to judge?) It gave an
urgency to his mission and made up for what he lacked in dynamic
with enthusiasm, a blindness with which he could approach the future
couched in what was right as could be confirmed by the indisputable
fact that others were here, doing as he did, following as he followed.

It was the intellectuals that inevitably led whether they held positions of power or not. Their insights could not be denied by the striving
masses that by far outnumbered the elite, even though they controlled
the lion's share of wealth and resources. But it was more essential than
even that. He had never guessed in his entire life up until this point,
there was never an inkling of how fundamental the real issues were
that determined who would survive and who would not. *We will not be
led like cattle,* he had heard, *we will not fuel the furnaces of economic
slavery!* The acrid smell of perspiration grew stronger in the enclosed
space and it mixed with dust and a slight odor of oil. He became more
anxious with each movement and his knees began to ache on the cold
sheet metal.

Ahead dappled yellow light filtered through a grating. It silhouetted the figures struggling before him with an eerie halo that burst through the dusty air in tiny moving beams that dissipated in the tunnel far behind him. Back where the life was out of which he had come where the thought of breaking the law was a concept too unnatural for him to consider. Perhaps it was just fear, too much pride in his physical self to be able to easily accept the retribution he knew would inevitably be delivered from acts like the one he was embarked upon at this moment. He thrilled at the thought, like the first night he had decided to go with the leader he again felt the elation of completely severing the ties that bound him to this society and in fact, as he had learned and come to know intimately, had chained him. *The Automatons want you purely as support of their electronic machines...the* infrastructure–*how many of you, how many have been displaced, dispossessed of the right of a man to work with his own hands for himself and his family?* The truth gave him power and with that newfound energy he became someone else. The élan vital coursed through his body as he hoisted himself up over the edge of the broken grating and felt his feet land firmly on the ground in the dimly lit room the location and significance of which he didn't know. But with trust he followed. Hadn't the leader given him enlightenment, and guidance with his philosophy in many areas of his life, his up to this point meager existence that no one before had paid any attention to? He would follow now into the heady realm of the avenger with his sacred burden secure in a backpack honored that among all the others he was chosen to carry it. *Death be dammed* he thought.

At that exact instant across the city Nash felt the shock of cool metal on his fingers as he turned the knob and opened the heavy, wooden door. They were all there. Only Anther looked up as he entered the room though he was still embroiled in conversation across the long table. The High Advocator, who sat at the head in an old wooden high-backed armchair in which he slouched resting his old frame with elbows propping himself up. His head, however, was erect and radiated the intense life energy that characterized his entire being. The gaunt and bony face was framed in long, straight white hair and was set in what appeared to be a moment of extreme and perpetual exertion–the eyes bright blue and electric. He had always been a strongly physical man until his seventieth year when debilitating illnesses began to take their toll on him. It made his already acerbic nature, with which he goaded his subordinates into compliance, more pronounced and gave him an unrelenting quality as a last stand against mortality. *Death be dammed*, was the most recent epithet, but only replaced others that had the same intention he used throughout his entire life that had no relation to his physical condition. He was, however, a keenly intelligent and sharp-witted man and so his directions no matter how difficult to accept by reason of their delivery were often correct and pertinent to the situation. No one would have allowed him power in the Church, even with its failing congregation, if he had not been right most of the time.

With this support and agreement the staunchly conservative *Old Religion* continued refusing in this congregation, as within others across the Western Hemisphere, to change as the times had changed leaving it an anachronistic island in a digital world constantly in flux. Nash scowled as he entered feeling the decay embrace him and the specter of doubt descend upon him again.

Sixteen others around the table were all men over fifty. No women had ever been allowed to become ministers despite extreme social protests. Only Nash, of all of them, had been allowed into the ministry at a young age and was admitted to the High Advocator's council at the Cathedral, the main church of the city, because the High Advocator himself had intervened from inside the Church hierarchy. Even he could not deny the purpose that burned in the young man. He could not deny it.

They were all well intentioned, but were forced to temper any liberal ideas in order to preserve the integrity of the spiritual union brought about by The Canon of the Church. It was written in old books, fragments that had survived the neglect and collapse and was in fact a catharsis of many different religious philosophies out of which the most important tenets had been appropriated and compiled into what was commonly known as the Old Religion. It had enjoyed tremendous popularity in the last century during the period immediately following the Kaiein when the economic structure had completely collapsed and men found themselves in a spiritual wasteland with no faith, no belief to carry them other than the median income standards and economic models developed with advanced calculus that were supposed to right every imbalance of the economy, which had gone with the wind. It was then the old men came into power, The Rememberers, they who had lived long enough to have some spiritual foundation were then looked to for guidance by the young, the strong, the lost. They became evangelists for the word, not of God in the traditional sense, but of the spirit, of the greater life force over and above the physical world containing possessions and all the sensations so rapaciously hunted by all the living before the collapse.

Due to this alone social order slowly returned. The economic base, however, was never the same. Gone were the institutions that had created men's lives and provided them with their values and slogans and their ethics to uphold...it was all gone. Since the vast honeycomb of interconnected quantum computer networks had survived all communications and then commerce occurred over these digital highways and so from birth each child was online, immersed in the nomenclature, the technology and the by-products of the post digital Armageddon. A new God arose from the moral ashes and decay, His face was electric with radiance, His eyes filled with the sacred numbers and from His mouth flowed all the knowledge of the universe in a deafening roar that made men humble and meek before Him.

Nash sat down at the only available seat. "Gentlemen," He said to announce himself, but more for self-recognition since no one had acknowledged his presence but Anther. Beside him the old cleric looked over and said "Thank you." And gave him a saccharine pat on the shoulder.

The room was a pastiche of many centuries with opulent trappings that represented different beliefs and pulsed with muted gold and polished ebony, silver and ivory beads now so obscure the animals from which they came lived only in myth. After the rise of the Rememberers all religious artifacts from many disciplines were meticulously gathered together and entrusted to the Brethren of the Old Religion, they alone kept the spiritual alive and each symbol was thought to represent the collective wisdom of man who through violation of universal law had brought about his own social collapse. Symbols of the mandate from God for the chosen to manage the religion as they saw fit. It seemed only just and was declared illegal for these artifacts to be possessed by anyone other than a Church representative, which immediately created a vast black market and fetched astronomical prices for the commonplace and the absurd. Here rested Orthodox Icons, elaborate Stars of David, ancient sandstone carvings of Vishnu and other deities, a huge Golden Buddha, a handwritten manuscript of the *Tào Té Ching* said to be from the hand of Lao Tse himself–and a thousand other relics obscured by clouds.

While it was true that many items had been disbursed throughout the Churches across the world and could be seen by any common man, but those of inestimable value were placed in sacred chambers such as this one for the privileged whose right it was to possess them or hidden away in even darker vaults. There were rumors, however false of true they may be, of vast treasuries stored at some undisclosed location that only the highest officials knew of and were sworn against their life to secrecy. Riches beyond price. With them the ancient books, literature and records that together made up The Canon. The Archives were a common fact, but just what was in them was subject to wild speculation. They were kept by a secret order in the Church, enlisted for life, forbidden to leave. All Canonical law came down from the highest ecclesiastical council in the form of Encyclicals and every matter of doctrinal law was put before this council as final arbiters.

"As of last month ending our books have balanced." The High Advocator droned with a wry deceptive smile. Around the table attention was immediately drawn to him and murmurs of "New donor" were exchanged in hushed whispers "Yes, yes it's true," replied the white haired old man, "but that doesn't mean anything has changed. Not anything..." he took a moment and glared at each of the seated men, "except of course that our books *are* balanced for the first time in some years. Our new patron, she wishes to remain anonymous, has indeed been generous...as I hope is a testament to our good works and those that will continue that align with The Canon." His cold eyes glared at Nash on these last few words. "We will speak of this later."

A stocky man removed glasses from the bridge of his nose and laid them on the table speaking as if from the middle of a continuing dialogue that he was preordained to complete against his will. Light reflected off his round cheeks "We have had more parishioners requesting counseling in the past six months than at any comparable period in our history. The income from this is up, but then," he put his glasses back on, "can we afford to turn those away who cannot pay? I think not." He ventured an opinion and frowned with a frustrated concern wondering if he had done the right thing. Without waiting for a reply, "We have discussed this and think the downturn in the economy has created these pressures. However, we are exhausted. We've managed to attract a few laymen for training but if this continues we *will* have to turn people away, even those who can afford it, and that's not good with congregations failing across the hemisphere. Perhaps," he offered, "we can afford to waive the usual fees..."

"Our overhead alone is enough to answer that." A man from the head of the table next to the High Advocator spoke. He still had jet black hair and it was slicked back neatly trimmed, which was a holdover from his term in the military prior to vows of the ministry, and for this reason everyone still called him Commander Rybin. "We can reach five hundred and thirty million people on the Web who seem to do nothing more than peruse the computer networks searching for entertainment. It costs money to be on that network, our parishioners are contributing to our missionary work they know what their money buys. It's tradition."

"Tradition dictates that a religious man does what's needed..."

The High Advocator dismissed the flare up with a wave of his hand "Please. Let's try to keep this meeting to the point. There is a new Encyclical that I wish to share with you after the normal business is complete." The two men looked up at the High Advocator and suppressed their heated feelings for the sake of conservatism tacitly agreed to be the best for all. "Now, I'd like a brief report from each committee chairman." He pronounced and waited expectantly for his wish to be complied with finding some satisfaction in the fact that it inevitably always would be.

In another part of the City another group continued on its predestined path because just as the cauldron of collected wisdom had spawned a singular religious philosophy so had the monolithic armies of technocrats awakened their nemesis. The seven made their way humbly through the dark on a self proclaimed desperate mission feeling their way along hands against the wall gripping for whatever stability might be needed to boost the resolve each had for success. They passed closed doors, locked and darkened for the night, hallways with dim incandescence meant only for emergency crews to locate the power switches and long corridors that led off into the corporate reaches of the building complex where administrators perpetuated the machine. The vast architecture of the server farm–thousands of quantum computers all linked and working together as one giant mind far superior to any human–kept in huge refrigerated abyss like structures.

He felt alone. But wishing for a God did not bring one into existence and the words he had heard still lingered making him feel empty when he needed to feel full...*If you are looking for God, look to the inner mirror; there is no help other than that which you give yourself and no answer you do not already know.* The utter bleakness of self-sufficiency did not fully hit him until now, when he needed his wits and ability. He never once stopped to ponder the question of sin, how could it exist without a god, how could evil exist without goodness?

Suddenly, and without any warning the Leader raised his hand in the dark as a signal and all seven men held completely still as one. Only their frosted breath betrayed them. Up ahead, beyond the three men in front a warm glow spread out from a side corridor. "We're going in now." Someone whispered. And they moved, a step at a time every instant perceiving the particles around them in the air, subtle fluxes in the atmospheric pressure, temperature changes, slight, nearly imperceptible noises coming from far off, through walls and ceilings and floors...he felt entombed and that was where his God came from, out of desperation, rage that reflected his own deep sense of frustration for disabilities that prevented him from the accomplishments he knew he had the capacity for. Holding fast as the waves of fear swept over him fueling the resolve, the rage, the moment he was living through. As they rounded the corner and headed for the source of the light he became acutely aware of the soft padded ringing of his footsteps upon the highly polished floor, and his staccato breaths that seemed to echo off the walls...(Will I betray them with the sound of my heart?) He was fully alive, only now, at this moment, all other moments ceased to have any significance for him and he surged forward with complete certainty, a certainty he had never had before. The weight of the explosives strapped to his back became suddenly lighter.

Down a long hallway they came to a window. There was a series of interconnected rooms with *Videtel* monitors, computers and electronic equipment of all kinds. And there were people, technicians driving the devices. This was not what they were looking for, it was not the source but only a relay point and they each seemed to know it not only because they had studied floor plans intensively, but also because it didn't surge with the power they knew the heart of the beast would. Light spilled out into the blackened hall as the seven darkly dressed men slipped by unnoticed as silvery fishes in the moonlight.

On the VT monitors danced sinuous images. Undulating rhythms pulsed through the fiber optic cables as numbers, zeros and ones in a billion different configurations. Hands of technicians on dials, knobs, levers, buttons controlled the flow as it rushed inexorably to the public who waited out there in the dark ravenous for sensation. The signals went to private pay-per-view clubs around the city the most exclusive of which were total virtual reality environments where the club paid a flat fee for the signal and their members in turn covered the charge with hefty dues. Here was the conflux, where the cold calculating figures of digital technology were translated into fantastic analog sights and sounds, which in turn were absorbed by entertainment starved people and adopted as their own experience. The Rex was in the old section of what was once downtown Los Angeles. The night enclosed as wind whipped against the sides of the old building, but not a soul was aware that the heavens danced in concert with the fleeting clouds in a spectacle of nature rare in any time and especially so in this age. People gathered at tables and donned the virtual gloves to be able to caress and fondle the perfect nude form displayed on the monitor for all to be a party to the imagined sexual depravity, or they were immersed head, hands and heart into an enclosed environment to fully experience the rage of passions, or perhaps the flaming crash of an Astrocruiser at three hundred and fifty miles an hour down the expressway only to emerge without a scratch. The narcotic drinks were soothing and enhanced the detachment needed to absolutely accept the electronic experiences as real, and reduced to quivering effect the strongest of patrons.

This social gathering was like those that were taking place all across the city, and indeed across the hemisphere in private homes, public space and exclusive clubs alike. The Trust had been the architects of On-Line VT, and this was its highest form…above the mundane information, the news, documentaries, entertainment programming of all variety…this was its apex, the state-of-the-art. The providers had invested trillions of dollars into the development of this virtual technology. The reason was simple. There was an inexhaustible, relentless demand for it from all quarters, all demographics and stratas. It was wealth, it was power, it determined the rise and fall of economies, the pinnacles of celebrity and the destiny of nations.

The elemental evil of this sin was a burden which each of the seven darkly clad men had assumed as penance for the remainder of the human race whom they pitied and were willing to sacrifice themselves for. At the end of the corridor they found the stairs. The certainty of this confirmed the fact that the plans they had studied were accurate. They followed them three flights up in the dark until they came upon a huge elevator whose doors were flush to the wall and locked with a digital combination and card key system. It took only a few minutes for the charge to be set. The Leader was an expert and even in the shaky beam of a flashlight the job was easy. The explosion was muffled, but still sent a resounding crack echoing down the stairwell and so they remained still and in defensive positions for a full five minutes. Advanced polymer devices actually weakened the molecular structure of the elevator doors so it was not force alone that gained them entry, a charge strong enough to blow the doors would have collapsed the walls as well. In moments the seven were riding the darkened elevator car to its destination.

The heart was an autonomous superquantum computer server farm system that was complete to the finest detail with a myriad of back-up systems, checks, balances and storage devices that all monitored themselves in a never ending self-inspecting corrective cycle. It was enormous, the size of several football fields yet completely unmanned. As testament to this new world men were superfluous, prone to mistakes, illness, politics and most of all they were not cost effective. To train and maintain a crew for this complex of digital equipment would double the operating costs and so it was that men were superfluous. That is as it should be in the mind of the futurists who foresaw the needs of living life anticipated and the futile labor of existence a thing of the past. It was the paradigm scientists had sought for ages.

Perhaps this perfection was foremost in the thoughts of the dark seven as the first charges were ignited sending showers of glowing particles high into the air when the optical cables cracked and popped loose giving each of them a rush of elation as their righteous indignation surged forth. Out of a thousand ways to bring down the beast the use of crass force seemed the most appropriate, the most fitting for the insidious and sublime sins that were perpetuated by the machines and those who fed them, perhaps fire and brimstone of legend could be the hammer of the future. Another explosion followed, and then another until the cavernous computer center was ablaze with flashes and the air filled with flying pieces.

He was knocked down by the first blast. It was not supposed to be so strong, but in the heat of the moment passion overtook reason and the desire for vengeance clouded good sense. The warm salty taste of blood was in his mouth and everything blacked out for a few precious moments–the display of exploding sparks, the sonic resonance of the deafening booms, the airborne debris– moments precious because he had never before realized how every instant of living could be used, how if opportunities passed without realization or inaction let the day escape it could never be recovered. He was sure there would be another day, but what was past would never come again except in the mind where the dust of many lost opportunities collected and inhibited him from inspecting it too closely. The time he was unconscious could not even be counted in minutes but when he came to all his muscles were flexed and he was bursting with life. *Finally,* he thought, *I am creating an effect, I am*!

"You'd better git goin'!" someone shouted from the smoke and the strong smell of cordite that now replaced the odor of fear that had vanished, "We're gonna really blow it now...gimme that pack!" He slipped the pack from his back and handed it to the fellow who had been shouting at him and who he had barely heard even though there was only about three feet between them. He watched the man set the backpack in the middle of some computer equipment and place a small electronic device on the very top of it, just perched it there as if it was a dresser stuck away in a quiet corner. Flames licked up the walls and live equipment still sparked and cracked. "Comon!!" The man shouted frantically and started running to the stairwell from which they had emerged.

He ran without thinking as smaller explosions were continuing to go off raising clouds of white smoke and a deafening cacophony. Running just behind the man he could see all six others in front of him racing down the brief flight to the elevator that would, hopefully, ferry them from harms way. Inside they all piled against each other the momentum of the run too strong to stop. Someone punched the button and the door slid closed. They looked at each other in the dark as the car rushed downward to safety, and for a moment, though they could not see each other's faces, they all smiled with gleeful elation.

"Amen," said the Leader panting from exertion, but prone to dramatics and not about to let the moment escape him, "We have struck a blow against sin tonight!"

Suddenly a tremendous explosion shook the building and slammed the descending elevator car clear through the wall. Fortunately, for at least six of the men, it landed on its side into an atrium of one floor with the car itself protecting them from debris raining down in the absolute blackness. The seventh man was crushed between the body of the elevator and the floor, gloriously, for the cause, his energy high and his blood racing with the headiness of the moment as all young soldiers go. Whether he felt the same after death about the purpose no one took the time to ask, they were too busy unpiling themselves and, after feeling the crushed skull and spurting blood determining at least one was dead, they reconnoitered on a flat plane in a corner. From above they could still hear the repercussions of the explosion and the sounds of building materials falling down the elevator shaft. The smoke and dust made it nearly impossible to breathe.

"It's gotta be a whole floor!" A desperate voice yelled.

"Gotta be...gotta be...I feel a wall here. How many are we, six? I feel six?"

He heard all their voices in the total darkness blood streaming into his eyes and for the first time he questioned the wisdom of his adventure. "There are *sis*, I know there are *sis*...the Leader's dead." He heard himself speak, with difficulty, there was something wrong with his mouth...missing teeth, broken jaw... "Find a door!!"

"Spread out now, slowly...don't loose touch..."

"Watch out for holes in the floor... it may have collapsed by the shaft."

"I feel something... something, I can't tell what."

"Well find out what!! Where are you?! What is it?"

"It's a crack!"

"He's right. I can feel it."

"Comon, the door opens in! It's gotta have hinges."

"Here we go. Got it!!"

"Lift!! Comon lift the damn thing, I know it's tight...ya wanna stay here?"

"OK, cummon...dammit, cummon!!"

For thirty-five minutes they struggled. Six men covered with dust and blood and sweat trying to get their slippery fingers on the edge of a hinge pin that was almost flush with its casing. Finally it came lose. The pins slipped out and the door was taken off the hinges and gently laid down to the left of where they were working. Immediately there was a shattering series of crashes as the heavy metal panel fell off the edge of a gaping hole in the floor not three feet from them where it had given way during the explosion and lie unseen in the pitch blackness. It fell into the elevator shaft and caromed off the walls floor after floor raising thunderous metallic explosions until at long last it reached the bottom with one final momentous crash.

"Might have been us," someone said.

"Maybe should have been after that announcement."

They filed out into the hallway, but still there was no light. Having the presence of mind and an unalterable sense of direction he began to lead them down the path that had led them in. Presently they found a stairwell and descended the number of floors they figured they missed, plus the number they had climbed. When they emerged again it looked familiar, there was a dim glow from the emergency lights and they could make out far down the corridor the glass windows of the control room they had passed on their way in. It was absolutely silent. The air conditioning had shut down and no other sound could be heard. Again they slipped like silvery fishes beneath the glass though this time there was nobody inside, the building had been evacuated and the emergency crews had not arrived yet. Through the dusty shaft they crawled this time without the smell of fear, or any smell at all and he did not even notice the dust or the cold steel on his knees.

The network went down. The signal ceased immediately cutting off hundreds of thousands of subscribers and blacking out the myriad of relay stations that acted as signal boosters. The real damage, however, was done at the highest levels, where people were connected to the virtual machines and had been mid-experience and completely oblivious to any outside stimuli. Lost. Enveloped in an artificially created world so real to them at the moment of blackout that unconsciousness was the consequence and their own memories paled in comparison to the experience they were subjected to. Panic ensued. Hundreds of bodies littered the clubs and private homes as people collapsed and the chaos ran from the sheer terror of being witness to a loved one mysteriously dropping away to the insidious terror of mass lawsuits and economic reprisals felt by the businessmen. Emergency lines were jammed. The

Parameds were in the streets and red and blue lights flashed against the sides of buildings everywhere.

Perhaps it was true that terror had become so common in people's lives that it no longer stood apart from the ordinary occurrences that together made up the collective experience of society. The terror of violence against ones person, of economic chaos, the flame of war over the horizon or simply the uncertainty of life on earth where even the invisible world seemed to conspire as when one virulent disease succumbed to eradication another one appeared more resilient and immune to our defenses than ever. Why it was then that Nash perceived the pain could not be easily explained, but he did while sitting among the others of the High Advocator's council and it caused him to keel over with feelings of distress. Reeling with confusion he sweated uneasily not able to know the source. The High Advocator had been discussing the local mission work and the scheduling of services in the Cathedral for the past hour with the heads of each committee. Nash braced himself fighting not to give his feelings away. He listened with a perfunctory attention but was filled with nervous energy anxious to get out and try to unravel the mysterious spiritual disturbance that hit him so hard.

"Now," said the High Advocator in conclusion, "having finished the business at hand, unless there is something I have missed...I will read you the Encyclical I received only yesterday copies of which will be distributed to you all as well as being posted and I expect you all to study and commit it to memory." It was a formally written tome expanding the Church's position on social values and the role a spiritual life takes in forming the foundation for those values. The old man read it matter of factly with clear diction and a detached, unemotional tone as if it was God's own truth restated and rephrased as only the Church's executives had the ability to do. Nash cringed as he listened to the rhetoric that was as meaningless to him as it must have been to the generations that had to endure the verbose aggrandizement of the middle ground for the past hundred years. Doubt and faith again clashed inside him.

It was a consensus originally formed from the opinions of the Rememberers, old men, on the virtues of considering all things before acting, but it failed entirely to be specific and was simply an ultra-conservative position on social consciousness and not a religious document at all. He sank down in his chair anxious to escape and hoping he could hold his feelings inside and avoid another confrontation with the High Advocator– because right now he was on edge, by the disturbance he had felt, and it made his naturally rebellious nature rise to the surface in an antagonism that people did not like. He resolved not to engage anyone in disputes for he wanted no interference now.

"Reverend DeCoucy there will be a service this Sunday, as is traditional for the Winter Solstice, and you will give the sermon." The High Advocator pronounced without looking up from his papers immediately upon finishing their reading and with a challenging tone in his voice that was not without a hint of malice. "The subject of the sermon will be from this Encyclical since I can see from your expression you are particularly captured by its meaning and its wisdom."

Nash was startled and sat upright in his chair, "Anther maybe, or Rybin I think would…"

"Aren't you able to speak publicly? I seem to recall a particularly eloquent discourse you gave to the press some months ago." "Yes… but I can…"

"Are you ill, you don't look that well…perhaps we are no longer part of your socially minded agenda anymore and if so there are smaller missions we can send you to where you will learn the true meaning of sacrifice."

He watched the venom expertly woven by the white haired old man who had not raised his eyes from the sheet of paper and was holding all at the table motionless by his insistence of subordination and acquiescence. "I'll be happy to give the sermon." Nash finally replied out of his resolve not to have a dispute.

"Splendid." The High Advocator looked up at him with a smile painted on his face with eyes like glazed marble, beautiful like a tomb. "I trust the wisdom of the elders will make itself apparent to you in your study."

That night Nash sat alone in his apartment reading the Encyclical and for all the words that lay before him it spoke of little that was spiritual, as he knew it. On the contrary, it seemed to validate and even support elements in society he had always seen as aberrations and opposed to the nature of the human condition. He tried though, he did try to fully understand the intention of those who had written the piece and completely duplicate the reasoning process that brought them to this point. Safety was what he finally deciphered, a safe solution in a volatile and up ended world where anything that was tinged with the spiritual was immediately suspect as a sham, a cult or a con. They were being safe. He had been at this point before and in fact so had most people who had endeavored to do something extraordinary that transcended the ordeals of daily life. The spirit, he trusted, would guide him now that he was twice confirmed as being unable to support such positions in good conscience. Only rhetoric. What possible effect could it have on a breathing life.

Out over the city was a slight haze that reflected the light back down again, the billions of lights maybe even trillions that radiated up from the streets where real people dwelt in the dirt and the sweltering heart and like the heavens one for each soul. He watched from the window as some went out and others appeared and thought of spirits in transition always moving from one phase to another longing for security they would not find on this ocean where squalls and waves moved to mysterious plans that seemed altogether random and all too often unpredictable. *Nothing lasts for long,* he thought. What then would faith have to do with it if there were no God and each needed to have his own reservoir out of which would come the power when called upon, the strength when needed and the character when all was falling down. It seemed to him then in that moment out on his terrace in the night where the real stars had given way to electric ones and had not been fully seen by his generation with their naked eye; out among the winds that stirred up the industrial pollution that had reached a critical mass in the last century and had forever changed the ecological balance of the planet; out shoulder to shoulder with the people who had not lost their inclination to violent acts and barbarism and savage emotions even though with their machines they had conquered the physical world, but who would still aspire to genius and great artistic rhapsodies; it seemed to him out there in the night that it was a question of faith. Perhaps his sermon should be on what, in lieu of God, to hold faith in. It was hope that people needed. A reason.

Sleep came to Nash on great fog waves as if spells were being cast each one deeper than the last. It was a singularly sound sleep where the echoes of the city were not heard, but the flights of angels could be perceived by the fluttering of their wings as they passed.

- V -

Sojourner

He knew in a moment there was no such thing as a near miss, it's either all or...hands that almost touch...hearts in counterpoint, one beats the other doesn't. "The well of spirit," he beseeched the gathered congregation with a naked honesty as if pleading his own forgiveness, "is character, it is the strength on which we can draw...a reservoir that dwarfs our surroundings, even though it doesn't appear that way at all. It is the breath that can ferry us through rough times and out of the labyrinth."

The true folly of his reading did not become clear to him for days as he tried desperately to come to grips with the disparity between what he meant and what was ultimately carried away with each member from his sermon. For some time previously he had wrestled with concepts too heady and sublime for the real world yet essential to him like a hand grasping a tool in the most fundamental of all acts as he grasped the pulpit edge now feeling its smooth, cool surface.

"How can one speak of faith?" he intoned and let the words echo into the hall. "How can one speak of belief if those things which you believe in and have faith in have never been defined?" He paused while his voice rang clear into the morning yet detached, and it was as if in fact he was also a listener. "These are the lights that guide the spirit." It was only later that he knew he was edging the limits of the possible and was trying to speak of things for which there was no language.

Even more disturbing was the clear vision that came to him while on high in the pulpit where by tradition the word of God was delivered. During that driven sermon it had arrived and left him shaken with doubt. It wasn't so much that it was a tangible experience that he could easily communicate but just that it gave him such a radical viewpoint shift that it seemed tangible. Words and deeds of faith were what appeared to him and balanced now precariously in mid-air as if in some graceful *pas de duex* frozen before him in an impossible paradox. The meaning of faith was not enough.

Even though this revelation came before he had finished his planned service he continued bound by a predestined plan baring his soul out across what numbers of the congregation had gathered to listen. He was the youngest of all the ministers in the old religion. He owed it to them. They in turn listened wholeheartedly gathering in the rhetoric, bits and pieces of which each individual latched onto in an affirmation of his self having hit on something he knew to be complete truth. The old familiar words were greeted with ease. However the bulk of his sonnet drifted among and around them as a grand yet abstract symphony of which some could admire the craftsmanship, but of its music nothing could be heard.

Somewhere in that group of people before him was the antithesis of everything good that was ever dreamed, he felt its presence as though it were a malevolent person yet looking into the faces saw only striving, as he was, as they all were. The odor of people reached him with its slightly astringent sweetness wafting up from the audience and he breathed it in secretly, as if he didn't notice, feeling too intimate with the crowd, too close to the human element when he was speaking of life on another plane. He knew then (words can never be enough) that the fundamental of faith, of belief was in the act and not in the meaning. All faith was in essence a relationship, a way of living with others and with the material world. Here old fixed ideas shattered into a billion glittering pieces and all that the church had taught him now lay open to inspection, to interpretation and he reeled with confusion. Dizziness swept over him in waves and he struggled to hold onto the pulpit without moving and not letting his voice waiver for an instant from its calm, certain passion. There must be more than just the idea of faith, he thought, there must be acts of faith, there must be truths hidden that would give a reason by changing a person's condition as a result of his acts just as surely as his face changes from the familiar one he had known in his youth to the strange and ancient apparition that visits him on his death. He knew this because his faith was like a hammer unlike the congregation whose belief was tested with each struggle for survival, with each contest and crisis.

At the close of his talk he left them with words that came out of his personal revelation and did not cohese with the rest of his message, but he was compelled to speak as if to make up for the faltering in his own character.

"Listen for the silence in your own lives," he said, "listen and follow without fear into the unknown that it reveals." And he left the crowd somewhat bemused while the more good hearted ones tried to make out his full meaning as they relied on the church for some guidance. These thoughts remained with Nash as he left the cathedral for his office feeling humbled that without warning what had been so clear to him before was now obscured by doubt and longing. He cursed the High Advocator silently for having forced him to face his own beliefs and now to shore them back up as if they had been blown away, tossed by a gale, sprinkled on the far off horizon line too distant for him to ever retrieve.

Sabiha was sitting in the wooden chair at his desk. "I thought you would never get here," she said sardonically standing up and collecting her ubiquitous scarf, "lets go." There was an edge to her voice.

"It was my morning to give the sermon, my time..." he said startled yet preoccupied as he reached for the coat that hung behind the door and then throwing it on turned the collar against his neck while the yellow light from the ceiling painted a shadow across his face, "was I expecting you?"

She shook her head looking at him, "I can see you haven't heard."

"What?"

"There was another bombing. The Phan."

"Again...?" He stopped to give full attention. "Where?"

"At one of the independent networks... Cyberwrks."

Like looking through a cloud he tried to relate to the hard news while circling down from the heights at which he had been perched dealing with concepts better left to immortals. "Was anyone hurt?" he stammered, the stirrings of a rage welling up.

"Yes," she hesitated, "and no."

He finished jerking on his coat and barked at her. "What do you mean, either they were or they weren't."

"It's a long story," pulling on his arm trying to get him out the door, "I'll tell you in the car."

He paused. "Wait a minute," a realization striking him, "when did this happen?"

"Last night."

"I mean what time?"

"Close to eleven I think..." she turned to him exasperated unable to get him to move, "Why for God's sake?"

His eyes squinted up as he remembered the disturbance he had felt, "What do you mean yes and no?"

In the car the city was so many lights and so many blurred faces all secure in anonymity. The sound of it was entirely muted and only the highest decibels reached through the shell they rode in; the conditioned air; the comfort made it all seem unreal and without teeth. Perhaps that was the reason Nash held onto his old vehicle because it still contained some of the discomfort essential to the human experience, in the overall blend of things where extremes were never measured and the only way there was of judging the value of something was by its opposite. She told him how they had come like silver fishes in the night and bombed out three floors of the Cyberwrks building that housed the central digital relay station for this sector of the city and then had faded away just as secretly leaving one dead. The only evidence of the Phan.

"How many people have died in the name of God," he spat out with distaste.

The Phan might have been predicted a hundred years ago. It was then that the twentieth century expired in fits of rage and disillusionment, when social disorder was boiling up into a venomous mix and spawned radical right wing religious movements from all cultures. But now, they were viewed as anachronistic and out of place with the digital photon-induced state of social consciousness that hailed itself as a golden age where men and machines had achieved a perfect equilibrium. They were a group that still held faith in a supreme being.

Sin had been the downfall of the one Rememberer who, after the fall, the Kaiein, followed his own vision of theology and refused the general consensus that violation of natural and scientific law was the cause of the collapse. His complex reasoning was never completely written even though many espoused its full understanding, but it was from him that the antipathy towards mechanical technology became integrated into religious philosophy and in fact defined sin more succinctly than anything found in nature. He was a well respected man who, though known for his tempered responses, began to be considered as more and more radical following his continued opposition to the Rememberers mission of bringing together the fundamentals of all extant philosophies, the universals that all cultures had found some truth in, into the one religion. It was a long and complex tale of old men and their struggles for power taking on heroic proportions because being old and human there was not much time remaining in their lives and so the desires of a lifetime were left to be realized in a few short and chaotic years. Like last embraces each sought to be the author of the new religion as a metaphor perhaps for a progeny to continue the father's name and memory long after his passing. Through council discussion the sublimation of God was a central theme following the religious wars and terror of the late twentieth century. Man, it was surmised, would be much better off without God and the chaos had revealed that the age of parable had come to a violent climax by its own flawed hand and each one in his own right had to take up the burden of viewing existence the way it was in its hard, cold reality despite the consequences. The Dhammapada; the ten thousand song Rig Veda; by the analects of Confucius; the Tao of Lau Tse; the unspoken law and the Apocrypha and the Tanakh and the Qur'an, tempered by truths of Western science that had manifested themselves in the healing arts as well as in the daily lives of each person on earth. It was then deemed a sign of heaven on earth (could it be denied?) that God the metaphor should vanish and God as man take his rightful place in the pantheon.

"This old anvil has seen many broken hammers!" He bellowed out in protest at the councils of the Rememberers where one by one the tenets of earlier religious dogma were struck down by democratic vote not uninfluenced by a philosophy even older than the ones they debated, greed. Here were voracious eyes glaring out of their sunken sockets riding the pinnacle of the moment that had thrust them into the confidence of a disenfranchised population whose culture and future had vanished in the smoke of the terror of nearly thirty years of anarchy. Their intrigues were legend. But that is a story for another time.

The Phan, so it is told, were people who rallied to this archangel descended as he distanced himself from the others. They at first were driven to extreme monasticism in the vain hope of keeping the wisdom they considered so sacred pure because as they thought that the common man had certainly lost his ability even to perceive it let alone uphold its virtues. It had become non-extant in the modern age through the falling from grace and they were bound by conscience to its salvation. So anonymous and benign were their beginnings that the sect was easily accepted and generally ignored as fringe dwellers refusing to change in the face of superior logic, yet still human and harmless to the general well being. They lived on the streets and in communal situations at their start often begging for subsistence in exchange for which they would share what remembered wisdom of their God they knew. Through the years however the reality of producing for a living made them self sufficient and sometimes invisible blending in with the general population so that when it would be discovered that a neighbor or acquaintance was one of the Phan a subtle shock ensued wondering what one so driven by ideals was capable of. Even when an income earned them nominal comfort they shunned material possessions because at the heart of their developing lifeway was the idea that all separation from God was a result of the physical world and when one could eliminate his desires he could touch the Infinite and would gain the power to be with God consistently. This revelation was to come in one blinding moment known to all of the Phan as *The Epiphany* and was the apex and goal for their strivings.

For many years this was their only aspiration and anything else was a distraction that was dealt with or tolerated as part of the sacrifice of their faith. Until they discovered the one true fact hidden by its obviousness, the results of which could not be denied, but were never discussed or written about. The discovery was a single way to achieve social change that was so compelling so overwhelmingly seductive no one could resist it. Terror. Fear of physical harm. They began to use this tenet, but since they were not necessarily evil men their acts were directed against facilities and only occasionally were people involved. To the Phan sin was the enemy of God, and nothing embodied sin more perfectly than computer technology which in its highest state was the networks on which the commerce and communications of the earth flowed. The Phan waged war against sin and were the nemesis of the modern world arising perhaps as a feeble act of natural selection balancing what was human with what was inhuman. It was as predicted in ancient Bali, a struggle between good and evil.

Riding through the blurred city Nash struggled with his own spiritual conflicts. He considered for a moment the act of terror. "What if..." he began full of coiled energy, "it was an act of faith, a seminal act, something that transcended all that we speak about our beliefs?" His voice was low and strong.

"I don't know what you're thinking about, but you'll see when we get there." Sabiha glanced skeptically at him keeping her hands steady on the wheel and her eyes flashed white against her brown skin. She saw the lights glow off the chiseled features of his pale face and his eyes dance looking at her then at something in memory never holding still for very long. It was as if he was inspecting things in his own world and his physical appearance was only a reflection of what was really there.

"Where?"

"Where we're going." She could wish (if silent wantings were worth anything) that she knew the riddle of the enigmatic man seated beside her that she so admired. He was a hard one to read. "Nash?"

"You didn't answer my question."

"Are you alright?"

Shifting in his seat to look at her, "Am I what?" he replied.

"You OK?"

"You mean other than the fact of being hit with the news of a terrorist attack, a bombing no less... and being whisked off to some unknown location when I should be..." he frowned looking back out of the window from where they had come. "What makes you ask?"

"Nothing, except that if you keep gripping the arm rest like you have been since we left the church I'll have to get it repaired."

"Nervous energy."

"I don't get that."

"What?"

"I can't hold it in. I explode."

"What if no one ever thought?" Nash said quickly looking in her direction, but not really at her. "I mean, what if no one ever... *thought*. If everybody just acted." He paused, held his breath as if waiting for a response. Sabiha rapidly formed the concept in her own mind to give some form of intelligent reply and was just about to do so when he continued unencumbered by no response. " Point 'A' to point 'B', you know...just did it."

"First impression?"

"Yes."

"Be a lot of damn mistakes made, fools too..."

"...but they'd define themselves immediately wouldn't they? ...no personal philosophy, it would be who they are."

"At that moment..."

"Yes, that's the point. Defined by the act."

"Very interesting. There's only one problem with it."

"What?"

"People don't want to be judged by how they act all the time. I think they have higher aspirations...ideals they can't quite live up to, but maybe would like to."

"Then they have something to reach for instead of falling back on words, maybe...something like that..."

"You're in a funny mood."

"Maybe I'm not."

They drove through the congested streets where the magnetic beams ended and the car was forced to make its way on its internal engine without relying on computer guidance. She homed in on the hospital without quite knowing where it was having never been there before, but finding it as if by some instinct of self preservation, genetic memory, or perhaps some residual knowledge of a former lifetime. Sabiha led Nash to the first floor trauma ward and after a brief discussion with a duty nurse, a phone conversation and final wave through, inside. He was expecting a rosewood appointed office with a large desk behind which a woman in her mid-thirties with gray streaked hair in a navy blue jacket with a white blouse buttoned to the neck and a tie held in place with a silver effigy of an ancient Indonesian God would sit. Instead they fell into a maelstrom. White light glared down from the ceiling fixtures and absorbed all the richness of the color until only the washed out bleakness of human misery remained. People were lined up at windows filling out forms, they loitered around some sitting some standing and arguing while patients were being wheeled recklessly to their destinations attached to tubes and wires and all manner of devices. Doctors rushed around at random in and out of doors and passageways. They passed ward rooms where the only walls were green cloth drapes hurriedly pulled to for a semblance of privacy, but everyone knew once you enter the trauma section all illusions of privacy vanish as you relinquish your body's functions to those whose job it was to sustain its life. Drawn, tired faces greeted them from every direction and it was clear the staff had gone far beyond overtime. It was the noise however that was the telling sign. Cries and shouts, whispers, barely audible words and the drone of conversations all blended into a humanesque harmony that wrapped its arms around Nash and brought the emotions to the smooth exterior where they were raw and vulnerable. He was drawn in against his will at once repulsed yet attracted by some mysterious purpose he had yet to fully know.

"Fionica," Sabiha announced trying to get some attention, "meet Nash DeCoucy the friend I told you about."

A woman turned around and looked him directly in the eye. Her face was vacant for a moment, rushing, full of a wildness he had recalled seeing only once when he happened upon a lone coyote late one night who peered at him in exactly the same way and he remembered thinking in that instant what it must be like existing as a wild thing and desperately trying to evade the complacency of civilization that numbed everything it touched. It may have been the last coyote. She must be forever on the run, he thought. She in her mid-thirties with a gray streak in her hair (as if lightening had struck) in a navy blue jacket with a white blouse buttoned to the neck.

"Sabiha and I are old friends," she said breathlessly and grasped Nash's hand with an unexpected firmness. It sent a shiver through him that he was not expecting. "Welcome to Cedars." In the background a woman's frantic talk rose increasingly louder with its helter skelter meanings ricocheting off the walls.

"I haven't told him yet."

"We'll sit down in a minute..." she glanced over her shoulder pausing to listen to the erratic woman poised to fly, "and I'll explain..."

Sabiha was anxious in the emergency atmosphere. "Fionica is the chief of the trauma ward here. We met in school and..." her eyes darted around nervously, "you're too busy, we'll come back..."

"...friends ever since," the woman calmly continued as if in her own home, "no, it's all right, it's always like this when I'm on duty, but the Phan's latest didn't help did it?" The woman replied with a slight hoarseness and smiled, "We hardly ever see each other, never professionally...Sabiha hasn't even been here before." "I have," Nash offered in a resigned manner, "but I don't know why I'm here now...I've been rushed down and I can only imagine..."

"You would have had business here before I suppose..." Fionica interjected with a hint of impatience and a furled brow, "of a spiritual nature."

Nash felt patronized, and took a moment to look behind the eyes of the woman finding them cool yet lucid with intelligence. "No, I don't do operations or set bones, but then I don't suppose many people offer up their confessions to you either."

She turned and disappeared into one of the curtained rooms as the cries of the woman rose to hysteria letting the words fly back to them from nowhere, "You'd be surprised..."

"She's just tired." Sabiha spoke quickly and held Nash's arm. "We all have a common interest."

He could see the weariness, not in her face or her look, but in the manner with which she attacked the environment throwing the curtain back and helping to strap down the wildly thrashing patient who was yelling frantically..."*I don't breathe this...way I don't!!* (Did you take some drugs?) *Really...I can't, I can't...* (Did you take some drugs? We heard you did...) *No, no it wasn't drugs...I can' breathe... don't strap me down, don't do it...please...pleeeese...* (It's alright... take it easy...it's OK now...don't worry we're not going to hurt you...) He watched her through the crack in the curtain from across the hall while Sabiha was riveted to all that was transpiring. He was more at home with spirits in need than she was, it was his mortar, but she... the long dancing scarf and elegant fingers that played on the flow of life, her intuitive sensuality. Presently Fionica returned, wringing her hands then pushing up her sleeves as if to signal a readiness for the next case. She looked again in his eyes. Hers were intense with purpose and when she met Nash's there was a slight instant where both of them felt a recognition spark between them like flint rocks in the dark, instant fire fleeting so quickly neither could testify to its ever having appeared at all.

"...my interest is purely medical," Fionica continued as if she had not been interrupted, "but since this is a moral issue...I almost think of it as a moral addiction...I, well, here you are," she gestured back to the woman now whimpering into calmed submission who just a few minutes before was enraged, "the latest gift from science."

"Yes," he mused in polite confusion. "What is it exactly we are discussing?"

"*Electrically Induced Neurosynapse Failure.*" Sabiha replied.

He looked at her quizzically. "Like in the translations you told me about?"

"Yes."

After a moment of silence Finoca leaned forward, clasping her hands together against her breast and gathering a composure to her expression that a doctor occasionally gets on discussing something of a terminal nature, which he knows he should be able to cure by all rational explanations, but by some random tumbling of cosmic dice and chance limitation of technology cannot and so the fact of it being out of his control perhaps raises questions of faith that leaves him uncomfortable. "There have been many incidents like this in the past thirty-six hours since the Phan's bombing." The condescension in her tone that Nash had detected at first now vanished and gave way to a slight desperation. Glancing at Sabiha, "We think it's the first really concrete evidence."

"It is! It is! But Nash has seen things too and..." she looked over at him, "It's indisputable, it's really indisputable now I think."

"This woman?" Nash asked trying hard to place the pieces together.

"Yes, she's coming out of it now...they seem to go through that when they come out of it...comatose before, completely gone and susceptible to any command you'd want to give them."

"Hypnotized?"

"In a sense, only with electronics?"

"Oh...maybe I'm dull but I don't follow you at all. I thought no one was hurt except the terrorist who died?"

"Come," Fionica took both their arms, "let's go somewhere quiet and I'll try to explain." She led them down the corridor past the wards and dimly lit computer stations built into alcoves whose attendants monitored everything from heart and respiration to drug doses, chemical analysis, blood, urine, cholesterol, cellular biopsy spectrogram breakdowns, genetic maps, viral structural component comparisons, admittance procedures and insurance forms. They turned right down a short hall and went into an empty private exam room.

"Can I smoke?" Nash asked.

"That's illegal isn't it?"

"So's war."

She flipped a switch and an exhaust fan whirred into operation. "Sure, go ahead."

"We've been watching this," Sabiha said, "Nash and I. Last week I ran across a document that mentioned *Electrically Induced Neurosynapse Failure* and I explained what *EINF* is, as far as my understanding goes...but there have been indications of it before."

Fionica leaned up against an examining table and crossed her legs letting her head fall back exhaustedly as she rolled it around to loosen up a tense neck. "You were right it's almost like being hypnotized. Imagine the person, you for instance, yourself, going to sleep, but the subconscious mind takes on its own life and continues to function and you appear to everyone else quite normal."

"Except, of course, when they began to act strangely." Sabiha interjected.

"Yes. It makes one very susceptible to suggestion and malleable so the techniques were perfected originally for programming back in the twentieth century and then have been used in social rehab work for many years, but with varying degrees of success which frankly means no one knows what it does exactly or why it happens. There's a wild card in the mind, you see, it's unpredictable..." she paused suddenly realizing that Nash, being of the cloth and having ministered to many people, probably in time of greatest need and probably already knew this more certainly than her, "...personally I think it's dangerous and only the most radical practitioners use it, or government doctors"

"I see..." Nash pondered the weight of it... "what does this have to do with the Phan and how did so many people become effected?"

"Simple," Fionica rejoined, "elementary even, I don't know why I didn't think of it before...we have you to thank you know."

Nash looked blankly at Sabiha. "They were all on-line," she said. "Don't you see? Most of them were from the clubs plugged into the virtual broadcasts. Hundreds of people were brought into hospitals across the city immediately after the bombing and the black out of transmission and they all had one thing in common. They were all on-line, on *videtel*." Touching his arm, "It proves it don't you see? They were fused, all along people were fusing, but now it's getting lethal for some reason and it was only this incident that made it clear."

Fionica squinted her eyes and shot a glance across at Nash while addressing Sabiha, *"Fusing... what's fusing?"*

"We have a theory," Nash replied, at that moment just beginning to smell the medicinal odors of the exam room, of alcohol, disinfectant, gauze and bandages, "that people are addicted to...light projected images."

"You mean like... *videtel?*"

He folded his arms and tensed the muscles of his jaw as his eyes narrowed. "It's got something to do with the light I think, the emanations of the screen are much stronger than they used to be now that holographic 3D images and 128-bit color is the standard. The people I've seen are completely fixated on it; I mean to the point where their lives actually parallel the lives of people on VT unaware of their condition. It's almost an exact duplicate existence, except it's virtual. A separate reality that only they know and it takes them over completely without any volitional consent and exerts force and the power of command over their thoughts and actions."

"That's not unusual in disturbed people..." the doctor responded, "we've seen it before."

"Not in otherwise normal individuals." He looked at her and continued as though he hadn't heard. "I've watched it develop for several years and it became so common that I tried to categorize certain points about it so at least I could cope with it when counseling these people. The first thing I noticed, the first clue, was the things people talked about in ordinary social discussions. They almost always took a tact toward some recent transmission, some broadcast they'd seen, some story they were following as if their own lives had no incident, no experience...or the VT news...and the fact that people always seemed to complain that they had no time yet I discovered they spent inordinate amounts of it watching the *videtel*. It distorted their time sense, gave them an artificial time span you might say, a virtual continuum in their minds"

"Still, I'd hardly call that..."

Sabiha cut her off. "Wait. Tell her about the kids."

"They started getting on the virtual VT machines at arcades and at other public places while on drugs. I suppose that made it easier for them to lose their sense of place and become completely enveloped in the virtual reality. They called it *Fusing*. Pretty soon, I don't know how, probably accident, they realized they could do it without drugs–simply with sleep and food depravation and long periods on the machines."

"That's when he called me." Sabiha said.

"Why?" Fionica asked, puzzled.

"I thought it was in the machines…"

"Most of the hardware still comes through the Eastern Metropolis and since I'm a translator at the United Nations…"

"I just wanted to know exactly where this stuff was coming from."

"Did you find out?"

"Yes and no, but it didn't matter. People have grown up on these things as you know, they're plugged in at birth and get so much information passed to them that they're in a stupor anyway, mentally… monitors in every home, in all public places, in the streets, public transportation…it's an underlying subtext to all our lives. But recently, for some reason, something changed; something has been happening that is pushing them over the edge…completely out of the real world and into a virtual one. We didn't know if it was possible, but the line was crossed."

"*Fusing*." Fionica said finitely yet still grasping for something, some sense of tactile reality she could hold and relate to.

Sabiha continued, "People are fusing. They discovered they don't even need depravation, they're crossing over into this virtual world randomly, all kinds of people, but what is startling is that they are getting *addicted* to it. Trying to see how far they can go…how deep into the subconscious…"

"…before they reach a place from which they would never come back." Fionica finished the statement with the obvious. She had seen it many times in her medical career, addicts trying to die, pushing the envelope. "*Sensation is the paymaster* they say."

"What's that?" said Nash.

"Oh, it's just a saying of some of the spacers who get addicted out there," she gestured to the ceiling, "they say there's nothing else it's so devoid of any semblance of life. The incidence of drug addiction is very high. That's what they say, *sensation is the paymaster*." She turned suddenly serious. "Do you really think someone's doing this intentionally? Someone's behind this?"

"I don't know," he replied, "People push drugs, have wars…"

"I didn't think so," Sabiha began, "when Nash first called me I didn't even think fusing was possible. Then I saw it with my own eyes… and the documents…"

"The ones mentioning *EINF*?

"Yes, it was too much of a coincidence, and now this…you can see why I wanted you two to meet."

They all three stood there for a moment each considering the consequences of what was unfolding. Fionica looked at her watch, "I've got to go." She said, and added that she would try to find out as much as she could about all the cases reported in the city and that she would be in touch. Nash imagined he heard a movement of wings and thought for a moment there were birds outside the window, but when he looked there were none. As the doctor was leaving she held his hand and gazed at him without saying a word, then was gone.

Also that night had been a room of subdued elegance. It was a chamber in one of the few remaining mansions that hovered as tossed spiders precariously clinging to the sides of hills that surrounded the actual city where actual people dwelt lacking the luster and the rarefied security that the select few enjoyed. They did provide a sort of hope though. From the streets if one looked up, at any time of day, they were always there lending their concrete edifices as icons to the possible saying *Here! Look at us! Want us!*–and those of little purpose would be inspired, at least for one more day by the fact that someone had done it. They looked best, as mansions do, in the flooded moonlight where imagination fills in the shadows and the only limits to what drama might be playing out inside was the darkness.

Two sleepers lay under worshipping cover on the long, white bed. It's pillars were of burnished ebony, the trees from which they came long since extinct, and totems of carved jade sat upon dressers and marble topped tables. His face looked like a bulldog against the snow white slopes of the pillow, and his lower lip hung down while saliva slowly dripped. Breathing was the labored wheeze of a man who has lived too well and his backside rubbed up against a fat, but healthy woman who he had some time back ceased to regard as his mate and simply taken for granted as a source of warmth in the bed beside him. All his life he had striven for this moment and had managed to subordinate his own ideals for the sense of security and possession that now enthroned them and lorded down over the denizens of lessor gods who dwelt in the flatlands. He was a merchant of the law. It was with this attitude that he approached it because he had discovered that within the administrative quagmire of the system anything, *anything* could be rectified and fully and completely arranged in the best interests of his client by reason of the complexity of legal language. He could bring up statutes and codes to cover any situation, any situation. For this reason he thought of himself as a merchant of the law and its rewards cradled him in opulence.

As the clock rounded 3 AM the telephone rang harshly by the bed. Twice more its shrill tones pierced the darkness and he struggled to come to and bring the receiver to his ear. "What?" He said forcing the sleep away. "Where?" He mumbled and listened intently as a tired scowl came over him but, at the same time a hint of fear shone in his eye like the cool glint of Jade in the moonlight.

She sat down exactly in the center of the long, sublime forest green couch and the shock of her white thigh radiated across the room as the dark worsted skirt slid up past her knees. Beyond her knowledge (however instinctive) a genetic impulse surged from her like a heat wave drawing each male's attention from around the room in an unconscious acquiescence to the ritual that demanded they follow the dance. She crossed her legs luxuriously in a room so quiet silk could be heard brushing against silk and nervously tapped the foot that dangled in the air.

"There's so damn many lawsuits we'll never see the light of day!" The man behind the desk said. He was turned away from the others in the large executive office and was hidden by the back of the chair in which he sat angrily staring out the floor to ceiling windows across an urban landscape smothered in a late afternoon glow.

"We've sent a barrage of press releases out..." one of the men pacing around the room responded.

"...and messaged to all the on-line services and other broadcast mediums..." added another.

"Legal has been on it since last night, since fifteen minutes after it happened." Still one more added.

"So has theirs!" rejoined the man in the chair.

They bickered hotly. The six men. Five on their feet pacing and the one seated facing the window. There was an air of impending disaster as if they were all waiting for the building in which they were meeting to be demolished from under them with only their ineffective cries of protest as protection. The worst scenario was unspoken though it hung on everyone's lips as if almost said, waiting for the right moment, a lull where it was the unavoidable conclusion and could be brought out and thrust into each one's heart an icicle slowly melting into a prolonged death. True in the back of their minds this hung, but none of them really consciously considered it possible even though it was the source of their anxiety. It was after all a terrorist act and they, as everyone else, were victims equally sharing the same trauma and loss. There was no possible way that the *Virtual* technology had been detected; litigation was just the automatic reaction to a catastrophic event. Just a reaction.

"It happens all over the world," someone added.

"Right, how could they know?"

The only variable was Hisham Mostafa 'Ali Fayed Al-Razio their silent partner. They liked to think of him as their partner but in actual fact Hisham Al-Razio simply viewed them as vendors, as a contract for programming to fill the immense relentless void that was ravenous twenty-four hours a day into which huge, untold masses of people dove with the rising of the sun and moon relying on its spark of nature, its friendly life essence, its embellishment of a nearly intolerable existence to elevate them above the droll monotony of living at the apex of the industrial age into a more exciting, enviable place. Nobody wanted to be common. Everyone wanted to be sexy. If, by some advanced technology they, Cyberwks VT, could provide an added incentive for people to watch, and indeed become willing puppets of, then the Provider would be satisfying its mandate to the public by providing what was truly needed and wanted in each concentric community. The fact that billions in revenue were to follow, moneys that would be deprived the other overlap Provider by means of a larger share of the fixed market, was only a consequence of their wise management. They all depended on it. Everything hinged on it. There was no other option, one was either in or he was out. Black and white. Life and death.

The chair slowly turned as the man in it spoke. "I hope we've covered every option. Wait! Where's that little man," he snapped his fingers twice, "the computer wizard, where is he?"

"Hidden."

"What do you mean?" someone interjected.

"You don't need to know."

"That little bastard!"

"Don't jump to conclusions. We've been doing *very* well."

"Up till now," a cynical voice added.

The man at the desk half stood and reached over to slide a note pad closer. "How many *up till now*?"

"What?"

"Lawsuits you idiot."

"Well how the hell am I supposed to know what you're talking about, osmosis?"

"Three hundred and sixty five."

"Oh perfect," the man said leaning back forcefully in his executive chair letting its hydraulics catch the motion and bounce him gently, "one for each day of the year."

"It could be worse."

"No it couldn't."

"Wait until tomorrow."

"What do you mean."

"What I mean is the court docket was full for today, but tomorrow more suits will be filed with the clerk's office."

"No! How do you know?"

"Reliable source."

"Your mother's one of the plaintiffs?"

The woman on the couch, Roxanne Helperin, still tapped her foot in the air. She was unmoved in her faith and oblivious to the posturing glances at her legs between the exhortations and puffing and antagonism brought about by a deep, underlying fear no man in the room would admit to having. She however had no fear, and being able to exist outside of its grip could view with complete lucidity the reactionary drama before her.

"You will not lose the *contract*," she said with particular emphasis on the last word knowing, as each one in the office knew, its utter significance. It was the one unspeakable event that was never discussed. Not that it was a written code, but in the same sense that the meaning of the Albatross spoke itself plainly to a hundred generations of sailing men who plied the waters of the planet prior to the existence of any written word. It harkened back to the mystic, the talisman, the seed, the gourd, the stone, the magic that made the difference between one man's survival and another's death, that silent unembraceable element which meant success and when missed brought on plague, pestilence, and famine to even the best, the most righteous, most gifted, most loved without regard and without reason. It is the secret face of the night that stares back at one when he is alone and on his last breath. "You will not lose the *contract*."

The silence that filled the room was pure. They tried, each one, to appear as though they had no reaction to the statement while in fact it mirrored each's most intimate concern and brought the petty bickering to an abrupt end. No one spoke for a long time. Roxanne continued to tap her foot in frustration, the man at the desk turned again to the window and the five others paced and fretted.

Presently the man in the chair spoke. "How can you be so sure?" His words wafted up over the high back.

"Because…" she answered drawing out the word and dwelling on it with pent up energy as if they would catch on any minute.

The man turned to face her. "Why?"

"…it's an affirmation. Don't you see? We knew that it was producing some effect, and pretty interesting ones too…but we never knew for certain how deeply the effect went. Now we do." She spelled it out slowly. "We couldn't buy this research…or the publicity for that matter…!"

"I don't get you." A man asked in bewildered tones tinged with antagonism.

"It's clear that it works beyond our wildest imaginings. Right now we have three hundred and sixty five positive results. Why do you think people watch? Why do they want a virtual reality? To escape their own existence! We've got the drug! It's legal, now it's tested and nobody can prove a thing because it's a confidential technology between us in this room and Hisham Al-Razio, and he certainly won't leak it, in fact I'll bet he hasn't missed the significance of any of this. Not any."

"And the wizard."

"The who…?"

"What…?

"He means Yzak, the kid, the programmer. Don't worry about him, he'll never talk."

"How do you know?"

"I just know."

Everything about him was perfect. He loved to see his reflection in a mirror or a window as he walked by and never missed the opportunity to catch his image and ensure its faultlessness, even if only a silhouette he could still correct its form. When he was a child he would go about and straighten things up instead, as is the way of most children, of spewing disorder and minor fits of chaos in his wake like dust clouds raised in the hot desert by a passing vehicle. "I just can't explain it." He would reply to concerned parents, teachers and the old Mullah who would ask *why*. It was now exactly as it was then and a matter of pride with Hisham Mostafa 'Ali Fayed Al-Razio that nothing would escape him because his obsession had continued all his life and what the elders had failed to observe was simply that a part of his character had revealed itself early. The darker rivers were to come later and perhaps that was nature's safeguard for his mother was too frail to face a harsher reality than the one she was already burdened with and certainly unable to cope with any hint of true evil. She lived an existence sheltered not by wealth or privilege, but by an unawareness that each crisis encountered along the road nurtured and so she emerged unscathed though intellectually duller and less perceptive as it passed. The scars were on her soul and she could not see them as others could and when she finally passed from this life no one was her witness but her son who felt nothing but obligation and that too was now fading. He had not failed to notice her spiritual demise. Perfection was to him the standard upon which everything, human or otherwise, was judged and he made no exceptions for kin. The star, however, that fell from the sky on that night leaving its tracer as a fleeting sketch on heaven's gate he missed entirely.

Sometimes he would be so filled with complete satisfaction that he would almost be moved to flights of ecstasy like from the *qawwali* songs of the ancient Sufi mystics he would sometimes hear in his sleep. His doctors, who conjectured that perhaps he had an anomaly of the inner ear although they could see no such aberration, could not explain the phenomenon to him. Because of the fact that Islam had ceased as a tradition before he was born except in the stories of a precious few Mullahs who though decrepit and old carried the torch of the Prophet to their grave it was suggested that the recurring dream was a repressed memory of his early youth too painful for him to remember in his waking hours. Hisham Al-Razio dismissed this evaluation and attributed the occurrences to a mysterious connection with an unknown god from a time he had missed by two generations but was destined for and perhaps, he thought, it was the seed of revelation just as it had happened to the Prophet in the past now obscured by the passage of time. For this reason he welcomed it and with each occurrence he felt blessed and treated the day following it as a holy time by fasting and meditating on perfection, because that was the closest he could come to any concept of God.

A clock chimed with twelve strokes. The sound the chimes made rolled lazily around the palatial rooms of his home of polished granite floors strewn with hand knotted rugs of subdued color. He would not flaunt his wealth by living in one of the few remaining mansions in the hills as was the custom of all men of great importance in the Western Metropolis, but preferred to exist in the center of it where the breath of the city was hot and its heart could be heard beating twenty-four hours a day. With complete anonymity he had purchased a skyscraper that sat on the concentric coils and shot up as a streak of light from the streets. Most of it he leased and its tenants were completely oblivious to his presence because his private world was the top two floors. The only access to them was by private elevators rushing from a hidden entry in the underground garage to the apex where stars brushed the ceiling. Now reaching down and bringing the sharp cheese to his mouth he broke the fast of the preceding day looking out across his highest floor where he had no walls and so could see in all directions for a hundred miles of glittering lights, seas and oceans of lights, cosmic ethers of lights, infinities of lights, a transcendence of lights validating the power he knew he held over people through the medium of light projected images. He raised an unleavened ball of bread made with rye flour to his mouth savoring its nut-like flavor and then drank of a cognac letting the rush of its fire overtake his senses. In the glow of a candle in the small hours of morning Hisham Al-Razio was certain this time where the mystic experience had its origin, but had followed the ritual of the fast just the same being without a God and therefore superstitious.

He had followed closely the news of the Phan's ill fated bombing and then even more closely the flock of lawsuits that flooded into Cyberwks corporate headquarters. There were detailed transmissions from his intelligence sources and even medical reports on each individual who had been taken into the emergency rooms that night and he had read every word of many of them fearing at first a disorder in the flow, a disturbance in the electromagnetic balance he had always perceived as existing between the broadcast signals put out by his contracted vendors as programming and the audience who was receiving it, a balance that reflected the positive and negative sides of nature, in a word good and evil. It was his belief that this balance was what kept civilization on an even course. For every action there was a reaction. The broadcast being the positive and the audience being the negative, outflow and inflow, it was in tune with universal constellations and the slightest wavering, he knew, would bring the world tumbling down from the moral equilibrium it was so delicately balanced upon.

At that moment when the realization hit him he had heard the singing while still awake and took it as a revelation of the truth. The extent to which his audience could be captured was nearly infinite and the vision of a perfect balance, which had always eluded him until now, made itself apparent. He knew that once a person became addicted to the *Virtual* technology they would become blank slates upon which he, or the Provider, could write the future. *Finally,* he thought enraged with the ecstasy of the moment, *God's wishes are being made known through me and I can speak them deep into the souls of men.* After a moment of gloating over this he added, *...whether they want it or not.*

- VI -

Each Light a Life

The last thing he remembered was the sound of footsteps running. It echoed off the walls with a hollow metallic ring into the street where he lay. His cheek was pressed firmly against asphalt. There was a salty taste in his mouth. He couldn't think of his name.

There were flashes, however, flashes of light he at first mistook for cars passing but as they continued he saw that they were tinged with color; magenta, violet, blue, each time a different one and he finally came to the conclusion they were not cars at all. There were no cars. There was no traffic what so ever and as he slowly regained consciousness it occurred to him the lights were in his mind. They shared the stage with the fear he could not overcome. He had lost control.

The first thing the young woman felt was a rush of cool air on her cheeks as she violated the double swinging doors at the end of a long corridor. They had the markings of one half an "X" in serrated black and yellow on each giving them the look of a pedestrian crosswalk. When the doors were closed a message lit up...*CENMED-VAN*, it said, *ENTRY PROHIBITED BY LAW– AUTHORIZED PERSONNEL ONLY*, and added, *VIOLATORS WILL BE ARRESTED*. Juggling two large containers of coffee, a bag of rolls and a brief case she had tipped the doors racing through after having gained entry with a code card and left them roiling in her wake flapping like crows wings in the wind their mechanisms whirring trying to properly seal the entrance again. It was cold. There was a thin row of amber lights drawn out against the ceiling that nearly vanished in the distance where at the end were other doors with the black and yellow "X". Two heavily armed guards stood quietly watching. Her breath vaporized in the air as she drew deeper into the tunnel and remembered being told that the center was surrounded by a cold zone for the electronics inside, it somehow insulated them though it never occurred to her to ask how. Things of a technical nature eluded her and so she didn't pursue them for very long, just so she could do her job and that was all. She wasn't sure if it was the complexity of the subject that threw her or the fact that there was something so fundamentally inhuman about it all that it instantly negated any real importance in the overall scheme of existence. *I'm not stupid,* she would tell them, but still felt blank. "Robert." She acknowledged the guard passing through the second set of doors. The burly young man whose neck was as wide as his head just looked at her and frowned without saying a word while the hydraulics hissed slightly bringing the doors back to position.

At the desk were more security personnel. The young woman went through an elaborate procedure of credentials, key codes, palm and iris scanning and finally passed through an x-ray even though she was well known. Once, years earlier, a disgruntled hospital employee had gained access to the command center and fired an automatic weapon randomly at the computers and delicate wall panel LCD and map displays. No one was hurt at the time except the man himself who was killed by security when he refused to drop the weapon, but the center was off line for 47 hours and there were 846 fatalities attributed to failed communication links. They all put up with the ritual and it was a matter of contention between the union and the city whether *time in* started before the screening procedure or after.

Finally she passed through the double sealed entry to the command center that kept the equipment dust and contaminant free. Inside there was low light and it cast a blue green field across everything. There was also a chorus of voices, a multitude–all calm, controlled and calculated for a specific result. The room itself was enormous with high ceilings and constructed like a theater in the round; rising cubicles equipped with computer workstations where the audience would be and long rows of built in desks across the stage floor where people sat side by side in front of monitors with wireless headsets on. There were little red lights everywhere. On each terminal touchscreen was a panel that lit up with incoming calls. Each one was on fire. Looming in the front of the room was a massive digital map of the Western Metropolis that reached from the floor to the ceiling...one red light located each emergency call, one amber light for those responded to and blue ones for terminations. Above the map was the legend, *CenMed Vast Area Network*. Other smaller maps lined the circle of walls representing specific districts. *CenMed-VAN* was the emergency call in command center for the city. It was a clearinghouse for disaster, a switchboard for despair and ruin and held all the vital links from citizens to police, fire, parameds and other emergency services. There were nearly three thousand people on line twenty-four hours a day, every day of the year, year after year.

She sat down at her terminal and adjusted the headset so it was comfortable. In front of her the red lights sparkled, blinking off and on desperately vying for attention. She considered them for a moment lifting the lid off her coffee and taking a vital sip in preparation for the night shift. The caffeine would be needed later. Her husband of three years was a detective with the police department and also worked at night, she enjoyed having some daytime free. *For each light*, she thought, *is a life*. With one final adjustment and another even deeper draught of coffee she mentally braced herself, said out loud... "Here we go..." and pushed the first red light of the night.

An eerie silence greeted her. For a moment she listened to the electronic stillness certain there was a presence. "CenMed..." she spoke in a calm measured voice, "what is your emergency?" The static quiet persisted but she held on. The rule was one repeat and fifteen seconds of wait. "What is your emergency?" Still there was no reply while she watched the digital clock count off the moments and plainly saw it pass the fifteen second mark. Perhaps because it was her first call of the night and she questioned her own alertness she held the line open. Internally the dialogue began weighing the value of her intuition against the rules that had evolved from hard experience knowing that a mistake either way she could not live with. Errors did happen. How many souls, she wondered, were losing their chance by reason of this one tied up line and bucked up against the mounting pressure that would not recede but build until her shift was over leaving her so agitated sleep was usually impossible. She glanced absently at the huge panoramic map that filled the front of the hall noting the green lights flashing on and off. Terminations. They ran in one of four categories; either they were dead, had been responded to and handled, simply hung up because the wait was too long and the tragedy too immediate, or they were what the operators called *hearts*, short for lonely hearts, people who needed help, but not the kind CenMed could dispatch and who, though equally desperate, wanted only to hear another human voice to ground them and give them the spiritual lifeline they needed. There was no telling which category an extinguishing blue light signified. The operators all liked to think they were responses; it gave their work a tactile reward imagining each light a life.

Time was running out. "It's a *heart*," she thought, "gotta drop this line…" but still she didn't. Finally muffled sobbing pierced the ether. "What is your emergency?" she repeated.

"…he's hitting me…" was the pathetic reply, weak, sobbing.

"We have you located." She said punching in code on the touch-screen that would route the call automatically to the law enforcement vehicle closest to the scene and simultaneously file reports with the precinct and district police stations and the local Parameds. "Is he there?"

"Yes." Screaming cut the woman off. "Stop it…help me…nooo…noo…" Silence.

"Is he right there? Is he right there?" A beat ensued. "Can you hear me?"

"Yes."

"Hold on, help is coming." There was no reply. "Can you hear me?"

"Yes," the woman replied meekly, whimpering, sobbing.

"Can you hold on?"

"Yes."

"I'm leaving you now…help is coming."

With a feeble hysteria the woman's voice cried "Don't…"

She pressed another red button cutting off the first call, the woman's voice, which was all the identity she wanted to give to it, just a woman's voice. She couldn't handle any more."

"CenMed, what is your emergency?"

She could hear a low growl on the line, like an ill and injured animal who, though cornered, lacked the life to try an escape or even attack but could only make disgusting grumblings. "Fuck you, bitch."

Unmoved she repeated, "CenMed, what is your emergency?"

"Fuck you in the ass..."

"Do you have an emergency?" After an instant of no response she moved on without the slightest reaction. Sometimes the trauma of the moment made people unsound, and it was this she would listen for (from their eyes). Heartless it seemed, but a person *may* exist at the pit of darkness (with the prince of the power of the air) so she made herself listen. Intuition was also present and those calls never breached the barrier as the first one had. Fifteen seconds of fame and they were history.

"CenMed, what is your emergency?"

"I'm lookin' for someone."

"What do you mean? Are you in trouble?"

"I'm in trouble... I can't find a' address..."

"What do you mean?"

"Can you send someone to help me find a' address?"

"Are you in trouble?"

"Yea...I'm lost."

"I'm sorry we don't handle that."

"Can you send someo..."

"I'm leaving you now..." She punched another flashing red light and felt the pulse of it beating, throbbing beneath her slim finger and it reminded her of the blood coursing through her body, through the collective body of the city. Red flashing lights, one light one life, clearly it was blood red; sanguine for the useless accident for the senseless violence. What of the human condition? The thought stood still and malignant in the shadow of her consciousness never becoming fully known and yet never really resolving, a thousand years could pass and this board of flashing red lights would be the same without interruption reflecting an unchanging condition that stretched so far back in memory it defined what is human.

Hands flew across the touchscreen without thinking connecting the cross thread fabric of those in need with others whose calling it was to minister to the desperate. The irony of it never once occurred to her, the absolute perfection of the microcosm that existed between the two could never be perceived by one so close to its core as she was. The cries to her were real, they could not go unlistened to or sleep, which was evasive enough, would be impossible. Samuel, her husband, a detective on the night shift heard voices too. His were harsh ones though, violent, staccato, demanding not pleading yet still in need. He was a minister too and perhaps, though they had never discussed it, their similar purposes drew them together stronger than love. After all love was a fleeting thing, but a purpose would revive the dead.

"CenMed, what is your emergency?"

A strong woman's voice this time with an accent. "They shot my boy!" English was not her first language.

"We have you located... is he with you?"

"No...get away from here!" She shouted off the receiver and street sounds could be heard. Traffic, voices, distant sirens, the silent sounds of milling people in the humid night. Suddenly the woman was back. "He's in the street."

"Is he bleeding?"

"Of course he's bleeding, they shot my boy"

"Can you stop the bleeding?"

"Someone's holding him."

"Can you stop the bleeding?"

"Yes. They're pressing a shirt into it..."

"Is there still shooting?"

"No," she began to lose strength and began to speak hopelessly. "They're still here."

"Who?" There was no reply. "Are the people who did the shooting still there?"

'Yes."

"Are you safe?"

No! No were not safe. We're never safe, we can't go out on the street, we can't even walk on the street without being shot...my boy's lying there with cars driving around him! They just shot him you know, they shot my boy..."

"Help is coming." Just then she could hear the sirens wailing in the distance in response to the call, the woman was yelling at someone again, yelling and cursing and she heard the receiver fall against metal as it was dropped. Voices in the mist... "I'm leaving you now," she said knowing no one was listening but unable to withdraw her attention without warning. "Help is coming."

Before the next call she drank deeply of the stale, bitter coffee, like water she drank letting it burn her throat and infuse her with its narcotic properties. By the clock she had been on duty thirty-five minutes and had eight hours and twenty-five to go. Her personal life was often surreal and dream like and only a brief respite from the rapid flow of events that fleeted by her barely touching often under the most tragic of circumstances–she didn't think she could approach the real, the sweet smell of freshly spilled blood the power of anguish and the absoluteness of despair. Only intellectually with computers and red flashing lights and telephones. There was a period when the city had installed holographic vidphones the idea being that the more real the person on the other end of the line the better the response. Shortly after they started losing lights. Terminations doubled. The trouble was they were not from responses but from disconnections...no one could confront that much misery. It became too real and people ceased to function. They finally gave up and reverted to the old system, the way it has been done for over a century. There are certain things technology cannot help. She knew she internalized the cauldron of feelings that surfaced like fire on the sea, even if she never consciously thought of each individual case in her own time it did effect her and drove her with relentless cruelty.

She wandered through the beacons that radiated each from its tiny lamp glowing sanguine, signifying the lifeblood. It was the essence that it symbolized; the blood of men, the blood of strangers, the blood of enemies, the blood of souls…all the same, élan vital, it was living and brought life and growth in mysterious ways she never presumed to fathom.

In the heat though she would testify her deep belief and call out for a witness when the ecstasy overtook her senses and she rolled with sweat running down between her breasts with her fine young husband. He was perfect. She could find no other symbol of the everlasting spiritual life quite as fitting as he when the raw energy flowed and they intertwined. She was lifted above the simple and mundane tasks of survival to those things that really mattered. The lingering moments of his touch filled her for hours afterwards and came visiting on feathered wings when she was in need of support facing the despair of the moment listening to the tales of the hopeless and forsaken. Even if he were only a taste in her mouth that swelled and filled her like rich hazelnuts and then was brushed away like the briefest spring, the frailest fog wisp, the most distant loon's cry…it would be alright, because she knew it was not her birthright. She was not born pretty, though fit by nature, well proportioned and ripe with a youth that had not fleeted away from her though she was pushing thirty, so she took what was doled out to her and neither lusted after what she could never have nor regretted what she often found herself saddled with.

From the start though she had wanted him. Never before was there anything to compare it to in her life except maybe the small purebred poodle her mother once owned when she was a child. It was a perfect animal, destined for the greatness of a flawless gene pool and so her mother had isolated it with plans and prejudice to be bred with only the most perfect studs. The poodle however had her own agenda, which included a rowdy, muscular, scruffy mongrel that roamed the neighborhood at will looking something like a cross between a pitbull terrier and a miniature Rottweiler and whose owners could only be guessed at. At least nobody would admit to it. There was no parting them and even a six foot fence and locked gates were not a match for the desire that possessed the two misfits. They were drawn together across worlds and no power under heaven could keep them separate. She would watch them from the window on cold winter mornings their frosted breath painting the air with a primal landscape of tiny clouds and would fall into a wonder at the mystery of life. It made no sense. It followed no rules except those that worked. It seemed to channel through material things without distinction for its own purposes without regard to whether it was at all logical or fit within the frame of reference with which it was being viewed. Life was its own master, it had no higher authority, it flowed into pools and eddies, the currents of streams and rivers, and into seas and oceans as vast as the ether. She was swept away into the roiling fever of her fine young man because that's where the mystery was. Sometimes at night she would come to him again and again unable to get enough as she brushed his marble flesh with her fingertips drinking in all, she thought, but he would turn to her again with rushes of a thousand birds racing through the wind until at last sleep came.

The one great fortune of her life was the enigmatic love she shared with her man. It was not questioned, nor obeyed, but ridden with one hand flying high above her head and the other fully grasping a tuft of his hair as if astride a lightening bolt leaping across the universe. She drank sex with him, she breathed it and sometimes didn't know if she was dreaming or not. It was uncommon behavior and she had never before in her life been so carnally drawn with full consent and in fact had truly desired few men preferring to live alone than to wander unfamiliar territory. There was no remorse for the way she acted any more than the dogs so mysteriously drawn to each other felt regret. Acts of god needed no justification.

She pressed one of the red beacons. "CenMed, what is your emergency?"

"Something's wrong..."

"Tell me," she replied crisply.

"He went down like he was...eyes are still open, he's breathing... just won't respond. He's gone...there, but gone."

Inputting the Paramed code, "Was there an accident?"

"No. He was on VT, might have had some drugs...I dunno, I don't think he does that anymore. I'm scared."

Sensing the fear she absorbed it. "What happened?" she asked to calm the woman down knowing that the Parameds would be there in a few moments, glancing subconsciously at the map on the wall, if there was not a backlog.

"There was flashing," a young woman began weakly, "...something, I forgot..." She could tell the woman was young because there was haughtiness, a forced irreverence straining at the surface. "His eyes are fluttering. Oh God...we were on the VT, watching it you know?" A long silence ensued. "Why is this happening? I don't understand it at all. Is he sick?"

"Help is coming. We have you located."

On the line the voice was quietly hysterical. "What's going on?"

Breathing. It was rapid and clearly audible over the optical connection. "Tell me." She asked again. *That's the trouble,* she thought, *it's too real.* Every nuance could be heard, every breath.

"I feel dizzy, you know? Faint." There was a moment in which nothing stirred. "We used to go to the North Coast..." she spoke in monochromatic hues letting her consciousness fill the waiting space, "there's a stretch up there where nothing is built yet. I think it's the only one...is someone coming? He doesn't look too good."

"Help is coming. We have you located," she intoned with all the compassion she could muster for the rote procedure that she was required by law to follow. Since the end of the Twentieth Century they were severely limited as to what they could say on an emergency line because of the litigation brought by citizens and carried through the streets as lighted torches by the hoards of unemployed lawyers whose ranks had far exceeded the demand for their services. That the citizens had ultimately bankrupt the city, so the story goes, is the reason why the name *The Angeles* was never used again after the fall and indeed it may have contributed to the ultimate collapse, the Kaiein. So the theoreticians speculate with the brilliant perspicuity that viewing the past gives to a mundane academic mind. The impulse of men to kill their saviors now forced the social services to protect themselves. "Help is coming." She repeated passionately.

"There were little tiny flashing lights that I saw out of the corner of my eye," the woman said, "like when I was a little girl and I would watch the lights of the city come on at dusk through my closed eyelids. I never knew whether I was dreaming or not so I had to open my eyes and make sure...only now I have them open but it's still..."she breathed in deeply, "will he be alright?"

She broke the rules then, "I don't know." *Never,* she remembered being told, *never under any circumstances give any evaluation of the situation.* "Help is coming," she once more intoned in an effort to redeem herself. The job was very serious to her, one light, one life.

"We're only drifting through the electronic fibers now..." The young woman continued playing out her own scene to her own rhythms. "if we had any sense at all we wouldn't be here, we wouldn't be doing this...would we?"

There were other lights beckoning, other lives in the fabric. "I'm leaving you now. Help is coming."

The moment he grasped the steel railing it gave him an overwhelming sense of place. He balanced there letting the familiar wash over him and soothe the unconsciousness away as he began to realize where he was and even though the location was unknown its similarity to other locations filled him with an inner peace. Looking down he saw the rail rusted through in spots, embedded in concrete that had been poured maybe a hundred and fifty years ago and he remembered seeing pictures of Mexican laborers working in the heat of the old Los Angeles. He blessed the Mexicans just now. It was still night though he didn't recall if it had been night before, prior to his memory lapse and the awakening on the street where he lay kissing the asphalt.

The blonde man with close cropped hair and a thick, muscular neck saw that his suit and shirt were torn. A long scar was partly revealed running at a forty-five degree angle across his chest, he couldn't remember how he had gotten it. The knees of his trousers were wet from puddles in the alley...*the alley!* he thought looking back over his shoulder at the gaping black chasm that led up between two long narrow buildings. "I must have been slumming." He said out loud, and then felt foolish for it. He couldn't remember his name, who he was or why he was in the Second City, at least it looked that way from his surroundings and he grasped the rail tighter until his hand began to ache, but at least it anchored him. There were still flashes of light, colored flashes sometimes as if he was being hit in the head and he was flickering in and out of consciousness. It was hurting him but most of all he was reeling violently and found it difficult to keep his balance. At first he thought he had been drinking, the effects were the same, like a drug, but he hadn't, not alcohol anyway, though the more he thought on it the more convinced he became that he had been drugged. *Why else*, he asked himself, *would I be here*. Where *here* was he didn't know, and when he realized that he began to question his inner identity, the self he had been conversing with for the past few moments and that, of course, made him feel worse. The man, who was tall and cast a long shadow from the street lights began to walk down the way because he was certain that whatever had happened he needed help.

There was a moon that night and it sent its beams as messengers through the permanent industrial haze that layered the atmosphere of this planet we of the past embrace with such rapacious hunger. Incandescent light painted the mans face from cheek bone to jaw bone with a pearl colored glow while the harsh reds, greens and blues of the street glittered in his worried eyes. If he had flown apart into a million pieces he would not have been more unnerved for as it was he did not have an existence and even with great effort and resolve could not bring up a memory from his past as a clue to who he might be. It was as if he could not focus his eyes and everything was indistinct.

He could see down the long thoroughfare. It was crowded with murky light spilling over from the street lamps sifting through the thick city air and down into the gullies of the buildings where there was no one except himself. There were no cars. The man noted their absence as unusual, but then he thought it may be the area he was in since he had no real idea where he was and the scarcity of traffic may be completely normal. This he told himself. Buildings were old, but all reconditioned with the utilities from the city. The external silver conduits filled with optical cables, network wiring and other peripheral connections ran up their sides and around them and stood out as alien objects, symbols of man's conquest of himself. He thought of hotel rooms. Suddenly he was flooded with memories of hotel rooms that had no place in time and no faces attached, simply hollow shells with the smell of disinfectant. He had to shake his head to rid himself of it. Also he was weak, which hadn't occurred to him before and he noticed how loud his footsteps were in the night. He told himself he was tired because he remembered somewhere hearing that extreme tiredness had almost the same symptoms as psychosis and that someone had cured it by just having his patient get enough sleep. That's why his footsteps were so loud, everything was exaggerated. This he told himself.

When the man reached an intersection he looked to his right and saw the red stream of lights that signaled a main thruway where traffic was crossing over. There were no magnetic beams on these streets, *that's why*, he thought, *that's why*…no one travels in the Second City off the beams at night…it's not safe. Then he spotted a Vidtel station and suddenly felt an urgency as if his life may be slipping away and in fact the thought struck him that he may be dying and how useless it would be if he didn't even know who he was when his time was up. The man started running, a lone figure with an ungainly gait sometimes dragging a foot until he reached the call station then fumbled frantically in his pockets, but had no money. He felt his legs give way as they buckled at the knees not having the strength to hold up any longer. Fighting his way to his feet he struck the Vidtel screen with his fist furious at his disability and finding that it gave him some relief hit it again, and again until his hands ached and started to bleed. In an instant the screen burst to life with the jagged symbols of the yellow "x" that looked like a crosswalk.

"CenMed, what is your emergency?"

Earlier in the evening, close to midnight, there had been an announcement over the CenMed VAN monitors. A police vehicle had been in an accident. Two detectives were involved. Their names were not known. Since it was customary to give information on all police emergencies to CenMed operators because they were the link, she had observed it on the screen during a call. Her eyes looked through it and for nearly the duration of the call it did not register until the final moment. "I'm leaving you now." she said, "Help is..." and left the sign off unfinished as a flush spread over her clouding the senses. In an instant all the sounds of the room were muffled and unreal and perspiration appeared on her forehead even though it was cold for the electronics. There were no names. To her, however, there was only one name. She thought of her fine young man who was a detective on the night shift the same as she working in the lightless hours.

Without hesitation she continued to answer calls constantly playing her fingers over the flashing red lights that never seemed to let up and were a perpetual reminder that the needs of people did not keep time but were relegated to other universes where the clock has no meaning. The momentum of her life ferried her past the riveting personal concern she had and allowed her to answer to the higher purposes, but it was not without effect and the straight rigid back, clenched fist, and position perched on the edge of her chair gave her away. Speaking calmly and with measured tones the emergencies were handled one by one without a single thought of why no one was handling hers...it was a long distance run she was on trailing through the distant countrysides with their fields of amber undulating beneath the caress of the wind and cities where the blue violet shadows were watched over from lighted pale yellow windows where souls embraced in the clarity of love.

"I'm lost." A man's voice said plainly.

"What is your emergency?"

Again he spoke, hesitating a moment as if looking for the proper answer, "I'm lost."

"Is there an emergency?"

He fumbled for words feeling the lifeline in jeopardy as he had when he rummaged through his pockets for change. *I must say the right thing*, he thought, *I must.* "I think I might die."

"Are you hurt?"

"I can't...remember."

"If you're just lost, we can't..."

"I'm hurt..." he said desperately, "I don't remember what happened." She thought of the hundreds of calls they had after the Phan's bombing and the VT went off-line mid virtual experience and drew the link between how this man acted and those responses. "We have you located." He was breathing hard and she began to wonder if he really would die. That had never happened to her except once though it was common with some of the other operators and she had wondered and tried to logically explain why it was but had concluded that some things just defied logic. There were no answers to some things. "Tell me."

"I'm sorry..." he said, "I feel so weak. I'm not like this, I'm dizzy, I can't see right...a minute ago my knees buckled, all by themselves they just...I'm sorry."

"Don't worry. We're here. Help is coming."

For what seemed like a long time there was silence. Only a few seconds elapsed but to her it was much longer each emergency having its own time continuum, it's own space. Perhaps it could have been measured in milliseconds and then there would be enough to divide up, to assign to specific moments, as it was now far too fleeting to be spoken of with human language. She relied on the heart, it filled in where other things failed. "Where are you my friend? Are you with me?"

"I am. I think I'm in the Second City."

"Yes," she said, and there was more silence. "Talk to me."

"I don't remember my name."

Alarmed, she was afraid he was in shock and losing ground so she entered the priority one code into the computer, which made the man's red light blink twice as fast as the others. "I wouldn't worry about it," she said breaking the rules again, "I do that all the time."

"What do you mean?" The man asked weakly.

"It happens," she replied matter-of-factly, "too much on the mind, so many things to remember, code numbers, sequences, serial protocols...we are human aren't we, you and I?"

He asked, "How did this happen?"

"We just let it get away from us didn't we? You and I?"

"Yes, that's right we did," the man spoke exhaustedly, "I wish it wasn't this way but it is."

In the background she could hear the siren. "Will you be alright? Are you with me?"

"I'll be OK...thanks."

Just at that moment a message flashed on the monitor stating that the detectives involved in the earlier accident were in good condition. Her fine young man was not one of them and for an instant her life hung suspended between the hope that we all live for and the despair that lurks just below the surface until it gave way to the flood of relief. "I'm leaving you now. Help is coming."

- VII -

Chasing The Muse

The clear, white wine was a chilled nectar and Sabiha drank it because she was at a loss and attributed her apparent lapses in memory to its effects. What never did occur to her was that anything was out of the ordinary at all. That should have been the first clue, and under normal circumstances it would have been.

Roses spilled out of a glass vase. Like black-red tears their beauty was a shock against the flat mauve wall behind them. Voices chimed in the air. It was cool. Sabiha felt as if she were gliding across the polished wood floor. Around her perhaps five hundred people flowed in currents, the silk of their garments making swishing sounds as they moved in flux as wheat in the wind gravitating to the sources of power and influence. The enduring odors of perfume, garlic and cooking oil were inescapable. She breathed deeply of them and emerged a hatchling salmon far upstream whose only thoughts were to run the mad river all the way to the sea and survive.

There was no memory of arriving. The diplomatic parties she was required to attend were so frequent they ran like a string of overlapping days with no intervals to separate them and so she imagined she found herself again spinning in the middle of the illuminati feeling light headed, but thought nothing of it. Through the sea of faces she moved subtly aware of herself as a presence in their midst and drew glances and occasional stares from men, middle aged and unappealingly

117

common as was the lot of the politic community. The din of the crowd, the crystal voices were unusually distant, like vapors, she could not seem to connect with all the lives who lingered close and felt as though she had just arisen from a profound sleep still unable to focus on the real world. Yet it was a glamorous, glittering, palatial landscape of breathing symbols each adorned as if a skyscraper with all the twinkling lights revealing the nuances of the lives inside, lives that needed form and most of all explanations to make them complete. Suddenly she breathed in the rich air of the sea filled to capacity with the blood of the earth and the billion creatures that shared its space. There was no clue why it had come to her in a crowded room and made her light headed. The touch of it and she tasted salt, the energy of her body coiled up in the belly like a starfish flexing its muscles and her legs like rippling sharks eternally hunting gave her a hunger for prey, equal prey, beloved prey. She felt a hand on her arm.

In her ear he spoke, "You are most attractive tonight."

She turned and flashed her eyes in a wild animal impulse at the sensation of the touch to find a man whose hair was briskly short and flecked with gray, broad, muscular and smiling judiciously having missed completely the danger he had just passed through. There was a familiarity, (she knew him), he waited for a response...(she must know him)...with a sagacious smile, "Thank you. I think I've been here nearly a half an hour and you're the first person...well," she surveyed the crowd staling for time...

"It's a diverse group. These summits always throw the oddest types together, don't you think?" he paused, "Well, I suppose you should know."

"I should?" She replied curiously watching his eyes transverse her body and feeling completely detached.

"I mean, your office," becoming aware he had been staring, "you must be used to it."

She seductively shifted her weight while looking at him through fallen hair and smiled because she had made him meek, "Yes, I am."

The man attempted a smile, but was nervous and perspiring. "I'm afraid I have to get back to my wife..." he absently glanced across the room, "she's entertaining the Works Administrator from Beijing." He looked at her with a blank expression hoping that she would give him some sensation so that he would know the feeling of living. "I can't leave her to him for long, it's just that ..."

"Yes...?"

"...you looked so lovely."

"Thank you," she frowned, bored and veered her eyes away from his. "I suppose anything's better than the Works Administrator. What does he do anyway?"

The man delicately pushed his way through the people. "Administers the works I guess..." and was lost in the room.

She still didn't remember who he was, but had the strongest feeling that she should have. She must have done business with him... he was familiar with her office at the UN, so it must have been business. She was pleased at the effect she had on him...and that was something that should have been a signal. However it slipped away as she strode into the mix of people and began to feel more in touch. There were many that she knew and would briefly stop to talk with, pass social banalities, which she didn't like to do but was as adept at it as she was at her job. The real talk, the talk that mattered didn't happen here, nothing really happened here except the intrigues of social intercourse whose real mystery was that there was no mystery at all.

The huge room was shining in its opulence. Chandeliers of crystal reputed to have been crafted in pre-revolutionary France over three centuries ago dangled from invisible optical cables under a post modern, post decline-and-fall ceiling of angles, of vented skylights, domes and shadows that marked all the public architecture of the reconstruction. It was a statement of breakage, of severance, of nearly complete disconnection from the past leaving nothing to the imagination that could remotely connect with it. Except the chandeliers, which no mortal could resist the beauty of, the resplendence or the association with civilization at its zenith prior to the proletariat revolutions and the industrialization that led to mechanized wars and carnage and above all death beyond the abilities of kings to imagine. Perhaps they were symbols of the flower of youth that was annihilated time after time by the atrocities of the machine age leaving the earth to the meek of spirit, heart, vision and mind. Beneath this legacy diplomats from every provincial arena waltzed around while their surroundings fulfilled the mandate to never remind anyone of the past, of the failure...except for the chandeliers that everyone secretly revered as a symbol of their lost humanity. A thousand hollow eyes were reflected in each crystal.

She was uncomfortable that she felt particularly sexual tonight as if the sea creatures inhabited her in their frenzy to propagate and left her awash in seed floating on the brine. The proximity to the crowd and the occasional leering glances of men who normally would not have been seen by her excited her. A frenetic, clawing, animal rapture grew from within that gnawed at her. She did not know why she drew this kind of attention, but once discovered it was sought out and she played with glances, bantered with sullied looks and did her best to make strong men uncomfortable.

The fact that she was not herself went unnoticed. In the unre-membered part of the evening she had dressed in an out of character manner, in a way that would never have happened except under exceptional circumstances. She caught glances of herself in mirrors, in polished windows...her thin, black wrap lightly hanging whose clinging synthetic material folded and caressed the curves and muscular angles of her body in a living manner at times appearing nearly sheer, breathing, in certain light, with certain movements...shimmering...it plunged to reveal the full length of her spine and the interplay of sinew, skin and bone of her back as it disappeared in the material barely within the confines of decency. It fell fully revealing her breasts when she would lean in a way that...or turn, as in passing or in conversation...her luxurious brown skin radiated the vitality of a woman overflowing with restrained sexual abandon. Her silent movements were an unconscious mating dance and commanded the attention of every male. The odor of intimate relations surrounded her. She wore no other garment than the thin, black, draped dress that could easily be folded and crushed and concealed within one small hand. The slim, rakish shoes elevated her from the ground, the movement of the fabric on her bare skin aroused her and she felt naked in the crowd. Naked and predatory.

Women with whom she was usually on good terms would not converse with her, but withdrew after a few cursory exchanges and excused themselves some timidly some with the hair standing up on the back of their necks…a few were aggressive and intrusive and like men they hung on her, like vultures waiting for the weakness. The men spoke honestly and openly and were effusive and drawn to her thankful for this private sin they could each indulge in without commitment or remorse. Yet all were harboring a secret in their eyes, each of them, meanings hidden but so obviously corrupt that they dare not reveal them even though they longed to. Each desired to be her paramour. She grew uncharacteristically antagonistic, and as she made the required rounds at the gathering she became more cynical and caustic. Sabiha was drinking too much, but even she could not ascribe her behavior to this. In the grand tradition of all insanities her behavior was ignored by the mind's eye like all aberrations and devils that have plagued men since before the beginning.

As the night frayed away she became filled with an agitated energy. It gave her strength yet at the same time a bewildering confusion. Her eyes darted around the room like minnows flickering silver in the mottled shafts of sunlight that bathed the deep and caressed the shallows and met other eyes equally agitated making their own desperate swim in search of only they knew what. She felt frantic without reason.

"Are you one of the diplomatic corps?" A malevolent voice spoke closely behind her and she turned to a man who was unshaven and sweating. He was young, younger than her and tan from carefully nurtured bathing in light. There was a sweet smell about him.

She shot back a reply, "Why?"

The young man stepped back a pace and blinked repeatedly, but then he laughed under his breath. "The cat's claws."…he muttered covertly.

"That's right." She swirled around showing him her back and his eyes traveled down the copper skin of her spine to the almost revealed and he began to sweat even more. Sabiha was not unaware of this process and let him stew ignoring any recognition, but could feel the heat of his stare as it traveled across her exposed flesh letting it burn into her like a narcotic. Her cloudiness did not obscure the fact that he was not of her breed but rather gave her license because of the difference. *How far would he go?* The thought occurred to her from out of some dark recess. She was entering the danger zone.

Sipping silently on his drink the man regarded every nuance of she that haughtily stood before him, inaccessible yet worthy of obsession. He absorbed her. The way she was standing, the weight on one hip making one shoulder a little higher than the other and pulling the fabric tightly across her buttocks; the smooth flesh of her back with each muscle defined; dark black hair tied up above the sweep of her long neck; the backs of her ears with large silver rings hanging from each one–suspended mid air not touching any other part of her. He wished to touch her just once like that, once and he would be satisfied because he knew she was not of his breed. The tall, slim woman gave him a voracious appetite and he longed to reach out his hand and place it under the fabric to feel the luxuriousness of her skin, and would have done so without hesitation under different circumstances. The brilliance of the moment made his heart race in anticipation. "My name is Justin...", he said breathlessly.

She turned to face him, "Sabiha Sahin," she responded before he could finish tilting her head slightly and avoiding eye contact.

"...Justin Coe. Algerian?"

"Ethiopian."

"Well," he said with a forced enthusiasm enthralled by her dark eyes, which would not look at him, "that's settled."

Regarding the young man contemptuously, "You work here?" she asked smiling.

"In a way..." he replied unaware he was being trifled with, "I'm a courier."

"What do you *courie*'?"

"Messages, documents..." his eyes narrowed to slits, "what have you got?"

Pursing her lips as if she had just bitten into a sour lemon she struggled with the young man, though attracted uncharacteristically. She faced him for the first time peering into the windows to get a glimpse, past the gates to learn his story and saw there his whole history exposed as if he had explained in detail every sordid encounter and dismal relationship. Beyond that there was no redemption. His eyes were lively like a dog when he is first called yet there was something intrinsically material about him, a paucity of spirit and an abundance of hormones. It caused subtle waves of excitement that were drug-like yet at the same time very separate from her. She let the sensation roll over her anyway, against any judgment that may have been present in normal times. There was an urge to flaunt the moral propriety of the instant.

"Won't you walk with me for a moment," he asked, "let me show you around." She walked just slightly ahead rarely looking into his eyes, once had been enough and she was afraid with one more glance the illusion would be gone completely and her disdain would show. "How did you end up here?" He blithely asked and she curtly answered allowing words to pass between them as objects each one having its own predictable response certain that he had no good intentions and she wanted to play along, to see how far he would go. They sat and talked for an hour, she disdainful, indifferent and distant and he insincere with hidden motives. It was a position she had never been in during her short life and one that she had gone to great lengths in the past to avoid, but the physical attraction was undeniable and though she viewed it as if it were happening to another, she was curious that she could feel anything sexual for someone so alien. Yet she did, a dull aching desire not at all like the fresh lightness of love she had known. As she became more agitated it got to the point where she was barely listening to him at all and only watched his body move the words insignificant. She placed her hand absently on his thigh and innocently watched his reactions as she subtly moved the ends of her fingers over him.

"This is an interesting residence you know," he offered desperately, "there are three stories where the delegates are housed, and each one is designed from a different culture...would you like to see some of it?"

Up the thickly carpeted stairs the young man followed. He watched her move, the delicate shift of weight from one leg to the other, the sliding of fabric across skin, the sheer mystery of it made him breath heavily, so much so that she glanced back at him following up the stairs and said, "You are out of shape, aren't you?"

He explained in detail the meaning of the interior schemes of each floor, corridor and room as they passed glad to be away from the crowd, if only briefly to be able to indulge in her privately. She felt intent on luring the young man even further and took every available moment to slyly entice him, to darkly ensnare him. They turned down one of the cloisters and through dim hall lights. Sabiha suddenly stopped and stood with her back propped against the wall looking at the young man. There was not a sound except for his breathing and she was surprised at how loud it was. The hallway was vacant.

"Come here." She said with authority and grabbed the top of his trousers to pull him close so his face was only inches away, and brushed her lips against his smelling the sweetness of the alcohol, the pungent odor of perspiration and feeling the heat of his skin. He responded slowly and pressing against her so she could feel his muscular stomach kissed her only lightly. She slipped her hands up under his coat where he was damp with heat and sweat. They kissed again and ground their lips together in the awkward passion that marked unfamiliar sexual partners. The young man's head spun with confusion as he tumbled without conscience into whatever might come seared by heat and heartbeats as his hands explored her breasts. Sabiha pressed back against him for no good reason other than the unconscious demand for sensation she wished would overwhelm her to oblivion, to find how far he would go as his hands coolly and smoothly ran across her exposed back and her breasts just as he had imagined. The young man felt her muscles contract and ran his tongue up her long neck until it touched the ear that he had lusted after in the crowd. When she shuddered he knew. For a long time they embraced, she drawing him closer while he grew bolder and more out of control. It was cool in the hallway; she could hear their breathing. Her body was in need. She watched it all happen. She was in the danger zone.

Sabiha senselessly let her hand run up his thigh as she leaned to one side while he kissed her neck and lightly brushed her fingers across him feeling the hardness beneath. His hands ran down her back along the sheer fabric across her buttocks until he could feel the bare flesh of her legs, then he brought his caress slowly up under her dress and was inflamed by the discovery of her nakedness. In the corridor, beneath the light which cast shadows upon the wall, by the rooms where the diplomats were housed he lifted the skirt away from her thighs, and ran hands across the flat of her exposing her sex to whoever might be passing by.

She felt dizzy and pushed him away. With heavy lidded eyes she wiped her mouth with one hand while she pulled down the dress with the other, "Just a minute now," she whispered hoarsely, "hold on there..." He fell on her again and with her head reeling she once again pushed him off and slipped through an open door whispering' "...wait a minute now, just wait..." The door closed silently.

Inside it was dark, and quiet. Up against her back she could feel the icy coldness of porcelain tiles and she slid in the pitch black along the cool wall until another door was felt, she entered and closed it behind her. There was no light switch that she could find even though she ran her hands along the walls close to the entrance where it should be, but she did find a basin and knew it was probably of one of the diplomat's bathrooms.

There was a glow coming under a door from a pale light in the other room. She silently turned the knob hoping to be able to see the switch, but soon as it had opened she knew she was not alone. From out of the adjacent space flew human sounds, animal whimpering rhythms, and rustling movements of bedclothes. She froze and listened. A slight moan cut through her unwillingness to hear it as if hot steel through ice and it seared the pit of her belly and made her legs weak. She listened unable to pull away absorbed by the privacy she had invaded debilitated by the moral dilemma. A man's breathing could be heard, heavy, in syncopated time with the slight moans...she listened against her will to the secrets being traded in the silent intervals. Rustling movements whispered and she thought she heard the brushing of flesh against flesh. An overpowering, unnatural sensation grasped hold and forced her to crack the door just enough so she could peer innocently around the corner into the dimly lit space where the rhythm of nature was at play.

The shock of that first sight sent a jolt through her like a fifty amp current making her gasp and causing her eyes to swell and her perceptions to become more clouded. In the room on a snow white bed two dark skinned people lay glistening beneath the dim light moving and writhing in time to each other. He behind, face buried in the shadows of her black hair. She could hear him breathing...she, lips upturned caught the light making them glisten as they parted to allow a low moan to escape as they moved, and a quick breath, her lean legs spread liquidly over the man's muscular driving frame. Sabiha could not pull away though every sense she possessed demanded it. The woman sang out with a long low note and then began to cry. The man moved furiously on her with quick, staccato gasps and guttural exhalations that sounded like a hyena off in the darkness, beyond human reach while the woman surrounded him in a death grip her breasts glistening with sweat and her arms spayed out frantically waving her sobs filling the air.

Sabiha silently pulled the door closed and sank to her knees against the wall feeling sick and drunk and filled with disgust at herself. In an instant strange images came to her, forced themselves on her and she closed her eyes tightly and covered her face with her hands in a vain attempt to block them, to hide. But they came anyway.

It was a dark hallway like the one she had just been in with the young man two men were leading her. She shook her head and pressed her cheek against the cool porcelain tile resisting the memory, which was revealing itself to her now. It was as if she was drugged, *yes*, she thought mirroring the idea of earlier that evening, *I was drugged*. The jarring pictures continued now with the man holding her arms, the dark room...she began to convulse as unpleasant sexual sensations rained upon her...*the machine*, she remembered and got the idea that two men had drugged her at an official luncheon and forcibly had taken her to a room where the VT was playing...there were pictures, pictures of sexual activity, it was virtual, on the screen. She sat straight up, suddenly stronger as her memory clarified itself by the true look and she consciously remembered. In a room she saw herself that afternoon in a semi-conscious drugged state while the VT played virtual sex on the screen. A dark frown covered her face. She felt no shame, no loathing or remorse, but anger ran through her in a raging torrent.

It was now becoming clearer. She remembered, their touch, their smells...and most of all one man's face. His hair was blonde and cropped close. Through the unconscious veil she remembered him as she lay helpless, vulnerable yet somehow fully perceptive. His body was wiry and muscular with a thick neck and strong sinewy arms. Sabiha tensed completely as the realization struck her that she had been implanted with sexual feelings from the VT that were not hers. The impossibility, the sheer fantastic thought of it defied belief, but that was the best defense, it defied belief.

Fusing, she stammered, *they used fusing!* Someone knew about fusing, someone was using it! The events of the evening became perfectly clear. Her appearance. Her behavior. A calm seized her and she felt immediately herself as if someone had lifted a shade and allowed light to enter a deprived space. A weight that had been unknown lifted revealing a lightness of being.

Suddenly there was a sound from the room where the two dark people had lain. Quickly Sabiha rushed through the door and slipped again back out into the hallway where the man was waiting. His dull eyes locked onto her. She could feel the cool breeze in the hall brush her skin through the impossibly thin wrap and she felt naked and ashamed. Crossing her arms over her chest she walked up to the waiting man, who still in the heat of passion, expected to fall back into the vortex and be swept away. He nauseated her. He reached out. She stopped him with cold, harsh words.

"Give me your coat!" she said venomously.

He froze where he stood and a look of shock covered his face, which was pale and bloodless. In a moment he handed over the coat. She grabbed it, put it on and then slapped him viciously with a resounding crack in the silent passage. He fell back against the wall stunned and wide eyed. Helpless he watched the woman walk away down the hall and disappear around a corner knowing that he would never see her again and for some reason never see his coat again either.

The cross burned itself into the floor of the cathedral. Its power stolen from the yellow dwarf star whose light fled over ninety-six million miles of lifeless ether to finally pierce the leaded glass high in the wall and etch the symbol into stone. It was imbued with even greater might unseen on this earth. It was without weight, without space, without any location in time yet of such magnitude lives were tumbled in its wake like so many autumn leaves. The Christ, of which generations had clung to with a desperate hope and belief only to become disillusioned, had passed. The churches with their martyrs, relics and universal dogma of the inherent evil of men...they too had passed like the burning symbol now slowly moving across the floor with the rotation of the earth. The mystery was that it did not leave an indelible tattoo on the masonry, but for all its force and brilliance it too was fleeting and ethereal. An illusion. The symbol, however, remained as a signal to all those swept into the cauldron of the material world. Its inhabitants who reached frantically for a lifeline, who held fast perhaps to the one spiritual thought that remained throughout their days higher than all the other ideals and kept them from complete oblivion. The cross spoke of the spirit. The symbol was the last best hope of men. Its power was immutable. While the ideologies ebbed and flowed the symbol remained.

The silver cross glinted as it caught a stray beam of light. It rested on dark fabric buttoned to the neck. Nash understood the power he dealt with and had freely accepted wearing of the cross as part of the canon handed down to him by the brethren even though many other aspects of it he could not accept. The trade off was that it gave him a conduit through which he could come to realize the essence if not the fact of his life's work with the organization of the Church and its teachings providing a spiritual base and a congregation already reaching. It was with this mission that he approached each day and as well overcame his own personal desires in order to maintain the discipline required of anyone who chose the way of the cloth. The conflict of passion and purpose tested him constantly.

He closed the door to his office. It scrapped across the marred floor leaving one more etched reminder of a day's passing. He flicked on his computer monitor. Immediately the symbol of the GIS, (Global Information System), appeared. After a few deft touches on the screen and answering the perfunctory voice prompts he navigated into the areas where he had been searching for information. Nash hated the damn thing and it in turn glared back at him with an electronic malice that sometimes made the hair on the back of his neck bristle. It was cold from the harsh realities it portrayed that had no tempering judgment of moral or ethical concerns such as a person might give. The result was a falsely created equality of ideas lending the same credibility to one as the other without any criterion to measure each's validity. The sewage ran with the wine in the cauldron of the digital ecosystem, which enveloped all who lived. People had become lost somewhere. The media portrayed all at the same wavelength, with the same hue and density, the same volumes and pitches and importance giving the impression that all things were equal and the mighty were the same as the meek save the exception of celebrity. It was not as Nash understood the meanings of individuals to be where nuances and perceptions were weighed, balanced and evaluated with the incredibly complex human mind that could handle more information within the intervals between the smallest moments of time than the most complex quantum computer yet devised or imagined could. Intuition, it was called, and even a baby had it.

The one thing he could admire was the instant availability of information. Fear had initially propelled the pooling of all extant knowledge into the enormous databases of the WEB, but now it was as if a new human right had appeared from the chaotic events of history and each new child drank of it like water and with the same expectation of its free use. What had started as the great equalizing effect of the media had given rise to the evolution of accomplishment from the privileged to anyone who possessed the courage to rise above their own station.

"Ahhhhh…" Nash exclaimed despite his animosity toward the virtual world. On the screen before him was a document that reflected in his eyes fragmented words partially transcribed and idioms of the day lost to generations. It was from before the Kaiein. He found it on a search string from something he had heard of only in stories and had keyed into the computer without any hope of response. However, here it was, a fragment yet a link. Over the optical cables many of which had been laid a century ago flew the images in shattered photons, in bursts of light, chaotic, random and traveling the virtual slipstream signaling a response to the string *"Golden XiOma,"* but the true significance, the astonishing part was that it spoke of it as *"The" Golden XiOma*. Nash felt as if he had found the one key thread by which the fabric, the woof and warp of the universe were bound.

Unknown to him in another chamber deep within the halls of the cathedral shadows were thrust across the smooth, gray brow of the High Advocator as he frowned with unfathomable concentration over words being spoken. Commander Rybin gritted his molars together, as was a habit, flexing the muscles of his jaw so that they sprang out in rhythmic spasms when he was silent and remained tense when he spoke giving his language a labored pedantic tone. His hair was brindled and cropped short in military fashion, his skin translucent defying any description of color and giving the impression of a membrane. The man was, however, strong and stood erect with posture that had once, many centuries ago, been imposed on all children from birth and gave them an aura of resolve and strength and an allusion of aristocratic nobility. Who was to say if it had been for good or evil that this discipline had vanished, for now despite his age and apparent infirmities the Commander was an imposing figure. He pinched his nose between thumb and forefinger and gestured boldly across the space. "He's not really one of us, thoroughly undisciplined and *erretic*."

The High Advocator who, though listening, was racing ahead into the worlds yet to be and so anticipated nearly everything said to him before it was voiced as the logical conclusion for each train of thought. "Erratic." He said correcting the pronunciation of one of the many words the other man had by inclination or accident fallen into the routine of butchering. To the High Advocator life was a narrative of which he was already familiar. He agreed with the Commander without allowing him the grace of recognition, but as a former military man it didn't matter and that was why the two got on so well.

On their breast too lay the silver cross that had become the symbol of the spirit. There was no telling whether they wore it for the same reason Nash did, but one thing was certain neither was ever seen without it.

"I've given him every chance, every opportunity..." the High Advocator explained hunched over rubbing his knuckles.

Commander Rybin interjected, "He's a damned dilettante."

A moment passed. "Perhaps too intellectual..."

"He bucks command, there's no denying that."

The High Advocator was amused. "We are religious men..."

"Bahh!" he replied dismissing the obvious effort to negate his perceptions and turned on his heels in crisp fashion to consider more carefully his next words. "We are in the army of salvation wouldn't you say? There's no excuse for lack of discipline...I see nothing martial about it, just common sense...he's flaunting us all. It's alright being individual until it interferes with the group. It happened before didn't it, individuals all after their own ends and see where it got us."

"But for fortune who knows that providence has not brought us here by plan. Perhaps, Commander, we are like all leggless birds destined to live on the wing, on the wind only to the extent we can navigate capricious changes."

The former military man pursed his lips as if in meditation upon the High Advocator's words, but in reality he seethed and recognized immediately the attempt to embroil him in obscure metaphor and was already planning his counter attack. It went like that, in his mind, he could not escape his past no matter how far or how fast he might run the ritual of military logic was too firmly ingrained into his psyche as a fingerprint of the spirit. Of course the argument might go that all men are victims of their environment to a degree, but there are also those whose calling is predestined and have only been waiting for their destiny and only appear indolent. It is overpowering, this terrible purpose, he thought, its lurking demons can only be guessed at. The echoes of former lifetimes were lost as he blustered out a response. "Our elevation from the muck is determined by reasoning alone," he said glaring at the High Advocator who was still amused, "even a fool knows which way the wind blows."

The High Advocator's bony fingers sliced through the air as he talked animating lost meanings and hidden innuendo that revealed the full richness of his mind. Inside were halls and archives and vast libraries of obscure information, labyrinths of details, chasms of knowledge all at play with each other in an impossibly intricate system of cross references, balances, checks and double checks, evaluations and categorizations of all sensory input. It was the infinite mind that he aspired to and the power of his intellect was truly impressive, even to the uninitiated it was said that his oratory was the inspiration for generations of converts to the Old Religion. He was a firm believer in the evangelical mission he felt was preordained to any man of the cloth. With this thought he guided the brethren through the shoals and helped them avoid the *paths to nowhere,* as he was fond of putting it, secure in the conviction that he had the insight others lacked. Rubbing his chin with the back of his hand he pronounced with simple finality, "He needs missionary work. Honest work." And then sat back wincing his cold blue eyes into slits, placing his fingertips together in a mock cathedral and staring at some far off place while intoning plans he had made for disciplining the young minister. "It's a simple matter of whether he will fulfill the needs of the Church," he muttered as more an incantation than a statement, "putting aside his own personal desires, or whether he won't..." the High Advocator rose up out of the chair enlivened by his own righteousness, "...by testing his dedication." He explained in exacting detail how the missionary program coupled with that of the donations were the life's blood of the Church and that no minister had the right to ignore those duties. Commander Rybin had heard the diatribe many, many times, but was soothed by having his attitude concerning Nash vindicated and so said little except for an occasional *uh huh* interjected as an encouragement when the High Advocator's voice lulled.

Secretly the Commander wished to purge the Church of all those who did not fall in line. It was not, he had decided, an open forum for liberated thought, but rather a place of tradition and values not to be disturbed. In fact he was of the opinion that the entire mission of the Church was simply and wholly relegated to the upholding of spiritual values and perceived himself as a soldier, a keeper of civilization. The falling off of congregations he attributed to moral decline drawing no parallels between the dogma and the parishioners. It was black and white. Believers and nonbelievers. "This obsession he has with individual counseling is something I've never understood."

"He doesn't seem to grasp the concept of fundamental belief, the comfort, the order..." The High Advocator spoke venomously, "people take great solace in their religion, he's looking for something else, something unknowable and we must disabuse him of it if he is to be of any use as a servant of the Church."

Commander Rybin added cynically, "You won't be able to."

"Perhaps not," was the reply, "perhaps not." The two men were sullen each with the knowledge he was using the other to his own ends, and each tacitly consenting to whatever may come. "I don't want him fooling with souls." The High Advocator continued vehemently, " It should be left alone, at least in the Church. Isn't it enough that we have the fruit of the Rememberers, the law of The Canon... where would he be without it I wonder?"

"Another convert for the Phan I should guess."

"Yes..." The High Advocator wheeled around and looked down on Commander Rybin who was still sitting with his eyes wide and full of fire. "I should guess."

The Commander gloated inside. It was only a faint shadow of the brazen emotions he was used to, nevertheless it felt good and as he rose and took two steps a perceptive man could ascertain the hint of a strut in his walk. Out of the High Advocators door he could see down the hallway and into the vestibule of the cathedral and was struck by the beauty of the late morning light flooding through the high windows like molasses. He suddenly felt at peace knowing the order would be preserved. His thoughts ran in rigid linear trails each of which left a mark that was straight and as narrow as the edge of taut wire. One thing followed another, it was progression as it should be…everything had a reason and could be explained given enough time. The rest, it was all pseudo theory and he didn't devote any time to conjecture as to whether something might come of it or not. That was not the issue. The basic principles were now as they have always been. If anyone had questioned him or even intimated how closely his own philosophy aligned with the Phan there would have been hell to pay, and so he kept his more essential ideas very close to his breast never fully letting them see the light especially among his peers. For now he felt satisfied with himself and without a word slipped through the door and into the morning not even feeling the High Advocator's all knowing gaze freezing the path behind him.

Nash placed his finger on the screen as if to touch the virtual, to dispel the unbelief and gain a tactile reality on that which was passing before his eyes like a vision. Though he dared not think of it, of revelation, and wanted any knowledge he absorbed intellectually to have its roots in practical experience. Life was, he knew, the test of any theory and the crux was if it worked or if it did not. Nash had no use for fallen bridges, there were too many scattered across the eons to count and as well far too many offers to help that had ended only in betrayal. The cool glass pressed against the skin of his finger and he could feel the radiation from the screen surge through his body in tiny waves as he stared wide eyed into the near void where fleeting impressions of photons burned their message home and then were gone, swept away into the continuum.

It was not a document in the true sense. It was not written for the computer. It was an image. The glow of it excited him. Two pages of a book lie open with a wash of yellow light across them. The lines not straight as if the copy had been made in a hurry, carelessly, copied and then left haphazardly in a file on an obscure, off the mainstream server under the tag "*Golden XiOma.*" Chances are he would not have found it in many lifetimes of searching the WEB, but for two brief references to a *Golden XiOma* in *The Canon*, and even then he might have missed it. The dichotomy that surrounded its mention intrigued him because at the time he had been pensive, anxious, hungry for detail. In one sense it was mentioned as an earlier reference source by an anonymous writer who implied that it was an endless reservoir of data the bulk of which had not ever been plumbed. Yet in the other mention, too distant in time to be remembered, too foreign in content to be connected the speaker condemned the *Golden XiOma* as being *the chalice of corruption* and its author *Azrael*. In the compendium of The Canon, which was comprised of many books pieced together from many reference sources all of which had survived the Kaiein, he had become familiar with the concept of no specific author, but rather a matrix of voices. In this way he had learned to study it and gather the remnants of civilized knowledge as it was and had been salvaged from the great social catastrophe. The Canonists, such as the Brethren, were endlessly engaged in drawing a finite line of knowledge from one end of the Canon to the other forming links, relationships and metaphors that do not exist. So here, perhaps, a discovery of the thread left untouched whose praises on one hand were infinite and on the other ascribed to the angel of death. The mystery of it lured him and for no logical reason absorbed his interest.

He had not even begun to approach the sheer volume of infor- mation contained in *The Canon*, but he had scanned its make up, its essence in search of keys that set off unconscious signals leading him on. Nash supposed he was driven by the same purposes that drove other men though he knew not the depths to which those unfathomable men had fallen. His desires like theirs were a burden, his unseen purposes a harsh master. He drank knowledge as lesser men did of wine, or the flesh with its rewards so immediate and available. It did not occur to him that there was anything unknowable or conversely that there were so many stray truths imbedded in nondescript data that the process of gaining full wisdom would be nearly an infinite one. To him there was the fundamental touch. The grasping of hands. The grit of the hazy sun streaming through industrial air. It was all very simple. The feel of feet planted firmly on earth. There was perfect sense and clarity yet the disability of some to come to understanding baffled and frustrated him. It was so apparent that he scanned the texts without a clear purpose, but rather searching for the nameless clue that would lead him to a deeper meaning. Knowing he would recognize it when it occurred. Certain he was driven by the same desires as other men. It would all make sense if living meant more than just passing through the Mandala, if there was a certain attainable end that somehow made it all worth it.

However, the image before him was even more of a mystery than he had imagined. The overall design of it was non-linear and read like a computer language with symbols, equations and directions as if some long dead architect were leaving a blueprint. He tapped his index finger on the desk. There were only two pages. The rest either unimportant or lost to the ages by a misguided or careless hand. His mind was washed with blankness and he could not fathom the significance of the *Golden XiOma* from these hieroglyphs, though he longed to embrace their meaning because without reason he knew this was the thread. For hours Nash grappled with the intangible.

With a great sigh the impossibility of the task loomed over him. He sensed danger without knowing the source. From the silence there was a shuffling sound at the door to his office, which he had left open. A figure leaned in. A hoarse voice whispered, "You've got trouble." He turned to see the red flushed face of Anther. The old man stepped inside the small office and pulled the door to.

Nash looked at him without expression thinking this was the last thing he needed right now. "What do you mean?" He asked.

"You've got to learn to take it easy... things come, you *will* learn if you can last, but they come slowly, in their own time. Everything has its own time. Just now you need to slow down, listen a bit, get the feel of things."

Nash turned back to the monitor on which the document was still displayed. He closed it down knowing that there would be no further useful work done now. "What are you trying to say?" He replied without looking back and reached for his coat.

Anther put his hands together as if preparing for a very serious discussion. "I like you," he began, "can see in you what I wanted to be when I was younger..." he lapsed into a long reverie as if the tail end of a vision were passing through or the memory of a poignant love that never was. "You may not realize it now, but once you loose it, sometimes you can't ever get it back." He gathered his long coat and pulled it up over his shoulder in an effort to ward off the chill that lurked in these back offices, the least desirable in the cathedral. There was a musty smell about him. "I'm reminded of the Canon chapter 878, verse 66," his voice getting deeper, "on the last King of Mycenae, who he was we'll never know, nor why he fell...the book tells us that with his fall the written word was lost for a thousand years..." his delicate voice trailed off into a whisper again, "Carthage was burned to the ground, its fields sown with salt, its people scattered to the winds mating and blending with all the other inhabitants of the continent until their identity was blurred and indistinct. It vanished and even the legend wears thin." The ruddy faced man looked at Nash with a compelling empathy. "You're like that."

"Sown with salt?" he rejoined bitterly.

"Yes!" Anther blurted out, "By your own hand too!"

"Sit down." He gestured to the natty couch shoved up against the wall out of the way of the door. "What is it you want?"

Anther spoke earnestly trying to impart something obscure that was clear to him. "You must know that...you've got to take the brethren's attitudes to heart, you are one of us and you can't be one yet separate."

"I am not separate."

"You seem so sure."

"I am tired."

"Of what? You're so young."

"The all consuming whirlpool of the Church that takes our lives as fodder, ingests us for its own use...no matter what I do it's never enough, and you..." Nash paused, reigned himself in with his hand poised halfway above his head, fingers curled in a dynamic yet futile gesture. His hand dropped to his side having thought better of his words. "I question my own faith sometimes and that makes me very uncomfortable. "

"You must give us a chance."

"I see plodders and shufflers advance, all you have to do is put up with it long enough and you're in, and then you don't know you're shuffling, and the plodding becomes a virtue…a saintly virtue."

"You must understand the economics."

"You must understand the purpose."

The air was electric with conflict. Anther could not understand it so he reached deep into his reservoir to come to grips with it, and like many things in the modern world it just escaped his grasp like a fleeting shadow. "Just now I was by the High Advocator's door. I couldn't help overhearing."

Nash scowled down at him feeling no personal animosity, but confined and useless.

"They won't have you following your own agenda."

"Who?"

"The High Advocator and Commander Rybin."

Nash sat on the corner of his desk. "Bahh… what can they do?"

"They don't agree with your personal counseling."

"Never did."

"You're going to be tested my son, tested."

"What do you mean?"

"Things come slowly, in their own time."

"How am I to be tested?"

"You'll see, if you last…it's not how bright the flame burns, but how long."

The ambulance screamed through the teeming streets like a banshee with unresolved agonies caroming off the canyon walls reminding everyone of how easily disaster can strike. A million lives balanced, teetering, flaunting the inevitable, rolling the dice, spinning the wheel, taking the ticket, buying the chance, betting the farm, shooting the moon…a million flaming lives set in a course of fire racing to their destiny. The terrible purpose guides them all…brilliant, inarticulate, creative, sensual, dull, flamboyant, weak…it cares not, for there is a heaven up ahead and in the end no excuses. *You can't fool yourself* an old saying goes. Those who shoot down children in the streets and feel no remorse are preordained to be free to kill again and are driven the same as any other man. There is no difference except the map in the head. For one man the next day has meaning, for another it does not. Good and evil is a question of survival.

The carrier raced into the emergency lane and pulled up to the airlock guided by hydraulic curbs against the beams. Red, blue and amber lights bounced from fender to window to wall and back again in a frantic rhythm that reflected the sound of the siren even though it had stopped. The whole of the back of the ambulance was suddenly lifted from its cradle as a pressurized, sterile environment containing the man who had been picked up by the call box unconscious with a scar diagonally crossing his chest and the two parameds who had found him. They had attached a complete life support system contained in the walls of the capsule so would not need to move the patient again as the container that held them was inserted into a giant receptacle on the wall and would quickly become an emergency operating room. Inside the trauma center on the second floor was a long narrow hallway above the walk-in traffic. On one side were dimly lit built-in cloud computer workstations where technicians monitored every minute detail, on the opposite side was a wall of tinted glass dividing the corridor down the middle and providing an hermetically sealed hygienic environment. Inside the glass were huge cavities where the capsules were plugged in from the outside. At each receptacle an emergency trauma team was assigned. On busy nights ambulances would line up in the emergency lane and the teams were dispatched directly to the carriers where emergency procedures were carried out on the spot. It was all very efficient. The technology was state-of-the-art. Hundreds of hustling physicians could be seen through the glass ministering to the acutely ill and injured. Still a human endeavor, the mysteries of healing had not yet been solved by machines.

Since Fionica's tenure as head of Trauma she had raised the survival rate of acute emergency victims from sixty percent to over ninety by defining the relationship of the medical staffs to the high tech machines they relied upon. She was credited with bringing medicine back into the healing arts and had created the most advanced and successful trauma center in the western hemisphere. *If you're in an acute state of trauma, accident, burns...* she would tell the press, *...this is the place to be.* Five years ago she successfully fought off efforts to close the facility in order to make up for vast city deficits and overspending by spearheading attacks against the old boy networks of the metropolitan government and in the face of death threats managed to get several of them removed from their posts. The trauma center still stood. It was still running in the red, but few people considered it a bad investment. Its reputation was now global.

A loud, low hiss signaled the attachment of the capsule to the docking bay on the second floor as the intermediary air lock forced trapped atmosphere out and from the vacuum filled it with sanitized air. When the inner door to the compartment opened its iris a gasp was audible over the voices of the trauma team and the hum of electronics. It reminded the uninitiated of a baby's first breath. The man was wheeled in on particle beams so not even the slightest bump was perceived and brought to rest in the operating bay under the lights still attached to life support. A pale face gazed toward the stars with eyes closed and measured breath surrounded by banks of electronics and eight strangers into whose hands his life was delivered without consent.

Gimme some numbers! a doctor barked impatiently, *it's weak,* was the reply, *testing, testing...let's bring him around...* The team moved quickly, surely, from long experience reaching out and finding things at their fingertips without even looking. *How much?... five hundred CCs... let's do it NOW!.* The monitors immediately showed increased activity as the drug was absorbed through his skin directly into the heart. Two members of the team cut his trousers up the sides and began attaching monitoring electrodes to his skin while another drew a minute quantity of blood into the probing arm of the computer that hung suspended from the ceiling with a hundred different kinds of sensors. Within minutes a complete biological roadmap of the man was displayed on the monitors in the wall and from it his physical history and future could be predicted with amazing accuracy thanks to the genetic blueprint disassembled from his living cells. The blonde man with the scar could be cloned down to the last detail without the slightest flaw or hair out of place. His proclivity for certain illnesses could be erased, his flaws and weaknesses destroyed and in truth his attributes could be enhanced. That is if it was legal. Food animals, endangered species, plants, crops, all things that were less than us, but of men...it had been done and was still done on the black market but the overwhelming majority deemed it an act of God. Clones were hunted down and assassinated by professionals. Not one could be allowed to ever escape. It was an activity with religious overtones, even though the belief in a God properly as it had been known in the past was an anachronism. Genetic mapping did help in the diagnosis and treatment of preexisting conditions. It was not a violation of natural law.

Into whose arms he might find himself the man had no idea, but somewhere there had been the decision to relinquish control, somewhere in the dim reaches of his mind lay the key that for now was hidden undisturbed and lost. He shuddered. Eyes opened brightly shot with the drug. He was agitated but did not speak, afraid but did not cry out.

Through the tinted glass Fionica witnessed his resurrection. On duty she was privy to all incoming case files and so would gravitate to the most complex or traumatic in order to ensure that it went well. It was her presence, she was convinced, that determined the outcome and experience bore this out, though she would not and had never discussed it with anyone. Medicine was a physical thing. She knew she could not violate that reality and survive in her profession, but of healing...some things are better off unspoken letting the result testify in its own behalf. She took notes on her tablet computer that were transferred wirelessly to the network server and saved as case files in her own personal storage area. The blur of code and numbers on the monitors spoke clearly to her of the condition and rapidly changing state of the man. He was responding. Shock of some kind she thought, though there was no physical injury, but for a few scrapes and bruises, and no drugs detected in his system. Fionica hesitated outside the barrier unable to move on to other patients. She became concerned only by one readout, the electronic field measurements showed highly random activity even though his vital signs were stabilizing from the anti-trauma procedures. It meant that his nervous system had been overloaded and the nerve synapses were broken down no longer able to carry the body's messages. So she waited. The same phenomenon was seen on accident victims and especially those who had experienced violence, but this man, it was not clear what had caused his catastrophe. There was one clue however that lingered just out of her conscious-ness and it was the fact that she had seen this condition before, and recently. It was exactly the same as the emergency cases brought in after the Phan's bombing. She was certain it was *Electrically Induced Neurosynapse Failure.*

Suddenly the man convulsed. His heart stopped and the monitor flatlined. Lights flashed and even from behind the glass she heard the alarm buzzers sound. Fionica ran. She didn't have to wait to see what the team would do. She knew. Her hand held computer crashed to the floor as she knocked aside two aides and dove wildly through the airlock door pushing aside the loitering doctors who were in her way. Frantically she input the code and waited a breathless moment hands and face pressed against the cool transparent wall helpless while the atmosphere changed and she was scanned with light sterilizing her body and clothing. The doctors three bays down had not decided yet. She could tell because they were motionless and poised, waiting. Into the glass enclosed hall she raced… "Number eighteen!" She yelled catching the startled attention of one nurse who only half looked at her charging helter skelter towards them. The lead doctor was just about to hit the man with the electrodes when Fionica roared up and breath-lessly ordered him to stop. "Get back!" She shouted, "You'll kill him." Mystified he stepped back and dropped the electrodes to his side and with a distorted look caught halfway in the jump between the world of the living and that of the dead exclaimed, "Are you crazy?!"

"Don't talk!" When the startled Doctor protested she barked again, "Don't talk!" and took up the patient's limp hands holding them firmly by their fingers. "Hit his chest!" She ordered, and when they hesitated she screamed, "NOW!" The doctor in charge pounded on the man's chest with his hands clasped together in a fist with exactly the right rhythmic intervals thinking to himself of the lawsuit he would incur by losing an otherwise salvageable case by performing this archaic procedure, which though he had been trained thoroughly on had never actually done before. The dull thud on the chest cavity was all that could be heard. The corridor went silent. Fionica held tightly to the man's hands and braced her feet. With each beat on his chest there was a blip on the monitor and his vital signs followed in staccato mimicry. All of a sudden there were small crackling sounds, all looked out of the corner of their eyes at the bank of computers to see if a short had developed and was sparking, or if some equipment were going down, but the answer came in a blue coiled flash so fast that not one person present knew what had happened nor would retell it in the same way. Like a bolt of lightening the man lying so passively sprang a foot in the air with his back arched, his eyes wide and his close cropped blonde hair standing straight on end. Flickers of blue static electricity came and went between his parted lips and he gripped Fionica's hands with the force of an industrial vise. She gripped back with all the strength she could muster just to keep her bones from being broken and though expecting something was not prepared for this. The wave of electricity surged through his body and into hers as a ground, she felt the numbing combination of heat and cold that was pain and ground her teeth together to keep from screaming. Her hair exploded from her head as if blown by a huge gust of wind and then crackled and flew wildly about her face.

As suddenly as it had started it was over. Fionica was thrown across the hall into the glass and lie slumped on the floor like a pile of rags. The monitors sang with the chorus of details reflecting the restoration of the man's vital signs as he painfully looked around delirious.

"Are you alright?" The nurses queried Fionica.

She nodded weakly. "What happened?" And looked up at the monitors, seeing that they were emblazoned once again with the man's biological data and just shook her head.

"Your shoes..." someone said.

She looked down to see that the rubber soles were melted nearly all the way through.

The lead doctor knelt over her taking her pulse and looking at her eyes. "How did you know?" he asked in complete amazement.

"I didn't. I just saw that the electrical field indicators didn't correspond to the physical signs."

"What happened?"

"*EINF*. His heart stopped because of an electrical standing wave. So you see? If you had of applied the electrodes…"

"…it would have killed him."

"…when you revived his heart it unbalanced the equilibrium of the wave and it…'

"…discharged." The doctor finished the sentenced in astonishment.

In her office she reflected on the night. The man had no memory. It was as if his history had been seared by fire and sealed. Physically he was improving and she could only guess at what cellular damage there had been while his heart had stopped beating. Physical disabilities they can observe, but of the spirit, the mind…she did not know what had happened to this man but could draw certain conclusions, the first being that he had experienced a tremendous amount of energy, enough to render him unconscious with ease. The idea of fusing kept occurring to her and was inescapable. The first indicator of the case was its similarity to the victims of the Phan's bombing. She produced a card from the file that had been given to her that night when all the people had been brought in and police anti-terror personnel had questioned her. The card was from someone else, a man who had little interest in evidence or circumstance. She had seen him around the ward that night and when challenged he gave her the card. *Call me*, he said, *if anything like this ever happens again.* She punched in the numbers on the Vidtel and looked at the word on the card. *VOX*, it said, *a division of the Metropolitan Police*, and she wondered what it meant. A man's face appeared on the screen, tired, bored, with an unexpressed hostility in the eyes. "McGilvery here."

He thought of the eyes, an old man's eyes, lack luster, watery blue, yet there was something indefinable present also, something righteous and terrible. Nash was furious. He slammed his hand down on his wooden desk so hard that it made his monitor jump. He contemplated the meeting an hour ago, but it was really more like an audience and perhaps that was what infuriated him being fundamentally egalitarian by nature. But that antique gargoyle, that self infatuated religious fanatic, he was a Canonist of the worst sort. In the High Advocator's office where walls were lined with religious artifacts salvaged from the centuries; icons, talismans, relics and symbols of other times in his private museum, in stately repose he dominated Church life from this inner sanctum where usually only the most senior of the hierarchy were allowed. *We have decided...* He began and soon Nash was to discover the *"We"* meant Commander Rybin and the High Advocator. *We have decided...* and he could feel the Commander there in spirit sending the young men to stand till death and give no ground ...that you need to more closely align with our purposes here.

"Purposes?" He remembered saying suddenly at a loss fearing the worst possible scenarios–if he should lose position...

"Our best interests are served by coordinating efforts and not individuating and that's why I've asked you here so we could put aside our differences for the moment and speak vis a vis."

Nash fumbled with the chair behind him having been totally unprepared for the encounter, although Anther had tried to warn him. He found his environment becoming indistinct, unreal. "What exactly are you getting at?"

"Your eccentric behavior."

Nash sat uncomfortably in front of the old man whose bony hands fingered the carved animal paw arms to the throne-like chair he inhabited. The indisputable head of the Church in the Western Metropolis his blessing was the necessary ingredient for everything and everyone involved in the Old Religion. He ran the Church with a dictatorial splendor abhorring any "worker oriented" ideals as pedestrian, decadent and ultimately destructive to their mission. Nash had long suspected that the network of the few remaining leaders who made up the hierarchy had another motive than the simple dissemination of the Canon and spread of the knowledge it espoused. There were, for instance, persistent rumors of investments, properties owned and great sums of moneys in foreign banks. Then there was the question of the vaults, the hidden treasury which held not only the original books of the Canon but supposedly the amassed wealth of many religious denominations collected since before the Kaiein. He certainly wasn't seeing any money, and hadn't for the ten years since he had been ordained as a minister, but it was only of consequence if he was being played for a fool. He first began to suspect something when he started chasing down clues on the WEB. What he had been told about the Church's financial standing and what he had discovered were at odds. Someone was making it big, and someone didn't like him looking too deeply into things.

"I think I'm..." he searched for the word, "down to earth. Simple things make me happy." He said sardonically sitting back more relaxed assessing the situation.

"We think it might be best," the High Advocator continued in a set monotone, as if he had rehearsed what he was about to say, as if it was inevitable and carved from the granite from which cathedrals were made, "if you helped out more with our donation's programs instead of pursuing your counseling agenda. "

"I like my duties now."

"I know you do, but here's my point. You see we all have to pull our weight, and we live on donations not good will alone. Do you have any idea the cost of running an institution such as ours? Why, the utilities alone are enough to bankrupt us."

Nash held his mouth tightly shut. "Yes I do. If you remember I spent some time on the finance committee." In his mind he was racing through alternatives and weighing what this man could actually do, he was, after all, subject to the same pressures any other man trying to survive was. It was the framework of the Church that gave him his rights as a man of the cloth for he had no credentials otherwise and his purpose depended on the elders good will. "If there's some way I can help you..."

"You can leave the counseling to the social services for one thing. It's not an activity we should be involved..."

" Only for the last ten thousand years," he interrupted sharply, "and now, in this time, suddenly it becomes a social service left to the government, the same people that administer sanitation and taxes!"

The High Advocator glowered over the younger man with deep furrows of concern funneling down his forehead like rivulets leaning over with his elbows on his knees, hands wrung with impatience at this impertinence. "This is what I mean, eccentric behavior." He said through his teeth.

"Dangerous ideas!"

The High Advocator sat up in his chair and glared at Nash as only he could steel eyed and towering. "Dangerous?" he said with quiet control.

"The work I do is an integral part of the relationship the Church has with the community, it's traditional...and I am not, as you know, a strict Canonist, but well versed in its teachings...otherwise I wouldn't be here, would I?"

"By whose authority do you presume to have any concept of what you are doing?"

Nash placed his hand flat against his breast. "By this authority, by every man's responsibility to minister to whoever might need it if he has the wherewithal...Good God! Every text, every reference of the Canon is overflowing with it."

The old man sat back and a cold silence ensued. "That's not the way I see it."

"Perhaps you're wrong."

"Unlikely, and at this point you might consider some soul searching yourself and since you are still young and I know a certain brashness goes with the territory I can allow particular indiscretions to pass, but only in the hopes that you will be of some service to the Church in the future. Wasting your time with this social work is not a part of the modern Church. History can attest to the futility of that, the same history that you use to try and justify your actions. We have a roll to play in the social hierarchy and the Canon makes it plain, in fact if you were more up to date on your encyclicals you might have a better idea of the intentions of the Church. We must fit in to the society in which we find ourselves...acceptability comes foremost in our relations with the public."

"I don't consider an interpretation the same as the source."

"No...?" he pondered a moment now feeling completely in control and having the attitude that he had rendered a venomous snake harmless, "we must have you work on the donation's programs. Let's see if you can match your fervor with concrete results and make no mistake about it you're being watched," he leaned forward pointing a bony finger and impinging into his space, "and I consider that lenient."

He was not resigned but infuriated and resolved to say as little as possible to not antagonize the situation any more than he already had. His flaw was he could not keep from speaking out, he was not ready to acquiesce yet...perhaps when he was older with many more failures chalked up he may began shuffling and hold more concern for his physical well being than for his ideals. It had always been that way in his life. All he had to do was show up and fingers pointed, people said, ...I've got my eye on you. Those in power didn't like him. He didn't understand it, but the fact of the matter was the world belonged to those others, those with the cars, and the buildings, the schemers and the sellers of dreams...he needed only to use this world to accomplish his mission not to posses it, as was the obsession. Certain compromises were involved, but life was a compromise. Outraged he returned to his office and rehearsed a million responses in his head that he would have liked to deliver but could not. He questioned his faith and pondered in his own mind his directions. Was the purpose worth the price? He didn't know the answer, but did know that excuses would have no place in the end. Failure has no mitigating circumstances. Every justifier is a condemnation of guilt.

- VIII -

The Gate

It was the first time she had ever felt true power. What she had known before and thought of as power was indistinguishable from the intoxicating experience that swept over her now like a tide pulled by lunar magic. It concealed the earth with a shroud of feathered white water restless and churning, bristling with living things. The certainty settled in that this was what she had been after her entire life and all avenues she had traveled led to this same destination, but only now had it become clear, only now had it been revealed. Her eyes danced with sparkling light and even down to the tips of her fingers there was a growing sensation that was positively electric and lured her, beckoned to her and demanded to be fed. The fire was all consuming. Dominating. No part of her being was untouched, nor undamaged.

"Dammit!" she exclaimed from out of her office; wounded, aggrieved and victimized by incompetence loud enough that her secretary would know the error. Roxanne burst through the door, "These are the wrong statistics!" she delivered with malevolence toward the other woman sitting at a desk whose startled eyes looked up frozen wide. True power had no regrets. Barriers to it could not be allowed. "I want the *express* demos for every day part outside of prime! I thought that was *clear*! These," she held up rumpled sheets of hard copy in her fist as if they contained the ultimate blasphemy, "are three days old!" The woman whose title was *Personal Assistant*, but who in fact was simply an extension of Roxanne's hands sat silent never having become accustomed to the outbursts common in the upper management strata at Cyberwks. "I want it! First thing after lunch I'd better have it." Then as a gust of wind she stormed back into her office with one dynamic motion slamming the door behind her. In less than a minute she was on the vidtel oblivious to what had just transpired while her assistant suppressed her grief long enough to swallow two painkillers for the headache she now had and then busied herself with the task assigned unsure as to whether her job would last the day or not. It wasn't always this way, only for the last year she thought; Roxanne had been possessed this last year.

The desk was as if a palatial mesa top balancing on its point like a severed diamond with facets cut deep down its underside. Its color was of jade and its stability owed to a small gyro implanted in its core that used the atomic fission from an unstable isotope as fuel. It was not expected to fall on its side until the half-life was reached, about 14,000 years in the future. "I've got back to back meetings all day..." Roxanne spoke into the vidtel while the holographic image of another woman shimmered radiantly in front of the screen, I can't possibly get away right now." The fingers of her right hand fumbled with the hem of her skirt. She loved to look at the deep plum-gray color of her suit; she nearly always wore suits, man-like, coats with lapels, but never trousers. Her eyes passed lightly over the exposed thighs of her legs and she crossed them as she talked. In the wall of polarized glass that separated her from the world outside the forty-third floor she glimpsed the flash of white skin reflected. The vision added to her already overloaded sensory input, but she needed much more fuel to feed the power–her skirts were always short, perhaps not appropriate for a woman in her early thirties who had managed to attain an enviable executive position, but it was her style and she did it for effect. Before she got the power she had begun to worry about the lines that had started to appear around her face, but now, with its transcendental influence she felt immortal. Her body was a business tool, something to be used for the maximum velocity that she could attain in life.

"You've got to take some time for yourself, Roxanne," the woman on the Vidtel was saying, "how can I entice you? We haven't even seen each other for over a week, what should I think? I've got it... you've wanted to know the new story lines for Magna's next season haven't you? Well...?"

"Not fair..."

"That's right."

Roxanne was nearly to the door collecting her shoulder bag on the way out, "I'll meet you in half an hour, we'll do it over lunch." and the vidtel went blank.

It took her longer than she thought to arrive because of grid locked traffic and the entire time she was concerned with things left undone at the office. There was even a slight regret at the way she had become angry, but it passed along with the other responsibilities she felt compelled about and the idea that she would gain some privileged information concerning a competitor's new productions justified almost anything. This last year she had developed a taste for the edge. Her total absorption with the network, and then with Yzak's discovery and finally nearly complete success created a dependence on the thrill of the unexpected and the wealth that accompanied it's arrival. The rush of power had come suddenly and without portent so that it overcame whatever native ability to moderate it she might have had and left her dazed, spellbound by its force yet in a state of confusion about her personal identity. There were times when everything began to seem unreal and she would go through whole weeks where she felt detached, as if viewing her own life from somewhere else, like a book, or a story. It was during these times that the obsessions began and clouded her sensitivity. Initially she thought that it was just a more vigorous existence she was experiencing, but then it took on the aspect of some tremendous game where life was the reward and death was to be flaunted and she was removed from all liability. This changed her whole perspective and she became much more aggressive than she had ever been and intent on experiencing everything she had disavowed before. The power made her invincible. No denial made her free.

Roxanne's friend, Elaine, was waiting. She with the long limbs, a delicate woman with pale blonde hair and equally pale skin that was as smooth as cream and gave the impression of being translucent. When she moved every part was balanced with an uncanny symmetry and the equilibrium of the motion of arms and legs reminded one of levers and pulleys and suspension bridges masterfully engineered to support enormous weights on seemingly impossible threads. Such were the illusions of her body. It was the most perfect form yet almost completely androgynous exuding no sexual radiance at all. Drawn to her initially by this ethereal beauty and then shocked by the revelation of what life force dwelt under the skin the clash of the imaginings Roxanne had placed on her and the actuality took nearly a year to dissipate so they could have a free and unencumbered conversation. Since that time they had become confidantes. Elaine was seduced by Roxanne's power the way she was drawn to her friend's beauty. Each a fleeting illusion.

They met in an exclusive club that specialized in virtual fitness. It was something that Elaine had introduced her to and then became routine in their relationship. Every month they would meet for this sole purpose. Once inside the whole environment was transformed into a dedicated ecosystem designed as the perfect setting for the human body. In every detail from the temperature, the optimum moisture content, the foliage and artificial sunlight as it might have been in primordial times down to the microscopic bacteria bred for the circulated air that promoted healthy skin and lungs. It was a primeval Eden as close as science could estimate. Regulars called it *The Womb*.

After completely removing their clothing they went through the chambers, which were glass corridors lined up one next to the other in a long glistening row. The first time Roxanne had come she was shocked to find two husky, naked men staring good naturedly at her body from another row in which they were being processed through the glass. Complete strangers of both sexes, young and old passed only a few feet from each other during the process where their bodies were being acclimatized and sterilized to keep the inner environment free from contamination. After the initial shock she enjoyed it, but rarely saw any men that appealed to her. She would never admit looking for them even though the occasional glimpse of a nude male form through the steam gave her chills with the idea that some unknown man was lurking about when she was so vulnerable. A wave of thick, humid air swept over their bodies caressing them like a warm lush hand and the smell of the thousands of plants hit them with a sweet, musky odor as they entered the ecosystem. The foliage was so thick as to create a jungle with its own canopy and generated all of the oxygen internally. An artificial sky could be glimpsed through the leaves and sounds of animals and birds sang in the background. Boiling pools of densely mineralized water steeped and filled the air with thick steam that spread out into a general haze making it difficult to see clearly more than ten feet. The paths, however, through this artificial primeval garden were marked with sign icons and illuminated with fiber optics for people to find their way.

Everyone was naked. The rich were unashamed and took it in stride as an expected condition for the luxury of getting back to nature. It did present surprises, especially with the steamy air and partial visibility and was not for the timid or reserved since given the opportunity almost everyone leered with sexual abandon making up in spirit for the lasciviousness they lacked in real life. Roxanne listened to her bare feet pad after Elaine's and silently watched the nude form in front of her partially obscured even though only three feet away. She saw perfectly sculpted shoulders cascade down to a waist that rose above hips and smooth, round buttocks with the muscular power of an athlete and it gave her a sensuous pleasure that she never got tired of, but as they walked it attracted others gazes too and she felt them inspecting both with caressing eyes. To deny that it was exciting would have been an obvious ploy, the whole setting was exciting and the illusion of some illicit sexual activity going on in the bushes only added to its allure as far as she was concerned.

They swam in a mineral pool like swans where the water was so imbued that it was slimy to the touch and very salty. Her body absorbed the minerals hungrily and gave her a feeling of well being putting out of mind any lingering thoughts of the responsibilities of the rest of the day. After that they wandered into a large clearing where they lay on tables and were given long, vigorous massages by two dark, shiny oriental men who could not speak English. Roxanne felt the man's hands race up and down her body now slick with perspiration and minerals and abandoned modesty as he kneaded the muscles and stretched her limbs with some secret expertise of the East. She was surprised and somewhat disappointed that it was not a sexual experience. Finally they reached the private recesses of the interior where the virtual exercise rooms were. They were circular chambers of glass that sealed them from the noises of the outer environment yet allowed the feeling of the jungle to invade. Here they sat back in large reclining chairs that were sculpted to hold the body like huge hands while a young woman attached the electrodes. They were placed at strategic points of conflux for each major muscle group where small currents of electricity would jolt them in precise rhythmic shocks fooling the body into thinking it was actually straining with motion. The result was exercise without work. The heat made them sweat. They were each fitted with a pair of virtual goggles so they could be enveloped in any natural environment while the body was put in shape and it was all accomplished without any effort whatsoever. It was complete. That was what Roxanne loved, its synthetic grandeur, the fact that it was completely man made gave her confidence in the human race as masters over unexpected adversity and also served to substantiate her own work. It fed her power and that made her deliriously happy.

She lay back lulled with the humid scents of orchids, animal musk and partially rotted bark. Beads of perspiration covered her entire body and rolled off her breasts and as the goggles were lowered over her eyes she took one last look at Elaine resplendent in her perfect proportions. Each time a different virtual experience was presented and she had always found them pleasurable. They were amateur, however, when placed in comparison to her own programming, which she helped develop with the magic of her wizard Yzak and his marvelous technology. It was true that they had synthesized his experiments and no longer actually needed him to produce it as it was recorded knowledge, stored and backed up many times in Cyberwks network vaults. Nothing was ever stored in just one place in the event of catastrophe or terrorism such as the recent Phan attack. Nothing of value was ever lost in the system. The WEB and its history had taught the lesson of having a network with multiple storage locations duplicating each other. She couldn't bear the thought of getting rid of Yzak, though it had been suggested, more than once considered the weak link in the corporate ring of secrecy. He was the only human link. The only real person connected to the increasingly virtual experience life was becoming and that was a reference point she subconsciously knew she needed. Desperately.

At that moment the *Almost* began. She called it the *Almost* to distinguish the commercial attempts at virtual reality from her own work. There was no comparison. The absolute absorption and complete submission her own programming subjected people to without their volitional control could not be compared with any extant technology, but still she enjoyed the lighter diversion and closed her eyes.

The forest. Light spilled recklessly through the dappled leaves of the canopy dashing against broad leafed trees, small rushing animals, giant ferns, and onto the floor below in an ever changing calliope of dancing motion. She smiled, and drifted, and felt the first series of electric shocks so mild as to hardly be there, but it made her muscles flex unconsciously. The virtual woodland's breeze fondled her body as she was running with abandon through the undergrowth and gave her a heightened awareness of every inch of exposed flesh. It was alternately cool then warm. She felt her hair matted with sweat and smelled the rich, heady scents of animals and decay, of heavily perfumed flowers whose sweet honey odor filled the senses so completely that it could be tasted, of pungent greens hiding slithering rainbow colored reptiles... a jolt of electronics as she splashed into the cold water of a virtual mirrored pool. Her tongue moistened her lips and though hot she was covered with goose flesh. Bare feet against ground deeply covered with compost kicking up bits and pieces of bark, leaf, mushroom, fern, stem, flower, insect, fur, bone, horn...up toward the sky from the viewpoint of the runner, she the fleeting one across secret groves, through thickets and stands of two hundred foot trees while in the distance drums, she barely heard them, and when it occurred to her wondered if they had been there all along. The jolts of electricity continued, each stronger than the last her body flexing to the stimulus...each time at a crucial point of the virtual movie, the virtual reality...she was breathless, she ran and heard the drums louder as she leapt over fallen logs rotting and sprays of green brush. Eyes closed and panting from the run she lay, at first amusement, then enjoyment until finally seduction and abandonment to where only the virtual was real. It hit her deep in the forest of her most private alcoves where she guarded the entrance and personal thoughts lay hidden and alone divorced from business and the earning of a living wage...a subliminal yet persistent sexual sensation. A shock. From the dimness of consciousness Roxanne thought they weren't supposed to place electrodes anywhere but at the muscle groups, but it was unmistakable. Her eyes became more heavy and the shock brought second thoughts about Elaine, and others who must experience these same feelings...intensely sexual, primal, animal...the drums grew and the virtual jungle she rushed through closed in on her forming a path through the green growth where vibrant bursts of colorful orchids hung and sunlight created glowing frames. Her whole body was flexing rhythmically and the sexual sensation burned up through her in a long steady current. Suddenly there were footsteps on the forest floor, many of them, faint yet...she couldn't be sure the elation of free running and the beauty of the scenery made her light headed so she kept running, but almost certainly pursued. Louder now the following feet snapped twigs, brushed against philodendrons, kicked up tufts of rotted floor. Looking back across her shoulder she saw sunlight fall on golden flesh, on straining muscle as hard as teak wood. The eyes in shadows followed her and she felt them on her exposed flesh as she flew.

The two figures lie reclining attached to wires with bright yellow masks feeding them the virtual light. Each was convulsed with the strain of the imagined workout stimulated by the electronic pulses timed to emphasize the drama of the virtual moments being fed them.

She felt the rush against her, so close she could hear the breathing, so near she felt the heat. A touch...a grasp...*why were they after her?*... and finally the fear only just contained by the slight realization that it was virtual and she trembled with its cold grip. Still she ran until finally it came, the hand touching her heel, the tumbling headlong into the open clearing, the struggle. Four pair of dark eyes glared at her, strong men, breathing hard from the chase, sweat streaming over their chests, arms and thighs. She pulled herself up against a tree, and they moved towards her. Exhausted, transfixed, unable to move anymore the men gathered around and held her arms...hands traveled the slick, moist skin...the sensation she denied so violently rose to such a pitch that it plugged her ears like high altitudes and just as she was succumbing to it and embracing it she heard the deafening roar of a large animal and the crashing of brush, an animal close by...the men fled in an instant with looks of terror and she was left on a pinnacle of sensation heightened by the increased electronic current that paralyzed her, immobilized her–she opened her eyes just in time to see the creature closing its jaws down around her and she screamed.

It wasn't at all what she had expected. There was no pain. The three inch long white teeth sliced through her body like butter and she just melted into the animal, overwhelmed with the joy of being eaten, of sacrifice. It was an intense yet exquisite pleasure.

Later over lunch with Elaine she was embarrassed, but her friend talked lightly of the Magna's production secrets and other social banalities with no mention of the virtual experience. So she took it in stride still wondering how she had been so vulnerable to the virtual adventure, after all they didn't have Yzak's technology. On the way back to the office she was exhausted and knew her muscles would be sore for a week, her head ached with a dull throbbing but she would return because each time it was better, and she needed it to be better to feed the power. Roxanne bored easily these days.

"He nearly died." The woman's hoarse whisper came out of the darkness where two figures were silhouetted by light streaming in from the hallway each shifting uneasily from side to side not able to stand still for long.

"Yea?" Came the husky reply. The man was preoccupied with some other aspect he suspected hadn't been brought out into the open yet. "You say he's been… unconscious?" he asked scratching his nose.

"Yes," Fionica replied, hesitating, uncertain if the man was sharing her concern or was a hovering predator like a hawk in the wind at a the crest of a butte, "except when we brought him around."

"What do you mean?"

The man made her nervous. She felt his danger. "He was awake then, I guarantee you…his eyes were like Christmas lights."

Derek McGilvery paused for a moment listening to the muted noises of the hospital that sounded like things heard while sleeping and looked at the physician. She held the back of her neck very straight, he noticed, with her long hair tied up with some wisps breaking free, her eyes were slightly hooded, "He's not much like the others is he?" Holding his breath and then directing his gaze back at the limp, blonde body sprawled across the hospital bed looking every bit dead, except for the breathing.

"Actually he is." Fionica corrected him, "Just more acute with him, more intense. Same symptoms."

The policeman inhaled deeply in an effort to relieve some of the stress he felt at being in a hospital room, in fact just being in the near proximity made his stomach tense. When his father died the experience left him bitterly sad. It wasn't the kind of lofty sadness of which the poets scratched out of a drunken night of madness and beauty nor that which warriors cart heavily with them from the smoky pandemonium of battles, but a meaningless loss of hope that came and went as a brief flight. He saw it in the eyes of that man, a stranger at birth and at death, going the route alone leaving what unrealized nobody knew. The wildness of youth abandoned him when that had happened, but was replaced by defiance leaving him running twice as fast afraid to stop for fear mortality might catch up.

"I don't understand how could that happen?" he questioned.

She explained the physics of the situation as well as she could in layman's terms not expecting the policemen to understand, but the fact was she didn't really have an answer.

McGilvery's team hovered around the workstation in the corridor that contained the complete bio-data of the man from the time he was picked up at the Vidtel box and attached to the sensors until the present. "Electronic phenomena is something I'm very familiar with, so I understand perfectly." McGilvery replied perceiving her skepticism. "The fact is electrical energy and life energy seem to have a great deal in common..." He sat down, began rifling code into the hospital's network and giving voice prompts to the holographic desktop trying to crack it's security system in the few seconds it took for Fionica to follow.

"You're not authorized ..."

He rose turning aside to one of his team whispering, *"I'm in... Doctor Donegal I don't want you to say anything about me being here today. I'm glad you called me, but for now..."* As he spoke his team began downloading to their remote optical network sensors which read the data, broadcast it wirelessly in a compressed algorithm to their vehicle out in the street whose more powerful cloud computer acted as a relay station to send it to their office network where it would be stored in a database, cross referenced, relationally compared and tagged for relevancies they could only guess at by the time they returned. The man helped himself to another computer while Fionica talked easing himself into its operating system and cajoling the information he wanted out of it with blinding speed only half engaged, possessing such command over the machines that they jumped at his wishes.

"I'm sorry but I can't give you access to the computer system..."

He looked at his team and one of them nodded affirmatively and then backed off from the station leaving the optical connection in tact, and he too abandoned the touchscreen though both downloads continued via the sensors unknown to Fionica. "OK. We're done."

At VOX he was used to the covert usurping of data from all kinds of sources whether legal or not. It was such an intimate procedure to him that he couldn't to think of it as a transgression. Information had taken on the essence of a life form with its own system of rights and moral codes and the courts were backlogged for years with cases of industrial espionage, pilfering of proprietary data and a thousand other illegal acts that one could commit against the wall of information that cloaked the civilization and every one of its inhabitants. Legions of lawyers were dedicated to its defense as the result of a decision made by the World Court in the case of Milhous vs. Tae-Hun Corporation in which a man was convicted of routinely accessing sensitive information concerning production and contracts the company was engaged in between the Eastern and Western Metropolitan Security Forces. Although the man was only a cracker and was exercising his talents out of curiosity and a fundamental belief that all information should be in the public domain the upshot of which is that he published much of what he discovered on Wikis and for that was sentenced to death. After fourteen years of appeals the conviction was upheld and the man executed. It set precedence. The court's decision was intended to send a message that with the complete dominance of the optical Web, where all communications and information storage and retrieval took place for the entire civilization, the right to privacy had come of age. Words became coveted objects. Concepts became things with hidden meanings. The legal community contributing to the momentum took the doctrine of privacy to it's *ne plus ultra, ad infinitum absurdus* finally weaving so many codes and laws into the culture that moral issues were left bypassed by reason of statutes prohibiting any kind of questions that violated the confidentiality of information. All the answers were there, but nobody could ask the questions. Consequent legal maneuvering and litigation presented a dazzling spectacle of language from all those trying to hide the truth in contest with those who were trying to discover it.

Knowing he operated outside the law perhaps gave him the spark that had kept him going for the past eighteen years and allowed him the fluid movement between different cultural strata. Life on the fringe of the information envelope where it was a no-mans land inhabited by misfit scientists and criminals each trying to gain some privileged insight, the only difference being in the nature of their motives, had its liabilities not the least of which was the heightened sensitivity he had developed as a result of the sheer bulk of data he synthesized on a daily basis.

However the most devastating consequence of his way of life was not even guessed at. The bond between Derek McGilvery and the collective mind of all the quantum computer systems on the planet was truly an act of God. A sacrament. He had begun his career as an intense and dedicated young man and it was those qualities that drew him deep into the abyss. The qualities of his character that may have, in other centuries, provided the seeds for nocturnes and sonatas, arias and rhapsodies that would elevate the soul sealed his fate with a relationship this lifetime that was inhuman. He flew upon the cyber-stranded optical highways that existed and did not exist in the same time fleeting through the mind as a magician's sleight of hand—now you see it now you don't. Every detail, every extant programming language, every particle of hardware from the earliest to the latest was a part of his repertoire as he gumshoed his way through streams of electronic haberdashery chasing the bad guy. Cybercops were an anachronism from a time where there was some distinction between the human being and the electronic instruments they had evolved to satisfy every urge for power down to the most minute detail. More than anything he was part and parcel of the computer networks that honeycombed the planet. His life energy was vital blood on-line.

It was for this reason that he felt threatened without reason when Fionica led him into her office, the sanctum sanctorum of her private musings when the aura of pain and death became too much to bear. The yellow light bulb from an earlier era shone down on the small windowless quarters, which were piled high with books from wall to wall making any visitor believe that he was in a museum storeroom not the office of a celebrated physician. She apologized dutifully and flung herself down in the old padded office chair that was haphazardly shoved behind the antiquated desk and listed to the port side attesting to the battles it had seen. "God it's good to get off my feet..." looking at McGilvery with a humorous light in her eye, "you'll never know." For him it was almost too human, but the danger signal passed unheeded ignored out of the desperation that accompanied the age. Even the smell was mortal not at all like the crisp cleanliness in the air of his computer rooms, which were kept at a constant 66.5 degrees with filtered air and low simulated daylight to allow for optimum viewing conditions. The world had been built around the machine and the allowance of spaces for people was only to maintain them at optimum so the machines would be operated efficiently and maintained correctly. Somewhere in the equation McGilvery had gotten lost. He had become a master at tracking down criminals in a technological age, but it was no longer clear why he was doing it.

"I am interested," he began, "in this phenomena from your point of view. Personally I'm used to the more mundane criminal types, you know…cyber-espionage, hyper-tiered embezzlement, copyright violations, code cracking, digital terrorism…the usual."

She sighed deeply furrowing her brow having to make a concerted effort to concentrate and overcome the exhaustion at the end of the night. "First I have to tell you that I am concerned," the intimation of confidence made McGilvery uneasy, "something seems to be effecting these people and although this one's the first, there have been cases, reports for years of specific phenomenon related to these conditions but they were isolated and usually accompanied by other symptoms that indicated it was more of a psychosomatic origin."

"What do you think we're dealing with?"

"Oh," she said blithely, "it's clearly *EINF*."

"What?"

"Electrically Induced Neurosynapse Failure. It's a condition where the nerve synapses collapse from stress sometimes, but more often from severe impact or electrical shock and render a person unconscious. However the difference is that it also places one open to suggestion, no one knows quite why, and all the stimuli of the environment are absorbed and go to make up a behavior package which the person then tends to dramatize after he has come out of the comatose state…quite opposed to his volitional control. It is similar to hypnotic suggestion except that random stimuli act as a command and cannot be resisted. You can see this places a person at a risk, he isn't in control."

He thought for a moment searching for points of reference, creating scenarios in his mind to visualize the concept, "How could it happen? All the others were doing was watching the VT, they were on-line virtual…"

"It would take enough energy to knock a person out, at least that much."

"There were no marks then?"

"This one's had some, he's had a rough time… but that's not what caused his condition."

"How can you tell?"

"The bruises," she said matter of factly shaking her head. "If he had been unconscious the blood pressure would have been substantially lower and the discoloration would have been much broader at each bruise. As it was they happened before he was unconscious, hours before unless I miss my guess…" she regarded him navigating the lines of his face and the shape of his skull as if determining his character by craniology and sank down into her battered chair and narrowed her gaze, "you see what I'm saying don't you?"

McGilvery sat down on the corner of her desk careful at first not to upset anything and felt particularly out of place as if they should be discussing the capacitating ratio of gigabytes as they dispersed information transferring over a high speed optical network connection. Then he would have opinions, on how the data would hold its integrity, of corruption either by reason of improper shielding or human intervention…but wounded flesh and the mystery that lie between consciousness and unconsciousness inhabited a realm that was of a higher nature and like love he categorized them under acts of God and so kept his opinions to himself. "I think so," he rejoined cautiously while his eyes darted around the partially darkened room at the titles of books trying to gain a glimpse of who she was. "But just for the record…what exactly are you trying to say?"

"What we saw before was an accident, circumstance…nobody knew the effects the virtual experience was creating on those people until it was exposed by misfortune. The fact that of the bruises on this man that indicate he was assaulted a substantial amount of time before he was put unconscious tells me someone knows what the power is, and what's more is using it."

"Why do you say he was *put* unconscious?"

Fionica blew a wisp of hair out of her eyes and answered quickly. "That much energy would have killed him otherwise. No, it was *administered*. It was given to him gradiently one level at a time until..."

"What?"

"You tell me, you're the policeman."

He straightened his back just now aware he was slumped forward listening to her and screwed his mouth into a firm line squinting his eyes casting shadows from the overhead light. "Transfer of information...? Deleting information...? When there's a surge of energy that's what we look for. Shows up on the security system, it's flagged as an unauthorized access."

"Too bad we can't plug him in...I wish people were that simple, unfortunately it's a highly complex issue especially this area of biocybernetics, body and soul."

"Yes, I find it so...I think of computers like bodies, the physiological...yet the prime mover is that intangible..." he spoke with unexpected compassion expressing the parallel with her, "it's a metaphor really, people didn't want just another device they wanted to solve the mind and they subconsciously thought that creating a machine which was identical to it in every way would give them a perspective they couldn't get on themselves in real life."

"It got out of control, didn't it?"

"I think so."

Suddenly she burst out filling the small room with crystal laughter. "They don't teach you that at Metro do they?"

Forcing a smile, "No. It's my own interpretation." He thought about what information they might discover on the hospital's server and relished the idea that he was already across the line. It never mattered once it got to court, then no one cared what he'd had to do to get the evidence, there were never any questions as if once the truth was unearthed its power was defiant.

"Do you live alone?" she asked him.

Looking across the desk for a moment he was utterly adrift and without any point to navigate by, out in the ether where once you get past this galaxy and things become unfamiliar one's essential being is tested as to whether life is ruled or is the ruler. *What possessed her?* He wondered, grappling with failing lives day and night. "Yes." Once he spoke he knew he had been revealed through the haze of anonymity and let his glance fall down to the floor even though he felt the bond, the human bond that burned through the wall around him. Personal matters were never discussed because he felt it compromised his professional bearing. "I'm not home very much," he looked up at her, "I suppose I'm like you...the city never sleeps does it?"

"It never does."

"What do you suppose will happen to people like us in the future?" A smile quietly appeared on her face with such subtle movement that it was almost magical. "That's a funny question." Watching him as he looked toward the floor, feeling the bond that had been made too, unsure of what it was. "People like us will always be here, we'll always be keepers of the city...there's always someone in need isn't there?"

"I always felt as long as one person somewhere is trying to do something about it all everything would be alright," The tiredness from the day seemed to well up in him and flow across his eyes giving a dream-like quality to her voice, the warmth of the small room lined with stacks of old-fashioned paper books and the streaming yellow light absorbed him into its womb. "the world would be fine... it's just that one person, but if that one was ever destroyed then the balance would be off and the..." he stammered at the personal beliefs surfacing not having spoken of them to many people in his whole life and now to a woman he didn't know... "I believe in an equilibrium of forces, a sort of static, a conflux between complete energy and complete potential."

"Good and evil you mean..."

She was so human it made him feel that he was an alien, which he may have been, a stranger to the woof and warp of people's lives. He was more at home on the information conduits of the society where the assets were measured and the conquerings discussed and battles waged by pundits. Where men lie scattered to the four winds who had tried to make it and had fallen short. The way was littered. He had become numb, but now the voice that sounded so musical to his ears, so absolutely feminine acted like an elixir. She even smelled good. "Those are relative terms, don't you think? One man's ceiling is another's floor."

In her private room with her feet up on the desk there was momentary peace. A glance down at her wrist where the comm-link pulsing at a moderate and steady rate assured her that she was not needed for now. "I don't think you believe that." She spoke in a kind manner as if already under his skin, or maybe, as he thought, just guessing what he was really like.

McGilvery looked at her and replied, "Perhaps." It was noncommittal and she didn't know if she had hit the mark or not.

"So tell me this, if it's so relative why are you doing what you do?"

"To keep the world in balance."

"Me too," she smiled.

At the other end of the metropolis there were still power lines strung up on wooden poles. They were not hot as once they were and had not been in use for nearly a century, but they remained as a relic of the people who now lived in the Second City. Not many of them were descendants of the original inhabitants, waves of immigrants had washed them up over the shoreline of the city where work was readily available and soon all the stones of the tidelands had been smoothed by the ebb and flow, the waxing and waning. Those who resisted the tides were burnished just the same in the end. There is no glory in being the last to go. Nash had not returned to the Cathedral for over a week. His mailbox was full of messages. Though it had never happened before he had absolutely no desire to communicate with the brethren and despite the obvious consequences was not deterred by any logic. It was beyond sound reasoning yet he allowed it to carry him along undisturbed.

The first few days it was as if the light had been turned out. He had no feeling. The nights passed as slow moving scenes encumbered with waking dreams. He spent long hours at the window of his apartment from which he could survey the street below, the life of the city, and could not conceive of himself other than as a refugee fleeing from the past having left behind all possessions that would remind him of who he was—though he knew things were only necessary if a man's purpose was not clear. His mornings and evenings blended together so after a few days they were indistinguishable and he walked between them as if on an hegira each step solemnly taken as an act of faith made in the world of men on which we agree and can easily observe. Even his collaborator Sabiha made no advances into his universe and he played out the wire until it was taut and reaching its tensile limits. The silence in the city was only found in the intervals between the noise; hovercraft searching for criminals in the shadows with arc-streams of light tearing the blackness apart and shattering the dark streets into thousands of refracted pieces, the comings and goings of the traffic below with anonymous people piloting automobiles each with their own complex lives composed of millions upon millions of threads crossed and woven into the fabric. Nash passed over its coarse surface searching for meaning. The reason.

On the third day he arose with wings. Without the slightest reason he began to feel confident and even the murky sunlight filtering through the smog laden air was as a blessing to him and he walked over to stand in it for a moment before any other event could sweep him away. Its warmth radiated to his bones and in the light he saw great expanses of long, green, flowing grasses that bent as the sea forming swells and tides under the racing hand of the wind. The cool smell of sage and wildness echoed through him and was still there when the first call of the day came. A man's voice... *Why in'a god dammed hell haven't you'ver come by!?* It was a call for help.

At first footfall on the steps the door opened. Up the flight before him stood a man in late middle age. He was tired, pale and unshaven. There was the cast of many storms over his face and lines from each harsh winter he had endured on a thread of hope that never seemed to materialize. The light shown out from behind him streaming through his thinning hair like a halo as he welcomed Nash, "Finally, you're here..." and by turning away and leaving the door open invited him in.

The apartment was orderly, but lifeless and without the grace of any home-like feeling to it. It reflected the man's eyes; lucid, gray and severe. In one corner there were pictures of a woman neatly and elegantly framed in perfect arrangement as if a shrine to one beloved. She had passed some years ago and left him in the time it takes to move from one step to the next; looking down for a moment, a slight pause, a glance away and everything had changed, in the time it took to draw a breath his existence was irrevocably altered against his will. Though he had persevered through the years with it was as if his life were being depleted a handful of spirit at a time and at last feeling it slip away he had called the minister of the Old Religion. This was not an easy thing for him to face, for he had always been a strong man full of vigor and had prided himself on his ability to make it alone.

The man was drawn to the cleric out of unfulfilled cultural longings. For answers he couldn't find elsewhere. In doing so he ignored the multitude of social services that had evolved over the centuries from the amalgam of all the most acceptable psychological techniques extant. There was no real help however; they were practices completely without value based on sympathy and adjustment and conformity. For these reasons, the field was showered with government funding and what was not subsidized was made up for in large fees that the practitioners charged transforming them, with the help of their tax exempt status, into a powerful social and political force. The rational for this elevation to authority was simple. To maintain a semblance of order in a massively overpopulated civilization *The Sympathetic Movement*, as it had come to be called, had been the only train of thought that did not pose any threat of instability to the reforming economic system. The popularity of scientifically based social services nearly eclipsed any remaining religious or spiritual thought after the Kaiein with government sponsored mental health that legislated whole sectors into the fold. Children were given drugs to lessen their activity, to stimulate their alertness, to make them sleep and to keep them awake. The biotechnology industry formed a coalition with practitioners and sales soared as nearly all living beings were subject to one drug or another. The term "psychosomatic" had fallen from the lexicon of modern men. It was all acceptable because of the scientists claim that all mental technology belonged in the realm of the medical sciences by reason of the specious nature of the spirit. This philosophy was wholeheartedly embraced by the educational system and that was the hammer.

It was, however, this argument that in the end gave the last great actual religious traditions social momentum. The Rememberers wisely maintained a silence about their work of collecting and collating all surviving religious writings in the civilization otherwise the strength of human greed would undoubtedly have stopped them. Some in their midst claim it was an act of God that there was a presence of mind to just form a place of observance and open the doors. As the bulk of remaining materials were synthesized the Canon was issued one book at a time and slowly people developed an acceptance of the hybrid elements of Islam, Christianity, Judaism, Buddhism, Hinduism, Shintoism, Taoism, and a hundred other religious practices that had come forward in time to the present as living legacies. Congregations started small, but grew unopposed to a strong international base until it was a global social institution. But as the Old Religion reached its zenith a divergent branch of religious thought suddenly gained momentum. Then it struck like a tornado. The *Evangelical Fundamentalists* swept society with a home grown liturgy that required little inductive reasoning, no grasp of metaphor and nothing but a literal interpretation of imagery. Known as "The Great Awakening" it was as if the age of reason had collapsed and like Mycenae the written word an all it symbolized lost for a millennium.

The Old Religion remained, but its numbers fell into a decline from which it never recovered. The conservative backlash of its hierarchy was the result. Now both religious traditions were obsessed with the creation and increase of their wealth through donations, real estate holdings and other more secular means. But what no cleric had foreseen was the rise of the third and most powerful theocratic idea of all, one that could possibly be older than any other tradition and is at the heart of most men's lives. Greed. Greed and the lust for wealth it generated. It was a reverence for all that constituted the economic foundations and was the ideology the vast bulk of humanity fervently believed in and carried as a faith so close to their deep spiritual essence that they would and did give their lives for it without hesitation. Economists became the highest savants of the era. It was the new religion, but not the new God for it arose of a darker nature.

"I've needed to call you for a long time but I haven't been able to..." the man confided finally swallowing his humiliation and defeat in life. He sat comfortably in an old straight backed chair that appeared as if it could have been made by hands living in any of the millennia that spanned the wastes of time. The lamp that flooded light across the man's gnarled and bull dog like features was abstract, an eclectic interpretation that stood awkwardly mounting the cream colored wall with its gaunt frame to throw shadows over everything within its reach.

"We've spoken many times." Nash told him.

"...when Katherine was alive..." he stopped short and sucked in his breath closing his mouth tight lipped letting a cloud overtake him. Then he bolstered himself and continued. "What does a man say to a someone like you? I'm not really expecting anything..." He took a moment and then with great dignified sadness said, "I just didn't know what else to do."

Nash clapped him on the knee. "You did the right thing." he said, "You're just a man aren't you...like all of us?" For the next six hours he settled in and listened. The man told him his story. It came flooding out, rushing out boldly fearing nothing now that the gates were down and the sentries had retired and he knew that the need to purge his soul was more important than any other consideration he had held in the past. Once he could see death's face, his eyes, and smell the rank odor of his breath and the stench of his presence then he knew the time had arrived to make peace one way or the other. Nothing stays the same. Nothing lasts for long.

He talked of his life as an aggressive young man who took to architecture with the idea of recreating the environment in which people lived, of elevating it beyond the school of functional structure and into the ethereal. *For men to live in an environment of compatibility with their powers of reason and creativity*...he told Nash with a dim but steady light still aglow in otherwise cool gray eyes. It took him a long time to become disheartened, even when his beloved Katherine had left him he managed to move through it with the buoyancy only a deep sense of purpose could support. Then there were setbacks, failures, dashed hopes and as he grew older the cognizance of dreams unrealized and that would not be realized in this lifetime. That was the point of embarkation. As Nash listened he simply nodded and made occasional comments to let the man know that he was attentive and he began to see a picture of Luis, the man, as he perceived himself. He arose and walked around as he spoke and appeared out of place with the material surroundings, as if he were an anachronism, a mirage, an apparition whose very presence could be questioned by people with different points of view. There are those who are not like that, of whom there is no question and whose existence is so utterly strong and visceral that no one, not even atheists can deny it. Luis was a man in flux. He had thinning hair and loose teeth and muscles and sinews that did not work as once they had, but the most important thing in his past was that he had lost Katherine and with her passing so had gone his mirror and his way of viewing himself and gaining perspective. Nash knew that the man had begun to leave this world even though he was still a long way from death and that his departure had nothing to do with Katherine.

The night, whose delicate fingers have woven their way into every corner and have done so in the same manner since the days of the Assyrian kings on the dusky sunset plains of Babylon and beyond had now infiltrated their tower. The two men sat facing each other, Nash in one straight backed chair and Luis in another hunched over resting their forearms on their knees, talking with their hands, illustrating the space between them with images that came and went with the fleeting of wind with no remembrance, no permanent meaning leaving only temporary impressions. The man struggled to make his intention clear, not being as articulate as he wished and the muscles in his arms rippled with tension in the dim light. Nash could smell bitterness, just as if oak leaves had been crushed and then lain out on the floor to dry.

"I had designed a building once," he began, "beautiful speckled granite from the old quarries where the stone that build Chicago had come from–that building rose up from the ground like a fist. Just like a god dammed fist!" He smiled broadly and the gesture lit up his face. "It was the greatest thing!" Luis stated loudly. "It was brought in from a quarry in Ohio and was the last of it... after that they closed it down and used the holes to dump nuclear waste then filled it in. It's impossible now; there are no new quarries..." he stretched his arm out curling his hand, fingers upwards beseeching heaven, or trying to grasp hold of the intangible, "a monument." He sat there for a moment with a lean determined look on his face that revealed the inner power of resurrection.

It was not lost on Nash who sat with him through the night hanging on to every word Luis grappled with in the effort to come to a life's resolution. In the end there was no more to say and he had been unable to offer anything so just continued listening. At the door when he was leaving Nash was about to apologize for his inadequacy, for the lack of power he felt to truly bring about a change in another's life who had come to him in need...he could only listen and offer that up as consolation for a lifetime of disillusionment. Luis, however, smiled warmly in the yellow light of dawn and with an embrace awkwardly spoke, "I don't know what I would've done without you. Don't be a stranger."

On the way back home Nash could not shake the image of the outstretched hand. It seemed somehow to define who he was with its intangible, never to be spoken reason reaching eternally. It was the mystery that had been present when the Bishop of Rome had finally come to sanctify the Carolingian kingship in the eighth century or that walked with the Mayan rulers for generations on the Yucatan. Mortal kings passed through the silent gate and it made them more than human. Days drifted into days as he was summoned by distant cries coming over the wires as winged birds whistling down the wind. The gates had opened. There was barely time to rest as he rushed from one place to the next each a crisis waiting for resolution. It confirmed his commitment to the counseling of spirits, to the religious tradition, which had been betrayed by the business of religion. Even when his resources ran thin, and his credit was used to the maximum he still responded when called and into whatever house he entered he took from them whatever they offered in return for whatever he could give. He had not returned to the High Advocator, Commander Rybin and the others though they had attempted to contact him many times. One night they even sent a delegation to his apartment, but he happened to see them coming and managed to escape down the back stairs before they reached him. It was not out of any plan and in fact he was just following the flow of events that had begun to build as a crescendo and tower over any other personal feelings sweeping him into the labyrinth. This was the way of it, he thought, the constant turning of the Mandala out of which cultures arose silently and without warning to overtake all in their way with change either empowering people or leaving them wasted in a crushing defeat. It was the enigma of civilization. Men with their insufferable, vainglorious righteousness know they have everything under control, but in fact life simply carries them along with the tides as all flotsam and jetsam depending on which way the wind blows. Nash had no plans to permanently leave the Cathedral. The act of avoiding the brethren was done more to prolong the interlude than to escape detection, his self-realizations were evolving and he could not allow anyone to interrupt them.

Out of the turmoil that had denied him sleep and then enveloped him with the demands of those in need a catharsis was occurring. Nash did not feel it was an act of God because even as a religious man he had never formed a concept in his own mind of a *God the creator* as being separate from *God the metaphor*. The moments of enlightenment were spiritual beyond question and he instinctively knew their fruition happened in their own time and could neither be rushed nor denied for either way the moment would be forever lost. The Cathedral was not a place he needed to rush back to in order to perceive the connection with the spiritual world, the Basilica was just another icon as all the others that had been gathered up and collected by the brethren over the past century. He carried it with him. The house of God, unlike the Canon would have everyone believe, was in the universe of individuals carried along with them from place to place through all the times of their lives and beyond from one lifetime to the next. It was the essential, fundamental belief in oneself that was the redemption demanded by all religious dogma from the beginning of history. The awareness of that made him wonder who was demanding that men redeem themselves and what were the intentions that inspired the demands upon others that did not result in a further and more stable belief in oneself. If there was a God, he thought, surely each man sheltered him.

On the third day of the seventh week he arose and returned to the Cathedral with a new belief. The others were for some reason not surprised to find him sitting in his office again at the far end of the long dusty corridor appearing to most of them just as mysteriously as had disappeared. The High Advocator, who initially had been infuriated by his inability to bring the recalcitrant minister back into the fold, cautiously walked down the hallway to see this miracle for himself and once laying eyes on the young man through the door left slightly ajar went on about his business knowing that for some reason everything was as it should be and the constancy of no change that he had enjoyed during his thirty-five years as High Advocator would no longer be disturbed. Commander Rybin refused to allow himself to be drawn into the controversy and told those who reported Nash's presence to him, "It's none of our affair what that heretic does..." and stormed off.

The eternal circle. A wheel within a wheel. Nash continued to minister to those in need applying what he knew of the laws of the spirit to their traumas and no longer looked to the hierarchy of the Old Religion for approval. He followed the rituals demanded by the church and those demanded by his own purpose finding that there was no conflict in his duty to either feeling deeply that reform was needed and that it could never be accomplished from the outside. He had found a common ground and in exchange his eccentricities were more tolerated. The High Advocator, however, did not ever trust him and haughtily assured the others in the hierarchy that he would never be allowed into the upper echelons of the church, after all he was not producing his share of income and "...how can you trust a man whose commitment to duty is interfered with by an unauthorized departure." Nash was barred from certain ceremonies, certain rites and would always feel the sting of his own actions as determined by the church management. At the same time their most inner beliefs spoke to them and implored them to let the young minister follow his own purposes for they all instinctively knew that he had a more fundamental grasp on the mystery than they did. It was because of the mystery they all continued in the grand religious tradition with divergent beliefs all leading to the same salvation.

In the dark three men whispered. One gestured and mouthed the words, *You two, down that hallway…and I don't want any god dammed noise either!* They separated, three dark shapes in the shadows the two going to the left and McGilvery to the right. The moon had just risen to its apex and hung there suspended freezing time. There was a glow that shone through the murky olive haze of the night casting a yellow-cream glow on the building and it came through the high windows as a luster. It was dead quiet. McGilvery didn't like this, he didn't like it one bit. He had stopped serious fieldwork years ago and preferred to pursue the guilty through the networks online that made up the WEB and all the other conglomerate systems that honeycombed the planet and just kept expanding like fission out of control. There were times however, like this one, where the opportunity could not be passed by. He crept down the darkened corridor his back sliding against the wall. It was cold. He knew that the building housed computer equipment. Even if he hadn't seen the network branding by the entrance the temperature was a dead giveaway. It was an environment he knew well. It was his habitat.

The weapon was heavy in his hand. It was brand new and had only been fired on the test range at the manufacturer and once again when the department had received it as a final check on its workmanship. He had never used this one before and it had remained in its holster just where he had placed it two months ago. It was made out of a synthetic compound that had originally been discovered while researching a substitute material for silicon to use in quantum computers. It offered almost no resistance to conductivity and so was ideal for microchips. They had spent untold millions to develop it. By the time it was put on the market optical quantum computers were taking over and electronic chip models were instantly obsolete. The material then went to industry and one of its uses was in weapons because of its inherent tensile strength and its almost feather lightness. To McGilvery though it was heavy, too many meanings, too much significance, it had no regard for life. Up ahead was a faint shaft of light. As he moved closer he could see a stairway leading up to the mezzanine level that divided the two story warehouse. When he reached the top of the stairs he waited. There was no sound. He could not even hear his own breathing. Then he slowly went out onto the landing, which was composed of a wall of glass lined offices facing out to the open space of the building. Inside the cubicles he could see computer equipment, banks of it, tiny red and green lights betrayed its presence.

He pushed up against the glass and peered secretly into the first office allowing his eyes time to adjust to the dim light the equipment made. He could see no one, yet he knew someone was here, or had been here...they saw that at Cedars, someone was on-line trying to access the same file of the man who had been admitted that they were interested in. It had originated at this location. He was certain someone was here. McGilvery inched his way to the next room and peered through the glass repeating the procedure down the row. Each one was empty and the equipment was simply operating as unattended servers. Then it happened. Suddenly he heard a noise. He froze, listening, poised. It came again. A soft footstep. He debated if it was one of his men–unlikely because they knew better than to make noise, especially a careless footstep. He crept to the railing on the edge of the mezzanine without a sound and looked down. Below was the figure of a man dressed in black. He was visible only because the dark clothing contrasted with the luminous glow on the highly polished floor from the moonlight coming in the high windows. Instantly the man looked directly at McGilvery. He hadn't made a sound, but knew he didn't have to for the man to know he was there. He was gripped with fear as he swung his weapon up and aimed at the figure's heart. Neither one of them moved. The air was electric. Finally, he yelled to the man, "Hold it...police!"

Then all hell broke loose. The noise was deafening. It jolted the air around him and hit his ears as if with hammers. Glass from the offices exploded outward and a large piece nailed McGilvery in the back of the right shoulder. The blast knocked him down. He felt the terrace of the mezzanine give way beneath with thunderous cracks and all of a sudden he was floating endless to the earth as if by huge wings. The insulation from the ceiling below broke the fall and saved his life–though he didn't consider his good fortune lying on the top of the pile of rubble a jagged piece of glass stuck in his back and dust and debris raining down on him from above. The walls held, only the landing was destroyed and all the computer equipment inside. He lay there in a fog for a long time until once again it was totally silent and dark except for the luminous moon glow coming through the high windows.

"McGilvery!" The voice drifted past him as he lay there semiconscious covered with wreckage, blood beginning to soak into the dust that had fallen on him and he questioned whether he had really heard it or not. "McGilvery!" It came again, and this time he knew he had heard it. "Up here." He answered weakly, even though from where he called was no longer up. "Up here."

Nash had not touched a computer since he had been gone and was now faced with the dilemma of whether to violate his principles and again become immersed in the virtual world or not. It seemed unavoidable. He embraced it as part of his philosophy that change could not occur from the outside and so from the moment he touched it and the monitor burst into life with photons dancing across the screen he felt the electrons surge through his body drawing him ever closer as if it were a magnet to the soul.

As he followed screen after screen of reference he took notes and jotted down virtual pathways that he would follow up later in pursuit of the *Golden XiOma*. There had been several references to it in the books of the Cannon and from each one of these he chased down leads and found more references until it became clear that a circular path was being taken that always lead him right back where he started and began to wonder if it was by design to further obscure the secrets. He spent every spare moment on the search and soon was going without enough sleep as the obsession grew with the revelation he would surely find. Finally, very early one morning after a full night online he had pinned all his notes up on the far wall of his office and was engaged in a thorough study of them to see if he could discern any patterns, any common denominators that would somehow help the endless search. Then there it was. The circular route that he had imagined showed itself plainly when all his notes were pinned up to see and touch with fingers and breathe upon in a human manner and not a virtual one. Plainly each reference was interrelated and by following up any of them the route eventually lead in a circle as if each search was answered by its own question. The vast amount of time it must have taken to devise this secure strategy, which was far better than any encryption scheme he had ever seen, was a dead giveaway to the value of the secrets he sought. Through all the networks and photons glaring in fractural glittering displays of light, color and darkness he could finally see a fingerprint and it was decidedly human.

It took Nash seven days to discover the secret of the scheme. During all that time he ate little and slept in his office in short naps following his obsession to the limits sure this time it would pay off. The brethren would occasionally shuffle by his door down the hallway unsure whether he was in the office or not and indifferent to what, if anything, he may be doing. The High Advocator came to the door one night and by placing his ear very close could hear Nash moving around and inputting commands on the touchscreen thus confirming his suspicion that he was up to something though he could not imagine what it might be. The Church had little connection with the online networks and so he went away clutching some comfort from the thought that the young minister was simply wasting time.

Nash had determined that in order to unravel the secret of the circle he had to find a signature, some idiosyncratic marking in the data or the code that was distinctly individual and could not possibly be generated by the coding software or the programs themselves. He had no idea what it might be, or if in fact it was possible to find some human mark among the thousands, even millions of characters in the code strings of each document, but he meticulously scoured each screen searching. Then at last he found something. It was a symbol, or more exactly a kind of character that seemed to have no roll in the overall function and one that kept reappearing in the code. It was a sideways 'V' followed by three dots. He thought of it as "The mark", and when he had discovered enough of them in each document and made certain they were not part of the code's function he input the mark to a search program that would scour the WEB automatically seeking out and reporting any identical marks anywhere on-line. It would take an estimated thirty-seven hours for any results to be known, so he slept. For fourteen hours he dreamed of a world where electronic memories were given to people through the VT and that their behavior was monitored by the command value of these images below their awareness level and so by the time he awakened he was in a cold sweat from the chaos that ensued and it took him hours to shake the lingering thoughts from the night. The one idea that remained with him was that the world of the mind and the real word had become confused, their borders obscured and that somehow the *Golden XiOma* held a solution.

His door burst open and Sabiha stormed in with a scarf loosely flying around her neck and black hair ablaze. "I hear you haven't been eating," she said throwing down bags of take-out food on the old couch that was shoved up against the. "Hu-nan..." she said elocuting it dramatically as if it was the answer he had been seeking and she was finally delivering it, "you still like Xaing cuisine don't you?"

Nash looked up rubbing his eyes half asleep. "I thought you'd forgotten me."

"I've been busy."

The aroma of the food made his mouth water. "I don't remember the last full meal I've had." He said anxiously unwrapping containers suddenly aware of how hungry he was.

"I've got news," Sabiha said sitting down on the couch, when I couldn't reach you at your apartment I tried calling here...your vidtel's disconnected."

"No it's not," he replied with his mouth full, "I've been on-line and it's overriding the circuit. God this is good!"

"For a week?"

"Well..." he said sheepishly stuffing food into his mouth, "yes."

"I can't believe it..." Sabiha said mocking disgust, "they told me you had left the parish."

Nash scowled, "We had a falling out," and turned to the computer monitor to watch the digital read outs of the search program as it relayed its progress. "

"...I've got news,"

Nash replied abruptly concentrating on the screen. "I can't now."

"I think it's important and I think you'd better come with me."

"Not now."

"What do you mean?"

"I'm waiting."

"For what?"

Nash told her all. He told her all that had happened from the meeting in the High Advocator's office, his weeks away and finally his return and search for information about the *Golden XiOma*. He told her all, except the realization he had experienced because it was far too personal. "I'm glad you came..." he offered warmly, "I was pretty hungry." Nash smiled.

"Fionica called, there's been another event." She told him about the man brought in to Emergency and the strange energy phenomena that had been encountered. She wanted to go to Cedars now while he was still there, while events were fresh. The depth of emotion as she spoke left Nash a bit bewildered, unknown to him she had omitted the incidents that culminated at the embassy party. She thought it far too personal.

They waited for the search program to offer up its results. When finally the list of references to the mark were revealed, Nash ran them through a database of addresses and managed to trace a majority of them down to a specific server. He was elated to learn that it was in the Western Metropolitan area. Its suffix was ".YZK". When he ran a search on ".YZK" there was no response. Not even a negative message. It was as if it didn't exist and so looked like another dead end.

"Yzak?" Sabiha said out of the blue.

"What's that?"

"Yzak." He's a programmer for one of the networks. A whiz kid... they say he's an honest to God genius...that's how I know the name... from a blog."

"I wonder if it could be..."

"Sounds like it... y...z...k, Yzak. "

"What network?"

"I don't know."

"Damn! How about your friend Iverson, would he know?"

"Yes," she thought fleetingly, "perhaps, I'll give it a try, but...can we go now?"

As always the halls were teaming with the overflow of misery from the streets and they waded through throngs of people waiting to be seen by some anonymous doctor–it didn't much matter to most as the only ones who ended up in emergency were those who had no other alternative. When they finally spotted Fionica she was down a long corridor moving busily between rooms. They caught up with her managed to corner the harassed doctor in a supplies alcove where the noise and fury were least intrusive. There she told them both the story of the man who had been admitted with all the details of his appearance and symptoms in a clinical and academic manner just as she had related it to McGilvery. Then illustrated the electrical phenomena he had exhibited and tried to give them a lay explanation that made it most clear.

"His case is similar to the others," Fionica said, "I immediately thought of you," looking at Nash and pausing for a moment, "this is what you've seen isn't it?"

"Close," he replied uncomfortable yet attracted under her gaze, "but not so violent."

"Can we see him?" Sabiha asked.

He had been moved after he was stabilized. All three of them stepped into the glass enclosed computer station that was, like all the others they had seen on the floor, an adjunct to the room. A young woman at the console in a white nurses uniform indicating the case was critical and needed constant monitoring. Fionica began discussing the man's vital signs and the nurse gave her the readings on the screen pointing out what was changing and what was unusual for their benefit while the doctor clarified points too technical or too brief to be well understood. Sabiha peered through the glass watching the sleeping man. Unnoticed by the others her face had grown dark and hard. She pressed her palms against the window. Her breath fogged the glass– muscles grew tense and she was breathing heavily. Then she screamed in rage, burst into the man's room and began beating him savagely on the chest, flailing on his face with her fists and tearing at his hair.

Startled out sleep the man was desperately trying to fend her off tubes and wires flailing, and falling off the side of the bed tried to grab her wrists, but she was too erratic, too out of control. All he could do was protect his eyes as he fell. Nash grabbed her from behind, hugging her close holding her arms to the side as he drug her away from the man with the help of the nurse.

"He's the one! He's the one!!" She yelled, "Don't let him just sit there!"

"Hold on now!" Nash did his best to calm her. "Quiet. Calm down. It's alright..." And sat her slumped over in the hall alternately crying and then furious until finally after much coaxing she was still.

"What that was all about?"

She whispered so softly he could barely hear her. "He violated me."

"He what?" Nash replied incredulously.

Sabiha cried. She looked directly into his eyes and spoke in a measured business like cadence. "He drugged me. Violated me! Understand?" Then she broke down. Nash had never seen her cry and he just held her in his arms as her body convulsed with sobbing against his shoulder. When it had passed, she told him the whole story, at least all that she herself knew since much could not be remembered at all after she had been drugged. She did remember the man's face with the scar running across his chest, the one who had put his hands on her, had violated her. "He's got a scar across his chest doesn't he?" Fionica nodded.

"I'll call McGilvery." Nash comforted her white faced and scowling.

"Derek McGilvery?" Fionica asked.

"That's right..."

"He just left." She told him of McGilvery's interest in the case and how he had contacted her after the first incidents of the Phan's bombing and how he and his team had come earlier that day and had plugged into the complex's computer system.

"... that's McGilvery."

"I had to stop him... but I wanted to help..."

"Did he go back to the precinct?"

"...I don't think so. I think they found something in the hospital's computers before I could disconnect them. They left in a hurry."

"Something about this man?"

"I don't know."

"Any idea where he went?"

"Oh... yes, I forgot," she pulled a card out of her coat pocket, "he gave me this address and told me that if the precinct called that's where he'd be."

Nash looked at the card and disappeared down the hall.

- IX -

Virtual Redemption

When he was twenty-three years old his eyes were clear and he spoke lucidly about public responsibility. He had come from a tradition of civil minded ancestors and was not about to lose his place in the family annals by not bearing his burden as they had before him and hopefully would after his passing. It had been said that a person's socioeconomic background had little to do with his calling and success, Charles Iverson didn't believe in that for an instant. Breeding was everything. His career had begun based on the two fundamental principles that remained with him throughout his life, money and connections.

Many had said about him that he was the only young man on the political scene whose forehead didn't wrinkle and who could look you straight in the eye. *He was honest,* they said, *honest, scrupulous...*but Charles didn't listen to any of it because he knew that they were stupid, and he knew that the public at large was stupid and that it was moved in great waves and migrations and tumult that swept one way or the next reacting to the currents and flows, the tides and eddies like the massive kelp forests that were harvested hovering dreamily over the sea bed. Called by a manifest destiny to lead his fellows he rose up at a young age and listened to the aristocratic whisperings about the right to rule that had lingered in his circle from the time of early boyhood and helped block out any awareness of the simmering cauldron of revolution that boiled in the masses ready to engulf those who would be saviors in a vitriolic rage. Here lay the essence of his personality so plainly visible that it was misassigned to youthful enthusiasm and then later to eccentricity and tolerated only because of his wealth and stature. Any ordinary man would have been ostracized if not verbally then by ignorance and if not that by the mechanics and laws of life which swirl around us all, rich and poor, unseen yet omnipresent like the ether. Who better, he thought to himself, than the wealthy to rule when they have the time and the wherewithal to educate themselves, to follow the civic sciences and do justice to the intelligent ordering of men's affairs. God's death it would be to leave it in the domain of common men, those who work with their hands or even worse technicians whose sole purpose he saw as the equalizing of all classes and abilities of people into one mundane strata where no individual has the opportunity to rise above another by reason of technical equity. His mission was preordained from birth, and perhaps he had been on this tack for many lifetimes each one learning more and garnering more power for the final climactic realization of all that he had been striving for. These were the reasons that he was now so enraged that his face flushed red and the color crept all the way back from his forehead filling the bald spot like the flooding waters of the Nile.

He picked up the vidtel and heaved it across the room into the only wall that was not made of glass watching impassively as the machine burst into a thousand pieces and then clenched his fist flexing his arm and yanking it back in a defiant gesture growling… "yeeaa!"

"Ah for chrisakes Charles," interjected a worried looking pale faced man in a dark business suit placing his head in hand obviously shaken by the noise and violence. "I wish you hadn't done that?"

Charles Iverson slowly turned to the man and then walked the twenty-five paces across his office and brought his face down close to the man's ear… "Really? Would you like to see me do it again?"

"There is no vendetta, believe me… it's coincidence."

"I don't believe in coincidence!" he replied quietly and firmly his voice quivering at the edge of loss of control.

"Trust me."

He looked at the man incredulously, "Of course you know that means 'fuck you'?"

The man sighed heavily and slouched down in his seat. "You're hopeless."

Roxanne Helperin entered the room. The charged energy scorching the ozone that would have made most people turn their heads in a sheepish, disapproving manner only fueled her need, which had grown more desperate since she had gained the power. "That's quite a mess," she said walking directly between the two men disregarding their highly emotional state. She sat down and crossed her legs letting the skirt slide up over her thighs as she moved and without adjusting the degree of exposure simply looked at their faces for reaction and added, "Am I late?"

"That depends…" Charles said and he, now exhausted by the expenditure of such a high volume of emotion, walked over and sat down in his high backed chair behind the wide, square desk. "…if you could have warned us about this latest outrage you are, otherwise…" looking at his watch, "no, you are not."

"I was just trying to explain to Charles…" the man exhorted with a restrained exasperation pausing mid sentence for effect and looking over at the other man who wasn't paying the least attention to him, "that there is no conspiracy against Cyberwks and that it's just a coincidence."

Roxanne looked at Charles and pursed her lips seductively seeing right away that he was in one of those moods. "Charles doesn't believe in coincidence." He glowered and muttered about the vindictiveness of people and the all trouble they caused while she found confirmation from his response that his soul was tainted with a malignancy like an irrevocable birthmark. Blue water vistas filled the remainder of her consciousness with its cool landscape out of which dolphins could be seen in the distance leaping into the air. She viewed everything as if it were trivial and only a passing two dimensional scene projected for her amusement because the power had endowed her with the ability to see, to truly see and with that came a profound dissatisfaction with the ordinary things life is made up of. In earlier ages she might have felt herself visited, blessed by a spirit of the air and would have gone to any length to secure her ascension to the divine, but things being as they were she prayed to the ratings bureaus for viewer share. Her program development for the vidtel revealed a prescient knowledge of hidden desires waiting in even the most common person. Every piece of programming, every effect she touched was consumed rapaciously by a public so starving for entertainment they could not get nourishment enough with a normal dose, it had to be extraordinary. Whole populations had grown on the vidtel, they were intimate with the electronically projected images from birth and relentlessly pursued every evasive sensation. Roxanne was a woman of her time and found relevance in her work.

Charles Iverson sat gripping the arms of his chair. His knuckles were white. His jaw was clenched with determination. His thinning hair swirled in permanent disarray. He was a man who confided in no one with his motives more secure if they remained hidden and known only to him, though if he had recognized the same characteristic in another it would have been grounds for suspicion. He rose up in the stately manner he knew had a calming influence on those around him and shook the wrinkles from his trousers as a signal that he had come around and now realized how outrageous his actions had been. In truth it was measured business. All his life he had been emotional and had also been witness through those many years to the disdain most people held toward possessors of emotion as if it were a dreaded crippler. Perhaps it reminded them of how they longed for the feeling of riding an unleashed passion and it was their inability to touch the fire of living that caused the frustration, but he knew each man had his own devils.

The meeting had been impromptu and Charles did not like to reveal his volatile nature to anyone because he had invested years in the collected and purposeful public identity that most knew him by, but he had been promised a revelation and unable to control his curiosity he had taken an unscheduled meeting. On his route to power there was little that could deter him. "I'm anxious to hear your news," he said to Roxanne momentarily allowing a smile to brush across his face like a flash of light. He could feel what was happening to her and acknowledged it as a kind of power, but not a true power, not like what he was seeking. It was only a shadow of his destination. She, though unaware, had formed the bridge from where he had been bound up against an impenetrable barrier for years in Purgatory desperately seeking the higher realms of ascendancy that he knew existed, but for some unknown reason could never quite reach. *How valuable she is*, he thought letting his gaze linger over her exposed legs allowing the full, rich possession of her to seep into his consciousness until he could feel it solidly. Her eyes met his and it was like the first time, the energy that passed between them elevated both and at times made him weak and his eyelids droop like a young boy. There was something profoundly sexual about power and it was a passion they both shared feeding off each other's lust for it in a perfect *pas de deux*.

So near that sometimes he trembled, so close he could feel its hot breath, its fingers drawing him in, seducing him completely allowing an absolute abandonment... Why then did the Phan attack knowing he was almost there? In his mind he could not imagine even the furies issuing such a warrant against him for having the desire. "Could it be," he asked them, "that some competitor is directing these attacks?" Raising his hands in the air in a futile emotional gesture stopping mid point unable to express the thought, "I think it's too coincidental."

"They're trying to break the Trust," the man in the dark suit said with finality. "It's not a vendetta, its chance... you're just nervous."

"I have every right..." Charles suddenly dropped the thought impatient with the man and turned again to Roxanne, "We'd better hear your report, I have a full afternoon of meetings with the outer affiliates, they're trying to gain syndication rights for their territories you know due in large part to Cyberwks' success. I think they're trying to break the Trust also...too bad."

Roxanne sat gracefully before the man and listened to his hostile diatribes with humor and politeness. It wasn't her depth of under-standing that made her so tolerant, but the fact that she was truly excited and the feeling radiated through her body like electricity. The sense of having her finger right on the pulse, on the edge, of being in the future while the remainder of the human race had to be content with the present until she allowed them access flooded her with overwhelming sensations. At first she assumed it would go away, or at least ease up as she became used to it, but it didn't. From the beginning of the application of the virtual technology over the vidtel she had been in a state of arousal that had remarkably increased as time went on and left her pulsing with desire despite herself. Roxanne assumed it was a part of the power. Unwilling to change her course she resolved to get used to it and to direct its force to her advantage. As a result her behavior changed, she found herself more stoic and she needed more and more stimuli to perceive that she was really alive. Old friends noticed the difference, but said nothing. As Charles Iverson settled down into his seat and gave her his full attention she felt a surge of energy. It had happened once before when they connected and she knew it was the gift, he still had the greater and so was envied, however subliminally, by her. Slowly she produced a palm sized tablet computer from her case and connected it to a terminal on the conference table. She powered up and immediately the back wall radiated with the Cyberwks logo and a blast of music filled the room. Leaning forward she passed her hand over the laser aerostat bringing the music down to tolerable levels and smiled seductively at Charles secretly coveting all he had. Her smile filled him with a strange sensual confusion.

The pilot she had created was only twenty minutes long. It had not been done for content, but to showcase the new technology, which now flooded across the darkened office like a lethal gas enthralling the two men who sat slack jawed within. Roxanne gloated as she witnessed their reactions. The short dramatic teleplay was a scene from a popular show of Cyberwks that had evolved out of the *Hypereal* movement and was characterized by the heightened effects of reality within the production, each sensation and emotion enlarged and microanalyzed to fully envelop the audience in the fictional world. It was the essence of technology, a concentration on the minutiae. The story was simple; man wants woman, woman wants another man. Some things never change; only the telling was radically different.

Two hundred years ago the nature of art had changed. Humanism had simply followed the sciences until the two were indistinguishable and lead exactly to the same conclusion. The absorption of all personal identity into a common virtual identity. The argument went that evolution had finally caught up with the fundamentals of communication and so even before the Kaiein the old rules ceased to apply. Some would protest the absence of criterion to their death, the loss of a standard, while to others it meant new freedom for all individuals allowing the art they were destined for to come into a world that was clear of harsh judgments. Psychologists taught that every person was an artist inside and finally, with years of theoretical integration it came to pass that every person *was* considered an artist and that every work created by these individuals *was* considered to have some merit of its own even though to many it may have been evasive. The world, aided by the advent of more consumer oriented computers, became immersed with art, flooded, engulfed, saturated, overwhelmed and finally the aesthetic senses completely numbed by the deluge until everything, but everything was considered art. The professional artist as traditionally known for millennia ceased to exist or as the revisionists preferred to describe it had *divested their talents into the collective mind that was humanity.* Evolution had claimed another victim. Technology rode the dominant pinnacle in the social hierarchy. Tech talk was more important than almost anything, except money talk. Commercial artistic endeavors vied for the enhancements that equipment could bring to the project and the most sought after artisans on the planet were the *sFx Technos,* special effects technicians, who were the closest thing to hardcore code writing programmers possible. Roxanne knew with complete certainty that she had them now, all of them, for she had possession of a completely new technical tool that somehow bridged the indefinable void between the world of electrons and the world of life energy and made an ineffable connection. With that came the power for they would all want it, the creators and the consumers alike. She exulted with an inner greed so complete that it threatened to consume her in a white fire.

In midair before the illuminated screen danced the figures. Their lines undulated through the empty space like waifs of smoke winding sinuously, dangerously among the real. They were not solid yet appeared so as to enchant the viewer into a suspension of cynicism and with the addition of the virtual technology, the high wavelength light flashes, the subliminal messages, the experience was complete and even the harshest of critics would have difficulty telling the cinematic from the actual. Roxanne blessed Yzak as she watched the piece unfold in full holographic dimension being careful not to become too involved so she could keep her wits, the meeting wasn't over yet. In the floating space hands caressed smooth skin and breaths intermingled in timeless ritual then carefully the fabric slipped down, exposing just so, enough...wisps of golden hair strayed across the man in the dark suit and she could see his perspiration even in the near dark, and was barely able to contain herself at the true meaning of authority that had been revealed to her. Charles Iverson's attention was riveted on the thighs, the hands on flesh, the inaudible murmurs... He was a man whose constant passion had met a match without his volitional consent. Roxanne closed her eyes in fits of exaltation.

Yzak. That funny little face, studious yet intense, so intense that she could not look him in the eye for very long fearing that perhaps he had hold of some elemental truth and by the sheer force of universal law it would sear her, weld her to him in a primal bonding no mortal could ever fathom. She smiled remembering the plan and how sophisticated and subtle it was yet how naturally it came to her. Women were meant for such things, she thought to herself smugly. In the darkened computer bay she recalled watching him for an hour in the silence of the cool air before even speaking, like a lioness waiting for the exact moment–she had remembered the past when there were wild hunting cats, before they were all extinct except the ones bred in captivity and kept in zoos, that they only succeeded in the hunt once or twice in every twenty attempts. That justified her waiting, her patience for the kill. She had watched him working in the dark, as always at the computer console engrossed and pathetic, she had thought, as a human, no blood must run through him, no vital breath.

When her hand touched his cheek like blue flamed hot steel and when he turned to her his eyes were electric and charged with the mathematics of hidden universes. Roxanne had turned away unable to look, but kept her hand on his neck feeling for a pulse perhaps, testing if he was warm, was alive, knowing she must possess him in order to tap this unnamable resource for her own purposes. What more natural way she mused and recalled how she let her hand drop down to his chest and felt his skin, Yzak's flesh, brushed his ear with her lips, hot to cold, and he so startled that he could not move or speak and then she kissed his mouth fully…his sex was cold and flaccid yet he was flesh and blood and she brought to him sensual delights long denied by arduous study that night in the darkened control room as the flickering screens of the two dozen computers washed their naked act clean of any sin before the virtual god. In the end she had seduced him, a complete woman and a boy-man who had no business in the real world. She feared at one point that she would hurt him, but went ahead and took her pleasure like an animal the faint hearted be dammed. When she was leaving, disgusted yet somehow erotically charged by her own power he said, *I'll see you again?* And from that point on he belonged to her. He would come in the middle of the night if called, would put aside anything he was doing, would alter the laws of nature. She the drug, he the addict, but she still could not look him in the eye.

It was perfect then, this scene she had pieced together for the demonstration of the new *virtual dimentionalism,* as Yzak had called it one night after she had worked him into a sexual frenzy. At first she thought sex would smooth him, make him more social, more malleable, but it had a most unexpected effect. He was dependent, that was a given and the single reason she had touched him in the first place because carnal acts were her best weapons, but when she had him, really had him where the hot wind whipped them both into uncontrolled fury he would mysteriously began to have visions. They were not religious insights in any way but glimpses through some secret window to the inner workings of the universe. He would climb on this mysterious Pegasus and spend hours sitting in the nude expanding on the nature of quark radicals, chaos theory or the inner connecting relationship between Photonics and the illusion of time and once rambled on and on about the difference between theoretical solidity and actual solidity, which was only illusionary all things being suspended particles postulated by an x-force that he, for some reason, could not define. Roxanne would usually end up asleep, frustrated, deeply ungratified and completely oblivious as to his meanings knowing only that this was who he was and if only she could harness this unfathomable raw potential then she might began to realize the *Power*.

Finally something real occurred. One stormy night, when she had maliciously brought him to erotic peaks so frighteningly fragile she thought he might shatter like an ice sculpture and climbed over his pathetic frame like a beast in heat willing to experience anything to satisfy her overwhelming desire for power, he rose up before she could possess him and described to her in infinitesimal detail the theory of *virtual dimentionalism*. He explained how holographic images could channel the virtual technology and form a direct connection between the light emanation point and the x-force, by which she gathered he meant a person. Roxanne listened exhausted with sexual desire unrealized, but eventually through the numbness of sensation began to perceive the gist of what he was saying and then visualized it, the perfection of it, and suddenly could see the absolute pinnacle of the power she had been pursuing which drove her to an intense climax that shook her body for a full ten minutes.

Eventually, after selling the agenda to the management at Cyberwks, keeping secret of course her own plans for use of the new technology, it was built and she developed the test program for this very use choosing as a subject the one thing she knew best. Sex. It was an effort to narrow the odds of failure taking a lesson from the great wild hunting cats that the kill only comes once in every twenty tries.

In the executive suite at the Global Communications Commission of the United Nations Charles Iverson was immersed in a sensuous virtual world that at once attracted and repelled him. His morality was somehow violated and though he never considered things of a moral nature somewhere deep within his makeup festered a resistance to that which he was so completely experiencing. With lecherous interest he watched the actors bodies writhing in sensual embrace the holographic images completely replacing his perceptions of the physical world, their feelings were his feelings, their thoughts, their actions... He vicariously pursued the sensations that were denied him in real life by circumstance, disability or aberration with complete impunity without the slightest responsibility for what was taking place thereby fearing no liability. When it was over and the room again went dark he slumped down into his chair and rubbed his eyes not entirely sure what had happened. He felt oddly disoriented, found it hard to focus and the sensation lingered from the experience, which was the one thing he found irresistible.

"Who knows about this?" he asked in a monotone staring straight ahead.

"Myself, a few of the management at Cyberwks...and of course the author."

"Who's that?"

"Yzak."

He pondered the significance of the moment, a slight smile began to creep over his face and then he asked quietly, searchingly, "Does anyone at ComNet know yet?"

Inside Roxanne glowed with a warm fullness that made her light headed and had to exert all her will power to keep from becoming giddy. She took a moment before answering. "I wanted to show you first," she said matter of factly, but with the precision of a perfectly placed scalpel slanting her eyes and watching his reaction, "I wanted your impressions and feelings as to what we might want to do with this."

Turning to her he beamed with the radiance that only happens a few times in anyone's life at moments such as the first realization of love, a windfall inheritance or the release from some onerous debt. It was at that moment both of them knew exactly what the other was thinking. Power would come to each, in different inexplicable ways, but undeniably their lives would change. "We must discuss how to present this to mister Hisham Mostafa 'Ali Fayed Al-Razio, we must plan our strategy very well."

"Yes," she said, feeling complete in every way knowing that the first hurdle had been overcome and with the tacit consent of the government this new technology would position them years ahead of the competition and would give them undreamed of ability to persuade masses of people for political, commercial or even personal whim. It would permanently secure their contract with the provider. The specter of the future loomed over her like a black albatross, and she gloated in its shadow.

It was a weak hand that passed with benediction over the crowd of hungry faces. He shook intermittently and his stomach was tight. Though he had taken the time to wash his body clean from the all night vigil at the hospital some things were indelible, tattooed on the spirit and he felt unclean and violated. The taste of dry antiseptic air lingered on his tongue from the emergency room waiting area where he had hovered in a cloud of doubt watching for a sign from down the long, scrubbed hallway. Each time there was movement, *as in the wild brush from the corner of the eye,* he peered deeply into the cavern trying to usurp knowledge from the space, purloin it from the essence of being that lingered from an anonymous passing. It was a void, but he had refused it and even existing within its boundaries for the short hours seemed like eternity observing the other souls in purgatory like him, waiting for word, unable to get on with their lives until the word was given. For once he was not nameless and merely a worker but a partici- pant in the tapestry gazing with hollow eyes at hollow eyes gazing back. It was an indulgence for him, a luxury.

The voice was rich, humid, soaring... "It came from so far away, as if music through an open door and I was unable to tell if it was real or I was only imagining it..." he reached for the inner strength that he knew must be there in vast reservoirs. He struggled with the shadow of failure that brushed across him and left bruises, atrophied, cancerous scars until with effort the mask lifted and the flesh was reborn. "It was hard to tell if it was real," he said, "hard to tell..." Nash paused, and searched again for the life force. Eyes watched him. There were people who still came to listen to the words of the Old Religion, and they came with an unquenchable thirst that he could not satisfy no matter what level of brilliance he might attain and he knew that they knew he could not, yet they came anyway. It was a mystery, but he took it as a sign that it was human to be less than perfect and that his flaws formed a bond of trust between him and his parishioners because they also were imperfect and so saw something they could relate to. Nash resolved then that he would never reach the potential of his vision, but struggled anyway grasping for the unobtainable perfection that was not man's lot to possess and this caused him great inner turmoil that left him so incapacitated.

The dust odors returned to him as he spoke and overwhelmed him, with it came the smell of blood. A vision of the man lying in the rubble with a shaft of glass piercing his shoulder, the only light in the whole ruined building converging into a beam that glinted in sparkling slivers off the jagged broken edge. He recalled placing his ear by the man's lips to listen for Derek McGilvery's breathing and hearing nothing.

He had not slept but rode the night ferry with his friend through the danger until he was certain it had passed and only then did he leave the bleak, sterile desert of the emergency room to re-enter the land of the living. "…the more I acknowledged its presence the stronger the sound grew until I was certain of its existence and the fact of universal truth became obvious, became…" and now he lifted his hand with his fingers upturned trying to pull the words from the air and at the same time beseeching the heavens for strength, "it is as if my existence has direction and is in tune with universal constellations," he pronounced with finality. "So I am certain that whenever a man is in jeopardy a universal truth is absent. This is something you can hold in your hands and something you can act upon without faith."

As he spoke the sound of his voice became a catalyst for the three dozen odd people who sat in the ancient wooden pews that had given comfort to the wicked, support to the morally lost and cradled the weak for so many years and whose collective sins had been absorbed by the dark, hard wood that now shone with a deep and lustrous patina only the rubbing of a thousand tired shoulders could give. It was a catalyst for the sun streaming in the high windows from out of the crisp chill of the morning air and mingling with the breath of living beings in a fantastic dance of light and life in which his words, the constant run of them following his thoughts in helter skelter chase, brought those who had come to an unexpected place. He could tell just by looking at them. Eyes brighter, more attentive, expression now where there had been none. Nash had learned to watch for the signs because in the field of souls who was there to say whether one was worth his salt or only a charlatan playing on hopes.

"It is a struggle against desire," he found himself saying while he gathered his strength, "When you give up the struggle, you give up life and even though it may seem that prosperity has no moral guide and in fact those who gain are often those who are ruthless..." The momentary pause hung above the slight congregation like a breathless summer storm with black, tumbling clouds suddenly motionless in the race across the sky reaching the final point in their ebb, collecting power for the onslaught against the earth lying far below impotent in all its technological fury against the touch of the elements. "It's in your eyes," he spoke resonantly, "only in your eyes will a life take form, will there be a judgment on victory or defeat, success or failure... look around, observe, we are all asking if it's worth the effort, we all want to know this, you are not alone... where the good are swept away without reason and the bad are free to bring ruin again, it makes one wonder, question the fabric... I say it's in your eyes. Perhaps the reward is in the struggle and not in the gain at all? Perhaps it is in who you are, every instant of your existence that is whole, integral, without compromise... who else would know these things? If we each are responsible for ourselves and our conditions alone, then it must also be true that only we can judge ourselves."

Nash stood resolutely before them his vision blinded by the terror of the night into which he had cast himself. Who was he to speak of others' existences, not a guide nor a holy man in the historical sense, he was not a messenger or a prophet or even a very good teacher. He was a worker, a man who toiled with the souls of men as others did with the things of life with sinew and sweat and longing and the most he could offer was what insights could come from his learning and his questions and his ability to listen. Nevertheless people did listen, they were thirsty to be told the things that they already knew and to have their own wisdom confirmed.

His breath mingled with the people who walked past him and he shook hands with some, embraced some and only slightly smiled at others. Beneath his feet the wood floor had been worn down by generations of believers who stood where he was standing and followed the ritual of the shepherd, only he felt just hovering above, not really touching for he could only be grounded if he firmly believed. Nash could never have faith. This flaw he carried with him like a burden of sin and though early in his life he had desperately searched for some reason that would prove his case, some point of spiritual law he could argue and at last bring about resolution to this insoluble moral conflict of disbelief, it was not to be. Their eyes bore into him as they filed past like flocks had done without question through the millennium having all tacitly agreed by some subtle telepathic means that this one was to represent them in all religious matters. One who had the number, no different nor better than the rest just another working man plying his trade among spirits, and no matter how meager or thin he saw his worth he could not withdraw and simply leave. He had tried it before. It was certain as a result that he was consecrated by his appointment to God, one that he never asked for and did not pursue, but one that evolved slowly around him and through familiarity with it began to impose its responsibilities upon him, which in turn he took up as a matter of course never once thinking about it or questioning. Now he could not forsake them. As the light from the door fled the open sky and shadows were cast across his eyes hiding perhaps the foreboding that echoed through him with every voice that passed, every hand that touched. Inexorably he was being drawn into the future long before he was ready to go. Familiar things slipped away unnoticed. Men and women passed and others were born further along. An old man walked up to him and put out his hand holding his wrist with the one and grasping firmly with the other while Nash raised his focus to meet the face and stare into the maelstrom of contradictions and complexities that composed this human symphony. The man simply smiled and held fast to his hand anchoring himself with resolve as if finding the beacon of a lighthouse. The life was purloined from him as all the others milled about and slowly shuffled away through the single arched opening, he felt it flowing from him in rivulets as he watched the knowing gaze. It occurred to him then that there was something he had to give, and it came in a tidal surge that enlivened him and made his back more erect and gave the inner strength he had been searching for during the sermon, despite the fact of having had almost no sleep at all. If he would have tried to explain what had happened he would have said that it was like being an endless reservoir. What ever was taken away there was more to give. That was as close to faith as he ever got.

Nash quietly wished for a sense of belonging that he had never felt, unable to put it into words. The world he had been brought into was electronically charged in constant evolution never settling long enough to fulfill its promise and even now, at this instant he could feel it changing again, slipping, morphing uncontrollably into... *where to? what next?* He questioned with those who came to listen. *You are not alone...* he said to himself. A storm was brewing.

He felt a hand on his arm and turned quickly, startled. He was expecting no one else and was too involved in his own thoughts to hear anyone.

"Sorry," Fionica said embarrassed, "I didn't mean to surprise you...you looked so...like you didn't want to be disturbed, but then I've come all this way and..."

"Of course," he stumbled, unsure, searching for a foothold, "I... I'm afraid I get too...entangled."

"A sermon?"

"Yes."

"I'm afraid I can't get used to you being a minister, you seem so... earthy."

"I have no pretensions. And you..." concern clouding his face, "Is this official?"

"He'll be fine you know." she said breathlessly seeking with inexperienced hands for the magic that would resolve his fear, the heartbreak, the devastation she had been witness to so many times in her career, "People just don't understand the...how advanced medicine really is...I, we run the finest trauma center in the Western Metropolis and there's hardly a case we get that is still alive we can't save. The statistics are striking, absolutely, you wouldn't believe if..."

Nash responded with a massive sigh of relief mixed with grief that swept through him in waves. "Thank God." He said as the churning devils rose up in him like thermal prairie winds to the sky tearing dry grasses, dust and sage and carrying birds and other flying things along with it. "He's as close to a best friend as...I'm relieved."

"I wanted you to know. He was conscious, sedated but..." She watched without changing the stoic expression that gave her fresh scrubbed skin a sterile look. Her lower lip was swollen slightly and made Nash think of a pale, fleshy rose with a new bloom fragrant and delicate yet surrounded by thorns. Waiting for the faintest disturbance in his vital signs she secretly scanned for perspiration on his upper lip, for yellowing in the whites of the eyes or the fluttering of the irises. It was second nature like breathing, though Nash only noticed that she was surveying him and attributed it to her clinical manner. The truth was that it went far deeper than that.

He turned from her unable to let the anger finally rush from him under her gaze and stepped out the door into the light where he could look up into the sky and let it go. "The whole world seems to be passing by and it's moving so fast. I don't look out there and see buildings any more I see an interconnected, fibrous infrastructure that supports layer upon layer of people all totally dependent on overwhelming technology. Somewhere we went terribly wrong..." he looked back over his shoulder to face Fionica, "don't you find that something's...missing in dealing with your patients?"

"I'm afraid I'm the wrong one to talk to about that, you see medicine is all technology and if it were not for its advanced state...well, your friend McGilvery for instance..."

"I know." He allowed a smile to appear. "I am grateful you came to tell me."

The doctor clasped her hands behind her back suddenly uncomfortable. She felt vulnerable. "That's not the only reason I came." She pronounced with clinical detachment.

"Oh...?"

Looking up at him in vain for a lifeline she did not really want, "I am disturbed by something, it has to do with our earlier conversations." Suddenly she was aware he was listening, and smiled. "... that's not so strange is it? You are a minister."

"I get the feeling this is not a spiritual problem."

"Well... perhaps it is, you'll have to tell me."

"What is it?" he asked.

"I am convinced now that *Electrically Induced Neurosynapse Failure* is intentionally being created in people." And then she added, almost as an afterthought, "Possibly even on a mass scale."

He held his breath and the silence of the Hall that surrounded them expanded out into the street, and further. "If this is your trouble, it sounds like you need someone from VOX."

"I think it's bigger than VOX."

"Why?"

" McGilvery told me he had been warned off cases..."

Nash was instantly alert. "He told me that too..." suddenly the alarming possibility that the explosion may not have been just a random Phan attack occurred to him.

Fionica paced into the atrium still clasping her hands behind her back with the chiseled, expressionless look upon her face. "We get statistics," she continued, "every month from CedMed-VAN." Looking at him matter-of-factly, "Number of calls, lost calls, terminations, sectors the calls originated from plotted against maps, types of emergency, medical procedures and other biotechnological data you wouldn't be interested in. The point is... I think there's a pattern."

"...and you think the patterns I've been seeing with *fusing* have something to do with it?"

She looked at him strangely. Her eyes seemed to sparkle with a slight glint of emerald green and he felt an ominous wave of apprehension sweep across him making him cold even though it was warm. With it was a compulsion, an attraction he couldn't name for this austere yet delicate flower who held so much power over life and death. "Meet me at CenMed-VAN tonight at eleven, I'll wait for you and we can enter on my credentials."

"I..." He started to make excuses, but Fionica lifted a finger to his lips as if taming a precocious child or soothing one in her care who was about to die and then turned to disappear through the door.

The limousine appeared like dew. Though a modest vehicle it still radiated with the glamour one imagined enclosed secretly within its womb. It was so quiet hovering on the magnetic beams that when it passed its only sign was a whisper, and then it faded into the murky ultramarine a silver fish sinuously gliding through the air. Roxanne sat poised in the back knowing that she was entering the cusp of ascendancy, a strata where she had never been before, but had postulated into existence throughout her whole life. Now the sensations were overwhelming and made a roaring in her ears like the rush of wind or the cacophony of the dammed. Lightly she brushed her hand over the real leather that had been stretched tight across the rear seats and barely touching let the feel of skin against skin exhilarate her insatiable desire for richness. The fact that leather as a commercial commodity had been internationally banned for decades because of the depleted animal populations made her almost thrill with the perversity of possibly having sacrificed the last of a species for her comfort. The ubiquitous VT kissed her with light as she constantly compared the PIA access channels and the competition's commercial offerings with that of CWVT by compulsively switching back and forth in an endless stream of light, images and sound dictated by the remote, which was always in her hand and which she carried with her so that she could flow through the virtual environment with any VT that was close enough to receive her signals. Tonight, though, was different. She only half absorbed the flickering, holographic montage and her eyes darted from place to place like a caged bird watching points out the deep tinted windows and details of the limousine and people passing by without letting any of their images make an impression as she was preoccupied with the absolute thrill of imminent victory. It was thick with its honey-richness and strong with its velocity and infinite in its expanse and made her shake with its grandeur. She had been blessed. She had received her communion. She had partaken the body and blood and by the grace of Hisham Mostafa 'Ali Fayed Al-Razio had been financed by CommNet.

Of course she had lied to Charles Iverson, she had even had sex with him and raked his back with her nails leaving long red welts as a brand knowing they would always be visible as he hunkered over her in a greedy sweating mass while she lay disheveled across his desk for the birds of the air to watch through the wall of glass to his office. The indignation was a small price and besides, he was an easy mark. She could have seduced him with her eyes only, but she wanted the touch, to sear him because it was one thing to betray someone from a distance with the firewall between and quite another to feel the hot breath of the victim and lie vulnerable under his hands. "Tell them to leave." She remembered whispering to him in a thin horse voice, and he looked up from his desk with that bewildered middle aged look needing explanation. "Tell them to leave!" She recalled insisting impatiently under her breath.

The day before she had taken the *Virtual Dimentialism* presentation to Hisham Al-Razio and watched for his reaction as he sat through it. She even toyed with the idea of seducing him, but when it was over and he rose there was an unmistakable look of power, one that was so much more pure and true and essential than the harmonic that Charles Iverson enjoyed and she could not. It was hypnotic. As much a sensation as existed between her and Charles, this was beyond description. Many people would actually die for the power this man held, the contracts he could dole out, a gateway to the Trust. She wondered if he imagined it in that manner though it never even occurred to her to ask, that being so familiar with the furies it made her afraid. Perhaps it was that the essence of all the workers' souls who had clamored up the track of history and embraced the devil working just to stay alive to work another day that resided in this one man. Here possibly was the highest point in their evolution, a being so superior in his concepts that with one word, a gesture, a thought lives could be made or ruined, civilizations changed, futures created or cities turned to ruinous blackened hulls of economic chaos.

The building at whose entrance the limousine had come to rest was an uninspiring structure in the media production district where the atmosphere was rarefied by the presence of the digerati, the computer special effects magicians that had proliferated since the Kaiein and had blended all the arts into one churning virtual cauldron of digital noise through a mysterious process of fission and the public relations of the computer companies. Roxanne slid out of the car feeling the cool leather brush her bare thighs and as her lean legs emerged from the opened door slicing white knives in the light painted dark the chauffeur blinked his eyes. Nothing was lost, the details were her tools, the media with which she cast her spells and so the exit from the car was a long sensuous movement for the sole purpose of arousing a need in the driver that could never be satisfied.

She stood on the walkway for a long moment while the chauffeur held the door motionless and consciously absorbed all the living air of the night. It seeped through her skin and, opening her hands with fingers outstretched, it flowed unhindered and gathered in he. She knew it might be her last moment alone in her own space before the ascension. A taste of the industrial smog and the electric tingling sensations along her back reaffirmed her presence and for a brief, fleeting almost nonexistent instant she questioned if it was really worth it and wondered if she could ever retrace her footsteps and erase the events that had brought her to this point. Regret welled up inside, but it was too late.

The entrance to the building was slowly opened revealing the lavish, austere reception of the studios and from then on she was lost, surrounded by fawning, adulating sycophants whose mission it was to satisfy her most subtle and unexpressed whims. At that moment Roxanne let herself be swept away and absorbed into the future. It was a conscious choice and was final to the degree that the past and what would come held no relation to each other and she was reborn into the next incarnation, which was, in her estimation, one step closer to the true power.

Once the twenty foot high door to the street was sealed and the light extinguished the driver was left holding the car open and gazed after the woman who had ascended behind the gates where he could only steal glimpses and imagine what it might be like. There were always radiant young women rushing and serious young men posturing with long hair and disheveled clothes like advertisements and they seemed to be doing something that was so much more important than anyone else that even he found himself feeling intimidated. There was no sense to the impressions, no continuity or reason. When the throng had come pouring out to meet his passenger he had faded into the walls and asphalt and distant buildings becoming invisible as the rest of the panorama and clearly outmoded serving no purpose other than that of icon that came with the limousine. He too knew he was being drawn into the future against his will though unlike Roxanne it held no promise and the truth be told he could not begin to duplicate the ecstasy she felt at having been brought into the fold of the Trust and given *carte blanche* financing for the development of her new projects. His eyes viewed things from the other point–on one side of which lay riches beyond imagining and dreams so desperately beautiful just one glimpse left a person snowblind and jaded forever–on the other was scarcity, futile wasted efforts and longing for worlds that could never be. Somewhere in the middle lay the secrets of life.

The company called itself sFx Technos. It was not a clever name because *sFx Technos*, which stood for special effects technicians, had become a generic term representing the ever increasing hoards of computer whizzes that appeared to materialize out of the ether and range on the planet for a brief tenure until they mysteriously vanished somewhere before the age of forty under circumstances that no one could explain and few noticed. They were a corps of youth that continually lost sight of precedence in the arts by reason of their built-in obsolescence and so with each new generation had to reinvent the principles usually with much noise and confusion. The result was a menagerie, a panoply of unrelated ideas all called art because the fundamentals had been lost to the ages in times so obscure that no one remembered.

Down the long corridors she waltzed with the enthusiastic voices of the entourage echoing off the high walls. She felt their energy, their pulse and verve, but knew it could not match hers and so considered them warmly, like pets as they led her to the conference room laughing at just the right moments and twittering amongst themselves over witty, covert comments. They walked by massive digital editing bays whose tinted glass windows housed millions of dollars of digital imaging equipment and were arched up to the ceiling forming a luminous tunnel through which they passed. Inside cavernous rooms teams of sFx Technos toiled together shoulder to shoulder at work stations configured for the convenience of the equipment, the users being only secondary peripherals in the overall plan, expendable and replaceable at any given instant. She could not see the hypnotic expressions on their faces however as they were transfixed to the monitors, light guns bombarding them with rays inches from where they sat as they speeded into creative oblivion. They only saw the images, the god-like creations that flitted across the screens and came and went with the inexplicable ease only a supreme being could accomplish and were so enamored with the prospect of instant creation, change and destruction that most worked for low wages accepting the impossibly long hours demanded and unquestionably sacrificed much of their lives to their mission. The fact that their employers became rich off their labors seemed to bypass them completely, possibly because it overloaded their aesthetic senses.

An angular, young man followed her too closely down the hall assuming an intimacy that did not exist, "I'm so excited about this I can't tell you..." he exclaimed, "we just got in the 8000,s and you'll be the first commercial..."

"...victim!" a woman's voice interjected. "I'm Ghina," she continued directly, "we spoke this morning."

"Of course." Roxanne replied walking briskly in the midst of adoration enthralled with her own ability to create an effect and not really knowing who the woman was or remembering any conversation with her, but from the tone and manner assuming she was a rep for the studio and affording her the disregard this position required.

They entered a chamber at the far end of the hall. Roxanne was ushered to the head of a long polished stone table that was made of a thin slice of basalt taken from over a mile up a mountain and which held the fossil remnants of crustaceans of the Mesozoic period. This relic representing hundreds of thousands of years of preservation became the resting place for papers and binders, small computers along with various beverages, rolls, pastries and other delectable foods specially ordered for this meeting–and the small personal belongings people carried such as keys, electronic message units and portable vidtels. As she sat Roxanne looked up into the vaulted heart of the room. It was clearly three stories high and was enclosed like a gigantic cocoon with tremendous unfinished beams reaching up the sides in arches to the apex giving the impression of a spider's legs. Layers of rusted, tarnished and corroded metal formed the walls and ceiling and were tiled upon each other in shingle fashion the only breaks being the beams and a dozen vidtel monitors, which were placed intermittently like stars, all displaying the same montages of the studio's earlier work. She was in the presence some one's artwork and didn't know how to respond feeling she had been thrust suddenly and uncomfortably into this rustic warehouse yet knowing at the same time that it was supposed to be art.

"Frank Cosimo designed it…"

Roxanne looked blankly over to the girl next to her pouring coffee.

"…Cosimo, the famous architect." She continued blithely and looked up with dreamy eyes, "It was just temporary while the studios were under construction, but when the rest was finished… well, as you can see he decided to leave it as statement."

Ghina added cynically, "Sort of a work-in-progress I think." She was bemused the way that all sales people were in an attempt to show their humanness, their vulnerability and to ingratiate themselves with their prospect. "I don't care for it myself. I think it's too…erudite, you know… elitist. What do you think?"

Venom rose up beneath the surface and Roxanne realized that all the years of putting up with someone she didn't like were over. She looked back with steel blue eyes and smiled with no warmth, "It's perfect. I think it's perfect."

"One of the things…" a very young man with black, slicked back hair and seated at the opposite end of the table began to speak authoritatively, "…we'd like to acquaint you with is the full range of our capabilities." He was smooth skinned and still had that child-like look to his eyes and nose that seemed to linger in some people too long giving the impression that they were unable to make the transition from adolescence into adulthood out of a fear for the inevitable. His clothing reflected the chic abandon that money and youth engender. "We have the new 8000's for instance..."

"The first installation." Ghina added.

" ...and their capabilities have not even been taken to the limit yet. We can create virtual environments with resolutions so fine that they will stand up to photographic images not only in their color bit depth, but in definition as well. We can create high motion 4086-res, three-dimensional environments on the fly, in real-time. That means we can show you immediately rendered images exactly as they will be online."

As people settled in and began devouring the delicate foods Crayton, the young man at the end of the table, pointed to a monitor with a laser control. The lights dimmed and sound filled the room from all directions as if the ocean had been let in through the floor and was rushing. Images tore across the screen in life-like scenarios with excitement and all the emotions of living amplified by the dynamic sound and meticulous detail of each sequence. Repeatedly he pointed from monitor to monitor as each demonstration helped cover the entire range of experience—graceful, violent, romantic, hideous, mysterious, sensuous, beautiful and often distinctly repulsive images. "Everything you see," he said, "everything you are experiencing was created entirely from ground zero out of our systems. We use no other external image sources at all. What you are seeing is an absolutely original composition more real than reality itself, because the artists make it hyper-real. Imagine a world where everything you saw and heard and felt was crystallized down to its primary essences, its genus and all the superfluous information such as extraneous visuals, colors and sounds that were not integral were eliminated until everything left contributed to the ultimate viewing experience, which is a condensed concept, an idealized version a hundred times more impactful than real life. This is what we can do," he raised both his arms gesturing to the surrounding monitors like a feeble Moses parting the waters, "We make life...or at least a life better than most people perceive their own to be and that's why we call it a hyper-world." And then he stood smugly folding his arms, "No one can do it like we can."

Roxanne did not speak at once. *If only...* she thought, *they aren't even close to the power...*but she needed them, or at least someone like them and so feigned herself to be deeply taken while inside she grew more confident about the forces she was dealing with. "I am impressed."

After the meeting, which Roxanne put up with in the interest of productivity, and after fielding all the banal questions she would never have bothered with under normal circumstances she finally reached a point where the need to get on with it overpowered her practiced social graces and so retired to a private conference with the young man Crayton and his trusted colleagues. The room was whisper quiet and glowed with low ambient lighting the source of which was indistinct and was crowded with large coal black polyethylene chairs that had an amber halo on the their backs from the single light that focused down from the dark reaches of the ceiling. "I am developing some very special programming," she announced amid nervous fidgeting and excitement, "programming that is unique and more absorbing than anything that has ever been done." Roxanne hinted as her listeners slyly looked back and forth at each other with knowing gazes feeling themselves the power of the Trust. Holding court perched in the round of the chairs circling a flat, low table she looked in their eyes, "But first," she said with the light spilling down her face off the cheekbones and across her dark, tailored suit glowing slightly green from the background illumination, "I must be certain I have your confidence." At that instant they replied in uniform chorus with oaths and promises of absolute faith. Out of her thin, black brief she withdrew a folio which was laid gently on the table and from which she pulled a series of documents, one set for each person present. "Please bear with me, but I'm afraid that isn't enough. I'll need signed affidavits, bonds and waivers, non-disclosure agreements and contractual statements from all the key players, and a blanket document signed and filed with the GCC from everyone involved or aware of the project." The room went quiet as Roxanne looked around expectantly and though they were eager to do anything for the business it was an unexpected event that made them slightly crestfallen. Then as if the shock was too mild she added, "I'll need optical imprints on each of you as well before we can continue."

There was some trepidation at the demand, but with the signed forms and the optical keys, to obtain which each person had taken a retinal scan exposed upon a self developing holograph integrally affixed to each document, Roxanne felt more secure though not at ease and still guarding her intentions closely. Any reference to the Virtual Dimentionalism technology was entirely veiled. That would come, she thought, but only in post production and by then they would have such a huge advantage in the market no one would be able to catch up. With these constraints she began to try to explain what she wanted to accomplish hoping that her enthusiasm, which bordered on fanatic, would be accepted at face value without question. "To draw a picture in the mind." She stated simply and emphatically, and then tried to engage them in the overall purpose while keeping it loosely defined and of course benign. "We want the audience to feel exactly the way we intend, to guide them and give them new ideas..." she thought of the conversation with Hashim Al-Razio, "this is a new art form and I have been chosen by CommNet to produce it. And now you," she gestured with her hands, "are part of it."

It wasn't easy to forget the clarity in Hisham Al-Razio's eyes that towered before her like the whole of interstellar space with its silent winds cold beyond the capability of mechanical devices to measure, its spectrum and panoply of color so infinitely dazzling and its distances so absolutely heartless. "Do you believe in fate?" He had asked her with his richly accented deeply melodic voice that rolled up around her like the singing of the mullahs calling all the faithful in his private dreams. With both of his hands he held her by the shoulders and then without the slightest hesitation folded his arms around her and held tightly as one would a lover. Roxanne was overpowered and did not move limply listening to his breathing and felt the surge of emotion and sexual energy that flowed through him and became deeply embarrassed as if she was being violated in some perverse, indescribably demonic manner. "Allah be praised." He finally said in her ear. "It is like being spoken to all one's life and then suddenly without any warning...you hear it, really hear it." His eyes burned through her as if focused across the room, "I know what I must do now, I have been spoken to and clearly this time... I'm amazed that this did not occur to me before, a messenger…of course, certainly a messenger." He paced while he talked and she, meek and out of character stood by in obedience because for her Hisham Al-Razio was the Trust not just a representative of CommNet, he was perhaps one of the three of four most powerful men on the planet and she felt blessed to be in his presence and graced by the power he held and she most desperately lusted after.

Then he planted the seed of an idea in her mind. It was a vision of a world more perfect than the one in which they both found themselves and the crucial essence of the plan was that people were not capable of making their own choices. "They are in fact incapable!" He emphasized with considerable violence, and then for the next three hours outlined his strategy in one continuous narrative fearing to stop for even an instance to catch his breath for fear that the spell would be broken, that the communion with God would be swept away and again the doctors would tell him it was trouble with his inner ear. This time he knew they were blasphemous. CBVT was to be his vehicle, and she, with Yzak's Virtual Dimentionalism were to be the voice of the Prophet so long ago lost to dust.

Roxanne was dazed and frustrated clearly aware of disturbing forces far beyond her control and completely beyond her comprehension. The intensity of nature had been unleashed twice now, before at the peaks of sexual heights when Yzak had taken off on flights of existential physics and now so close to the power she had envisioned once again the earth was crumbling beneath her and like a dream she slipped between the illusion and the real. She had been somehow empowered by her meddling actions, by her tempest, which acted as a catalyst on inert dynamism allowing it to rage into action and bring about what she could only call evolution. For the first time she had just the slightest inkling of what her power was and at the same time became aware of why she had not seen it before and why it was so elusive. It was quiet. Roxanne guessed that others had it too, or could regain it as if the ability and potential that welled up inside her and filled her with life so invincibly was the birthright of all. This thought she quickly suppressed fearing that if someone else gained the power she would be crushed and resolved then that with it came the fear and one could not be achieved without the other. She accepted that with finality.

"What... exactly is our role here?" Crayton offered up in a polite confusion not completely able to follow her stream of consciousness though he prided himself on the non-linear nature of his reasoning power. "Are we in on the creative or just production?"

Roxanne emerged from the reverie fully aware of the intention with which she was being questioned and regarded the young man with a patronizing look knowing essential details had been left out but wishing to secure the relationship so she could put her attention on something else. "I want you to produce the first project series," she said, and then added with flourish "exclusively."

Ghina was completely at ease now that the conversation was drifting into her territory and had the good fortune of possessing a talent that only master salesmen had, complete indifference when everything was on the line. "A contract?" she inquired nonchalantly.

With eyes narrowed Roxanne looked to the left without moving her head and spoke. "Details," she mused, "others can work that out. Lets just say that you'll be plugged in as an extension to our system and receive original rough programming and then work your magic on it. I expect extensive interface of personnel, and especially you Crayton."

"We're happy to play any role at all in the new projects, but you make it sound as if you are utilizing a new technology when our facility..."

"Exactly."

Crayton was stunned. "Is it possible?" To his knowledge the technology, hardware and code of sFx Technos was beyond anything else being used, over 95% was proprietary and they had dozens of the hottest young programmers writing code for them exclusively. "You didn't mention this." He added with a certain dark overtone that sounded suspiciously like artistic integrity and made all the members of the sFx Technos delegation cringe in unison.

"A pivotal role."

Ghina was the first to realize the enormous opportunity and glanced harshly at Crayton. "Key players...?"

"Crucial."

The young man began to get the message with the help of prompting from under the table by Ghina's foot and insistent looks all around and so responded to the proposal in an aggressive yet ambiguous hand-shake with the representative of the Trust. It was her position though not outwardly spoken of as if she was in league with Dybbuks and the mention of their names would unleash their fury from the netherworld coming one after the other reigning in their horses of fire and destruction upon all those within earshot. Her hand was cold and he took it as an omen.

It was raining. Ominous clouds had been forming all day high up in the northeast. The usual murky sun was absent and since dawn the weather continued to build not caring what technology was far below where humans scurried about oblivious to the signs from heaven. It rose up in a great, sheer wall of dark swirling fog dwarfing the insig-nificant metal ships that soared aloft. With darkness thunder boomed. It sent shivers through the infrastructure of the city and sparked power surges that caught out the unprepared and fried their systems, but for the most part left the electro-optical networks undisturbed. However, men withdrew and became gloomy and quiet. A few morose. Some-thing called to them from the unknowable hinting without saying that somewhere a wrong path had been taken. It left them feeling disquiet and slightly frantic. The thunder named each person one at a time as it traveled through the megalopolis connecting each with the other and drawing boundaries around the multimillions of inhabitants with rain causing each to feel especially singled out.

In the global village, people spoke. In mass transit vehicles they commented to each other, on platforms and in offices they exchanged views, in homes they traveled down deep mysterious pathways into their loved ones terra incognito and on streets they were compelled; in bedroom and parks and shopping centers the effect was universal. If there was one thought that came to the surface and remained ever present though unspoken, it was the fact that things didn't have to be the way they were. It was a choice. The sense of community engendered by the rain for an imperceivable instant caused a near cathartic human experience requiring just the slightest religious overtones to make it a revelation. There was no sign from God however so the moment passed. The apex of the storm came and went only a steady drizzle remained. It soaked Nash through to the skin as he stood outside the building waiting.

High concrete walls soared featureless and disappeared into the weather. At the very top, hidden from the ground, written in small, municipal lettering that was meant to be utilitarian and Spartan was the legend *CenMed Vast Area Network*. It was a huge bunker with walls twelve feet thick reinforced with metal and carbon fiber so it could continue to operate regardless of any disaster that its designers could foresee. There was a moat-like bed surrounding it that kept vehicles to within two hundred feet that was usually empty, but now glistened with run off. Only one bridge crossed to the large entrance doors, which were black with a distinct serrated yellow cross and there was a gate with guards on the near side. Nash nodded to one as he stood uncomfortably inside and thought he saw a slight smile in recognition, but decided it was only a trick of the yellow light that came streaming out into the dark. A steady stream of people came and went across the bridge hurrying to their appointed destinations, at which he could only guess, but they each stopped at the guard and slid their magnetic passes across sensors and submitted to iris scans. The heavily armed guards ran them through like clockwork.

"I hope you haven't been here too long...I just couldn't get away..."

He looked instantly to eyes filled with remarkable clarity. "Not long, just wet...I'm very wet."

"Come on then." She pulled at his arm and led him to the guard-house where she slid her magnetic card and briefly discussed their documentation; then they were subjected to the iris scan. Moments later Fionica and Nash were passed through the large black and yellow doors and cool air rushed across their faces bringing a chill to wet skin. Down the corridor Nash could see two other doors with the same serrated yellow "X" on a black background. An illuminated message topped them: *CENMED VAN - ENTRY PROHIBITED BY LAW - AUTHO-RIZED PERSONNEL ONLY - VIOLATORS WILL BE ARRESTED.* Fionica entered her code card and the barrier surrendered. The doors sealed behind with a muted, hissing whir.

A long thin row of amber lights trailed into the reaches where at the end Nash could see a set of doors identical to the ones they had just passed through. By these were two armed guards. Their hurried footsteps echoed. Fionica moved quickly down the hallway with an inner fury he imagined motivated her through long, emotional and demanding hours allowing her to regenerate each morning and began again. He admired this because of the truth he knew from his years ministering to spirits in need–strength was a virtue, perhaps the only one. In his view the bleakness of the complex was a perfect metaphor for the crisis of humanity in one forceful vision. He was in the heart of the beast, the center where lives balanced on the edge and those brought in by destiny had forfeit cause over their own existence and became dependent upon strangers. It was easy to let one's grip loosen and tumble headlong into the abyss, he thought. Crying out for help in the hope some hand may reach out and grasp your own was a roll of the dice. Nash couldn't refrain from believing this, even though he knew that there were those who needed salvation just as there were those who needed to save them.

"Who's this serious fellow?" muttered the stocky guard whose neck melted into his shoulders making his head appear too small for his body.

Fionica gestured to Nash anxiously. "Show him your ID," then added, "he's on a Cedar's case."

The burly man stood square in front of him looking alternately from the ID to his face while the second guard scanned his body up and down with an electronic detection device finally pronouncing with detached indifference, "He's clean." They were both given another iris scan to be compared with the one from the front gate as if a body snatching could have occurred in the last fifty yards of straight hallway. When they passed through the second set of doors their credentials were all checked again by a bored, surly, overweight woman and then they were x-rayed before being allowed through the double sealed entry to the command center.

Inside it took a moment for Nash's eyes to adjust to the low blue-green light and the almost antiseptic, dust-free atmosphere. Fionica forged ahead of him freely at home in the institutional environment so similar to the hospital. On the far wall a map of the city hovered over them clearly a hundred feet high and it twinkled with red, amber and blue lights like some fabulous galactic landscape. Each light a life, he thought, and was overwhelmed at the prospect of so many people in need all at once. "A direct hit," Fionica wondered out loud...couldn't disrupt this–it's amazing isn't it? Like watching the heartbeat of the city." Nash could feel the pulse of it, the unmistakable churning river of emotion that coursed through the isles and over the lines where voices thin and strong spoke the language of desperation even if it was hidden by the calm, studied cadence of the attendants. Words levitated all around them as if they were swept on the sea of voices each one a violent, passionate plea for survival–as if they were driven by gusts across the white arctic landscape with swirls of snow leaving only indistinct images of the circling white wolves their song piercing hearts tearing souls asunder. Here in this room he felt the fabric, the woof and warp made up of living thread unseen that cradles all our lives like cocoons coming unraveled and he knew there was only fortune between himself and the anonymous numbers on the lines. He knew this as well as he knew himself.

Hundreds of attendants were occupied at the terminals in the gargantuan space intent to their task and not even glancing up as they passed. As Fionica lead him through the maze of isles and workstations to some unknown destination the overbearing feeling of emergency permeated the place and Nash realized that war zones raged outside the walls. Here were the crossroads of lives and the current flowed through him in a raw and violent river.

He followed her down the long corridor and through a door that lead into a myriad of passageways all lined with offices where others toiled. At the furthest end Nash was ushered into a small crowded room. The walls were lined with the peripheral devices and their simultaneous whirring droned out a single note and made it necessary for people to speak louder and more clearly than usual to be understood. There were at least a dozen flat monitors mounted on brackets at ceiling level, in addition to those built in and others sitting loose. Across their screens flitted columns and streams of data, charts and graphs, maps and sector headings with relevant demographics of the population that inhabited them–changing in real time as people were reported deceased and others born. There were evaluative charts of CenMED calls, the received ones, the handled and lost ones and the hearts, those who had gone online just for company. There was only one person in the room. He was engrossed with human stories jumping from one touchscreen and monitor to the next and then back as if he were tracking a race being run in different places at different points in time.

Fionica stood behind the man with her arms folded and did not speak. Nash hovered in the doorway still not knowing why they had come. The man caught them out of the corner of his eye frowning at Nash then seeing Fionica and lightened up, but only slightly. "You can see what a god dammed mess I've got here and it's only the tip of the iceberg…" He was at some indistinct age between the late forties and early sixties where intent men seem to be anonymous and lose any evidence of their age becoming forces of nature driving through the years with an insouciant smirk daring mortality to catch up with them. The man grumbled half to himself and half to his visitors. "…the *tip* of the iceberg." He looked up expectantly and gestured, "Sit down."

Fionica smiled at some private joke as Nash looked in vain for a place to sit in the cramped and cluttered room. "Rozemund and I are old friends." She said as she introduced Nash and they shook hands in a distracted awkward way the man not having the inclination to free up his attention completely. She explained to Nash that he was the archivist in charge of tracking all the information flowing through the CenMED network; storing, evaluating and graphing statistics for use by government and private agencies. He didn't have to be told that it was an overwhelming task. "Just a minute here…" The man said quickly entering some passwords into three of the systems and immediately their screens were filled with a patchwork of red crosses on a black field with the inscription *SYSTEM MAINTENANCE IN PROGRESS*. "Shut the door I need a break."

The doctor smiled at him and they regarded each other as equals. "I told you I'd be back."

"Aren't you afraid you'll miss something?" Nash asked gesturing to the screens.

Rozemund looked back over his shoulder unconcerned. "Naaw... it's all tracked automatically. I've set up scripts and code...god have I written code...!" he added with exasperation and then looked back at Nash, "So, you're probably wondering what the hell I do do?"

Nash noticed a Baltic accent for the first time, just slightly, "Do I look confused?"

The man smiled. "He looks confused."

"Alright then," Nash replied, "what the hell do you do?"

The older man smiled self-consciously and sat back in his chair hooking his thumbs under his belt. "I cover the city." He pronounced and then paused with absolute silence for a moment until Fionica interjected he had better explain since Nash was a minister, she added "in the old religion" with a certain tone that made it sound like a cult, and was not as familiar with statistics as they were. He frowned, looked back at the equipment and then to Nash and seemed to be mustering up the energy inside needed to explain something so remedial yet so intimate to him that it had transmuted from the realm of data to the realm of complete understanding where words were superfluous. "It's very simple really...now, it didn't used to be, but that's where I come in I suppose."

"Rozemund's been here over twenty years and is primarily responsible for the network systems at CenMed."

"Until I got tired of the bullshit." He crossed his arms and made a face, disgruntled yet good humored. "They don't know what they've got... I created a self perpetuating, fully enclosed network system complete with a highly intuitive non-linear viable, human-like personality at the core that responds intelligently to requests and situations; redundant optical back-ups to non-centralized locations, graphic interfaces with help categories according to ability, automatic troubleshooting, repair, archiving, data collection, evaluation and report generation... In short the heart, the essence of the command center. But the real beauty of it is that it is an intellectual model, it is completely enclosed within its code developed more with calculus than algorithms and is autonomous of any hardware or specific operating systems. This means that it never again will go down because it is not dependent on the physical structure. It can run on any hardware. If a disaster occurs like the terrorist act of some years ago the CenMed VAN code is simply transferred to another system in another location with no noticeable depreciation in service. We are on-line permanently."

"The center went down about ten years ago, remember?" Fionica added.

"Yes," Nash replied, "that's right... how many...?"

"I hate to admit that it spurred me to genius..." He interjected cutting of the obvious question.

"Can I access this information on the WEB?"

Rozemund looked at Nash blankly. "The CenMed VAN is years, no light years ahead of the WEB and it may never catch up."

"Then you're not part of the global system."

"We're a parallel, autonomous, dedicated cloud network. Besides, the protocol used is so advanced WEB object models couldn't' read it."

"What he means is, we've come to the right place."

"Depending on what you've come for..." The man looked at Nash used to zeroing in on trauma and turmoil and squinted up his eyes. "Everything is god dammed publicity, PR...if they'd just let things alone they'd run themselves."

"We've come about that."

Nash looked at them both frustration growing that he didn't know what was going on or even what the reason was that he was here. "I'd like to get down to 'that,' he said, "What have we come about?"

"I've had someone break in the network." Rozemund spoke out.

"We've had a working relationship for years." Fionica interjected. "As I was building the Trauma Center part of my strategy was to track the types of cases, where they were coming from and all the other stats that could draw a demographic picture for me–including any other external influences in the city that may contribute to particular emergencies. He built the system. After Sabiha contacted me, I spoke with Rozemund, which of course made him curious and he began to find correlations in data that indicated a particular set of circumstances occurred just before certain emergencies that ended up at my facility. This made me began to suspect that *Electrically Induced Neurosynapse Failure* was being intentionally created by special video emissions. Then something happened that clinched it..."

"...the network break in!" Rozemund exclaimed. "In admiration I have to admit that I was knocked out, my firewall systems are the best, simply cutting edge stuff, the most advanced on the planet...but someone broke in. I couldn't fucking believe it! There was no malicious damage or theft. Even some of the proprietary code available was not disturbed...and that was the clue! It would have been worth millions on the commercial market. What was done was to alter the logic string of some databases obscure any relationships between particular events and particular types of emergency situations. The cause and effect line of probability was kept within reason, but changed just enough to hide the fact of any true links. In a word someone was covering up something they didn't want known."

"Wait a minute," Nash started confused, "I thought CenMed was a closed system, not on the WEB...how could someone gain access?"

"...I ran a full check on the system and then sent up an electronic spider to locate aces points. You know what the damn response was? That I had a glitch in my code! Me! A glitch in my code...! I couldn't believe it! I've been writing code since before they were shaving, before they began to sweat...I don't have glitches!!"

"...but, how did they get in?"

There was a silence, a morbid drawn out moment that held no life as if a sacred trust had been violated leaving the souls of men in jeopardy. "That's the point." The older man spoke gruffly with a low growl in his voice. "It had to be from within the network."

Nash felt a sudden wildness, an excitement, an out-of-control reeling, an instant whirling that ran up his body and made his ears ring. *Something*...he thought, "Maybe we should start at the beginning, what is it you wanted me to see?" Then without an answer he immediately thought aloud, "Was it changed?"

"You're just lucky I'm here." Rozemund said turning to the systems and deftly putting them back on-line. "Some asshole could break in maybe, but they were too dumb to figure out the architecture, the non-centralized redundancy..." his hands flew across the keys and screens came and went and flickered through the room, "the hardware autonomy, the integrity of the code..." In a few minutes a series of charts and graphs came alive on the screens with numbers and statistics being updated in real time. "The code's the blood you know, all the rest... well," he turned and looked at them with a slow grin, "I've got backup. Someone breaking into my system is like taking one leaf from a tree."

Rozemund explained the graphic presentations and what they represented and went on to show how to find the correlations. In a moment the immensity of what he was looking at struck Nash. He was witness to the tragic passing of lives at the instant it was happening, with each reflected change, with each new CenMed call listed. He felt the force of it, the power flowing from their lives to his, to the living. The relationships in the statistics were clear, and like the influx of medical emergencies after one VT network went down here was an affluence of them all coming out of one relative source. The independent network CWVT. The graphs clearly showed that after early evening access time, the most popular online VT viewing period, of those connected with CWVT there had been a forty percent increase in CenMed emergencies in the past twelve weeks, and of those nearly eighty percent had the signs of *Electrically Induced Neurosynapse Failure.*

"Is this accurate?" Nash asked.

"It's perfect." Rozemund replied.

"You remember the new "nanoflat" panel technology that went on the market a year and a half ago? The 3D screens that were only milli-meters thick? Well, it turns out that it had no government testing and was railroaded into the public by CommNET and the GCC. Fact is we did some testing on it ourselves. It's based on new light wavelengths and its emissions ostensibly are a lower wavelength than the common monitors, but only in the spectrum of visible light. We found radiation potentially over 5000 times that of the standard VT panels with a wide spectrum of invisible light–including some hitherto unknown light particles! The huge difference is that it can be modulated with a variable frequency response and the fact that it's from an entirely unique light spectrum."

"What does that mean?"

"It means," Rozemund answered, " that they've got enough power to knock you out with the right signal."

The implication struck Nash immediately, "...and you think..."

"...that CWVT is sending the right signal." Fionica replied. "Almost certainly."

Suddenly Nash turned to Rozemund, "Did you find anything, any signs, signatures...sometimes hackers leave a mark."

"Yes." He said. Picking up a pad of paper he showed it to Nash. "Here, this is the symbol." On the pad was scratched a sideways "V" followed by three dots. It was the mark exactly as he had found it.

"Have you ever heard of a programmer named 'Yzak'?" Nash asked without taking his eyes off the paper and at the same time wondering why anybody would want to knock out a viewer.

- X -

Hegira

"I have a small problem with this." A Chinese man spoke in Mandarin through his teeth. The tight white collar of his shirt bit into his neck causing his face to flush with suppressed indignation at some insult imagined or real. The glimmer in his eye was the reflection of holy imperial dragons that ages and revolutions could not wear away.

Through veiled meanings Sabiha saw the men clearly. Each as if sculpted of ice portraying things not germane to their nature, but how they wished to be perceived. Nothing was what it seemed. Smoke wisps. Mirages. Her brown hands danced with the phantoms and she knew their subtle moods and secret faces so well that she could speak the language of diplomatic correctness with keen insight into the inflections, the importances and the hidden intent of those who came to the table. Voices mingled in the air. Some with a high tension whine taken to the emotional edge by pressures from within, others deep and mellifluous, patronizing, condescending and steeped in the ease with which words come to those who have never had to worry about survival. They crossed in the ether as shockwaves from different worlds traveling with speeds too great for the human mind to easily comprehend and would have sailed off into oblivion had it not been for her. The translator. The medium.

It was the quicksilver that she was most at home with, the shifting words, languages and metaphor that floated up and roiled with the fury

of the ruling class no matter from what economic strata they had originally sprung. Wasn't it true that the right to rule was the first mantle of
assumption? That it descended from heaven to the shoulders of those
who had the wherewithal, who had answered or had conned their way
into a position? So this great towering purpose whose monument is and
will ever be the pillars of rhetoric and the innumerable diplomats whose
only products were words and more words enchained all of civilization
with its pretense.

Sabiha knew in the subtle and unexplained regions of her being
that men were waiting for the slave revolt. Each, she perceived, was
a willing arm in the struggle for freedom if only another would take
the first move, strike the first blow. It was buried in their genes just
beyond the surface, a reflection of an inner meaning as if some secret
knowledge lay so close to consciousness that its whisper can be heard,
but looking finds it gone. She knew that men never lost heart. For a
purpose they would rise from the grave.

Sabiha translated without emotion. The conversion to Hijazi was
not difficult though she always had trouble understanding why there
was a holdout on the Arabian peninsula as it had been annexed to the
Eastern Metropolis for nearly a hundred years and *Gwo yo* was the most
widely used language on earth. English and Mandarin vied for dominance even if they had each borrowed so much from each other that
the modern dialects could be scarcely understood by early speakers, or
so her professors had told her. Understanding their changes was what
gave her the ability with languages. She had been branded an intuitive genius from an incident that occurred at age eleven when her only
blood relative had forsaken her. *Too delicate,* was the pronouncement,
too sensitive and hard to handle, her mother had told them after the
seventh or eighth time she had run from home finally committing her to
a juvenile correction center. There, through some vast and mysterious
plan that was irreconcilable with the real world she began to heal the
other girls, the ones who came to her as if she was a messenger they had
each secretly been waiting for. Laying hands upon them their illnesses
vanished, listening to them their troubles eased. She never saw her
mother again and since then had been the sometimes unwilling pupil of

the brightest academic minds in the Western Metropolis. Sabiha's skills lay in her ability to interpret the next vector in a series of related variables with unnerving accuracy. In short, she could predict the future. But only in a brief span of time, such as within a conversation, and only in a series of tightly related changes such as in a language system. Her mastery of any given dialect was far out of the realm of mere humans. Consequently she was in demand by the United Nations, which acted as a commerce clearing house for the planet working out trade agreements and details of economic free zones.

"Ask him," the man said in Hijazi, "if he would be gracious enough to make his meaning clear because we cannot read his mind, and though it's becoming easier I cannot yet claim that I am clairvoyant." The Arab man did not change the scowl that swept across his dark heavy brow and did not move his eyes though the other men at the table shifted uneasily. The expensive fabric of their suits slid across their smooth, alloy chairs. They were clearly frustrated with the proceedings.

She translated, but changed the insult to humility with a simple inflection of tone.

The room was hushed. A quiet hostility permeated from men who were forced to confront one another over fundamental disagreements. There were no imperialists now, no expansionists and no victims. No colonized masses were seeking retribution, no inferior third world prejudices. Each nation was equal either in the orbit of the Eastern Metropolis or the Western Metropolis and was subject to equal exploitation.

The issue was water. Since the turn of the century what little fresh ground water there was on the planet had been polluted with chemicals and petroleum by-products, not to mention the radiation leaks that had occurred from the early nuclear waste and weapon dumps, and the lakes had been tainted by acid rains, irradiated rains, metalosis rains and enough chemicals to make them nearly indistinguishable as $H2O$ and only by the furthest stretch of the imagination could they be called water. Scientists normally viewed the natural fresh waters of the planet as a chemical brine cocktail not dissimilar to that soup which it is said living organisms first sprang from, though that view had lost adherents with the 20th century resurgence of fundamentalist religion. The word *water* now stood for the bottled liquid that everyone kept in their refrigerators. Though it was still possible to drink from a tap somewhere, it was not advisable and doctors were taught that it was a health risk just having faucets accessible to children and one possible solution was to change the word *water* as it related to the chemical liquid that was used for washing or other industrial duties to something completely dissrelated and that discouraged drinking. A proposal of *"scum"* was made at the World Health Organization, but it did not translate well into Mandarin.

The water that was consumed by billions of humans each day was manufactured. It was one of the largest and most profitable industries in the world. The aerating and desalinization of sea water on the Arab peninsula had been pioneered over a hundred and eighty-two years ago and after the oil fields had dried up and synthetic petroleum manufacture was monopolized by the Indians, the Arabian water distilleries became their greatest asset and their proprietary technology was guarded under harsh laws.

Mainland China on the other hand had become the agricultural capitol of the world as a result of the aggressive gene research programs from the early 21st century, an effort to end famine and feed its explosive population by mapping all the genes of the most common food plants. As a result of the genetic maps perfect fruits and vegetables could be produced from synthetic chemical gene structures. World hunger effectively was at an end.

There is an old Chinese saying that where need ends greed begins and so the imperfections arise when all problems were solved. The food production facilities needed one vital element they could not make enough of–pure, drinkable water. And the Arabian peninsula could not sustain the enormous population and infrastructure created during its oil producing heyday because it could not produce its own food. For the past one hundred years there had been meetings like this one to hash out the minutiae of details over the complex and incomprehensibly ornate protocol of exchange. Each was trying to gain the other's technology so as not to be dependent, each was trying to develop an enormous profit margin without letting on that there was fat, and each secretly wanted the other's power, or whatever was possessed that was not shared. Simple human animosity and greed that gave rise to interminable negotiations.

His hairline was receding yet his face was still youthful. The lights from the ceiling caused his forehead to shine. His cheeks were fat. The expression on his face was that of the bronze lions reclining outside the Forbidden City flanking the stairway to the heavenly throne where his ancestor had ruled as Emperor. Perhaps in the night when the wisps of cloud and mist swirled in puzzling circles hiding and then revealing the moon floating in indigo skies and causing apparitions to appear and vanish in a heartbeat; perhaps in this time when he was not quite asleep yet neither awake and his thoughts ran the length of his life and beyond to earlier lifetimes and dynasties now forgotten; perhaps then while he was reminiscing he felt the burning bitterness of loss that brought him to this state where he had to grovel and scrape and bargain and ply the trades of a merchant to his eternal disgrace. It was *joss* that no one knew him...that no one really understood to what depths he had slunk.

He listened sourly as Sabiha translated the Arab's words and knew that they imparted his meaning, but not his intent. "The detail I am looking for is what could possibly lie so close to the shore that our ships cannot come within a ten mile radius of it? Merely an inappropriate ruling against a partner in trade...*and* the hub country." He expiated in heavily accented English, which was briskly translated.

"Purely a matter of territorial waters. The custom for centuries, even since before the Kaiein..." the Arab looked politely at Sabiha ensuring she was allowed adequate time to effect the explanation into Chinese, "and we still are sovereign though annexed to the Eastern Metropolis. There is an identity to consider."

"Money" The Chinese man hissed again in Mandarin. "It's money."

Ignoring the insult the other man, who was in his late fifties and though fit and vital realized his treading on borrowed time called for some risk, some rashness, spoke. "That's foolish!" He replied in harsh, melodic Swahili, a dialect he had learned as a child while studying in North Africa at the university in Cairo. "Your distaste for trade is not shared." He said looking across the table with dark, brooding eyes, "In fact you are quite alone in your views. Your mandate is simply to come to an accord, not to aggravate an already festering situation." Others in his party smiled slightly with smug, self-righteous pursing of lips, turning of heads, lowering of eyes.

Sabiha delicately put across the words in a way not to cause a breakdown in the talks. It had been made clear that her job was simply as interpreter and she was to relay the intention of the speaker as accurately as possible without any inflection that could be construed as a personal opinion, which in the case of Swahili to Mandarin left considerable room for interpretation because of the four major tones of the Chinese with a fifth light one, and the complex albeit less classical inflections of the North African dialect. She surreptitiously took matters into her own hands with the good of the state in mind.

The Chinese man sat back in his chair clearly dissatisfied with the tack the discussion was taking. He turned to an aide on his right and conferred with him in a hushed mode while a briefcase was opened and papers fanned as if to refresh his memory, and then to the others in the party he nodded. "You are mistaken." He said directly, "We already know that you are stockpiling water, and that you have misrepresented your supplies on the world market and in fact have something to the effect of an embargo placed on water predestined to the Eastern Metropolis."

The Arab brushed his hand in the air to the great frustration of the Chinese delegation. "Idle…Idle talk."

China. The word is a conjuring, it is an imagining, it is a vision. The concept of it in the end overwhelmed the industrial machine so desperately forced upon it and the iron will of the people spoke with a democracy that had no voice and as gentle waves upon the shore wore away the rocks. There are rituals to attend to, urgencies of the spirit that have greater meanings than just food on the table at regular intervals. The same faceless people had endured communism just as they had endured the dynasties and emperors and conquerors one upon the other down the years until the religion of money brought about disaster. No one can enforce an agenda forever. China lived in the mind and was reborn. But there was a long legacy of having been a victim that could not be forgotten with ease. The man considered deeply, he gave an equal weight to the viewpoint across from him as he gave to himself. He did this out of an inner need for a moral equity, a cleansing of the soul and a conscious attempt to uphold some values that had become indistinct. There was no denying, however, that he did not have the confidence of the Arab. A fact that rankled him. Though he tried to maintain a high minded attitude it was nearly impossible because he hated the thought of someone doing something to him, especially if they thought he didn't know they were doing it.

"It is true." He replied with equanimity. "There is an identity that I personally believe is inborn. You are an Arab, I am Chinese." He fiddled with his hands and made a feeble attempt to smile in a disarming, humble manner he thought would appeal to the men across from him. "Nobody here is foolish enough to believe that civilization began with the Kaiein, as you pointed out...we are, out of necessity, one world, but not one people." He paused for effect holding absolutely still with the frozen words. "Trust must be a given for we each have something the other needs."

"But we trust you..." The Arab replied.

"Of course." Looking down at the hands on the table and suddenly feeling the coolness of the air conditioning and wishing he was in the mountains where he loved to walk among the trees and even feeling the spring of the earth beneath him with its blanket of pine needles imagining that the cold draft from the vents above the table was a freshening breeze down the eastern slope carrying the pungent evergreen smells. They were the saw-toothed jagged peaks of memory that had haunted his life since childhood where he had been raised in their shadow. He recalled the reflection they made in the Yellow river whose primeval sinewy arm had been the highway upon which many had built their homes and had depended upon as tribe for their lives being the means not just of trade, but of social contacts so important in the advancements sought through the years. How detached it all seemed to him now, even the river was like a postcard having no real relevance to anyone's lives anymore now that it was not used for commerce. It had become a sewer for the over populated, post industrial holocaust they called civilization. It made him sad without knowing why although he could have explained that something irretrievable had been lost, but just what that was he couldn't say.

"We have trouble bargaining in good faith when there is a ten mile limit to our embrace." He added in the *Hakka* dialect of Kwangtung, Kwangsi and Fukien. Sabiha, fortunately, was able to translate by her perceptive ability and the fact that the language was close enough to Mandarin for her to understand.

Bristling with suppressed indignation the Arab man bit his lip to maintain composure and managed to shape a response that was close enough to his feelings. "What we do is not your affair," he intoned in a stiffly formal manner, "it is of no responsibility to you or your country our sovereign actions on the peninsula."

It was translated word for word in measured cadence and she could feel the animosity rake through her and for the moment jar the more sensitive thoughts out of existence. She came to grips with the single minded focus that was needed to properly attend to the discussion in progress. Each ambassador's entourage sat erect in a staid orthodox way that suggested an obsession with protocol and an attempt by all those present to display the fact that they all were still needed. It had been suggested that logic boards could take over diplomacy and political summits when they involved concrete decisions relating to the survival of large masses of people and by the simple matter of feeding in all the relevant data and cross referencing it in a hyper relational databases the computer programs could divine the optimum solution from the random bits down to their essence, as few humans had the capability or the desire to do, and then presenting a simple range of solutions. Nobody wanted just one answer, the optimum was thought to be three, two might cause indecision, but three... It was finally agreed after long and costly legislative debates that a living being was to be present at all crucial decision making meetings, and if one was not, to allow an oversight committee to have the opportunity to review the digital files and make recommendations accordingly. Professional diplomats and politicians were horribly chagrined at the prospect of being reduced to data input terminals, and the result was obsessive protocol and secrecy mandating many levels of confidentiality. This gave rise to a strata of those in the know who were either given a level of clearance, or knew somebody who had one and the far larger common strata of those who had no access to public policy whatsoever.

The other effect that occurred was quite unexpected. A dark and foreboding distrust of code writers developed in the cultural psyches of many continents. Perhaps in some prescient way people saw through the apparent good and realized they were being manipulated for profit. Also it had finally been realized in official circles that computers were not the omniscient machines they had been touted as by their marketing people, but rather expensive hardware in the form of a consumer product only as good or effective as the intention of the code written for it. The programs. The software. For the past two decades governments had been actively recruiting and contracting code writing programmers with deals so attractive only an altruist would hold out. Or an amateur. Or a hacker. They became the most valuable assets of the governments and private sector because unlike hardware they were malleable and best of all, expendable.

The Chinese man hung his head and looked to the left and to the right at his colleagues. "You are quite wrong there." He began speaking in the *Amoy* dialect of his childhood. Sabiha knew this well having spent a year in Singapore working at the consulate and could bring to lucid Arabic the subtleties of the rural inflections. "When I was very young another boy in the province where I lived was accused of murdering a fellow in a fight. He was older than I, but this I knew about perhaps the way all young boys know about what happens to other boys by way of secret talk that is outside the realm of adults. The word among those boys was that he had not killed this other boy, whom it was said he had bludgeoned with a pipe, but had discovered the assassin himself." He looked up with a pained expression leaving the Arabs unclear if it was the memory that made him feel that way or the discomfort of speaking so frankly. "You must remember that I was raised in a very rural area. The corporate farms of course had completely obscured small landowners like my father, but at the same time had kept the lands open so from my town to the next was a half day journey. The tribunal came from this other community, which was larger and a municipal hub for the region. I still remember the day they came down the street, all six of them in their black suits walking to the court. It was sunny, but cold, and winds came up from the east." He stopped for a moment and looked straight ahead as if the cool air was rushing up over him. "It was clear to us boys that the fellow they charged with murder was innocent and we each predicted a short trial endured for the sake of face. After all, someone had died and so there must be concern otherwise... What was not clear was our responsibility in the matter. Nobody was moved, though deeply touched...perhaps all feeling inadequate, or too insignificant...even then young boys did not interfere in the affairs of men... nobody was moved to speak out on his behalf."

Overlapping words filled the room as the Chinese man spoke in one long narrative monologue and Sabiha scrambled to keep up stumbling occasionally with some of the idioms and colloquial expressions. The music of his language echoed in counterpoint to the harsh melody of Hijaz and the sweetness to her voice added something to the telling.

"To our shock he was pronounced guilty. At the appointed hour he was taken to the far outskirts of the corporate lands, up against the mountains where the foothills just started, and shot. My father went to help the father of the condemned boy and though I was too young I remember their small truck carrying his body through the streets and off across the country to his birthplace so they could bury him with his ancestors. I recall all this so clearly because the weather was exceptionally cold and clear without the faintest hint of clouds. In a few days they returned and everything was back to normal except for one important thing, nobody felt the same."

"I see..." he said stiffly. The Arab man was quiet and sat with his elbows propped on the table before him, fingers all touching, palms together resting his chin against his thumbs. He frowned in deep concentration letting the telling of the old story wash over him and for a moment lift the burden of responsibilities that plagued him, drawing his attention this way and that and making him do things that were against his own moral code and that he would later regret, still knowing there was no other choice. He remained this way for many long moments.

There was not a sound save the incessant hissing of the air through the ducts above them and he was transfixed, locked in a spiritual grip with the Chinese man. The others did not move for fear of violating some unknown protocol though none of them knew why the story had been told. Perhaps, one thought, it was just a reverie brought on by frustration. The Arab man waited for the end of the story, but it did not come. For a few moments longer he waited and then realized all attention was on him and that he risked appearing a fool if he did not respond appropriately. However he did not by his life understand why the story was told, and then to him at least, left incomplete. Across from him the face of the Chinese was completely motionless and his eyes, like those of all the others, were on him. The hair on the back of his neck bristled at the thought of being the brunt of some intellectual pun and he suddenly broke the frozen instant by shifting uncomfortably with a jerk in his chair. "That is unfortunate, but then we all reap our own consequences don't we."

"My point exactly," the Chinese man replied.

With more than just a little relief the Arab relaxed secure with the confidence he had understood after all and glanced surreptitiously to each side at his cohorts to find that they were at ease and even smiling now. "Yes," he reiterated, "a man must be responsible for his own destiny."

Sabiha had difficulty translating the subtext of the exchange because of the harmonics of inflection that came so easily to those brought up in the native tongues, but it was clear the communications transcended language and for some reason had brought about an understanding that was lacking before. From that point on the negotiation went much more smoothly the Arab agreeing to review his regions statistics and to come back in a week to address the allegations, and if true to rectify the situation not wishing to alienate itself from the central Hub authorities, which he knew any country or region may come to need in a brief calamitous instant when God and the elements conspired against them. The Chinese man for his part was honored that he had been able, through his cunning and excellent wisdom, to bring about a complete reversal in the attitude that confronted him.

She had planned this. It had come in a vision, a complete and comprehensive plan. Before her ordeal it had only been an intellectual understanding, though she had empathy with the unwilling victims of *fusing*, the impact of its maliciousness had not been driven home. Until now.

As soon as the Arab and Chinese delegation departed she had set off through the labyrinth of halls and interconnected buildings the United Nations' complex had become since the Kaiein. It had been estimated there were over fifty-seven miles of passageways and tunnels and no one except engineering corps personnel had ever traveled them completely. There were people from all over the earth inhabiting the honeycomb of offices. It was a long walk, but lean legs glided through the vast spaces leaving the impression with those she passed of one on a mission. She imagined scenarios trying to devise a pat scientific method for the task she had embarked upon knowing that with each step retreat became less an option and commitment to the act a certainty. She was not used to lying, but Sabiha was not accustomed to flinching from absolutes either and she had reached a complete understanding. Her life was a sequence of strivings and longings, the one was for the attainable and the latter for what could never be reached–to give up the enchantment would render life flat, dull and devoid of risk. She prided herself on knowing what she knew and what she didn't. It kept her honest.

At the same time another was navigating the maze. The same one who had penetrated the network tower and taken out its transmission center and who had watched the leader die a martyr. He too paced the distances with long measured strides that drew him closer to his destiny and farther away from the mold to which he and everyone else in the modern world had been born. Footsteps in counterpoint to hers.

His heart had been seared and still burned from the wound. He used the pain to ferry him through the difficult hours balancing the passions with which all humans had with the duty only a few would realize.

A vision had come to him in love's aftermath. One dark night where no moon or stars could be seen and the pulsing light from the city radiated on the underbelly of the low lying clouds. She lay next to him with one snow white breast exposed and slept; lips parted, with hair covering half her face. Drawn without reason he had been swept up by her voice. Under impossibly gentle fingers she had tamed his powerful, stocky frame and he felt temporary relief from the storm. All through his most violent love making, muscles rippling and straining and gleaming with perspiration in the streak of pale light from the crack in the door while he gasped and assaulted her small, soft body she kept her eyes on his as their breaths intermingled. When he would turn or roll away in passions grip, she would follow piercing with her eyes inches from his face not letting him escape for an instant. As he climbed the ladder, he knew that the woman had harnessed his power for her own and was certain he had fallen under a spell that now held him immobile and captive locked in nature's vise. When he climaxed he remembered eyes were the windows to the soul and was terrified at what she might have seen. Later sated and exhausted was his vision came. He saw the world as an interconnected, fibrous web of wires to which every man, woman and child were bound against their will from birth. For a moment he was startled and completely unable to make any sense of it, but then he began to get the meaning and absorb its significance and suddenly knew that something of great importance was happening to him and he could not let it pass without gaining its full benefit. That was the instant. He looked over at the sleeping woman just to reassure himself that the vision was real and felt the warmth of her breast under the palm of his hand and finally understood that she was a messenger.

The world was connected with wires and had been for a long time. The optic highways of the quantum computer networks and the Vidtel to which every living being was born into not ever having known true life, pure life, life in its natural state. He listened to the voice of God and it said that men were enslaved by a vicarious existence and had indentured their souls for sensations of the networks, the Vidtel and all the other connections to the virtual world. What was a man without creation, the voice echoed, without tactile longings, without the danger of defeat or the euphoria of victory?

The power of the vision propelled him and nourished him giving strength to his sinewy frame and direction to all his energies. He rounded a corner deep in concentration nearly toppling a woman he brushed against in his hurry and finally, down the long corridor, saw his destination. It was a door with serrated yellow and black edges marked, *No Admittance - Authorized Personnel Only*. Man was a prisoner in a virtual web and he had been chosen to find an exit point.

All through the morning Sabiha had been gripped with a premonition. It had come where the line between sleep and wakefulness was indefinable and the sounds of the night could be heard along with the sounds of dreams. The earth trembled with slight but powerful hands and though it cradled her for an imperceptible instant threatening to destroy, it wasn't that which brought her primal memories to the surface. With her spirit eyes she could see far outside her window across a strange and ominous city that was unlike anything she had ever known. Yet it was familiar. All the windows were tinted with gold and the air was thick with pollution and tinted a pale yellow-green. How easy it would have been to have risen and gone to any destination in the city with unerring accuracy even in the darkness, without a guide, and never for an instant have lost a sense of direction. It was a place of memory where the small details came back to her; the cracks in the curb at a certain intersection; a rough length of road; an underground cafe where one chair at the bar always squeaked because of a leg that was loose; the short cuts across town when the streets were gridlocked, and where not to venture at night alone. There was something else however, something black and mysterious and deadly that hung over the city like low slung clouds threatening rain. She sensed in people the deep traumas that wrapped all the living in their web and it made her restless. She turned again and again in her sleep trying to escape the brutal vision. By some prescient curse she knew what had happened to people in the city and saw it as an overwhelming silent menace that crushed the free will of its victims. Whether tied to the living wage or to the chain either way it usurped self-determinism. She could not deny the fact she was a witness to these mysteries.

Sabiha knew it was the future foretold. It was her native ability soaring having broken the bonds of wakefulness and entered the parallel world of amnesiac spirits. Here where the shaman and mullah live side by side; where the spiritualist and the priest vie for converts and the disenfranchised run along with the ruling class shoulder to shoulder in a dead heat. She touched it with her finger and withdrew seared to the bone and tumbled delicately into the morning.

The presence of her ominous vision had not left her. In the streets, as she drove to work, along the sidewalks crowded with streams of people in faceless moving currents–out of what wellspring of purpose was anybody's guess–she saw the pattern and flow of things to come. If nothing changed, if things remained constant in their flux then the random chaos of the world would conclude in a parallel of her vision. Perhaps man, as a species, was motivated by a death wish and that explained why his saviors were always murdered.

On the first level below ground the man hovered near the door with black and yellow serrated edges. He smelled ozone like the odors of arc welding. His heart pounded. Far below, two stories down in the catacombs, was his rendezvous. Past the door once, then twice and a third time he walked in rhythm with others except that he was waiting for his moment, the precise instant when his destiny would begin to unfold. Silently as predator hidden by the cloak of anonymity he settled into waiting motionless while he was racing. *What if,* he questioned, *no one came to the door? What then?* Though he could not imagine the entrance not yielding to someone during the daylight hours. Down the stairs behind the door were three stories underground. This was one of only three entrances; of the other two one was a formal, full security entry, and the other a massive industrial ramp for emergency evacuations and heavy equipment movement. All were distinguished by the black and yellow serrated edges and were officially off limits to all except those with a specific level of security clearance. He walked back and forth invisibly in front of the door ensuring no one noticed anything unusual about his presence. Once a young woman watched him walk by twice, three times–he had to throw up his hands, look intently at his watch and march away as if the appointment he was expecting had not shown. On his next run by the door she was gone.

The time it took to move from where he was at any moment to the entrance was measured to the last instant. It had to be exact. No mistakes. No failure. Suddenly a pallid nondescript man approached the door. He was wearing a pale blue shirt with blue trousers only slightly darker and had red hair with pale freckled skin. As he approached he placed his face close to an Iris scanner. A slight flare of infrared violet light escaped and as the technician was placing his key card in the slot the watching man was already in motion. Without a breath or a sound or a whisper he glided the distance across the crowded hallway weaving in and out of pedestrians and as the pale man disappeared and the door inched its way closed and was almost sealed with just the slightest shaft of white light escaping the man slipped a paper thin sheet of molecular silicon between the door and the jam. Because of its properties it conformed to the finely engineered tolerance that the closure was machined to, but did not distort laterally and that prevented the latch from securing and the bolt from falling into place and at the same time allowed the electro-optic impulses to transmit across the gap normally, the material having almost no resistance, so that in its brain the security system did not know it had been breached. He slid inside and hunched up against the wall as the door closed behind him leaving no way out.

Approaching the last corner of the tunnel before the elevator Sabiha suddenly paused and savored the last moment before she was totally certain she would go through with her plan. Here, far below ground in the massive United Nations structure, she considered her choices while the stream of people ebbed past in their mad rush to nowhere.

At the door of the thirty-seventh floor suite of offices was a placard with holographic symbols of the United Nations and the GCC across which was written *Charles Iverson, High Commissioner for the Global Communications Commission*. In reception was a huge circular leather couch above which a dozens Vidtel monitors were suspended each displaying a different channel of PIA programming the same as that which played at every street corner, in every public space and on consumer Vidtels as well. PIA government programming was mandatory for all private sector service providers if they wanted a license.

"He said to go on back." The receptionist droned nicely. "Have you been here before?"

"Yes, I have." Sabiha replied.

"Then you know right where to go..." was the quick response. Too quick, brittle and tinged with an impatience for no observable reason."...don't you?"

His eyes were disturbed and agitated in such a way that it was difficult to tell if he was serenely happy or on the verge of a psychotic break. But there was a glint of pleasure that escaped the other complexities of his being and told her he was happy she had come. She was relieved, but just slightly.

"Sabhia," he exclaimed in a gruff manner asserting a disingenuous friendliness and lowered his eyes to her breasts, which immediately made her even more uncomfortable if that was possible.

"Charles," she replied briefly shaking hands in a crisp business like fashion to which his response was to pull her close and kiss her cheek.

"I am so glad the weather has cooled off," he offered in a vociferous tone, "the algae was turning brown in my kitchen because the window's facing west and gets the afternoon sun." Everyone grew a dark green algae in terrariums usually in the kitchen. It was nearly the only source of the B vitamins left aside from seaweed, and was used in just about all cooking as a supplement.

"I understand we were passing through a particularly thin layer of ozone and that the pressure areas have shifted bringing in cooler."

He just looked at her pleasantly dumbfounded and somewhat annoyed wondering what she was talking about. "Less radiation you know?" Sabiha said nervously.

"Oh...?"

She fumbled, "I saw it on the weather this morning."

"Of course."

Sabiha sat down opposite the wide desk from him. There were no papers or any other evidence work was actually in progress, but there were three monitors with Vidtel programming running in separate windows and a wireless touchscreen. He punched in a series of keystrokes and the monitors all silently changed to a new sequence of programs like a gallery of quietly blinking eyes.

"Well, at any rate... I am happy you've come by. We don't see you enough around here." He said patronizingly with enough indifference and condescension to wither a stone.

"Actually," she replied dryly. "I'm here officially." Sabiha's nails dug into the artificial leather of the armchair, but otherwise she was unmoved as a result of years watching the best negotiating politicians on earth and absorbing their finer qualities.

"Officially?" he inquired gently, suddenly wondering why she was here.

It was the story she had to be true to, the plan, the one that had come to her after the cathartic experience and the vision of an enslaved city. "Yes." She said knowing full well that Charles Iverson really had little Idea what her function was at the UN and the only context he could place her in was at consular and embassy parties where she mingled with the power brokers as if one of them. Like so many others he did not know the bureaucratic nature of the Security Council and at what level of bureaucracy decisions were made or what her responsibilities were. She savored the moment. "I am in possession of some information *we* though you might be able to shed some light on?"

"Me?" He chuckled taking the high ground immediately and alerting Sabiha to his danger. Yet at the same time he became suddenly cautious as to what powers she might have and gave his full attention.

She perceived a weakness. "Well, we often call upon our more influential colleagues to help us with things that, say, *normal* men cannot."

"What things?"

"Things," she replied emphatically.

"Ahhh...yes I see... security matters."

"Exactly." Watching his eyes for the onerous burden of self importance rising up like a massive dragon to slay or be slain by. Power like his must be fed, demanded to be fed and the poor soul who was its addict was its slave. It must take an awful toll, she thought,

"Alright... alright." He cleared his throat and glanced at his watch impatiently, "What would you like to know?"

Now she had him. "We're in possession of some information regarding..." she stammered momentarily as she rummaged through her brief to produce some paper printouts, hard copy... "...regarding a series of network events." And without looking she caught him sitting up straight in his chair fully alert and focused.

Far below it was so quiet the man could hear the sounds of his own breath against the walls. It was frightening. Any extraneous noise could betray him. He was surprised there were so few people close by. That too, however, had been taken into account and with some difficulty he pulled an ID badge out of his left front trouser pocket and attached it to the magnetic strip on his shirt just in case. Luck was never his strong point. This had been a gift from an ill tempered old man who was the greatest forger he knew, which was divulged confidentially to him by the old man himself: *"I'm the last of a breed,"* he had said, *"after me..."* he paused and looked straight ahead with dying beauty, "...there won't be no one." And then he confided, *"I'm not feelin' too good lately."* He said the ID card would be good even in the magneto-optical slot used to gain admittance. He didn't need to use the card for admittance, everything had worked out perfectly, but the preparation gave him confidence.

It wasn't clear which direction would lead down to the third level, the place where he was destined, so he turned left and followed his instinct breathlessly moving as fast as he could without attracting attention. The corridor was sterile. Light from offices spilled out into its bleak interior and across the worn black tile floor that was not the quality of the rest of the complex being at the heart of the infrastructure. Here the pipes ran for miles with water and drainage and the conduits where lighting and phones and conferencing sped from one point to another at 299,792,458 meters per second. In the cubicles were engineers, technicians, plumbers, electricians, construction and maintenance managers and support personnel of every variety most of whom came from a military background giving the place a crisp, martial feel. Those offices he chanced to look in were institutional and cold.

His vision hunted him in bleak vestiges that swept across with dream-like intoxication leaving him jarred and agitated. The closer he got to the source the more anxiety welled up inside for it was the massive, multistrand, network optical cables that lay deep in the third level where the real power was concentrated. It was there millions of voices spoke in unison day and night.

Others walked and he mimicked them. They all moved in the same direction. He was thankful no one was coming toward him and felt anonymous. The sweat had soaked through his heavy cotton shirt even though the temperatures were low enough to make his breath condense, but no one noticed and so he concentrated on complete invisibility. There were recessed lights along the edge of the ceiling illuminating the hallway with a pale cream color and the glow from each open office flowed out into the soft haze making the end of the way visible yet indistinct. He saw the other people in the abstract, as representations of living beings, icons, but not real. There were three colored light strips embedded in the floor to give direction in the dimness; light cyan blue for the first level; a bright lime for the second and red for the third. He felt a flutter in his stomach as his foot touched the crimson strip and he followed it down the wide stairs until he arrived at the second level. There were more people here. He knew on this landing all the real work was done and that on the first had been only managers, those who had plodded long enough for promotion and were finally taking it easy getting someone else to work. This was perhaps the great achievement of the twentieth century. But the man was not an intellectual. History had no meaning to him. There was nothing more that he loved than to feel the strength flow through his body and to exert himself in honest work. His mission now was an anomaly, a short circuit in nature whereby he was the vessel of divine intervention to come down like a hammer upon the Philistines.

"Network you say..." Charles Iverson's eyes narrowing into mere slits as he peered across at Sabiha, "which network?" he asked pointedly.

She gazed up absently dropping some papers at the same time, "Oh, why Intercon-FTT," she paused and looked cheerfully at his surprise, "It's a military optic-server network used primarily for purchasing."

"Oh..." he said visibly relieved, "I thought you meant..."

"Yes, yes...no..."

"What can I tell you? It's really out of my jurisdiction. And, what type of event?"

"Espionage," she replied matter-of-factly without the slightest hesitation.

"Really." He was unimpressed, and in fact showed a disdain for the subject giving the notion that if it wasn't Network Vidtel and somehow linked to the world of entertainment it wasn't worth knowing and barely worth the time to discuss.

"Yes..." she continued doggedly not allowing his attitude to interrupt her, "you know of course that the vast majority of the virtual hardware comes from the Eastern Metropolis though much is repackaged under different regional brands."

"I hadn't actually studied it, but..."

"And that the military used these same machines for training and is a major player in the purchasing process?"

"No...I didn't know that."

"It's how we came across the break-ins."

He looked incredulously at her. "Hackers?"

"In a word."

"On a military network?"

"Yes."

He laughed despite himself. "I though they would have the most complex and impenetrable firewalls in existence."

"They do."

Charles Iverson regarded her for a moment and took in all that was being said and what was left unsaid to try and gain an insight into what data she wanted from him. "That good huh?"

"Must be the best there is." She held up sheets of paper, which actually contained nothing more than routine back-up records of office protocol. "Time after time he'd slip through the most intricate traps and network tracking using remote access, routing his calls through a hundred other networks before accessing and then covering his tracks with encryption."

"Why me?"

"The way we figure it, Charles," she used his name intimately now feeling him in her grip, "he's a professional, not just a hacker, someone in the business. Your business."

"Ahhh... now it's beginning to make sense.'

"And we thought... well, I thought..."

"...that I would know something you've overlooked."

"Exactly."

"It's not that simple," he said with a snap directness that was too quick.

Sabiha fell silent unable to formulate any words in response. She sat there and stared at him with a raw and open expression betraying none of the racing, computing machinations that were occurring in her mind as she tried to adopt a strategy, to improvise and pull off a live deception before the inadvertent blank spot in her composure betrayed her. "Why not?" Was all she could say and felt a fool for not grasping what to Charles Iverson was likely the most fundamental dictum in the global communications business.

"Layers. It's all layers you see." He smiled comfortably as one would to a small child inquiring about something she had no business knowing–even possessing the knowledge would be of no use.

"Yes..." Sabiha said half as a statement and half as a question in an effort to get him to explain, following with her eyes as he rose from his chair and walked to the window.

"There are many kinds of power." He turned with his back to the air thirty-seven stories above the streets below where traffic flowed like honey on a cold day. "Mine is...position, dependent upon..." he hesitated, "...a group. Like laminated wood each layer adds to their strength."

"I see." She said, but she didn't.

"The point is I can't just make something happen directly. I simply set the machine in motion; I'm the driver...what happens in the engine...? Well, you know what I mean."

What he meant was that any further discussion would be futile. "I thought you were...wasn't it you...they say you're responsible for the global network. That without you it would never have happened."

He looked at her as if for the first time with a halting self absorbed thirst and in the moment it took him to come to a full realization of what she was implying Sabiha knew she was feeding him, the fire raged alone inside and like an insatiable addict one taste was all he needed.

"Do they? And where do they say this?"

"Members. In the council."

"The Security Council?"

"Of course."

"Really?" His face flushed and he took short little breaths feeling for an instant that he was closer to the pinnacle than he had realized and the romance of it validated his every move up to this point and finally justified his existence and all that it took to create who he was. "That is nice isn't it," he said.

"I told them you'd be the right one to ask...if anybody would know...?"

"It's all economics. At the top money never changes hands. Just percentages; interest, fluctuations of stocks, regional bonds and virtual money transfers–numbers only. We decide and the machine moves. It has no loyalty, it's fed by capital and answers to its current master." He looked directly at her, "It's like telekinesis, we don't do much. But the next layer," he said emphatically, "*they* organize and develop groups of contractors who in turn work on a credit system, once their bids are accepted, and hire many levels of contractors below them in each strata with specific areas of expertise. It goes from the credit system to local currency for whoever does the project. Even barter I understand. There are so many supervisors on any given point that they comprise clearly two thirds of the work force."

"Isn't that a waste of resources?"

"Of course, but that's the way it works. This is what I'm telling you. I don't know who dug the trench or laid the submarine optics, or even who the contractors were, but I can tell you the routes and trace each line with my finger on a map. I can also tell you how many packets of information travel the route at any given hour, where the bottlenecks are and which part of the Trust owns what and which is sub-leased…so you see, there are many kinds of power."

At the top of the stairs to the third level the man paused and knelt down to fix his shoe. There were no elevators between the three floors below the street. He was happy there were no elevators. Pleased that he could look down from his vantage point and see the security desk at the entrance to the third floor. Each person there was x-rayed and scanned top to bottom with a magnetic imagining resonator one of the security officers held in his hand and then his optico-magnetic card slipped through for a final verification. He thanked whatever God there might be there was no second iris scanning.

With each step his heart beat in time. Slow like a drum beat, like the tattoo of a gun. His breath stopped for moments in time.

"Hey guys," he said amiably as he approached the two guards. They were middle aged and looked like brothers, surly but uncon-cerned. Their skin was leathery like they had spent too many hours in the sun and they moved with slow deliberateness of someone who was preoccupied with their mortality. He raised his arms to be scanned as he had seen the others do before him.

"You in Sys-ops?" one said to him in monotone as he moved the hand held device up and down slowly over his body.

"That's right." He replied keeping an eye on the other officer who was intently watching the monitor that showed the scan in real time. Suddenly the thought struck him that there may some type of physically implanted identification they were looking for. It had never occurred to him before now. *Why not,* he questioned himself, *it's the perfect security device...maybe even something that was chemically unique to each individual so it couldn't be cloned, isotopes for instance, what if they were looking for isotope signatures...*

"Are you hot buddy? Jeez...I'm always freezin' down here. You look hot."

He realized he was perspiring. "Yea, well...I'm late. I was runnin' up there. Can't ever seem to be on time."

The security man finished his scan and glanced over at the other one who was still looking at the monitor. He slowly brought his face up and after a tense moment nodded.

"That's too bad," the officer said perfunctorily, eager to sit back down and not have to confront another living being.

He took out the optico-magnetic card the old man had given him. His hand was shaking slightly as he slipped it in the slot and he hoped that it was not noticed, but in moments he was through and following the crimson strip again having forgotten the fear that had gripped him. He was still sweating.

The taste of the beast clouded his vision and bore him on terrible wings racing far above the din of people and made his heart beat strongly and rapidly even when he was not moving. There was a metallic feel to the air, a current that made it thick and his arms sliced through as he moved further on down the hall to his destination. His vision was compressed into a narrow field so that he was completely unaware of things he passed and perceived himself as a glowing flare of blue light arching out in perfect horizontal beams to each side. Before him lay the glass surface of an azure lake upon which he glided like wind barely causing feathered ripples. There was a distinct sense of being someone else, as if he was viewing all his actions from over his own shoulder and not really experiencing them at all. It gave him an attitude of immortality, of invincibility knowing that nothing could harm him worse than he had already been harmed and so buoyed him above any personal concerns for danger. There was the life behind him and that before him, but the void of the present within which he traveled was all consuming.

The walls of the corridor were painted red and there were no doors or openings of any kind from the security desk to the harsh glow of lights flushing of out an opening a long way down. It was the light of destiny (he knew) and so it was more startling when he suddenly heard voices from behind and realized he was not alone. It wasn't that he had expected there to be no one in the busiest, most central hub of communications it was just the shock of it like Icarus descending. He tried to filter out any extraneous sounds knowing that any discovery would be unlikely until the final moment. And then it wouldn't matter.

The closeness to the optical conduits, in which flowed millions of packets of information sealed tightly in encrypted little envelopes, seeped into his consciousness and sent a chilled wave down his back making him shudder. It was the seductiveness that drew him, the lure was a drug, like pipelines of heroin or liquid sex too enticing for a man to withstand without his sanity breaking down and so he became tense and clenched his jaw with determination, clenched it so hard his teeth and jaw ached. *This Godless place*, he muttered to himself drawing near the entryway where the streaming light was. Slowing down he knelt to fix his shoe letting the two men behind him pass. They were discussing software, comparing notes in binary short talk, quick elliptical sentences only tech people could understand. He hated that, feeling like he was on the outside and missing some vital information that would let others advance leaving him behind. He knew if they got more powerful them him...he would do the same, crush the enemy.

His fingers slid along the cold brushed metal railing. Each groove and mark could be felt distinctly from each other one. Inside the lighted entry was a clear wall sealing in the thousands of illuminated glass conduits through which optical cable flowed like glowing ribbons of pulsing light. On the other side of the wall were technicians in silver heat-radiation suits with the life support pack fixed on the lower shoulders making them all look hunch backed. As far as he could see the optical pipelines stretched in both directions with the digerati wrangling the data flow between the massive terminals which acted as signal boosters and sophisticated filters against the exact element he had come to free. Human communication.

His diabolical plan would work because of one fatal flaw. Not long after the discovery of industrially useful superconductor materials it was found that when allowed to flow freely with no resistance the atomic structure of particles changed. It had remained a complete mystery why and was widely regarded as just an anomaly of nature with the closest explanation being a quantum physics philosophical treatise on the relation of change of position in space to subatomic structure. Resistance was far more easily dealt with for photons could be shot through a vacuum, but their signal also became faint with distance and through research it was found that photons underwent an atomic transformation with the lack of resistance the same as electrons. Using particle beam technology a solution was developed to increase the volume of the propulsion until it could break the light barrier. Then the true discovery was inadvertently made. When photons break the light barrier, move faster than 386,000 miles per second, a chain reaction is begun that rips through the ether along its path of projection and the explosion tears through the fabric of the material universe. A complete city was destroyed this way during development and it took a decade to decipher what had happened and to harness the phenomenon.

The man knew they thought it had been forgotten, erased from the collective memory by long years and the benign nature information technology had taken. It was so pervasive that there was literally no differentiation between it and the fact of talking face to face. With his finger he felt the cool glass and remembered that it was forty degrees cooler behind to allow for the massive power in the terminals. Electronics fueled the filter system which caught the photons at 386,000 MPS decelerated them and then reaccelerated them boosting the signal still maintaining the integrity of the data. Stopped just short of chain reaction it was a feather's breath from disaster, and the whole infrastructure rode its ungainly back perched at the river's gate waiting only for a flutter in the cosmos for destruction to reign. He was the fist that would shake it. There was a sharp, fine edge to the envelope. Razor sharp.

The men in the silver suits knew it. They called what flowed through the clear glass vacuum conduits the "Soup" knowing that it could spill and tear at the fabric. It was a quiet trade off for the infinite bandwidth demanded by voracious consumers, addicts the man thought, who were so enamored with the instantaneous, real-time optical wonders of the Vidtel that any mention of security issues was heresy. He wanted to unleash its power, its infinite justice in rage at sin.

Charles Iverson's office had the crisp feel of newness. It was as if every object was a work of art and had been purchased out of an inde-fatigable money source and still had the smell that all fine new things had. The rich environment shimmered around her making everything else seem small. She could not reconcile the opulent surroundings, far too rich for a public servant even at Charles Iverson's high level. Sabiha concluded that he was just a front for the Trust. This somehow made her feel better as it placed her charade in an innocent light compared to his sins. When she looked across she could almost feel the wall between dimensions, one side evil, the other good, and felt an overwhelming urge to enter the other side and become feral and lose all sense of responsibility. It was the battle that raged within her between desire and purpose. Instead she calmly spoke.

"Have you ever seen this symbol?" she said holding up the mark of the sideways "v" with the three dots trailing behind it.

He squinted up his eyes across the desk from where he was standing, and then moved to her side holding the paper up for a closer look. "What is it?"

"A signature."

"A signature?"

"Of the hacker."

His interest was piqued. "It is? Fascinating."

Sabiha quietly folded the piece of paper and placed it back into her brief. She scanned his eyes for any recognition and saw only the intensity that simmered behind the falsely pleasant facade and recoiled spiritually from the power that lurked unseen in his universe. It was a dark, nameless force without moral equity that was somehow connected to the opulence and a feeling of danger she had perceived since first walking into the room. It was an unannounced presence.

"By the way," she asked innocuously at the door as she was leaving, "do you know which network Yzak is with?"

From the desk where his attention had returned the black eyes rose instantly to meet hers and through the ether that separated them arched a flame of burning intention that chilled her. She did not move and prayed the placid, friendly expression on her face would not change.

"Who's that?" he said unable to withhold the menacing quality from his voice.

"They say he's a genius," she blithely replied, "Yzak's his name. I thought you might have heard of him."

"No." He offered bluntly, out of patience.

She started to leave. "Thanks for your time..."

"Who says he's a genius?" he called to her sharply.

"What?" she said.

"Who said he's..."

"Oh, someone in the council."

Deep in the heart of the complex the man's face glowed bathed in the myriad light patterns created by millions of sounds and images transformed into pulses of photons flying through glass tubes and it gave him a saintly aura as he strode in confident steps along the clear wall. His right hand lightly touched the brushed metal rail with the ends of his fingers. The floor was a grid composed of a fibrous, non-conductive material through which neither light nor electricity could pass and the ceiling was black to hide all the pipes and ventilation shafts. People walked up and down the passageway paying no attention to him. Why should they, he mused filled with an overwhelming and arrogant confidence that had come upon him in the last few hours. He was aware of being someone else and justified the strange mental phenomenon that accompanied it with the idea that if things were to change then he must change first, and that meant being someone else. It made him feel antagonistic and physically strong even though his sense of reason was muddled. Voices drifted around him but lost their significance as if they were just static in the ether and he watched people's eyes surreptitiously as they passed looking for any sign of recognition.

"Hey!" Exclaimed a technician as the man suddenly bumped into him and knocked the glasses from his nose. Sweeping them off the grid he cracked, "What the hell, I wanted to get..." He looked at the man who had bumped him, "Sys-ops, right?"

He froze. Kept a straight face. Nodded.

"Thought so, in a hurry and no white coat!" he laughed.

The man feebly tried to smile, but the most that happened was a slightly worried look that crept over his face. He had not seen the two technicians standing in the middle of the corridor talking and cursed himself through clenched teeth for being so stupid. "Yea, I'm under the gun..." he turned and spontaneously picked up the electronic data board hanging by the door and scanned it studiously as if making sense of it. "...sorry."

"Don't worry about it." The technician said pulling his magnetic card from a pocket reaching for the door. Instantly his heart raced, without moving his eye followed the motions of the men, first both through the iris scan and then the cards. A satisfying hiss was released from the door and as it began to open clear light escaped brighter and fuller than could be perceived in the hall and he realized the glass was polarized. *Now*, he thought, *now*... but could not move and instantly was caught in the moral turmoil he'd been through when first deciding to take action. *Now!*... he thought again harshly to himself as if the command would jump start the body to act against the dynamic of life. As the door was swinging to be sealed again and the white coat began to disappear behind its veil he dropped the data board absently as if he hadn't been paying attention and leapt forward and caught the corner of the door just squeezing inside before it closed.

"Hey!" said the man whose glasses he had knocked off looking back at the sudden motion, "You can't do that! You need a suit, and your own scan...the alarm..."

Instantly a loud, shrill alarm pierced the environment and knifed through him with a painful thrust. Without thinking he pushed his way past the two men throwing them to the ground and ran, ran as fast as he could down the narrow isle that bordered the radiant tubes. Other technicians looked up from their tasks, shocked and startled. Another tried to stop him, but his momentum threw him aside him and he fell with the wind knocked from him. As he ran he reached inside his coat for the instrument he had prepared for this moment. He felt its coolness as he raced forward. He had to make it to the exact point just between the terminals where he had figured maximum effect would take place. Now there were men chasing him, amber and red lights were flashing on the terminals and a group was speeding to meet him head on. He halted short of midway determined not to be stopped. With two feet planted firmly at right angles to the glowing conduits he raised his clenched right hand in which he held a short length of common water pipe. Crude, blunt and heavy. And then he froze motionless for an instant the whole panorama of his existence before him in three dimensional color with each instant happening now in present time and all the voices and sounds of lifetimes were screaming in his ears like the cacophony of hell. Men from both sides were yelling at him too; to stop, to hold, to not move. Perspiration streamed down their faces despite the near freezing temperature and in their eyes he saw something he had never seen. There was life there; raging, tumultuous, vibrant, ragged, bold... He saw the whites of their eyes, wide and frantic. This, he finally thought, was real. And with a golden rush of energy that brought to him a climax, a fulfillment, a sense of attainment and meaning that had always eluded him he brought his hand crashing down upon the glass conduits where the optical cables and photons raced so close to the edge of disaster oblivious to humanity.

There was a blinding burst of light. He was swallowed. It was like liquid. Tangible and thick. All voices screamed at once, men from both sides sensing what was about to happen lost all thought of themselves as individuals and immediately threw themselves into harms way hoping their frail biochemical bodies would block the beams of light that shot from electronic cannons at thousands of miles per second. The first dozen or so were incinerated so quickly and thoroughly there was not even the slightest hint of ash or any other sign remained. Great plumes of spark and steam rose from the escaping energy hitting the moist bodies. The beam then skewered the next score of men who tossed their lives so carelessly away for the greater good with a clean hold drilled through them painlessly before a breath could be passed. Then it began to slow, and disperse and only knocked men over, pushed them aside, threw them up in the air brutally and with almost infinite force to the last man standing. His face was grim. In an instant he had leapt without a thought and faced certain death even with a family whose love and dependence weighed in his mind at all times. Now he looked to see the riveting beam of light strike his belly and singe through his silver suit and his cloth shirts to sear his flesh with a perfectly circular brand. The mark of God he would always call it after that day, for that was where it stopped ten feet short of bypassing the terminal and transmuting into a chain reaction that would have disintegrated the United Nations complex and much of the surrounding city without a trace. The back up system instantaneously absorbed the load of communications and there was hardly any noticeable interruption to the service except a momentary pause in the transmission, a surge and a low audible hum of sound.

Shadow and light, the last man thought looking upon the path the beam had taken to the now cooling terminal out of which it had come, over the burnt and mangled bodies of nearly a hundred men like himself, *shadow and light.*

On the floors high above insulated from all infrastructure details Charles Iverson still sat at his desk fuming after Sabiha had gone. He stared absently at his computer monitor and the Vidtel and wondered how in the hell she got the name Yzak. It made him furious. He did not believe in coincidence. Somebody would pay; somebody would bear the full brunt of his rage. Lifting the receiver from his Vidtel he entered the code that only he knew, the private line of Hisham Mostafa 'Ali Fayed Al-Razio and waited. Nothing happened. Then there was a momentary pause in transmission, a light surge and a low audible crescendo of sound. This fed his fury. *Those god dammed sons of bitch techies always fucking up even with the best resources in the world Jesus Christ…!* And he reentered the code. This time a heavily accented voice answered and a face appeared on the monitor.

"I need to speak with mister Al-Razio."

The swarthy man on the monitor began to explain in droll, dry and condescending terms, "He is not available now may I…"

"No!" he interjected violently. "What I mean to say you greasy weasel is that I need to speak with him *right now!*"

- XI -

Tempest

They descended on the night like rain, like fog, like the darkness. They scattered through the city. Each searching. Lights flared in the streets off the moist evening air and the dense industrial air as cars sped to their destinations while behind the wheels rode men of conscience and men of forgiveness and men of evil either running from the real or heading into its arms. The sun was forgotten. It was night.

"My legs are sore, they're really sore," said the woman, "I worked out hard and shee... I shoulda' taken' it easy."

"You'll be alright." A man with slicked back hair replied from the driver's seat of their car racing through the darkness cloaked in anonymity amongst all the others in traffic. Strangely, they felt superior; isolated, protected, "...few drinks... some laughs..."

"Yea... funny, you think it's funny. I remember when you wrenched your–what about that time you twisted your ankle and it swelled up like a melon?"

"That's different."

"Yea. I'll bet."

They sped past a corner on the magnetic beams still in the newer area of the metropolis where the buildings rose straight up out of the ground in alloy and fabricated graphite or granite or burnished copper oxide flushed with blue green and bronze. They shot up like stele all of the same mold only with different appointments. Recognizing one from another was a job for urban dwellers who came to know the subtle innuendoes of their neighborhood architecture that passed the uninitiated by. It was the rhythm of the city taken as a whole where entire epochs could be divined from the style of buildings that cohered like forest groves and ran through the warp of the environment like earth strata each one offering up its tidbits of plant life, pottery shards and bones. Those were not left to tell the tale. The only works of men that endured were artificial and idealized because the real had been shunted off to the grave with the Kaeien.

"Doesn't she live around here somewhere?" Straining her neck, looking out the window, "I'm sure this is the neighborhood," and added without pause, "she had her breasts done didn't she?"

"How would I know?" he replied in amused exasperation.

"I'd say first hand. One day slim, scrawny, the next... Did I make a mistake not dating that plastic surgeon?"

"I thought you didn't on moral grounds."

"It's relative."

"To what?"

"Will she be there tonight?"

"Who?"

"Comon'..."

"Probably."

He breathed deeply of her scent in the car. It was a mixture of green rose hips and spice, just what nature of spice he couldn't ascertain, but it was very appealing to him and in fact it was what first attracted him to her. It was as if her hair was curled cinnamon bark and her clothing woven comfrey leaves.

"Do you dream any more?" she asked absently.

"I do, sometimes."

"Not all the time?"

"I don't know. I'm asleep."

"I don't."

"What?"

"Dream anymore."

"At all?"

"No."

"I don't believe it."

The woman was silent for a moment. She watched the structures streaming by and within each street she knew were thousands of stories and was suddenly gripped in the sadness that she had nothing to do with most of them and nothing at all to do with the creation of the buildings or the streets or the lives that inhabited them. It was just too big, too overwhelming and entirely out of her grasp. She had long ago decided to settle into her existence and make a place for herself from which she could fend off the rapid change and chaos around her and have a proud story, which she had not yet written. The dreams were the first to go so she just slept, coldly and without vision of any kind.

"I had a dream the other night," the man offered up as if proof. "I was sculpting a huge stone, massive, ten or twelve feet tall, without any plan or drawing of any kind. I just picked up a hammer and chisel and went to work."

The woman looked at him as if expecting a punch line, but nothing followed and the man just kept driving. "So what happened?"

He looked over and smiled. "I spent the whole night doing it."

"How did you know what to do?"

He frowned, looked straight ahead, "I dunno, it was like the figures were trapped inside straining against invisible bindings and all I had to do was lay the chisel to the stone and let the magic happen. To release them, I just had to release them and so I never stopped working until I died." He just kept looking straight as if trying to glean its meaning from the air.

There had been huge excitement at sFx Technos for the past three months. The talented had been hand picked from the masses of digerati artists; the 3D animators, programmers, wire frame modelers, layout geniuses, digital motion specialists, compression technicians, sys-ops, colorists, conceptual art directors, designers, interactive writers, ad infinitum– hand picked by Crayton who, although only in his mid-twenties, had achieved a status among the computer imaging literate of Guru, Major Domo and Grand Poobah combined into one gloriously advanced package. Creative teams were formed around the requirements dictated by CWVT and, of course, Roxanne who was the *Angel*, omnipotent and sublime.

Crayton had agonized over the thousands of applicants, but in the end was exceedingly proud that there was no one past the age of twenty-nine on his staff and because of that absorbed the glowing tributes and sycophant fawning that he believed anyone with his exceptional talents deserved. It was because of this hidden addiction, this silent and unwholesome need that he felt threatened whenever Roxanne would visit or even when she had the dailies downloaded to her own private server to inspect the progress of the work off premise. Her calls ruffled him, her comments designed with such barbs, careless and cruel without the slightest awareness or remorse at the other end... as if he needed to be told what to do, to be creatively directed ten to fifteen times a day whenever the spirit moved her, even in the middle of the night sometimes when Roxanne's insomnia drove her to reinspect the preceding day's work and in the early hours found more to change, to alter and bring into agreement with her view of things. In the end he followed her instructions, was exceedingly polite and spoke through his teeth with such practiced expertise that on the Vidtel he sounded perfectly normal. He knew she was not perceptive enough to discern his real feelings. As such he knew that she held the power and he, contrary to the image he had carefully nurtured, was only one of the vast army of service personnel she, like all other sources of wealth, commanded. He hated the way she patronized him and grew more and more resentful as the project continued until some nights he couldn't even sleep, but stayed awake imagining terrible plots to exact his revenge at being constantly slighted and insulted. Nonetheless she was the hand that fed him and so he oversaw the project albeit with intense jealousy over his ideas as opposed to hers or anyone else's for that matter. Crayton soothed his wounds with the thought that, like all truly great artists, he had to sublimate some of his brilliance for the sake of cash. Money was, after all, the source.

"She's here!" Ghina face shone around the sculpted stainless steel wall that separated Crayton's office from the rest.

He sighed deeply letting the complete apathy of sadness escape through his lips and turned from his involvement with the computer and spoke in a low deliberate tone. "Make sure everything is set up. You know how upset she got last time when there was no coffee."

In the hallway Roxanne was already occurring. She no longer arrived or just walked, since her brush with true power wherever she happened to be was an experience, a presence that materialized on the spot in full force and radiance. Her entourage from CWVT floated close to her shoulders keeping one half step back and the digerati crowded around her in a throng coming down the hallway to the viewing room where the fruits of their recent work were to be critiqued. Already the mixed aromas of gourmet food, coffee and fresh cut flowers filled the space as the preparation for her arrival had been going on since early in the morning. For the patron saint of the house of sFx Technos there were no needs unanticipated.

In the darkened room with a huge circular glass table a shaft of filtered light spilled from the infinite blackness of the ceiling a full two stories above down in a perfect halo ringing the room and all who sat in it with the flickering of a late summer afternoon peering through Hickory or Sycamore leaves. It had been Crayton's idea and only a hint of his master plan to achieve the true nature of an interactive, virtual environment. The season could be programmed in as well as the wind speed blowing the leaves, and even the genus of tree. It was, he had said, a reconnection to the natural world that had become so foreign to most people since the Kaiein and besides it made the clients comfortable and gave him a chance to show off a little of their technology. He had a more sinister motive however, which was greed, the more at ease the clients the more likely they were to go with the program and not try to interject any of their inane ideas into the art. Roxanne however was different. She was immune, cold and oblivious of any attempts to subtly influence her opinions. Crayton sat beside her and despite his fury was strangely attracted to the woman.

Roxanne's fingers played upon her lower lip with her left hand and her eyes darted around the room enticing excitement from the space. She had become so electrified in the past several months that she could hardly contain herself and was constantly searching for the live feed where she could plug into the sensation she needed to fuel the power. Her right hand flashed up and with the ubiquitous remote control she always carried switched one of the Vidtel monitors suspended in the black space around the table to CWVT, and then absently cycled through all the other channels she considered worthwhile to view.

"Right..." intoned Ghina, "We should have had CWVT playing."

"Not really," Roxanne replied automatically with pronounced indifference.

Crayton was stimulated by the recent work they had been doing and was excited to show it, but tried not to appear over eager. "We've got some good stuff to show you."

"Good? Is that all?"

Swallowing hard to keep from any appearance of emotion Crayton smiled grimly. "You know what I mean."

Roxanne turned her full attention to him. He hated it when she did that, it made him uncomfortable and aroused when he did not want to be and he always thought of the friend's mother he had known when he was a boy who always made him have torrid sexual dreams and whom he could not face.

"I know what you mean, let's have a look." She placed her hand on his thigh touching it with just the tips of her fingers, which did not help matters. To her he was a malleable object and she viewed him with little contrast so that he blended into the environment having just about the same significance as everything else other than the fact that he reacted differently to her. Those were details she noticed and kept mental notations of all the different ways to make him sweat, like Yzak who she could bring to his knees with just the anticipation. She seemed to have become more beautiful since her meeting with the power, delicate and translucent with pouting lips and clear smooth skin a fully blossomed flower pregnant with sensuality. If there were any direction from God to the dynamic impulses that coursed through her she would surely have taken hold the hand of creation and followed it into infinity. As it was Roxanne could not understand why she hadn't been able to defile this boy-man and possess his conscience as well as his fealty and she imagined depraved acts she could bring him to that would ensnare him to the opiate. For this reason he was nervous around her and compelled to strange impulses that never before had crossed his mind and felt drawn to her and repulsed at the same time.

"Alright," Crayton said resigned to his lot, "here we go everyone." And the room fell silent with Roxanne's entourage sitting quietly in expensive business suits and the digerati pensively awaiting the verdict.

As the lights faded the sound came up with a deep reverberating wave that nearly lifted the furniture off the floor. The bass cut through to the bone. Light flared and all twenty-seven monitors suspended in the dark came alive as one with a flash of full streaming light. People slunk back down into their chairs gripping the armrests as the force of the moment took hold. Roxanne had seen the rough cut of the program a week earlier and on her approval had introduced Virtual Dimention-alism technology into the final digital edit passing it through to Yzak anonymously to work his magic on even though the technique was now finally stable enough for any technician to duplicate and create the same results, she wanted him to do this program, the finest yet. The the monitors had all been replaced with the new hybrids and the viewers in the small room were bathed in the mega-light radiation at maximum power just the way it would be shown in commercial Virtual establish-ments, or on a new home unit. The results were frightening.

Three people went unconscious within the first five minutes, with their eyes open. It was only for brief intervals fading in and out of awareness, but it was without completely realizing what was taking place all the while being fed the virtual experience in a continuous flow. That was the real art Roxanne knew, the unawareness, and why she had needed sFx Technos to accomplish it. There were three streams that composed the piece, the first the visually obvious that carried the story line and cohesiveness and it was a work of great beauty and sensitivity. Beneath this was a sub-text complete with fleeting images barely seen, subliminal and completely integrated within the digital picture sequence of the main program done with the 3D, holographic digital imaging processes pioneered by sFx Technos. Still further from consciousness was the core of Virtual Dimentionalism that had its base in pulses of light. Digital signals that along with the pictures made up a complete visceral and emotional package that could be recalled to the surface at any time with the right stimuli. Only Roxanne knew that, the others, the digerati and most importantly Crayton only knew of the highly complex imaging job where all their proprietary technology and hers combined to create a living story line that was so completely absorbing the difference between it and actual occurrence in the mind was nil. It was as perfect a virtual experience as could be imagined and certainly decades ahead of any other network and, much to the chagrin of Crayton, far superior to any technology he had yet developed.

Roxanne thrilled at the force of light and sound she was experiencing and felt more and more stimulated with each passing instant. The right stimuli, she thought, was something only she and a few others would know. And it was implanted there, in the viewer's minds for her use, or as the pact was made hers and Hisham Mostafa 'Ali Fayed Al-Razio. It was he who had the vision and the resources and even Roxanne had not the nerve to betray him. However not any single person other than she would fathom the whole key code and that was why the set up was perfect. The sFx Technos had their part, and Yzak had his, each autonomous of the other and each thinking it was their contribution that gave the piece its might, but it was the unknown that did that. Let Al-Razio dictate subliminal content, only one had it all. She exalted while bathing in the light as the realization came over her that true power came from possessing the key, the one element that nobody else had or could duplicate without her. It was her ticket to the future, to the blinding heights where the air was rare and lacked sufficient oxygen for normal people, dare she intimate mortals, to exist. Roxanne postulated herself in the shadows of the gods if not in their place.

The man and the woman had arrived and met their friends and now sat close together in a booth on the far wall of a virtual club called the *Iron Storm*. No one questioned why it was called that for things in the night needed little explanation owing to their phantom existence that vaporized with the light. Drinks were spread out on the table and there were two other couples sitting with them. The seats were high backed padded chairs the kind one would imagine to be found in a space ship, but never were, ringing a metallic table suspended over the center of which was a 360-Monitor whose picture tube wrapped around the circular set like a cigar band.

"I can't believe you were a sculpture," the woman lifted the man's right hand, "look at those hands."

"Sculptor," he corrected.

"That's what I said."

"No, you said sculpture."

"Same thing."

"Have another drink you two." A man from across the table tossed off.

The woman next to him sat back languidly in her high tech seat with a leg up over the arm rest slouched to one side as if she were more uncomfortable with the modern design than with the chair itself. Her hair was black and unruly and her hooded eyes shot piercing glances around the room. She sipped from her cocktail and watched people coming and going. "When were you a sculptor?"

"In a dream. It was a dream, that's all."

Across the table a slender young woman with very fair skin and straw colored hair brightly pointed out, "They say dreams are simply memories of other lifetimes."

"Who says?" asked her male companion.

A sidelong glance. "*They* do."

"I think she means it's a common idea." Said the man who sat with the black haired woman. "Don't most people feel they've lived before?"

"You can give me a break now..." the man said mockingly feeling a subtle unease.

The other man by the black haired woman looked at him oddly. "What?"

"Raiffe, were not kids... that's what they all think you know."

"Are they right?"

"I think," Harry, the third man said, "there's a lot to be said for having lived before."

Isabel the fair skinned young woman agreed, "Right."

"You're kidding. Have you all been holding out on me?" He turned to the woman beside him, "Well..."

"Don't look at me, I don't even dream anymore."

"You've got an opinion don't you?"

"Yea, it scares me. What if someone were after me from an earlier lifetime and I couldn't remember who it was...or worse, who I was?"

"What if you were after someone?" laughed Harry.

"Funny," she frowned, but then smiled and looked sideways at the man next to her, "but come to think of it...'

"I don't believe this. Have you all joined some cult?"

"Hey...! Maybe we're just more open minded than you." Raven, the dark haired woman quipped bitingly.

"Ha!" he said. "You're jealous that's all." The man paused for a moment, and then took another sip from his drink and was silent. He looked into the face of the woman across from him and felt a sudden wave of loss. They'd never been intimate, but that was what he'd wanted and she'd just drifted away without a sign to follow and beyond the barrier was the secret. He could never know it and now it was irretrievable so perhaps they were right, his thinking was too narrow. But he didn't really think so.

"Of what?"

"Questions," his head spun slightly with the effects of the alcohol, "never agree with anything without questions."

"Haven't you ever felt déjà vu?"

"Of course, but that doesn't mean I agree with it. It's just an illusion."

"Transitory reality is just an illusion," said Harry, "isn't that what the virtual experience is all about? The real is what you perceive."

"Maybe, but not if you don't agree with it."

The woman next to him was enjoying the whole exchange and watched it build with eyes slowed and made languid from the drinks. "I think you're just arguing for the sake of argument."

The man raised his glass in a toast. "There is no better way for students to learn from the master."

"I remember my past lives sometimes," the woman next to him said, "One I remember all the time."

"I thought you said you didn't dream."

"I don't. This is different."

"What do you remember?" Raven asked.

"A harbor town. A ship. Cool air, the smell of salt and the sound of gulls crying out over a still morning bay."

Harry asked, "How do you know it's a past life?"

"Right," Isabel added, "maybe it's just a…figment."

"It's a waking dream," she paused, "like I said I don't have them when I'm asleep."

"So tell us about it." Raiffe said in a deep, quiet voice and then sipped his drink feeling relaxed.

"The police come to my door to question me and I remember a sense of strength," pausing to look at them all, "tangible strength. I was full of energy. I recall the view down the dirt road from my house to the harbor and the yellow morning light just filtering through the fog. It was cold. I could see my breath. The policemen were wrapped in black cloaks. They stood on my door steps made of round river stones an old man who had happened by one day had built for me in exchange for a meal and a place to stay the night. He slept in the shed. Something about a man, a bad man…an outlaw. They were all sailors–sailors in that life."

"I like that," Raven said her eyes sparkling, "What else do you recall?"
"Someone had been murdered, a pirate they said, though I didn't think of him in that way…weren't there privateers? He had been seen with me, no… that's not true… we hadn't been see together for a long time, he came to see the dancer, the one in the smoky cabaret, I hadn't seen him since spring except when he'd set sail that… I told them Tuesday dawn. Besides… well, they accused me… I remember being accused and dragging me off to see the magistrate. I told them I was at sea, I couldn't possibly have murdered him, I was at sea then. Ask the dancer, I told them, go ask the dancer… she knows."

After a pause in the story the man asked, "Then what?'

"Then nothing. That's all."

Oh no!" Cried Raven, "Now we'll never know what happened."

"One thing I can tell you..."

"What?" asked Isabel, "Tell us."

"I would have died rather than go with them."

"See," cried Harry, "nothing like that ever happens anymore. When was the last time you were willing to give up your life?"

"Monday when I had to go to work." The man replied sardonically.

"We don't have to now, it's virtual."

"Yea, that's the point isn't it? Life without the pain?"

"We..... I don't see what this has to do with having lived before."

"Hey people," Isabel offered enthusiastically holding up the virtual goggles, "we haven't even tried the program tonight."

"Lets do it," agreed Harry.

Each sitting back in his chair and adjusting the controls in front of them with practiced skill set the canvas. The 360-Monitor came to life above them. Each put on the VR goggles that had up to this point sat unnoticed on the table. They were silver with a thin lighted band across where the eyes would be and from it came a colorful display of pulses and hues. It wasn't as if they needed the goggles, it was well known that the new generation of 36-Monitors could produce a virtual effect superior to any known up to this point without goggles, certainly enough for the normal person out for a night of fun. For the stronger drug, the goggles were essential. It was the first taste, the brush with something mischievous, a crossing over from the acceptable to the reprehensible. It was indecent, in vogue and as with much fashion had its origins in the street. To *fuse* was holy. To completely lose oneself in the oblivion was the ultra of sociability. Even if it was just done once, one could say he's done it, be in the conversational patterns and have the ability to complete the elliptical sentences everybody talked in and that made up the substance of the networked Vidtel. It was the feeling of in-context that drew people to the virtual machines in the beginning. It was social. The true alienation lay across the land like a cold metal blanket that enveloped every soul within its web and drew from them the warmth, the vulnerability, and the ability to foresee the future along with any reason to live. To have fused then was to have touched the pantheon of the wise and to come away seared yet alive. Loneliness was the draw, the loneliness of life where one was unable to face the real.

As the new programming was funneled through to them they sat limply in the chairs, except for Raven who had too much endowed life energy in the body not to fight it and she turned and grimaced uncomfortably as she face the virtual world unleashed. All across the club there were other tables like theirs, with people sprawled in their high tech seats fusing or coming close to it. The belladonna romance has it's allure in the brush with the cold one, the one in the shadows who had no name but knew all names and his footsteps were the last sound before the chasm opened up and swallowed consciousness.

Across the ringed monitor flashed the layered images so skillfully woven and so artistically blended only a sFx technos could tell how it had been done. And even he would have trouble discerning the layers of action, the depth of sound and sublimation. In the end the users were not so sophisticated. They used drink and relaxation techniques to lay themselves more open and susceptible to the virtual experience. Real fusing however was the point at which the true believers were separated from the disaffected and great debates ensued to somehow glean the points of realization that were peppered throughout the experience from the base sensations that numbed the senses and took over volitional control of the body until consciousness returned in an effort tom legitimize the experience. The artists were drawn by the money, like moths they flocked to the flames of wealth and security leaving any altruistic practices to someone else. Money was, after all, the reason. The deftness with which they created the virtual programming exhibited a complete mastery of sound, color, shadow and light, story and drama and all the digital arts that went into making a complete program. Their audiences, captive all, were swept away.

Roxanne apprehensively looked around the table as lights slowly came back up to the soft filtered luminescence they had been at before the presentation. Faces appeared. She wanted a first look at each person as they readjusted themselves after having experienced the final version of what she considered the highest virtual art. Flawed, yes, but that was inherent in the process and would be thoroughly worked out by Crayton and his colleagues...but she knew, only she had the complete vision and they were bound, not just by contract, but by the laws of nature to follow her lead into the labyrinth. There was an electricity in the air, a stillness that was in motion, a fleeting, raging, quickening impulse that ran before reason bring emotions to the surface, obscuring logic, laying raw. The feeling fed her. It loomed towering above and then poured down through her until each nerve was vibrating with energy and she had to catch her breath and concentrate simply to focus on the table and those around it. However the questions still remained and could only be answered by others and Roxanne knew that when she no longer had uncertainties and could operate autonomous of their opinions she would be much happier, but she still needed them and it rankled her. The eyes told her what she wanted and as she looked around the room at the dazed, euphoric and some bewildered expressions she asked Ghina, who was at her right hand, "Let's examine this." She didn't want to ask pointed questions because she knew what the answers would be, she wanted a technical discussion where she could judge real feelings.

One man who sat across from her rubbed his eyes and then replacing his glasses spoke to the room letting his cheeks puff out sitting back solidly in his chair as if it would steady him and keep his thoughts from escaping too quickly before he'd had a chance to compose them. "It works." He announced.

"Oh?" Roxanne smoothly replied, "I'm interested."

The young man smiled mechanically. "I don't know about every-body else, "he looked from side to side, "but I was moved. Truly."

"It had some moments, some... really... some moments." The woman by Crayton offered up in a confessional way, "I was spellbound... I...the truth is I uh...I can't remember some of it, but I can tell you the whole story. Strange I feel like I lived it a long time ago."

"Perfect!" Crayton exclaimed under his breath.

"Well I think laying the images across the fades at the transitions might have been a bit premature...It could sustain a bit longer..."

"Roxanne interjected. "Can you fix that?"

"Oh yes, that's easy."

"Crayton?"

"Could be right," he reluctantly admitted.

Roxanne breathed deeply. "Do it." Looking over at Crayton she saw him frown and then decided he could not be allowed any more slack or he would ruin things with his artistic integrity. It was all about what people wanted, and people, this she knew with such certainty that it could not be any more intimate than her own name, were vulgar. They were crass and rough on the edges and rude in their tastes. That great seething, moving, roiling mass of voices that all speak as one and ebb and flow as the tides or as magnificent flocks of birds soaring and turning and diving headlong only to pull up at the last instant, thousands all in the same breath, in the same heartbeat, that huge, inconceivably numerous group that she thought of only as the *Target Market*. That was the beast that needed to be appeased, the consumer. It wasn't art that fueled them, not aesthetics nor drama nor cinematic jewels filled with symbolism and deep running currents of subtext and unspoken innuendo nor grace, style or any of the superficial transient qualities of entertainment. It was the thrill, the rush, the seduction. It wasn't something she could speak of because it was too close to her and was an integral part of her talent, but she knew that when she touched the nerve there was a jolt and then it was certain the tack was right. Why it was that the world was this way, that people needed lives they perceived better than their own, needed stories and emotions much greater than they believed they could muster, adventures and ephemeral touches with greatness that could never be in their own temporal existences she could not say and had never even speculated on. For the one great truth that she had known and had pivoted her entire life around was that one discovered what was needed and wanted, and then delivered it. Simple. People needed life, and she gave it to them. And now, she would give them thoughts as well placing each like a polished sapphire into the psyche of her audience. One person at a time.

The indescribable ecstasy the surge of power gave her was finer, more malicious and certainly more addictive than any drug and though she could not understand why people were the way they were and why they wanted such things she would give them with blessings. No one could be allowed between her and the ascendancy, not Crayton, not anyone. But she knew what he wanted, better than he, for that was her talent and her art.

The meeting drug on for three hours and Roxanne was sure each person in the presentation had been deeply affected and had gone far into the virtual experience despite any reticence present at the beginning. As the time passed her agitation did not dissipate and she felt a wild emotional energy that gave her a sensation verging on the edge of hysteria. Her hand shook slightly, her eyes darted towards Crayton and their looks occasionally met, but he was uncomfortable under her gaze and turned away quickly. She played with him knowingly because this time he could not retreat, there was too much at stake and so when the others began filing out of the room she turned to him. "Stay," she said touching his forearm with her fingers, "I have work for you."

They sat in silence for a few long moments. She watched as the last person closed the door and he fumed at having to acquiesce to her again. His emotions were ambivalent towards the woman whom he saw out of the corner of his eye slide into a low, comfortable chair away from the table letting her animal-like legs stretch out making her usual brief skirt appear even shorter. It wasn't the sight of her exposed flesh that made him nervous, it was what wasn't visible–a current ran between them. He couldn't read her well if at all and what little acumen he possessed for judging people was short circuited when he was near her for he could never tell what her mood might be or what request she might have. He admitted though that the technology she produced was extravagant and far advanced of what they had been able to achieve and he began to think of his efforts as inconsequential compared to hers. At first he could not believe it, unable to grasp the fact that there was a more sophisticated programming than the proprietary brilliance they had used to stand the industry on it's ear and after the first edit was layered with the additions made by her code writer, the one she wouldn't speak of, that no one knew, they had tried to deconstruct it in order to plumb its secrets, but could not. The closest they had been to understanding its nature was the idea that it somehow depended on a hardware mechanism though they didn't know how or what that mechanism was.

Now he was a believer, but he had come through the humiliation and was still angry. Ghina was completely frustrated by the fact that he was irritated at the biggest thing to ever happen to sFx Technos, the client that was making them all rich. Crayton couldn't help it and though she thought it was an artistic altruism and constantly reassured him that the presentation of the work was at the height of vogue, that wasn't it at all. He just hated to be wrong, and hated somebody else in control. The dichotomy ate at him. Drawn by some mysterious genetic impulse beyond his understanding and repulsed by a need to be the only one with the answers she confused and bewildered him.

"I'm exhausted." Roxanne said, but she wasn't. She rarely went to bed before two AM and even then stayed up reading unable to sleep. There was just too much energy and she finally came to the conclusion that she didn't need sleep and that it was non productive and the only real good it did was to give her a chance to compose her thoughts. It was the potency of what she had tapped into that more and more ruled her life and gave her a physical vitality she had never had before. "I think it's good, but it needs work."

"What kind of work." Crayton tried to be civil but it came out stiff and ingenuous.

"The kind that only you can do," she replied with a saccharine quality to her voice. "I wish you weren't so hostile, nobody else around here is."

He sighed and felt humiliated. "Sorry."

"Sit down here. I think it needs...I don't know...what d'ya call it... jazz. Yes. It needs more jazz."

"Jazz?"

"Perfect. I knew you'd understand."

"But I don't understand."

"You just said...look, it's got the power right now and the emotional appeal, that'll get the women demos, but men...it's got to have more jazz to it. They're different at least in access and prime. I don't know about the other periods as much."

Crayton struggled to be civil and not let his emotions influence his vocal quality. "What's jazz?" He'd discovered years ago that if he could control his vocal mannerism he could deal with the most difficult clients and make them happy while still hating them. It was one of his most successful actions and had made him a lot of money and proved to him that most clients were fools.

"Jazz is what men do," she said bitingly. "It's a little risqué, it's got corners on it, hard to handle, it's bitter like black coffee."

"I didn't write this thing."

"It's not the script…"

"If it isn't the story line you're talking about then what do you mean?"

Roxanne looked at him with an expression of determination. "Crayton, you've got to get a hold of this thing it goes on air next Friday."

"I got a hold on it alright, I just don't know what *jazzzz* is!" He droned and immediately felt remorse that he had let his emotion betray him.

Roxanne smiled with her usually feminine lips drawn up into a tough little smugness pleased with herself. *It was the first piece crumbling,* she thought and said, "It's like fucking Crayton, it's like fucking."

He just looked at her for a moment, and then sighed a quick, impatient sigh, "Jeeeze! Makes perfect sense… really gives me a good grip on it."

"A woman makes love, she has sex, does something you know? There's an emotional attachment to things that is uniquely female. A man however is fucking someone. And believe me, we're talking demographics, it's in the nomenclature that men use, the frame of reference, they're not the same and there are certain things they respond to and the numbers reflect that. We want numbers on this, that's why we came to you in the first place. You're the best right?"

"I used to think so."

"I'd like to hear your suggestions."

"Do you want more subliminal in the piece?"

She regarded him for a moment while she calmly sat in the low chair with her hands folded in her lap. Then she crossed her legs letting the skirt ride up even more than it already was and carefully watched him keeping her gaze steady and saw his eyes follow her motion. "I want you to be creative."

In the shadowed room with the dappled light filtering down from the black recesses it was the mystery of the age that enveloped their conversation. They spoke of gigabytes, terrabytes and data streams, network connections and holographic layered digital transitions, they alluded to the symbolism that would reinforce the content and the compression ratios and how that would effect whether certain images and effects could be seen in transmission if their file size was too small to support the bit depth and image quality necessary for layered sublimation. Roxanne could see that he was not the intellect that Yzak was, but the challenge was somehow more stimulating because he had an attitude. She finally bewitched him into speaking openly, freely and creatively although he was by nature restrained and terse in his comments preferring to do his work alone and in his own universe. Now he spoke with a fluid quality and sketched out small likenesses on the napkins that were left over from the breakfast and even smiled slightly. She was pleased with what he had offered as solutions and came to an agreement on the changes to be made, but was even more pleased that he was closer to where she wanted him than ever before now that she sat by his side and placed her hand deliberately on his thigh touching him lightly with her fingertips. Roxanne could not help but notice that his eyes would travel down her legs when he thought she was not looking and she moved with a practiced expertise using her body as a business tool until beads of perspiration appeared on his forehead.

Then with her hand dangerously poised on the inside of his thigh she abruptly announced, "I have to go." And, after pausing a moment to gaze with coquettish innocence into his eyes she rose quickly to the door. As if her power now began to encompass the magic arts Crayton arose after her and suddenly was standing so close she could feel his breath on her neck. "Do you have something else to say?" She chided virtuously, "Have we forgotten anything?"

"I..." he stumbled embarrassed.

Roxanne quickly ran her left hand up the back of his neck and loosely grabbed a hand full of hair then pulled him very slowly close and touched her lips to his with her gaze wide open. He did not move, but closed his eyes. His breathing came in rapid pulses that beat on her lips like hot rain and she could not remember a man who had ever had such a high body temperature. With an imperceptible slowness she pulled him to her until her breasts were just barely against his and felt the roughness of his shirt through her thin silk blouse. Their lips gradually came together and begin to create a full kiss. She felt his heart beat. In an instant her right hand was at the top of his trousers fiddling with the clasp, pulling and twisting not knowing what type it was until finally it released and at the same time Crayton sucked in his breath. Still they kissed without moving their lips silently drawing closer, heads motionless in the way a hawk can ride the thermal updrafts with his feathers buffeted and wings splaying constantly adjusting for the right angles to keep him from diving to the rocks below yet keeping his head absolutely motionless. His pants fell open in one deft motion as her hand expertly moved in a way that he could hardly perceive and she felt the power grow inside her with this coup de grace quietly finding his warm naked flesh and letting her hand slide down his belly into the dense mass of fur. Her fingers encircled him and he stayed completely still. *He is hot,* she mused, *the hottest man I've ever felt.* Roxanne did not move her hand, but just held him gently in her palm letting his skin burn her and then slowly pulling away from the kiss watching his face, waiting for his eyes to open. And then they did. Crayton looked at her from under a hooded brow unsure of himself and not knowing whether to back away or press forward and feeling pulled in both directions at once suddenly reeling with the embarrassment of being exposed and under this strange woman's control.

Roxanne smiled sweetly, cruelly, and with the scent of her in his nostrils hoarsely whispered, "Your temperature's rising." And then was gone through the door leaving him with his shirttail out.

The man and the woman sped from the elegant neighborhood where the virtual clubs vied for the attention of the affluent and the well to do caring little where the money came from as long as it came.

Their car darted like a deep maroon arrow into the nightfall streaked with amber fog, cyan blue lights and the flaring of headlamps blinking across the metropolitan landscape. They turned and headed their own way with other drivers cloaked in anonymity racing to destinations that couldn't even be guessed at. Inside the air conditioning was still on from earlier in the evening, but now it chilled them and both turned up the collars of their coats not thinking to turn it off. A billion lights danced and flickered before them each a mirror in the darkness of a life in the fabric and symbols of the dependence of all upon raw electrical energy, which has one face of goodness and another of evil.

They turned at the rise of a small hill and swooped down the cataract that funneled over a thousand cars an hour into the expressway that was the vast network of arteries without which the city would fail.

The woman leaned back in her seat and let her head rest on the cushion. "I wish we were flying," she drawled in a nervous voice tinged with sadness.

"We are," the man replied, and when she looked over at him he added, "Magnetic beams...remember?"

"It's not the same...you know, I mean really flying so we could go somewhere."

They streaked past sections of the city that had become self enclosed environments sealed off by popular vote as a defense against crime or ideology, incorporated and defended against interlopers by private security forces. At the bottom of the off ramps were border crossings where traffic backed up for hours at busy times. The enclaves engendered political ideas ranging from the radical to the benign making them havens for the like minded, but the man and the woman didn't care about these places because fringe elements had little effect on the mainstream, they lived in the regular city where people just like them lived and worked and acted in almost exactly the same manner. If one were to describe people so similar to each other it would seem strange, but living amongst them it was a comfort because there was nothing out of the ordinary. The odds against two individuals being so similar and having so many identical characteristics were almost inconceivably huge as the one quality distinguishing a person from another is his individuality. Nobody, however, ever questioned this fact or ever saw it as unusual in any way. This was why the man felt compelled to speak.

"I feel sort of lost somehow, you know?"

The woman looked at him, but not with any glint of understanding or hope on her face just a grim determination and quipped, "In what way?"

"It's hard to describe." The car sped carelessly down the center lane of the expressway slicing through the night at high speed with abandon leaving the past in its wake. "I suppose it's a feeling of being without purpose, of having no roots whatsoever, in motion all the time." He replied wistfully.

She looked at his profile as he drove and thought how strange it was to be so close to someone and never really know them. "Like a bird that can't ever land?"

"Yea..." he considered it, "that's it."

"Me too sometimes."

He was having trouble focusing on the road and controls and was deluged with mental image pictures of the virtual experience they had gone through earlier along with waves of tiredness that made his eyes drowsy. The woman too was feeling tired, but for different reasons didn't connect it to the activities that had just happened. She had almost become accustom to the apathy that had set in over her life and a bit more now and again did not tip the scales in either direction. They kept searching for something that would infuse them with the vitality that had slipped from their grasp as they consumed more and more entertainment culminating in the virtual experiences and tonight fusing. At least she thought it was fusing. All control had been lost at one point and she had to restrain herself from going further under and in fact struggled back when she began to fall so deeply that a chill consumed her with the thought she may never regain consciousness. It was an ethereal terror, not a physical one that she had ever experienced before and affected her in dark and subtle ways she was just now recognizing. There was a pang of conscience accompanying the thought that she had been morally scarred by her transgression and had degraded herself irreparably that lingered.

The car soared effortlessly hovering less than an inch above the magnetic rails that kept it on its course and from caroming off into the guard rails or into some other vehicle out on its mission under the mantle of stars unseen behind the cloak of atmosphere three centuries of industrialization had created. They were quiet now, the man and the woman, with only the blanket of travel sounds around them alluding to any life force. The subdued hiss of the air conditioning and the whir of the droning engine mingled with the sound of the airflow outside the carefully sealed cockpit in a white noise that had no personality of its own. There were occasional sounds from traffic, which was nominally heavy, such as horns and exceptionally noisy motors–all of the engineering brilliance combined in order to create an environment separate from the road where the occupants were lulled into a sense of invulnerability by reason of their detachment from the exhaust ridden, dust filled, smog laden rough and oil soaked filth that was the expressway. Millions of vehicles passed over its surface without the slightest maintenance until some random disaster when politicians rallied to the cause quickly pointing out the culprits somewhere in the transit district bureaucracy. It is possible that some defect in the human makeup required this event to take place before any action with foresight could occur. An unconfrontable disaster with the wholesale spilling of blood and the tragic overtones of loss to the families and the society were the exacted price of progress.

Without any warning there was a noise. It was not a huge noise like the crushing sounds of granite being ground to powder by the shifting of the Earth's tectonic plates, but it was nonetheless substantial, and because it was metal against metal especially alarming while riding in a car hurtling through space at nearly 120 miles per hour. Neither the man or the woman flickered with any sense of recognition each lost in their own separate world attempting to figure out the complex puzzle of the mind that was invading their conscious thoughts with images of the recent virtual experience followed by earlier pictures of earlier similar virtual experiences. Each hoped they could cleanse themselves of the imperfections and find resurrection and renewal. The night grew darker and the gas lamps high above the roadway flared in the murky air an olive yellow casting their glow down upon the nameless travelers. Looming up ahead was the first of the Tunnels, the interchange of twenty-seven levels where the traffic was caught in the web, stirred and redirected toward destinations across the metropolis and as they, surrounded by a pack of other cars, were finally enveloped. They didn't notice the rooster tail shower of sparks that was trailing out from behind their vehicle and presenting a light show to other passing motorists, some of which waved and sounded their horns frantically trying to get the man and woman's attention. Their thoughts were already completely absorbed introspected into their own universes trying to sort out the images that ran out of control through their consciousness. The last thing the woman saw as she looked across the cab at the man driving was a faint, indistinct image of a person in a passing car frantically waving at her and somewhere in her consciousness an alarm sounded.

That was the moment it happened. All the expressways were flat, there were no embankments or allowances for centrifugal force because for eighty years vehicles had a gyro mechanism as an integral part making it virtually impossible to roll over or go wildly out of control. Speed limits had slowly been raised, 120 MPH was normal. A bolt that held the gyro mechanism loosened with vibration and finally let go. The system had immediately been caught by another piece of metal and that held it from flying out completely, but began to grind against it sending out the shower of sparks and quickly shearing it. There was a bone jarring vibration. The woman startled from her reverie saw the wheel wrench from the man's hands so violently that his arm bent back and broke and his face was slammed against the driver's side window. And then they were floating as the car became airborne on a turn clipping a truck as it lifted off and rolled in perfect form exactly once before it landed again, wheels down and skimmed sideways across eight lanes of magnetic beams heading for the wall where the pedestrian malls were and the train stops. She saw him bloodied and dangling limply unconsciousness as he was thrown around like a dead fish with the vicious motion of the car jamming into the ground, then other cars and ultimately the rampart. She imagined screaming from people all around her and for a split instant wished she could scream as well, but there wasn't time. The woman was thrown around furiously just held restrained by her seat and shoulder harness. The moment lasted eternally. An instant in the eyes of God.

They slammed into the wall with terrible force making pieces explode off the car and fly in all directions. Other cars that had been hit recovered their equilibrium quickly with the advantage of their gyros working perfectly, and aside from structural and sheet metal damage there were only minor injuries. Her sense of duty was empowered as they slid along the wall of the curve with a trail of smoke, dust and sparks rising a hundred feet in the air behind them, and she wished she could attend to everyone who had involvement and make them perfect again because she couldn't stand the fact of being responsible for injury to another. Just when it seemed they were slowing a bus full of people pulled out of the mall and into their path as she watched with infinite detail each consecutive instant as they drew nearer and finally hit their right rear corner. It was as if the world was suddenly illuminated by strobe light as the images of what was happening to her piled up one after the other in her mind and then replayed themselves as animation. The car hooked onto the corner of the bus and flipped end over up across the wall and sliding through the general concourse of the mall finally coming to rest wedged in a corner up against a retail arcade whose neon lights burned brightly through the smoke and debris.

Suddenly there was silence. It hung over her as a pall of smoke on a cold, windless day and was so filled with mass she could have touched it. A thousand hours passed in a breath. Her eyes looked at the man who hung lifeless from his seat held in place by strategic straps of the belting system. His face was covered with blood. She noticed the windows had not shattered and though she did not move her head could see the cabin of the car was relatively undamaged though askew from the sprung frame and collapsed roof and doors. Outside the sheet metal was torn and scrapped and ripped into tattered knives. She gasped hard. Then again. And called to the man, reaching over and touching his arm with her hand. He jerked back quickly and as he struggled back to awareness wiped the blood from his eyes with his one good arm. The first thing he saw was the woman looking back.

"What the hell..."

"Do you hurt?" she whispered intimately, urgently.

He shook his head in disbelief and confusion.

The woman repeated, this time more insistent. "Do you *hurt?*"

Looking down at his body which was soaked with blood from his head he kept shaking his head and finally looked straight at her and said, "No." with disbelief. "Do you?"

"I don't think so."

Then the realization hit them that despite injuries they were both alright, that whatever furies might have been abroad that night they had passed them over. It hadn't been their time. Suddenly they felt as if a monumental weight had lifted and the environment appeared brighter and more lucid than either could remember it being for a very long time. They both felt giddy and light at once and began to laugh, and kept laughing until the glee spilled over into hysteria. So when their rescuers rushed up to the crumpled mass of hot, smoking, jagged, ruined metal they were confronted by two bloodied people bound inside the death cage where rightly they should have had their final moments laughing frantically barely able to gasp enough breath to keep alive.

- XII -

The Egress

He remembered the trees. They had danced in the fierce wind that had beset the city for a week now that had tried to unearth their roots and let their feet take flight to follow the wild, thrashing arms deep into memories of earlier forests. The great groves had fallen. Long ago the last woodsman had his say and watched the sun roll off the tip of the earth through the twining aromatic wisps of pipe smoke.

Nash was cognizant of these things as he sat quietly with full conscience and listened for the woman to talk while the amber afternoon light seeped in through the windows. The room smelled with the musky sweetness of humans. The air was filled with the echoes of trees that lived only in remembrance. The woman cried out with a mournful almost inaudible tone that floated up into the air where the trees had danced and others had come and gone as shadows. Nash listened and though he experienced an overwhelming compulsion to reach out and in some small manner give comfort to the ageless turmoil he had uncovered in the her, but he did not. That wasn't the way. She fell silent again and Nash wondered what visions had passed unseen before her eyes as images in the mind and had violated her secret gate without knowledge causing her to murmur so poignantly. It was by his command that she sat so vulnerable and alone chasing down the demons in her mind and the minister felt the weight of it.

The woman before him was confused. Her hair was gray and dry and thinning. Her eyes were full of storms. She could not understand why her daughter had chosen to alienate herself. "I worked my whole...", she paused and raised her hands in front of her chest as if trying to grasp thin air, " ...life! God dammit!" she uttered in a completely futile gesture trying to muster up enough energy to overcome the sadness that was enveloping her. "She's ungrateful." In a moment added quietly, "I don't think I was," the word was difficult to say, "*rich* enough for her." She sat back in the old chair slouched down with shoulders hunched over and hands clasped together with arms straight between her legs and looked at the floor. It was the waiting that she hated and in the end dogged her as she now was coming to the realization that whatever it was she'd expected to happen was long overdue and the chances of it occurring were slim. Still she waited.

Nash truly didn't know the cause of the woman's bitter disposition though he had seen it all his life in one form or another and listened to the words having enough wisdom not to offer any of his own solutions. He had observed that no matter how much it was talked about and how purposefully he tried to solve the problems for someone else things never seemed any better and in fact sometimes they got even more distraught. So he was respectfully silent, but he couldn't help watching Sabiha across the room in the shadows behind them. The woman just needed a conduit to empty her spiritual baggage into and once having done so felt immediately better without knowing why. It was a mystery to Nash as well. He had learned to politely acknowledge the ones who thanked him profusely when he felt he had done nothing more than listen because if he didn't it would break the faith between them. Clearly there were mysteries of the soul that had not been answered. God was the cauldron into which all enigmas were cast through the millennium and he had to fight the urge to follow the tradition because it was so easy to reach a certain point and then declare it was God's will. Perhaps he was more pragmatic or at worst just an atheist hiding behind the cloth so that no one would know he was so vapid as to have a lack of faith. Faith not reason being the one quality that actually separated men from animals.

It had been three weeks since Sabiha visited him. She had come in her strange way and hovered off in the dark wings of the Cathedral where mourners at funerals sometime wept or jilted lovers stood during an unwelcome wedding. He attended to an early evening service having by this time developed a train of thought on the Canon and so could almost string his talks together as chapters hoping that in the end they would form a catalyst and make a profound statement on the nature of man's relationship to the universe. But somehow he knew it was in vain and the conflict between his own desires and the demands of his calling disturbed him. Afterward he sat for a time with a family he had a long relationship with and they explained plaintively to him the faults of a son with whom they had become estranged. That was when he saw her in the shadows. She may have been there through the sermon he did not know. It was her way. There was no darkness or any devious intent for her reticence around church functions–she just seemed uncomfortable. It was as if she knew that there was a divine way though exactly what it was remained obscured by failed help of the past and false promises of the present and so she held out for a clearer verdict. Nash knew the feeling well. His fingers could touch it as they would touch a clay pot and with the same cool, smooth certainty it embodied. He overcame those feelings, but it caused him a great sense of personal humiliation at times that he had not the strength to disagree and stand on his own, but only in the group could he fulfill his mission. The paradox of individuality and sublimation to the cooperative chaffed as flaws in his character.

"He knows." Sabiha exclaimed breathlessly while she followed him down the narrow hall to his office.

Nash shot her a look back over his shoulder, then continued straight ahead until he reached the door and asked while fiddling noisily with the lock, which he always set since the trouble with the High Advocator, "Did he say so?"

"Not in so many…"

"We can't be sure then."

Suddenly the door gave opening a crack. She pushed her way past him and sat sprawled in the corner of the old couch. "He knows," Sabiha said antagonistically, "it was obvious."

Nash sat down at his computer and absently switched it on as he was now in the habit of doing after spending so much time online searching the WEB for reference to Yzak, and more importantly the *Golden XiOma*. Then he swiveled to face her and held the bridge of his nose with thumb and forefinger. "What makes you so sure?"

Sabiha gasped impatiently exasperated. "Oh! Only the fact that he looked so startled when I mentioned the name, and questioned me about it...but it was his manner of intentional disregard that was the tip off."

"Really." Nash replied with interest.

"He's always nice to me."

"Is he?"

"Yes," she proffered up smugly and then with a hushed reserve, "He likes to sit near me...touch me..."

He just stared at her. "You didn't get any more information?"

"Oh!" she exclaimed with exaggerated offense sitting straight and throwing up her hands. "I was in the Under Secretary for Global Communications' office implying by my questions that he was involved in a mass conspiracy against the public and..." she fumbled for words her thoughts moving too quickly, "Isn't it enough that we know his reaction?"

"Then he's got to be with one of the networks."

"Iverson?"

"Our sideways "V" with-three-dots friend."

She frowned. "Obviously."

"What was it that Rozemund said?" Nash suddenly energized. "About the...uh...increased statistic in CenMed emergencies...? You know...?""

"CWVT." Sabiha pronounced with finality.

"Of course..." He pulled his lips together in a thin, taut line. "CommNET's got to be in on this...but why? What advantage could it give them?"

"Addiction," she replied instantly. "Nothing helps the ratings like compulsion."

Nash heard her, but did not acknowledge. Something else, something else I know..."

She shook her head and stood up to pace being more comfortable in motion. "Why? It's simple enough. If they get and keep the ratings then their contracts are secure."

"Because people always have an agenda."

Sabiha fell silent. She thought of the hundreds of eyes she had seen across the bargaining table in lost, hopeless negotiations where she was only a vehicle for words regardless of their intent. How many lives hung on the delicate threads of men's words. The ones who made the policy were the arbiters and by what means they reached their position she was never sure, where some gave rise to hope others to fear. It was random, arbitrary and had no basis other than the fact that it was the law and there were those who remained long enough, perhaps shuffled long enough or cajoled or connived or bought their way to become a voice in its making. What was the law then other than an agenda for special interests? She had seen it hundreds of times, the hidden plan, the unspoken covenant that stalled survival. "I'll go see Fionica." She said. "She'll be able to do something."

But Nash was on his own jag, his brow furled up into clouds of thought as he raced over memories trying to pull some sense out. "Do you remember what else Rozemund said?" He waited expectantly, and when he saw her dismay continued. "That this new flat panel monitor could generate enough power to knock people out?"

"Yes...something like that."

"I couldn't figure out why someone would want to do that. Now I think I have."

There was a cold silence. "Well...?" Sabiha urged.

Nash was not paying attention. He was talking to himself experiencing a chain cognition. "I think of... of course! McGilvery. You know he told me he'd been warned off certain cases of corporate hacking... what was it...? Oh! I got it. Until money was an issue. Money, do you get it? It's not the money."

"Would you tell me what the hell you're talking about because I don't understand a word?"

"It's ideas. Ideology. That's the hidden agenda! They're not worried about the money, at least...at least...he told me that as long as these hackers were only breaching the firewalls for data and code then he was not supposed to pay any attention, but when they got greedy...he got 'em! You see, it was easy; he could have arrested them any time. It wasn't money they were greedy for, it was information and they got too close."

"Don't you think CWVT is in it for the money?"

"Absolutely. But they're small time, they're not players here, they're being played."

Sabiha suddenly jumped up. "You recall what Fionica said about *EINF*? It laid you open to command, made one susceptible. Do you remember?"

"That's it!" Nash replied. "The means, the vehicle..."

"And the audience!" she interjected firmly.

"Somebody's implanting subliminal messages into the minds of the VT audience. What could they be?"

Sabiha added ominously. "Who could it be?"

In the silence Nash had time to inspect the woman's face. It was filled with stories and places and though she was not old each line spoke of her life, the exaltations and whispers and the breakings. He couldn't believe yet that his own life had changed so fundamentally, but what else could possibly have happened after finding the *Golden XiOma*. He was surprised that it was ordinary metal—gold in color, nothing special, just made to be durable, utilitarian. The woman's face was that way. Not beautiful but imbued with a sublime femininity that transcended the body and gave the impression of great loveliness. Her eyes were closed. He was taking her back into her past as he'd often done in counseling only now he had the technique from the disk, what they had managed to decipher so far from it at any rate the technology used to record the data being so long lost. The woman spoke, he acknowledged her just to give reassurance that he was still there. Whatever else he was with her. She may have traveled down the lifetimes alone for eons, but now... Patience, he could have enough to sit for the rest of his life and he marveled at the feeling always running before and never wanting to be still yet here he was, quiet, calm, competent. The others, the High Advocator, Commander Rabin, Anther... they had acquiesced to economics and opted for security. They would have disapproved of what he was doing, especially so that it was something new that nobody had ever done before, at least no one since the Kaiein. The disk was older than that.

It was only chance that they had found it. Nash had gone to VOX as soon as Sabiha left with the knowledge concerning Charles Iverson's tacit agreement and the statistics from CenMed VAN. Into the concrete canyon and through the labyrinth of offices he worked his way to the familiar dim glow of the computer filled cavern on the 87th floor that was VOX. Derek was at his desk, which was a cluttered maelstrom of devices and peripherals topped by three wide, flat monitors all of which he juggled with knowing hands. There wasn't anyone else who could have understood the insidious nature of what was being uncovered. But then cops got paid for that.

"Jesus god damned Christ my arm hurts!" He scowled up at Nash, "I bet they left some glass in there." It was the first time he'd seen his friend at work since the incident.

Nash was intent. "I hope you're getting what I'm saying, that it's not just..."

"I get it." He cut Nash off matter of factly, "When I bend over these damn monitors it hurts." He continued to keystroke data as lines of code raced across the screen while in the right corner a small window fluttered numbers tracking the myriad of networks VOX was connected to all at once. Though multitasking computers were common, nobody had equipment like VOX. They attracted the brightest young minds, altruists who came to test their mental and cognitive abilities against the finest in business and criminal empires alike. McGilvery said a VOX unit personnel wasn't made, but born. They were floaters on the networks and many of them never even saw daylight except once every few months. There were government apartments within the complex where they lived and since most were online up to eighteen hours a day there was no need to leave. Nash mused that these might be the next evolution of humans, immune to the effects of technology because they had finally and absolutely become technology with their language spoken in broken, elliptical sentences leaving it up to the recipient to complete the reference–but only if he was in the know. Outsiders could not easily understand them and when trying to be understood they spoke a muted version of English as if to a child or patronizing one less fortunate than themselves, but still faster than the average person.

McGilvery sprinted through the code being possessed with the dual obsessions of digital transcendence and criminal law. The latter had been long in coming. Though he had spent his entire career in the VOX unit perhaps it was the total mastery of the tech that finally brought him back to the fundamental underpinnings of civilized societies and the realization that people, after all, were the reason.

"Look," Nash felt angry, "it seems that *the mark* is somehow a key to this...it was found after the system break-in at CenMed VAN and I found it while tracking down the *Golden XiOma*. Sabiha is convinced it's an obscure code writer named Yzak, and as I told you the Undersecretary of Global Communications at the UN seemed to know it too or he certainly started acting strangely for nothing. Something big is going on. What are we going to do?"

McGilvery didn't look up from the monitor or even flutter an eye for an instant; there was not the slightest acknowledgment that a communication had been directed towards him, which irritated Nash no end. "There have been a lot of incidents..." he began as if mid-conversation, "you're right that fusing, *EINF* as Fionica calls it, is induced as a result of the introduction of the new nanoflat technology 360-monitors. Yes, it is confined to within those areas of product distribution, but soon it will be global because CommNET owns the manufacturing facilities, licensing and the copyrights to the hardware and hopes that the proprietary technology will make their networks so irresistible to the existing consumer base that they are projecting an increase of 30% in market share within a year." He glared sideways at Nash. "That we've known for a long time."

Then he returned to his computer. "There have been no fatalities that I can trace to the phenomenon except several cardiac arrests in people who had pre-cardiac conditions anyway...so were susceptible, but...there has been a distinct rise in domestic violence, suicide, homicide, people seeking counseling and sexual assault. Related or not...I don't know, but date coincident." He ceased the incessant keystroking and flicking from screen to screen, network to network. "Plus I have found the mark you speak of in several places, as have my colleagues for some time now...always obscure, always innocuous..." he breathlessly turned and with deadpan calm directed a question at Nash. "What is the Golden XiOma?"

Nash was floored. "How did you find all this?"

McGilvery shrugged. "You asked me to look into it."

"I thought you'd forgotten with the accident and everythi..."

"No accident, I was set up."

"What do you mean?"

"We had traced the mark you speak of to that location from the system at Cedars we had plugged into. I was drawn there." He paused with a gray, cold face and both of them relived the instant that night when McGilvery's life was on the threshold as the last dagger of glass hung from the ceiling after the blast and flickered in the air only holding on by good Karma. "What Golden XiOma?" Derek repeated insistently.

"It's a Greek variant for Axiom," Nash replied shaking his head, "...nothing you'd be interested in. There are references to it in the Canon. I don't know yet what the "Golden" has to do with it, could be just another legend...so much that has come down from beyond the Kaiein can't be verified."

"What did the mark have to do with it?"

"I found it in the code."

"You sure it was the same?"

"Yes."

"What the hell's the connection?"

Nash considered it for a moment, he had not realized until this minute the weight of coincidence between the same footprints being found at the heart of a religious mystery and involved in a virtual implant technology. "I've been on the WEB for months, at first to search out the Canon and all the related documentation I could find, but it kept leading me further and further down circular information strings– designed to lead in circles." He sighed with finality, his face turned dark. "There's a lot you don't know, a lot you can't learn from machines.

McGilvery leaned back in his chair with a bemused look of shock partly enjoying the unexpected outburst of emotion. "For instance?"

"I don't have time..." he looked at the cop and then grunted with annoyance and clicked his teeth, which he only did under extreme pressure. "Alright... it's dogma, philosophical religious texts." There was silence. His friend just looked at him expectantly without moving or saying a word. "Alright...it's common knowledge in the church that the Elders have kept an archive of treasures since the Kaiein. The Archivists order is bound for life to keep the secrets and once someone is accepted he's never seen again. The rumor is that unimaginable riches are contained in the repository, but the official line is that only collected information is stored there and the order of Archivists are engaged translating it all to modern language and recording it in indelible form... like modern monks."

"Fascinating." McGilvery uttered quietly.

Nash stood and turned searching for some kind of rational answers. "I don't think it's coincidence. If we're guessing right, the power of this new virtual technology surpasses anything that's even been approached before." He glared through his friend with a steeled gaze caught up completely in his own thoughts, "There must be some information drawn from The Archive, it's the only answer...even the most brilliant technician could not plumb the human soul, that's my domain...mine and the Church's. Someone has discovered some profound spiritual knowledge that makes this virtual technology work!"

With a flash of motion McGilvery's hands whipped across the touchscreen and began accessing the WEB. "Can you remember your path?"

"I suppose...but why? You don't really think..."

"Just tell me. This is my domain and if there are any secrets there... we'll see..."

Nash gave him the paths where he had found references to The Archive and found *the mark* as well as he could remember. Then he sat down and watched the master. A flurry of screens flashed before them with text, pictures, holographic animations, video and all forms of data flowing across the monitors like lightening while the small window in the corner of the center monitor logged every network path and tracked the search automatically. Soon the three monitors were working independently until all that was seen crossing before them were the flickers of light, shadow and colors in a mad race streaming millions of bits of information every second–information devised by humans, discovered and elaborated on and then expanded by computers and technology. It was first hand data taken to its intellectual limits where new information was postulated based on interpretations that were many times removed from the actual source, which was simply a man observing something for himself. It struck Nash that he was watching the unraveling of the universe before him where all the extrapolation and the compounding of information that had been the preoccupation for hundreds of years was being unleashed to fly out among the stars and become hidden and embedded in the physical world again. What was true and what was false was the real mystery. He knew there was a little truth in many things, but how to sift it out, to separate axioms from partial truths, how to find what was really valuable in the game of survival... He was burdened by information and realized that his whole life, and most people's lives were burdened with the data they had to know, or should know, or wanted to know, or were afraid they couldn't know...men, he thought, should be burdened by dreams instead.

Neither spoke for a long time. Both glued to the monitors as if the revelation would occur before them. Then as suddenly as the data stream had started it froze. All three screens displayed the same image. It was a long path name in code enclosed by a red box on a black field with shimmering, holographic horizontal stripes dissecting it. McGilvery turned to Nash for the first time in hours. "That's where it is."

Nash wasn't quite sure what he was looking at or what Derek was talking about, but didn't want to appear inattentive. "Yes?" He said.

"The Archive," his friend uttered bluntly keeping his attention on the screen fearing perhaps that the jewel would disappear back into the virtual ether from where it had come.

"You sure?" Turning to the monitor Nash looked in disbelief as the significance of what was being said finally sank in. Up until now it had been only a rumor, common as the knowledge supposedly was within the Church there had never been any hard physical evidence. Until now.

McGilvery just looked at him with an unabashed certainty. "There's only one problem."

Nash wasn't listening. "I can't believe it. You found it? Where is it?" Then he paused and slowly asked, "What problem?"

"Well, nothing much," McGilvery shrugged paying little attention to Nash, "it's on a network I've never heard of before."

"Oh." Nash replied calmly. "Well, lets find it."

The glance could have knocked Nash over. It was from an altitude that only VOX personnel could truly appreciate. "If I don't know about a network, it doesn't exist."

"What do you mean it doesn't exist," he pointed to the screens, "it's right there."

"You see, that's just it. You talk about *fusing* and new technology, but the damage was done a long time ago."

"Now what are you saying?"

"Just because it's on the screen you believe it."

He looked pensively up at the flickering monitor feeling the sinking vacuum of lost hope. "It's not true then...?"

"I'm not saying that, just don't assume it's gospel."

Exasperated. "Then what do you mean?"

There was no answer, McGilvery input a code to the Vidtel and in a moment a vacant room appeared accompanied by a voice. "Yaaas...?" it said gruffly. Nash peered closely at the screen image of massive network hubs filling a wall in the background while closer to the camera were tools, loose wires and optical cable and hundreds of metal boxes of all sizes that he knew housed digital peripherals of some kind or another.

All of a sudden a huge face filled the screen. The eyes were gray but bright, the skin brown and wrinkled and the hair white, unruly with an equally wild full beard. "Well…!? I haven't got all day!?"

"I'm lost." McGilvery said with deadpan seriousness.

The old man looked far into the camera and for a moment Nash thought he was going to get mad again, or slam off the crank call, but instead he just said, "Ahh you piss head, all right. C'mon over." And then there was blackness punctuated by the flash line of light across the screen and a small, quickly fading white static dot.

In the car they raced through traffic that never seemed to let up day or night and though it was nearly two in the morning it was as congested as mid-day. There were just so many people. Once when Nash had asked a Metropolitan Transit District manager about it he was told that people lived in layers in the city, a parfait of humanity, some slept, some worked, and always there were some on the road either heading to a destination, coming back or just wandering…*twenty percent of vehicle traffic at any given time are wanderers, no destinations, just people that have to be in motion.* Even the homeless had cars provided by the government, it was cheaper than housing and there was always the possibility they would relocate.

"Were going back in time." McGilvery said. "Mitsu Tokashi is a *cabler.* He's got to be eighty, eighty-five, but doesn't look it. It's the dark skin. He was a strong man…and don't let the white hair and beard fool you…he knows everything I know about the networks," he looked across at Nash from behind the steering wheel, "and much more."

"Then you think The Archive exists on-line."

"If anyone knows, Mitsu will…he can tell you how the planet got wired–he's traced the routes of all the cables from those done pre-Kaiein to the present, its all in his head."

The harbor was an unlikely place for the center of networking to exist, Nash thought, but as he discovered later it was the obvious choice being the entry point on the continent for the trans-oceanic optical cables that began to be laid in the 1990s. Driving down into the center of the labyrinth was like leaving the earth and traveling to an off world port where the industrial infrastructure was not covered with skin the way it is in the civic centers leaving the massive mantis-like skeletal structures exposed to let the light and the fog filter through. At the port's edge where the oil refineries had once been sprawled across the once flat marshlands under the hills where the exclusive homes of the rich were perched was the Western Metropolis' first major commercial spaceport. It was the best possible location where the commerce of the sea and that of cyberspace converged and now could extend to the limited peripheral that earthmen had managed to attain in space. On warm summer evenings when the privileged in the hills far above gathered in their splendor to relax on the lawns and terraces with chilled glasses of vintage wines they would watch dispassionately the intergalactic freighters arrive and depart far below in the twilight when the spectacle was at its most stunning. Since its inception other more chic space centers had been built so this one was relegated to the comings and goings of freight and heavy cargo of all kinds, but from a distance even the old corroded space hulks appeared magical. They passed a sign on the throughway that announced "Port Of Los Angeles" and was a hold over from earlier days, but since the continuity of ocean going vessels was never really interrupted by the economic catastrophe most of the ports of the world retained their original names so as not to upset navigational charts.

Nash followed McGilvery down the long tunnel that led into a honeycomb of passages under a huge bunker between the wharves of the sea and those of the ether. He had watched the lights strung from the huge loading cranes of the quays disappear still transferring cargo containers as they had been doing for hundreds of years leaving him with a satisfied feeling knowing that some things were fundamental. They left the thick air infused with pollution smelling of brine, oil and industrial foulness and entered the world of the *Cablers*. They were the legions of men who, since the 1850's, had made their living laying the trans-oceanic and transcontinental cables from the first telegraph experiment to the most contemporary optical spaced between transformers, repeaters and amplifiers and zero-resistance materials cooled by liquid nitrogen. The tunnel was about thirty feet high and a hundred and fifty wide and they were the only ones in it. After twenty minutes going down at a twenty degree angle McGilvery explaining that they were entering the intercontinental cable corridors and the bunker was built to withstand nuclear attacks as well as terrorist infiltration. They began to see light up ahead from around a bend. It was cold and damp as they descended below the sea level and the moisture from the deep pressed against the bare sides of the tunnel walls. In the piercing flare of lights they reached the security perimeter. MacGilvery produced his identification and the usual screening procedure began. The post was manned by military personnel and consisted of a heavy metal barrack built into the concrete wall an integral part of which were heavy linked gates that not even artillery could penetrate. Quartz beams were directed up the tunnel into their eyes placing them, and Nash supposed, any enemy at a disadvantage. When the gate rose shaking loose its salt accelerated corrosion the noise was like the chains of the dead. Then the huge doors began to move and the ground shuddered beneath them with a deep rumble.

"Water tight." McGilvery shouted above the noise. "That's the main tunnel...it goes all the way to Japan."

Inside the cavern was huge, and circular rising to a hundred and sixty feet at its apex. There was a tube running down its center through which raced high speed magnetic beam trains in both directions and the far wall appeared to be a glass-like substance beyond which were layers and layers of enormous serpentine cables illuminated by dim icy blue lights. An inconspicuous sign was plainly visible with an arrow pointing to the left with the caption *Asia*, and one to the right that said *Metrohub*.

"In the early days," McGilvery explained, "cables were just laid down on the ocean floor, given a life of fifty years and let go. Optics changed that, especially when the zero resistance materials evolved. Cables still had to be laid, but accelerators needed to be constructed at intervals, and amplifiers with repeaters plus the high-speed transmission generated enough heat to melt the materials so liquid nitrogen had to be used to cool it down. All that meant a way to access the machinery for maintenance had to be found since it was just too expensive to drop and give a life limit to." He raised his hands to the surroundings,

"The tunnels. They parallel all the working optical cable systems on the planet, under all the oceans and across the continents. The Earth is honeycombed in certain areas."

Nash looked in awe at the massive human feat of engineering and felt irretrievably small. "Yes." He said meekly. "I remember from school. Funny, I'd never thought about it much since then."

"Sure." McGilvery replied with a professional attitude. "It's infra-structure. It's supposed to be invisible."

They boarded a train and traveled toward Metrohub for what seemed to be only a few minutes, but on a train that can reach nearly Mach-1, just under 600 miles per hour, distance is relative. The station they found themselves at was an administrative center set back into the earth and the recessed wall was a facade for an underground office structure, which they were soon deep the belly of. Nash raced to keep up with McGilvery who naturally walked fast as he navigated corridors, desks and secretaries with practiced expertise.

At first the office appeared empty, but then sounds of someone rummaging around could be heard from behind a wall. Nash looked at a desk, which was completely covered with equipment of some kind or another as was most of the floor, even the chair was stacked with papers. On the back wall were shelves loaded with network hub stations filled with tiny flickering lights. "You must be thinkin' its a damn mess... huh?" The brown, wrinkled face peered from around the corner with pale, gray-green eyes. Gesturing towards the wall where Nash was looking, "Regional hubs. Part of the job."

"I'm more amazed to see paper." Nash replied.

The man entered the room. He was short, very short and broad at the shoulders and hips. The way he planted his feet squarely like a bulldog gave the impression that he had been heavily muscled when he was younger. "I like paper." He said.

"Nash Mitsu. Mitsu Nash." McGilvery said leaning back against the desk.

"You lost too, huh?"

Nash looked at Derek inquisitively.

"We've come up with a network I don't recognize."

The old man shifted his eyes to McGilvery and sneered a smile, "You think you know them all?"

He handed the man some sheets of paper. "Here's a printout of the screen."

He looked at it carefully, then up at McGilvery. "I don't know this."

"Look at it again..." he replied knowing the old man was playing with them, "at least tell us what do you think?"

Mitsu focused on the symbols again. He cleared a space on the desk and laid all three sheets of paper out side by side and smoothed their wrinkles with his hand. For a long time he looked them over. "Well..." he finally said drawing the word out with effort alluding to some upcoming struggle. "...we have to do some digging."

McGilvery glanced at Nash and with a painfully anxious look, nodded slightly trying to convey some relief and then began to follow the old man into the back rooms of the office.

"We'll trace it on his system, right?" Nash whispered to McGilvery following them.

"No," he said quietly without any emotion whatsoever, "we have to do some *digging*."

Nash didn't understand why he had emphasized the word *digging* until he rounded the partition to the back chambers and came face to face with the inner sanctum. It had once been a huge planning room and all along the far wall was a digital LCD holographic display of the complete network system of the Western Metropolis, but it was dead, there was no juice, lights were out and layers of dust covered it so thickly that some of the writing was even obscured. Standing in front of it were the sentries, oversized filing cabinets with extra large drawers, half of which were partially or fully open and out of which tumbled reams and reams of charts and paper printouts of all varieties. Paper covered the floor in messy stacks and in overflowing boxes that were crowded into the corners. There were hundreds of cabinets.

"Mitsu doesn't really believe in computers." McGilvery explained.

"This is nothing to the books I got at home..." the old man added mischievously.

They spent hours in the room searching, but Nash didn't mind at all. He felt as if he had entered an earlier century, one where hope had not been so thoroughly eclipsed and the slight glint that existed in people's lives was enough to ferry them through the night across storms and turbulence. Looking over the floor he saw men's breath in the yellowed papers and understood why Mitsu clung to them. In the virtual world were figments, facsimiles of knowledge and all the data extant was given equal weight and sovereignty as ones or zeros. A sheet of paper however still held the imprint of the man who made it and it served a far deeper purpose keeping a memory alive of the knowledge that had earlier been passed down from father to son thick with promise. Once it was easy to tell if a man's words were true and it was still possible when they were written by seeing with what value they were cared for on the printed page. In the information age if it looked true, it was true for within the computer everything equaled everything and with cold, precise cuts false information became mixed with true until there was no one left to pass along the wisdom wrestled from life in a human and believable way. How was a man to know that it was hard to survive and that the force of life bowed men's backs before their time because they had not their father's wisdom.

"We laid cable from ships." Mitsu said as he rifled through files pulling out charts and inspecting them, discarding some and keeping others as if he could carry on two or more tasks with equal importance giving the full weight of his attention to each. McGilvery tried to follow the sequence with which he laid out documents, inspecting them carefully some bringing recognition and others eluding his understanding. He organized them on the conference table after clearing a space while the old man told stories. "In those days we were doing it the way it was done before the Kaiein. Private investors would finance a line and we'd string it through different regions while the company would lease access to it at each entry point. I'd keep the charts. They'd just load everything into a computer and didn't want any of them." He paused and shot a glance at Nash. "That's how I got started." He continued to rummage through the files, jumping from one drawer to the next, from one stack to another in random patterns as he followed a line of logic that was intuitive and with each chart and piece of paper he was reminded of what he already knew. "Optical lines were there already, the cables go back three hundred years or more, the trouble is technology. Bandwidth was too narrow. Zero resistance changed everything...still happens though, by the time a full cable's laid it's obsolete. We're sort of an underground civilization down here...self perpetuating..."

He held up a particularly yellowed piece of paper and looked pleased as if both Nash and McGilvery would understand what it was too. "Here we are!" Then brought it over to the table and laid it out in alignment with the other charts, all of which looked like confusing engineering schematics to Nash. "See this?" He traced his finger down a line as McGilvery inspected it closely. "It's an old pre-Kaiein optical line. There's not much bandwidth so it's probably not used. Vidtel couldn't even connect with it and the networks abandon what they can't make money on. But maybe someone..."

"...hacked in an access and took over the network lines." McGilvery said.

"No reason why not."

"Is that the network?" Nash asked.

"It's the domain area, but I can't guarantee..."

"Close enough." Said McGilvery. "Where is it exactly?"

"Lets see..." The old man scrutinized the maps. "The hub is somewhere in these hills, see here..." He trailed his finger along a line, "...under some sort of structure, a tunnel maybe, the old Metrorail maybe from before the Kaiein."

As they drove back to the center of the city neither one spoke. The charts rested on the seat between them and burned with the heat of mystery. McGilvery was tense. He rolled over the endless scenarios of every time he had been stopped in pursuit, the unfinished investigations leaving him with unanswered questions. It had to do with issues more fundamental that just money, but cynic at heart he knew that it was probably just a scheme for generating money, which was the only thing he could think of that was more important to people than actual life. They, the masses who were incidental and indispensable at once, who were a polyglot of whispers and faces and aspirations blended without distinction by the lords of business and politics, without whom none of the contrivances had any meaning yet individually were completely unnecessary. Regardless of who a man was or what arts or genius he contributed, there was another who waited in the wings perhaps more talented, more ambitious and whenever one faltered by reason of age or infirmity or self doubt the other would step in line without missing a beat to uphold the machine and march into the future whispering his illusions to himself. McGilvery felt all the shadowmen and knew there were layers and layers of them each striving and longing and kicking and scratching his way to the front of the line. He knew he was expendable and perhaps that was why he had allowed himself to be derailed by his superiors. Some things were beyond life. He glanced over at Nash who was sitting still and staring out the window at the passing landscape and mused at what possible compromises a man of the cloth had to make to survive. One thing he was certain of, this time he would not fail himself.

The woman spoke more freely now. She could remember incidents that had been occluded before, moments when her consciousness had lapsed while fusing. Nash followed the procedure he had found on the disk, the *Golden XiOma*, and though some of it seemed strange he adhered to the course that was laid out. He felt the urge to deviate, to interject his own interpretations when what he was doing seemed to go against his own judgment, but as an experiment he did not because it was written that way and within the writings was the proviso that the system was axiomatic, based on self evident truths and so could only give results it followed exactly. He did not know completely what he was trying to accomplish other than to help the woman who had been traumatized by *fusing* yet had nothing physically wrong. He reflected on the circumstances that brought him to this point, the chance events that uncovered this long lost wisdom.

The night McGilvery had come to his apartment there was a terrific windstorm that seemed to threaten the old building to its foundation. Icy fingers found their way through cracks whistling around corners so that no matter how high he turned the heat it remained cold. Sabiha had arrived earlier and he had just finished explaining what had happened at VOX and all about Mitsu and the charts of the ancient network when Derek suddenly burst through the door his eyes erratic and bright.

"I've got the Metro maps." He was excited; there was a nervous edge to his usually measured voice. He awkwardly spread them out on the floor. "It was the old tunnel! Mitsu was right... look..." He pointed to reference marks and streets and boulevards. "I stole them from City Planning...pays to work for the government!" He did not smile. "We're going there tonight."

"Now?" Nash exclaimed.

"Yes," he answered insistently.

"Not without me...!" Sabiha falling in behind.

"Wait...I've got to get a coat..."

Derek looked at the woman whom he only knew slightly, "You can't..."

"That's what you think." And she slid out the door before them.

McGilvery looked momentarily bewildered "Sorry," Nash said coming from the other room, "she does what she wants...works for the government."

There were still small sections of the hills surrounding the city that were vacant. Everyone assumed it was privately owned land waiting for the highest bidder, or that it had once cradled building sites cleared before their memory and the owner greedily priced it too high to sell and the estate was too greedy to lower it. Still others thought it was government land and leaving it vacant was part of a conspiracy. In these ways parcels could easily escape attention. When they arrived, after leaving the expressway and driving for an hour on surface streets that had only magnetic rails and not the newer particle beams, they were not surprised that the car had to traverse the last few miles under its own power using its own wheels. A gust of wind hit them as soon as the door was open bringing a freezing cold waft of ozone in its wake. From long before the ozone layer had been depleted industrial centers all across the globe had been producing the gas and infusing it into the atmosphere, especially at night when the cooler air would help it rise to the ozonosphere. It gave off the smell of electrical sparks.

The landscape of night enveloped them in it's wildness and lights of the metropolis could be seen in all directions twinkling through air that even high winds could not totally clear. The car was parked in a cul de sac facing a chaparral covered hill with nothing else around them except lofty Eucalyptus trees that swayed in huge arcs and roared with gusts of wind.

"Now what?" Sabiha stood shivering in the rushing air speaking loudly to be heard.

Nash stood with the door open while McGilvery took a last look at the maps he had spread out on the car seat and wasn't at all certain of the wisdom in coming this night. The light went out and the car locked.

"I've been studying the maps and the network charts from Mitsu since we visited him," McGilvery said loudly in Nash's ear while Sabiha tried to get close enough to hear, "if they're right, and I think they are...I know where we can start looking."

"What are we looking for?"

"An entrance of course." McGilvery replied as if Nash should have guessed.

Three dark silhouettes, black against black, hidden by the moonless night and silenced by the roaring trees moved secretly into the brush unsure if they needed to keep out of sight or of what exactly they would find–if anything. They struggled through the chaparral up the hill and then followed it as it swept down into a small meadow at the base of an even higher rise where the bushes grew so tightly together they could only push their way through slowly feeling each step for a foothold in the pitch black. Sounds from the city below came and went with the streaming of the wind gusts. Helicraft could be seen layered one against another off into the distances beaming their arc lights down into the streets looking for trouble. It was impossible to feel isolated in the center of the megalopolis where so many lives were intertwined and the population density didn't start to thin out for over a hundred miles in any direction, except of course to the West where the sea lay churning with its own denizens who spoke the language of silkies no men understood.

There were old foundations tangled in the undergrowth through the cracks of which vines, grasses and small trees grew. It was an illusion that no one had inhabited this land as they traipsed across civilization's leave behinds as if a cemetery was being violated in the darkness and each had an ominous feeling that the mission they were on may be a link to answers that each had sought, but perhaps was best left alone.

"Look here!" McGivlery called out and Nash and Sabiha hurried up the hill to see what he was pointing at. "See it...? There...?"

High above huge clouds raced illuminated from the radiance of city lights running from the approaching day, still a long way off, and deeper into the night where they might spend eternity as they kept moving like shadows in a dream. In the lightless field with the wind churning up the brush no one was certain what they were staring at.

"It's the foundation of a drill platform."

Both looked again and still no shape was discernible. "So what." Nash replied loudly over the wind.

"Metro used them to drill air and power shafts into the hills when they were constructing the rail system. It means we're close."

"To what?" Sabiha asked.

There was no answer as McGilvery was off again winding his way through the bushes carefully inspecting every foot of ground he passed over looking for some kind of sign. They followed him for hours as he wandered across the hillsides until finally he stopped.

"Here." He said pointing to what looked like another flat, cement foundation remnant. Pulling out a light that he had not used before for fear of giving them away he knelt down and shined its beam while he ripped away vines and weeds and dried grass until all of a sudden there it was. The unmistakable evidence that they were in the right place was a huge, round, rusty iron manhole cover set into the cracked cement and in rusty, corroded, deeply embossed letters was written...*Metrorail - Los Angeles Metropolitan Transit Authority - 2021.*

"It's the tunnel?" Nash said not ready to believe it would be this easy.

"Yea."

"Let's open it." Sabiha commanded kneeling down to brush the hardened soil away.

It took all their strength but they managed to pull the cover up over the lip of the hole enabling and slide it aside a few feet, just enough for someone to climb inside. McGilvery peered into the darkness and then shone his light down into its depth.

"What's there?" Nash's voice trailed away in the wind.

"Well, it goes down quite a ways, but there's a passage at the bottom...pretty clogged, looks like mud's gotten in there." Then he looked up. "You want to try?"

"It's abandoned." Sabiha added ominously. She looked at Nash and each felt their hearts beat in their throats and they nodded yes at the same time. McGilvery handed lights to both of them. After grappling in the gloom for the iron rings set into the wall they struggled down into the murkiness where it smelled moldy and damp and close like no one else had been there for a few hundred years.

Nash cursed himself for being so unprepared and hoped it was only a short walk through the tunnel. The route was rectangular with walls and ceiling of concrete sealed at intervals by what once was probably a flexible substance to allow the cement to give with the stresses of earth movement though now it was cracked and brittle and most of it hung in crystallized stalactites that met at the floor with stalagmites rising up. There were mounds of dirt at the intervals where the soil had eroded in and a few small, weak plants sprouting in corners that were completely white and waxy looking. The silence was resounding. They had been transported from the city and sealed off from any external stimuli and the effect gave them sudden buoyancy being cut off from the continuous spiritual drain of the megalopolis. They flitted quickly through the corridor with stealth like footsteps not knowing what they might be afraid of, feeling trapped yet strangely drawn by what they might discover.

Sabiha froze. "What's that sound?" Whispering hoarsely out of breath from the fast pace. They stopped. It was silent.

"I don't hear it." Nash replied.

"C'mon." Said McGilvery.

"It was there."

Nash walked very carefully trying to separate his own footsteps from those of the others, then trying to distinguish Sabiha's and McGilvery's so he would have absolute certainty of every sound. He spread his fingers as he moved trying to sense danger from the air. Stale and damp air. He thought momentarily about being overcome by methane gas, but after a while feeling no ill effects forgot about it. Three light beams cavorted around the chamber bobbing as they walked swinging in each different rhythms like huge, long white canes tapping their way through the alien environment. Then he heard it. Unmistakable.

"Derek...!" He whispered forcefully. There was no answer as they walked and so he implored, "Do you hear it?"

"Yes."

It sounded like the far off throbbing of an engine. It sounded like a ship at sea in fog where the vibrations of machinery were absorbed by the deep and the pregnant air and kept secret while leviathans slid further down to hide their wildness from men. It sounded like the heartbeat of a giant, or an enormous animal whose vital organ was so strong it only required one massive constriction every few moments to send blood gushing in torrents through the gigantic circulatory system.

"What is it?" He asked excitedly.

"Sounds like..."

"...maybe a pump?"

"Don't think so... what would a...?"

They were walking faster now and stumbling over debris they had missed with their lights as they nervously speculated on the sound.

"Could be just some machinery from city engineering."

"Sounds like a repeater." McGilvery said.

"A what?"

"A signal repeater for optical networks."

"Then were on the right..."

"Only trouble is, they don't make sounds."

"Great." Sabiha cried in frustration. "What the hell are we getting into?"

"I told you not to come."

After a moment she barked, "Let's go see what the damn thing is!"

"Hold on… don't get too far ahead."

"Wait a min… do you see that?"

"A light."

"Is that a light… hold on… looks like…"

"A light. Now who…"

"Quiet! Something's coming."

They all flattened to the side of the wall and stopped breathing in one deft, hushed movement. The sound of a small vehicle could be heard approaching distinctly up the way. They waited.

"There's no lights."

"Quiet!"

"There's no lights…!"

"What do you mean?"

"It's not on this level… it's beneath us."

They stood noiseless against the wall and felt the vibrations as the vehicle passed directly under them with the whir of a small magnetic beam engine.

"Must be the network cables…the access tunnel." McGilvery exclaimed.

"Yea." Nash whispered feeling a strange familiarity and an apprehension at what he imagined he was about to discover. Long ago he had dreamt about this and now began to wonder what it meant. Was it fated to happen? Or if it was simply imagination why did he remember it so vividly? Or, perhaps he was still dreaming and this was just part of it and the momentary recognition was just a partial waking from a long slumber where life rolled by in predetermined sequences which he could either accept the role of or rage against.

"Somebody's here. Unless its a robot."

Silence. As soon as the sound had passed they again raced along the tunnel certain they were close to some sort of exit each dying to be free from confinement. A visible glow in the distance grew stronger as hey approached and soon as they rounded a slight bend the dead end wall at the end of the shaft was visible. A light had been jury rigged high up its surface directly over an entry door, which was ancient rusty metal and stood down at the end of a long, concrete ramp. McGilvery stopped and began to examine the fixture and harness commenting it was a late addition to the tunnel. Nash rapidly dropped down the incline and placed his right hand on the door feeling the cool metal with Sabiha close behind, her long brown fingers on his shoulder eyes flashing in the shadows. At the first touch he experienced a surge of energy and paused questioning whether he should go further or not. He was unsure if he really wanted to know what was on the other side because if he opened it he would be burdened with a responsibility he may not be ready to assume.

The decision was made for him. McGilvery had the door open and a staircase leading down to another small tunnel much like the one they were leaving was revealed. This one however was cleaner and newer with comm-link boxes lined up along the walls. It was the access way. "I think we've found the network." The three silently descended the staircase wary of the sound they had heard minutes earlier. McGilvery shined a light on the floor and a thin metallic strip was revealed that appeared to be foil blended into the concrete. "Wait." He whispered harshly. "It's a robot, magnetic beam...don't step on the strip it might detect us if anyone's monitoring it."

The passage was only about six and a half feet high and equally wide allowing just enough room for a work crew. After a moment to reconnoiter Nash and Sabiha followed McGilvery off in the direction the stairway had been pointing. The air was electric. None of them had any idea what they would find only that the urge to know was over-powering any fears and with each step a destiny was being fulfilled. They had walked briskly for about thirty minutes when the passageway began to change shape slightly. The left the wall was partitioned by a series of inset chambers that were a foot deep and appeared to have a rectangular hatch at the back long sealed over and covered with corrosion. Their lights grazed the edges and cast pitch black shadows in the frames that made them seem deeper and more dangerous as if one would burst open and they would be found out before they had a chance. In the darkness imagination was heightened. The senses were alert to the extreme. Even the sound of their own hearts beating in their ears as they rushed forward was loud and exaggerated.

They stopped at one of the comm-link boxes. McGilvery was determined to get something out of the adventure and ripped off the sheet metal cover to connect his hand held computer to what his guess was the main optical network cable access lines. Carefully he linked up making sure he did not cause any fluctuations in the signals that would be seen or at least recorded and later found by the sys-ops. He began to scan for the data stream hoping he could transmit at least part of it back to his system at VOX.

Then, so suddenly they almost past it, their lights brushed across one of the inset frames on the walls. It appeared black from floor to ceiling as it was revealed without seeing any interior.

"Hold it." Sabiha said tapping Nash's elbow.

"What?"

"We passed something." Shining the light behind her she could plainly see the opening of the vestibule that absorbed the glare into its dark recess and beckoned them. "Look, a chamber."

Excitedly they turned to investigate, but found that it only went back for ten feet. At the end on the floor was a hatch, stamped metal with the same markings that had been on the manhole cover above. It was obviously an original entry portal from the Metrorail tunnel around which the access passage was built a century or more later. Nash knelt down and began working to unfasten the latches that were screwed down against the edges thinking they were probably too old and rusty to budge, but to his amazement they slowly began to turn and showed the wear of occasional use making it certain someone else had used it not too long ago. They doused the lights and for long moments struggled in the dark to raise the cover trying at the same time to remain absolutely silent.

As the grate began to move McGilvery quietly joined them. "That might trigger an alarm..." and though he didn't know who he might fear the blackness around fueled the imagination. "...take it real slow..." He knew someone was operating the network. The cover creaked with metal rubbing against metal as they managed to crack it open a few inches. Then they stopped cold and listened for any movement or electronic alert. There was silence except for a low, continuous hiss that escaped from below through the inch and a half at which they held open the hatch. Sweat rolled down their faces and Sabiha began to shake involuntarily straining to hold the heavy object motionless in the awkward position.

Nash leaned down putting his face up close to the crack so that he could see the chambers revealed. "My god!" he exclaimed in a raspy whisper. "It's huge!"

Below lay an immense cavity, which he viewed from high up in some corner...probably a maintenance access point. "Lift it a little." He said without regard as to any danger they would be revealed and the three struggled once again finally raising the cover high enough so they all could see what had excited Nash. The panorama was unearthly. A huge chamber lined with rows of what appeared to be cargo like storage containers well over two stories tall and each one capable of holding rooms full of material. The facing of each was cobalt tinted glass with doorways framed in titanium colored metal. Alloy structured stairs and walkways crossed their fronts. The whole place was bathed in an eerie ultramarine, infrared light that absorbed all colors except those within the blue violet spectrum. Out of the glass doors came a deeper, more saturated indigo luminance that was thicker than any light any or them had ever seen. At the far ends of the chamber were walls at the center of which were immense sealed gates trains could run through if necessary. It was clear the old tunnel had been appropriated and sectioned off.

"I'm going down." Nash said.

""No!" McGilvery exclaimed in an excited whisper, but it was too late.

Nash slipped his legs through the opening as the others held up the cover and let them dangle hoping he would find stairs or something to light on. Finally his foot came to rest on a steel rung that protruded from the wall identical to the ones they had come down beneath the manhole cover and from there he began to lower himself. The air was cold and had the artificial dehumidified feel that was the same he had experienced in CenMed VAN and made him certain it was the center of considerable electronic equipment or something else that required a tightly controlled environment. He was breathless with fear, but quiet and stepped lightly on the footholds so he would not attract any attention, though he did not see anyone. Finally, his feet stood flat on the floor and he looked far up the ladder to the hatch he had lowered himself from and could barely see the crack in the ceiling where he knew McGilvery and Sabiha were watching. He waved his hand once slowly over his head to signal he was alright, then turned to the environment around him.

The isles between the containers were immense, much more expansive than they appeared from high above. He was dwarfed by their size and intimidated by the massive setup still in complete mystery as to what it was. He walked down the center path peering through the glass walls of the structures, but saw only more chambers inside as if the storage compartments were all separated for airflow. He tried the latch to the closest door and unexpectedly found it was not locked. There was a slight hissing sound when he opened it breaking the airtight closure and equalizing the pressures. Stepping inside and passing through two more chamber doors until he was in a securely shelved room with only the slightest violet glow. He switched on his light and gasped in awe at what he saw. On the shelf in front of him was an ancient Eastern Orthodox cross that stood carefully secured by intricately constructed stands so it could not be jarred loose by earthquake or other disaster. The finish was gold leaf with lapis lazuli inlays and a huge fire opal at its center where the cross bars met. It was displayed as in a museum, painstakingly placed by human hands and guarded against the ravages of atmosphere and time. He shone his light around the shelves and other precious objects were similarly positioned, all meticulously cared for and most all of them crosses or icons bearing a distinct similarity to one another. It was a cache of artifacts like none he had ever actually seen, but had only viewed in books that had survived the Kaeien. He moved through the chamber inspecting the contents careful not to touch anything then moved on to another chamber where he found similar artifacts only these were not crosses, but boxes with religious symbols on them. It was as if each chamber held a category of object each similar in some cultural way.

Nash was refusing to believe what his intuition screamed at him. So he inspected several more main storage containers and peered into the smaller chambers inside. The inestimable riches of the artifacts drew him with a transcendental power making him linger much longer than he knew was wise. The precious metals and jewels were paled by the art, incredible workmanship and detail that had not been seen on Earth for centuries...because no one could afford to put that much time into creating art and no one could afford to buy it. Even amateur artisans had given up long before his birth for want of demand. Here was a complete record of mans spiritual roots and the more he looked the broader area the cultural frame encompassed from the primitive to the sublime and he had only spent minutes flashing by the treasures, only touched the surface. The thought struck him that if the tunnel had been sectioned off and he was only in one section...how many other sections and what inconceivable wealth was contained in these secret vaults hidden away from the entire world?

There was no longer any doubt. It was surely the legendary Archives of the Church of the Old Religion. Deafening silence surrounded him. He stood for a moment and let himself believe. He felt the life force being drawn from him as if a man who had suffered such complete betrayal was rendered nonexistent before God. He breathed heavily. An image of the High Advocator's face intruded upon him. It was true then, it was all true...the Church was truly stockpiling riches, but that was not the issue causing his grief. It was the hoarding of sacred lore, it was the denying access to wisdom and whatever truths may be contained in these artifacts and thousands of manuscripts he had seen archived away and carefully preserved for the select to study and utilize that they may survive better than others. The facts were being edited for mass consumption. It was business, not religion. Like a huge technology company managing its licensed code...he grew furious at the immensity of it. The truth, he knew, belonged to those who would use it and as sure as the sun filtered through the polluted atmosphere those who withheld it from people were acting in hidden terror that others may rise up against them if strong enough and vanquish them. He trembled with uncharacteristic rage.

Suddenly, he was afraid. McGilvery and Sabiha were worried and they were all in danger. If this was the Archive, and it must be for nowhere else on earth could be like it, no one discovered here would be allowed to live despite it being of the Church and this he knew as well as his own name.

As Nash headed for the exit he entered a final container against all good judgment and even while he did it knew if was a fools errand. Life, as he understood it, was separate from the material world. They were independent universes that played upon each other and things that happened in one were not always rational to the other. He had stopped questioning himself, wondering how he knew or where the information had come from and had accepted the fact that some things just had no reason and transcended the act of human living. This was one of those times. He had to see what was in the container, what was filed in these particular chambers. Entering he noticed it was set up differently than the others. This one had a series of openings equally spaced along its front as if it were ordered rows behind the wall like a library of columns of files. And when he opened the third door that was exactly how it was. There were rows of small drawers lining both sides of the long chamber and the blue-violet light radiated from above. Though it was too dark to read, he saw that there was writing on each register. He shined his small light down and gasped in shock at what he saw. Etched into a metal tab was the inscription, *XiOma - 01960 - 01965*. Slowly he reached up and pulled out the drawer which slid with effortless ease floating on reverse polarity magnetic pulses so that there was no metal touching metal. Inside were three golden metal disks measuring about eight inches in circumference. They each rested on a magnetic field hovering in the center of the drawer. *If he moved one,* Nash wondered, *would it set off an alarm, would the slight fluctuation in the field show up on some sys-ops monitor setting off consequences he wasn't prepared to face?* He gently lifted up the center disk and slipped it into his coat pocket, then closed the drawer as carefully as he could realizing that he had stopped breathing–he gasped for air.

His heart was now racing with such speed that he was blinded certain nothing could happen to him. But his usual caution overruled exhilaration and he stealthily made his way back to the far corner from where he had first come and no alarms had sounded yet. Then he froze. There was a sound. He listened but could only hear his heart beat. Then it happened again. A thud. Muted. Far off. Then another, closer and another like doors closing in succession...suddenly and instantly a shaft of yellow light violated the dark infrared for a moment searing halfway across the space, and then disappeared. He was certain it had been a door opening and closing. Someone else was here. There was silence.

Detail was obscured in the dim blue-violet light and shapes came and went in the shadows, figments, tricks of the eye and the soul. His first urge was to run. He wished he could run. His heart demanded that he run and outdistance the danger, but he knew he could not. So he waited. Listened. Wondered if McGilvery and Sabiha were still at the crack watching and if they had seen the light. Could they watch the intruder? Slowly he inched his way along feeling exposed and completely vulnerable and though it was cold began to sweat. At last he clung to the wall and could just make out the rung ladder about ten feet away and within moments was climbing finally trying to breathe normally paying to nonexistent Gods he would not be betrayed by a sound.

Suddenly voices were beneath him. He froze and was completely motionless. He saw nothing. Sweat streamed down into his eyes stinging. Then Nash saw the two figures materialize from the shadows walking toward the ladder. Each ambled with a lanky, limber walk that made them look like their arms were too long or their legs too short–simian like slender orangutans. Whispers came drifting up the twelve feet where he was perched above them on the ladder and as the two stopped just a short distance from where the rungs began he started frantically searching for options.

"Shhhh..." one of them whispered below him, "Did you hear anything?"

After a moment the other answered. "Naaa..."

There was an audible sigh. "What a god damn waste of time. How could anyone get in here?"

"You remember the rats don't you?

"Rats are rats. I also remember the piece of concrete that fell during an aftershock. That kept us going for ten hours."

"Personally I could use a vacation."

"I got one."

"What do you mean?"

"Just that. I've got a leave coming up."

"Oh man..."

The figure on the right tilted his head back and mockingly placed his thumb and forefinger on the bridge of his nose. Looking down motionless Nash saw the white helmet with the small gold cross on the front, but uniform decidedly military...and the clerical collar...the same clerical collar all ministers of the old Religion wore. He could see their sidearms, short bulky ones carried on a strap over the shoulder, and one holstered. It was a strange and unnerving vision to see the symbols of life with those of death.

The guards stood talking. Bored, lackluster and neither one expecting anything out of the ordinary unaware of the access portal far above and the rung-ladder on the wall obscured by faint light and deep shadows. Nash noticed that they also had night vision goggles hanging around their neck, but thankfully did not touch them and as they slowly walked away routinely scouring the area he momentarily suspended his disbelief in God. One step after another he moved up the ladder with motions so smooth he would not have attracted attention even in full light. When he at last reached the top two pair of arms grasped him and yanked him through the opening.

"You're one lucky son of a bitch!" McGilvery whispered peering down from the opening to see if he could make out the figures any more

"Don't look at me..." Sabiha spat out, "I could just kill you."

Nash sat back against the wall intoxicated with fear and glory, drenched with adrenaline and testosterone and smiled sloppily like a drunk and held up the metal disk. It took a moment before either one looked at him and when McGilvery finally did he was not happy. "Now what the hell is that?"

"A Golden *XiOma.*"

"Jesus!"

Astonished Sabiha said, "You got it?"

"Just one."

"One?"

"There's drawers full of these things."

"Tell us later," McGilvery said emphatically, "we got to get out of here."

They waited for the yellow shaft of light to reappear and then vanish signaling the departure of the two figures and slid the cover back in place. Then they ran. They were careful not to step on the magnetic strip, but as they rounded the slight bend and finally had the stairway in sight they heard it. The sound from before. The robot maintenance train. Looking down from where they had just come the faint glow of light was suddenly blocked and the specter of the train car nearly filling the square passage as it rumbled mindlessly toward them left no doubt that there wasn't enough room for the robot and them side by side in the tunnel. The closeness of the space suddenly impinged. They sprinted for the stairway and ran frantically from the terror of bone and flesh being scraped and broken against concrete. Finally Sabiha and Nash clambered up and just barely managed to pull up McGilvery by one arm as the train clattered by knocking against his foot. Once above ground again they replaced the manhole cover just as it was with dirt and brush to cover their tracks.

Cold wind washed over them. The night was raging. They looked up into the sky and were humbled by the extremely rare spectacle of stars cast across the horizon as jewels glinting and shining bathed in luminant streams from suns light years across the galaxies in interstellar space where spirits dwelt wild and fine, restless and free. If there was fate it had occurred. If there was destiny it was happening. They all felt somehow blessed. The sight of stars was an omen.

The disk, as they later discovered, had been an ordinary metal alloy only plated with gold and was probably manufactured sometime in the late 20th century. It was a primitive storage disk recorded with a technology that had been long forgotten and though there may have been more information about it in the Archive, they did not have access to it. So McGilvery and some technicians at VOX took it as a supreme challenge to unlock the wisdom of the past and after hundreds of hours devised a method to retrieve the data off the metal disk without harming it. It was simply a matter of refracting laser light off the etched grooves at the exact right angle and then capturing the reflection with an instrument sensitive enough to translate the signals into digital information. The data was then decrypted and deciphered and run through translations programs until it appeared in English. There were no hard copies. Nash had studied it on his computer in the refuge of his back office surrounded by his old couch and wooden desk. He memorized it. As far as they could tell from the disk it had been a part of a huge body of organized knowledge that had been lost, or purposely obscured, in the Kaeien and had not been seen for over a hundred and fifty years.

Much later, after Nash had a chance to study and work with some of the information he experimented with it in counseling. The woman before him at last raised her face and smiled. It was a warm, disarming and distinctly human gesture. It cut through everything. A look of peace enveloped her. Nash struggled to keep his emotion hidden at his first apparent success with the new techniques he had learned from the disk. There was something in the woman's expression that made him certain a life had been changed. Something transcendent. He knew there was nothing of greater value.

- XIII -

Spirit's Breath

The economic beast lay sleeping just outside the gates. The fetid odor of its presence was a source of disgust and the panic it engendered when it rolled on its side at night and emitted deep and resonant groans at nocturnal visions playing before its brutish eyes and the huge taloned maw that struck out in fits of anxious dreams that maimed and terrorized were not so intolerable that anyone dared wake it. At least there was some economy. When there were masses of people they were expendable. Human beings were a commodity. Their purpose was to provide a buffer between the elite and the harshness of life in the real world.

Asia was old. It encompassed a way of life that was more ancient than anyone knew and the steps to its dance had their genus in primeval ritual. Yet all the eyes of the East looked up.

Preparations had begun three weeks earlier, which was unusual for the normal period had been known to exceed three months and sometimes even longer. This time was different, there was an immediacy demanded by events that were unprecedented. People lingered in the streets around the *Zhejiang Peiching,* the finest hotel in central Beijing and possibly in the entire Eastern Metropolis. It was originally the Continental Hotel based in the old Shanghai district designed and built by the British over two hundred years ago in what has come to be known in architectural texts as "The Masterpiece" of late colonial

318

architecture. Twenty-five years ago it was moved, or more exactly, grafted onto the latest technological infrastructure in the center of the Eastern hub by a group of entrepreneurs who saw in its legacy a priceless conceptual theme central to help them create a grand hotel for the new age that would be the most elegant, refined and expensive destination in the world. Relics of the Forbidden City adorned its lobby and its deluxe suites were authentic recreations of the Emperor's chambers down to the last details with what actual pieces of furniture had survived. Concubines, of course, were included in the price for those so inclined. It was layered and completely reconstructed around components, which at the time were experimental, and through the ensuing quarter of a century were absorbed in the technological mainstream making it no more than a node on the networks completely wired with optics ready for the most advanced computing and virtual hardware available. Since its inception, the experience had been the prime mover and the marketing strategy behind its development all fueled by greed– the prime mover of economic advancement. Early full size holographic virtual conferencing was a key draw to business and corporate meeting planners. With the advent of matured virtual technology and the perfection of zero resistance optical conductors its core technologies were complete.

The hotel was themed around royal life in ancient China. Famous screenwriters and directors were commissioned to create running operatic dramas for each section of rooms where entire walls were projectors and characters holographicly present populated the halls and suites. The term "Living Drama" was coined around the world. Guests were witness to all aspects of life and at any moment may walk in to a turbulent confrontation, a power struggle or some of the more intimate acts that were believed to have occurred within the Forbidden City centuries earlier. Time was suspended, but could be controlled by remotes that guests had the codes to and which could completely turn off all the effects. The *Zhejiang Peiching* was an immediate success attracting the wealthiest and the most influential clientele from both East and West and though their target audience was the business traveler, tourists overwhelmed the place in search of the unusual vacation.

Within a block of the most magnificent living experience money could buy people lingered. The streets were full of the sounds and smells and the hustling, bumping seething, serpentine flow of humanity that no amount of technology could ease. It had been tried. People lived. The traditions were essential elements indelibly tattooed on souls like the mask of each one's character that through pretense, guile and evil could be denied but never vanquished. So it was with the technological age where a man might operate a quantum computer system so advanced that it took many generations of geniuses to evolve it, not one of which could have done it alone in his own lifetime, and then turn to an animal deity asking for success in the future. Such were the elements of joss, luck and fortune.

Strange men had appeared in the neighborhoods surrounding the hotel. They were mostly Western, though some were oriental and obviously had no intention of keeping their presence secret as they spread out in a net of reconnaissance becoming omnipresent. Whenever anyone looked up, there one would be. Nobody paid the slightest attention to them however because so many dignitaries and corporate leaders occasioned the hotel that security personnel of all variety were no more unusual than a black haired woman with almond shaped eyes. Defenses were strengthened at the gates and walls around the *Zhejiang Peiching* which was done secretly and completely escaped the prying eyes of those neighborhoods who were so jaded as to have become bored with celebrity, as was the intention. The hotel employed one of the best security forces in the world in addition to those that accompanied government and private sector leaders because the Phan was always active and the facility was so wired into technology it represented all that was an anathema to them and everything they were against in modern society. The strange men paid attention to details that standing security forces could easily overlook. They were very highly paid and considered themselves professionals on about the same level as a surgeon.

Inside the hotel preparations were subtler, but nonetheless meticulous. It was understood amongst the staff that the conference guests were of number one importance to the management who traditionally pandered to pockets of wealth and power and had made a success of it.

The assistant managers for accommodations, food and catering, meetings and conventions, concierge services and technology were inspired to new heights of excellence and drove their underlings with merciless demands until the very sight of any one of them approaching was cause for a mass exodus. Special foods had been ordered and two of the main parties arriving were to be accompanied by their own chefs, which was causing the usual ego bruising turmoil in the kitchen that operated under the ageless philosophy that too many cooks spoiled the broth. The maids, valets and other service staff were forced to endure hours of drilling until it was certain that upon entering the hotel a person could theoretically never have to lift his own hand any higher than his elbow and still have all needs, wants and desires anticipated and served to perfection throughout his stay and when leaving would never think of the servants because they had been completely invisible. A spec of dust could result in a dismissal.

One key player in the conference had requested the entire upper floor of the hotel be reserved for his own use and so reservations had to be changed, rooms switched and eleventh hour public relations campaigns launched to handle disgruntled patrons who had to be bumped entirely from the roster. Two other players found out and demanded floors of their own and the whole charade had to be repeated. The hotel charged double for the spaces partly in recompense for lost business and partly out of the greed that had been the cornerstone of the whole *Zhejiang Peiching* project from the beginning and the fact that the participants were so rich it would make no difference to them at all.

The first to arrive was Hisham Mostafa 'Ali Fayed Al-Razio who was whisked in long after midnight under a cloak of security so tight not even the night porter realized he'd come and took up residence in the top floor apartments while his accompanying staff had accommodations elsewhere. His personal chef immediately went to work in the kitchen purifying all utensils and cordoning off exquisite food stores, which he considered, to the great consternation of the hotel chefs, far superior to the existing fare he found they had purchased. With his arrival an aura of grandeur and excitement fell over the hotel that was in excess of the usual celebrity bravado and down to the last manual

321

laborer the power that was now seated in the upper stories could be felt to the bone. It was like magic and made the weak giddy and gleeful and the able become irresolute and sad or antagonistic knowing intuitively that power of that magnitude does not come alone, but on the backs of many individuals who were sacrificed that the one may ascend and that it was unnatural and that no matter how hard they might try or how long they worked it would elude all but the blessed of them and like the throwing of the dice would become their addiction. Hisham Mostafa 'Ali Fayed Al-Razio knew all this. He did not care. He had been chosen.

Chaing Li-jen Monlin was thirty-eight years old and had been general manager of the *Zhejiang Peiching* for twenty-two months. He considered himself deeply honored and unworthy of such a responsibility even though he came from a wealthy family and success was expected if not guaranteed. He was not highly educated such as his sister who was an Ophthalmic surgeon specializing in aesthetic reconstruction of the eye, or his brothers all of whom were engineers involved in one way or another in the creation of the digital infrastructure or his father who was a propulsions systems analyst with the Space Agency, but he had skills they lacked. He was good with common people, and he liked to live well and be consumed in the circle of the rich and powerful so that even though he did not and would not ever possess their resources he could, with just a little effort, imagine himself one of them and if he was very lucky would be mistaken for one of them from time to time by an unwary tourist. This image he nurtured and had since he turned twenty and decided that his success in life would come from associations rather than through his own industry and so advanced an aggressive PR campaign within his peripheral sphere. To his superiors he was a model of efficiency, tact and decorum never raising an eyebrow at complying with a command and always looking out for the interests of those higher up than himself. He was also an intensely practical man and so through the network of Chinese workers in the hotel had developed the most complex system of graft ever devised within a commercial institution. He had his hand in everything and secretly employees called him, "Mister Ten-Percent." Chaing Li-jen

Monlin believed in preparing for the future. Everyone's bank account could use a little padding for lean times.

He had the employees organized into blocks. The bellmen's block, the food workers' block, the technical support group's block, the local gamblers' block and of course the best women for hire in the city. He scratched their back, they scratched his. It was run with the same efficiency, attention to detail and financial scrutiny as the hotel and the guests were served better with every need anticipated and so frequented the resort resulting in the lowest vacancy rate of any establishment in the Eastern Metropolis and everyone profited nicely.

Chaing had known since day one about the meeting of the Trust and had alerted his network that something tremendous was going to happen. He also knew that it was an urgent conference called by two of the three Providers and that there was concern in the global access community about a power push by one of the big three who had made significant technical advances that threatened to eclipse the other two, or at best relegate them to second rate status. Who specifically had called the meeting and who the one with the most power was he did not know, but he could speculate and with his keen insight into people felt certain he knew the one who would surface as the true Emperor. The consequences were obvious even to him, the Provider with the superior technology would gain more market share and become *the* global power. The opportunity was tantalizing. The amount of money that would flow through the hotel in the next few days would be staggering. He intended to have his fair share. All services would have to be exquisitely carried out to perfection not only for the sake of his network, but to maintain face, which was more important than even money.

In his small, unassuming office behind the front desk Chaing first received word that the second of the Provider triad was arriving from an associate limousine driver. A lump formed in his throat and even though he had witnessed one Provider's arrival, this was not the same. This man was Chinese. Impeccably dressed he arose and quietly spoke the name of his head bellman into the air. Instantly the man appeared as if he had been in the room all the time. "Number two." He said simply and then seating himself returned to his papers with an air of certainty that intricate details of protocol for which the hotel was famous would be carried out to the letter. He knew that under his employ were ancestors of the Emperors' household and perhaps a few who had come down the lifetimes to serve again as they had centuries earlier drawing the wire straight and preserving the continuity of a people who had been driven and beaten by a maelstrom of ideologies at the whim of a long chain of warlords. He was Chinese and the thought of it made him feel secure within the order of the universe. They were Emperors, he mused as he busied himself with last minute details of the impending events and smiled at how clear his perception was and attributed it to his not having an advanced education where he would be so filled with arbitrary ideas that all sense would leave him for the sake of ordered rationality like his brothers, his sister and his father. They were the illiterate, he thought, for in order to be truly learned one must know people, how to read them, to control them and to use them. His skills were senior in the divine order and because of this knew that though there were three now, there could be only one Emperor. He must choose wisely.

At precisely the right moment he stepped from the service stairwell of the stars he had climbed so he would be full of physical energy when the moment arrived. The carpeting, whose cost per yard was so high he could not afford to purchase one room, absorbed his footsteps and gave him a satisfying feeling of luxury. The walls with their delicate shades of color and fine hand rubbed rosewood and ebony moldings accented by the marble and alabaster pilasters and window sills curtained with fine silk drapery hand woven just as they were in the Ming dynasty would never grow old for him to whom this place was a living monument. At the end of the hall he turned expertly on his heel and took exactly four steps, reached out and opened the massive doors in front of him. The air was instantly filled with voices and a throng of people. He turned to follow a tall, broad shouldered and elderly Chinese man who was gracefully dressed in a dark blue suit. An entourage of people orbited around him vying for his attention and talking business. Chaing Li-jen Monlin was not the slightest bit interested in anything any of them had to say as he reached out and deftly opened another door for the elderly man whose long, firm strides took him sailing through its opening without the slightest hesitation as to whether it would be opened for him or not. Once more Chaing was there holding open the hallway doors and then raced ahead to open the first suite of rooms that had been prepared as the principle area for the elderly man who was the chief officer at the Provider for most of the Eastern Metropolis. His power was legendary and Chaing felt it flow through him as he made the suite come alive escorting a legion of bellmen into the room with flowers, fine wines and delicacies. Sashes were thrown back from the windows and all stood at attention as if for a white glove troop review while the man and his entourage flooded into the space. The old man smiled at Chaing as he entered.

Pleased for the rest of the day at the performance and that he was, as usual, present and the master of ceremonies seen by the most powerful and even smiled at he knew he had judged the event with the precise aplomb needed to gain the respect of the one who would be Emperor. The first to arrive was different. Hisham Mostafa 'Ali Fayed Al-Razio did not need pomp to obtain respect as his presence was imposing and aloof enough without it, but with the ascetic of a holy man and that unnerved Chaing, though he had been there as well in the middle of the night orchestrating the covert entrance, racing ahead to open doors and serve unseen as he had prepared unleavened wheat bread and the finest old brandy he was told was customary he did not enjoy it. Not in the same way he did with the elderly Chinese man. The Arab was different, obsessed in a way unfamiliar to him, antisocial, but the sense of power was unmistakable and he could not bring himself to look the man in the eye for he became dizzy around him.

The final link of the Provider triad arrived later in the day. She was a short, powerful Japanese woman of about forty-five. Her dark eyes were bright and unwavering and Chaing had her greeted with perhaps even more ceremony than the Chinese man, but it was with sympathy he fulfilled his duty to her for he felt she had fallen from grace and could never be an Empress. She ventured where she did not belong, but her power was equal to the others and Chaing was open to reevaluate his opinion if the turn of events called for it.

Dusk had descended upon the streets and eventide swept its blue violet shade across the land. Children were not yet nestled in their beds, but the young ones knew the inevitable was approaching and that the one thing unchanged throughout the centuries was that night remained a place for those who were stronger and more able to handle what lived there. The daylight was still for growing things and with the nightfall the virtual universe provided total escape for those who could not confront the force of living yet desired all its sensations. Nash had never felt more alive. His body bristled and seemed to have more vitality than he could remember since being a very young man and with every long step he took the consciousness of the earth beneath him and his connection with it gave him a sense of well being as if he possessed it all. He was holding everything in place by his thoughts so it would not float away out into the ether and leave him alone on this playing field barren and clean. The street leading up to Cedars was full of errant breezes and they brushed coolly across his cheek and tossed his hair and made his long coat fly out behind him like the standard of a ship racing off into the distances. This was the way it had been with an almost euphoric sense of discovery from the moment the first of the translations from the disk began to fall into place for him. It took a long time to realize the significance of their simplicity, but it came to him late while sleeping causing him to rise straight up out of bed and spend the rest of the night coming to grips with the consequences of the new realizations. Not until he observed it work for himself was the excitement complete and did he fully come to know how his life would change forever and see the *Golden XiOmas* as divining rods for his almighty purpose.

The lobby of the Trauma Center was overflowing. There was no ceiling on human misery and it filled up as fast as they could expand it until the financial oversight committee finally reached the same point all societies had reached painfully realizing that they were the chosen to draw the line as to who would live and who would die. It was etched out not by any arbitrary means, but simply as a confrontation with the economic reality that resources were never infinite no matter how wealthy the civilization was and in the end despite many good and humanitarian intentions it was money that determined individual survival. The doctors who fed the beast, save the altruist few who worked for the common benefit and not just for the stratospheric fees that were the rule, in the main refused to compromise their income demands and so the whole system revolved around the financial desires of the practitioner. Service to men based on the ability to pay was a concept as foreign to the medical profession as it was to business. Medical care that should by rights be an accessible commodity was a luxury and the profession had captured the market long ago having the one thing that human beings all needed contributing heavily to the economic collapse of the Kaeien.

The image of the *good doctor* remained though Nash did not like the specter of medical procedures that were half electronics, part drug, part surgery and only infused with a small amount of common sense. It rankled him that medical doctors refused to acknowledge the realm of the spirit in healing yet attempted to remedy religious and psychosomatic problems with physical medicine. Cleared by the desk he walked quickly through the ward down the corridor past the waiting rooms and emergency docks toward Fionica's cluttered office where he did not hope to find her, but knew she would retreat to eventually that evening. The enigmatic bond he had with her was something neither one of them could help. It was a mysterious accidental chemistry involving their mutually aligned purposes that had grown stronger with the recent revelations until he found himself here, in her territory as an emissary from the other side bearing news that he hoped would be as consequential to her as it was to him.

After an hour Fionica slipped inside her office. She looked tired and there was a mask of concern across her face that obscured Nash sitting behind her desk waiting. Her hands fiddled with the light auburn hair trying to pin it back up out of her face. Nash was struck by her beauty, which he had not noticed before. It wasn't a cosmetic loveliness, but a glow that came out of her being. "Good evening." He said.

Startled she looked up frozen in position with her arms raised and an expression of surprise. "I didn't see you." Then, after a moment, an unexpected smile.

"Sorry," he said starting to get up feeling suddenly uncomfortable in her chair, "I wanted to talk to you and it seemed like the best ..."

"I'm glad you did. Derek told me about the disk. A lot has happened hasn't it?"

Nash went on to explain in detail exactly what transpired that night in the wind up in the old Metrorail tunnel and about the Archives. "It was the most amazing thing I'd ever seen–especially since it was only rumors that I'd heard until tracing it on the WEB". He told her about the disk and the drawers full of other disks and then went over exactly what they had done to decipher the data and extract it. The story of what that data was and his subsequent efforts to apply it in real counseling was an explanation he punctuated with earlier experiences in helping others so she had something to compare it to. He saw people when they were at their most vulnerable and it gave him a very intimate view of human nature and he talked as one member of the healing profession to another. "Fusing. People were traumatized. Isn't that what you found? Doesn't seem to be physically damaging, but the experiences change people's behavior."

"That's it," she agreed. "There are physiological changes of course, some damaged nerve endings and a cessation of endocrine function in the affected area, loss of blood pressure, but that accompanies all shock...and in some cases severe damage purely from the electronics. The effect on the mind is more devastating than drugs in my opinion."

"I think I can tell you why."

Fionica regarded him curiously for a moment nervous at being drawn into waters deeper than she was used to though understanding the implications of his statement. It excited her with the possibility of underlying causes that she had always suspected and for two centuries had been studied as psychosomatic illness and faith healing. "Go on." She urged.

"It was purely by accident that I uncovered it. Using the technique as I explained the woman seemed to become..." he grappled for the right way to describe it, "calmer is the only way I can describe it, it was easier for him to communicate with me, he was more comfortable and laughed. And then it just...came out. He had been given a command while fusing, it was part of the transmission..."

"Like brainwashing?

He considered it. "I suppose, only it seems more deeply imbedded. I would never have discovered it without this new information."

"That's fantastic!" She rose and began to pace the small office between the stacks of files and books and medical magazines. "Can you imagine the ramifications of it? In the transmission? Must be that new nanoflat panel technology. It's unbelievable...! Who would...?" She stopped suddenly as if realizing something amazing was being completely overlooked. "What was it?"

"What?" Nash asked.

"The command?"

"Something about 'obeying God'..."

"Obeying God?"

"Yes. I had trouble getting it all as she couldn't quite recall the exact wording, but it was to that effect."

She shook her head with disbelief. "I don't... did McGilvery tell you about the rise in the crime stats coincident with this fusing phenomena?"

"That's right."

"...how could 'obeying God' make for criminal behavior?"

"That's an easy one and any student of religion should be able to tell you."

"Tell me then."

" Men aren't bad."

Fionica waited and when Nash did not elaborate she nudged him to continue in a way that appeared she was following him, "Of course...?"

"Simple. If one assumes a person is motivated by evil then it holds he would have to be forced to act in a good way. But most people aren't motivated by evil, even the worst ones I find are just trying to do what they feel is right to survive. They're just full of conflicting intentions and can't think logically...can't predict consequences." Then seeing that she wasn't quite understanding, "It's like this, if you force a man to do something he's already doing he'll protest...and if you force him into unconscious to do something he's already doing...it's the root of madness. Think of it! The behavior makes no sense because the cause is hidden. It's a hidden influence."

"...and it makes them dull."

"What do you mean?"

"We've had a lot of accident victims come in here, stupid things, like they're not paying attention or drowsy. A whole spate of them."

"Makes sense, just the same as someone coming to after being knocked out..."

Fionica looked intensely at Nash as one who had a complete grasp of the physical sciences to his counterpoint in the spiritual universe and imagined a bridge between the two. Her mind was churning with data being aligned, reevaluated and shuffled into a new order with a new hierarchy of significances and she sat on the desk her left hand aimlessly fiddling with small objects while she was adding pieces to the intellectual puzzle. There were long minutes of silence when she suddenly realized she had been lost "I...sorry, I have a tendency to intellectualize..."

"Me too." Nash smiled awkwardly. He always had a hunted feeling. Sabiha, while attractive, was but a good friend who perhaps had been drawn to him as a result of her own eccentric abilities that did not fit in and so required him as a sounding board. There was a dual nature to her, one side was coping with her unusual abilities and the other sought out the tragic and borderline of life as if she needed the dichotomy to balance out her existence. Her whole purpose lie somewhere in the development of the Trauma Center and anything outside of that had no relation to her existence. Nash could understand the similarities between them and the bond they had, but not the fact that each of them was missing something essential in the process of being alive.

Two spirits were transfixed. There was a moment when it seemed the world was still. For that time nothing moved. The great herds of migrant animals of memory ceased in their tracks, the heaven aflame with a billion winged creatures held its breath, clouds were motionless, babies stopped crying, clocks stood, the breathing, dreaming, sweating masses momentarily withdrew from their endless search for happiness. Nash struggled, if he did not seize the moment it would slip silently by into the stream of all other moments and the world would continue on its journey unaffected except that he would have let it the moment pass on his voyage and it would never come again as long as he was alive. Perhaps he had reached the point in his long track of lifetimes where he must change, where the demands of him were new.

He was surrounded by a pristine night. Through the desert and across its endless vista he could see the edge of the cosmos beyond the horizon line where one bright star hung near the bottom of a crescent moon. He imagined himself a Bedouin. The unrestrained feeling of freedom possessed at owning little and being one's own master in an existence amid the broad flat expanses where the unparalleled open space allowed one to be simply as God's instrument with amnesty from the petty worries that went with the cities. The sounds of camels growling as they settled down for the night lingered in his ears along with his expectations of hearing the Voice. Hisham Mostafa 'Ali Fayed Al-Razio wandered through the upper floor of the *Zhejiang Peiching* amid other wanderers in kaftans like his own. He could see them spread out across the campsites and through the oasis and they gave him comfort even though they were avatars, holographic virtual people each with an identity much like his own only synthetic. The walls projected the images while the sounds and the odors were produced independently synchronized with the action. The breath of another world came and went as desert breezes.

The special program had been opportunistically placed by General Manager Chaing as second nature without even the slightest thought if it would be appropriate or violate the hotel's ambiance by supplanting ancient Chinese culture for that of the Bedouin. He was anticipating a very important guest's desires and had the foresight to arrange for one particular director who was especially covetous of a contract with the networks to have an opportunity for a nearly personal presentation in the form of his work. Very intimate work that was of the blood.

The man in the upper stories had much on his mind. He had been having trouble with his hearing the whole week in anticipation of the hastily called conference and so was expecting the Word to be delivered in an exalted mystic instant that came unexpectedly and passed too soon. The avatars wafted by him affecting little more then a pleasing sensation such as a painting or a work of art does to a room, but the highly skilled, state-of-the-art technical aspects of the production like the random facial characteristic changes or the glow cast by the starlight that was entirely computer generated eluded his consciousness. Pressing matters occupied his higher faculties and so he paced throughout the hallways and rooms of the upper most floor as he was accustom to in his own palatial spaces. Trivial concerns such as cost per diem and the army of support personnel that attended his every whim, composed of his own and the hotel's staff, did not enter his mind because, if one were to ask, he was occupied with truly important issues. Of the highest consequence was his secret weapon in the unspoken war between the providers, which had been going on since the early 20th century, but he knew it went far deeper than that. He waved his hand with the remote and the fleeting images of the desert faded back into their virtual void to sleep for some future occasion when they again are awakened to their duty having neither aged or reconciled their precarious position in the hierarchy between the souls of men and their minds and will take up their train of thought right where they left it as if no time had elapsed whatsoever. Electric dreams.

He thought the message was upon him and so had wanted to prepare by eliminating all distractions, but it was only some of his senior staff for an impromptu meeting. Rattling up the hallway outside the huge imposing entrance he imagined them like a coven of skittish witches hiding their devious plans and incantations so that they may pass by a superior power undetected to be free to exercise their evil another day. They had been beside themselves for weeks in frantic preparations for the conference afraid someone from the other providers would outshine them and gain an edge on the market. Ultimately their stock options would suffer so the incentive was monumental. They were hawk nosed and sour but he put up with them out of necessity. One has to pass over many rotted trees on the divine path.

"Iverson's here. I saw him in the lobby." A man with receding hair complained with a fish wife's edge to his voice. They were deployed around a huge kidney shaped table that was made from a slice of igneous rock so thin that it was translucent and had to be sandwiched between epoxy layers. It was as slight as paper yet could hold the weight of a car. "I hope he's not talking bandwidth redistribution again."

Nods and grunts of agreement met his comment from the others around the table...most with the marks of too many years of good living; big bellies, sparse yet healthy hair and soft, pale skin that glowed from being well rested except for the slight bloodshot eyes and red veins at the ends of noses from too much alcohol...as spirits and wines were passed from one end to the other. Hisham Al-Razio disapproved and they all knew, but allowed it because each needed the jolt to bring their minds fully alert and perform the way he expected them too. "Popular pressure..." a man answered, "he always comes around." He spoke unconcerned as if the certainty of their hegemony were etched in the cosmos, an attitude that was reflected in their love of material possessions. The rewards were unimaginable to even the rich because the Providers had ridden the sublimated urge of mankind to immerse itself in a complete vicarious environment and obliged by funding the development of technology that made virtual worlds virtually irresistible. The result was that they had clearly become the dominant economic force on the planet. People behaved like they could exist on entertainment alone and placed it above food and shelter and even family. These men were at the top. Each of them was worth more than many small countries and the array of glittering wrist watches, sublimely tailored suits fashioned from fabrics of infinite exaltedness and state-of-the-art high-tech gadgetry strewn across the table in personal service was truly awesome.

"Terrorism works!" Another said throwing up his hands in mock defeat. "The Phan hit so many times this year it made us look bad...

liberal journalists..." he turned to the side and spoke in hushed mock confidence, "like there must be a good reason...right?"

Hisham Al-Razio listened from over by the tinted window through which he surveyed what he could see of old central Beijing immersed in the ubiquitous gray-green smog that hung in pockets over all industrialized areas of the earth. It made the sunlight appear a murky orange fluctuating to a near olive by the late afternoon. He had always thought that they were providing a better world for those whose lot was not as rarefied as the ones in this room. *Men did it to themselves,* he bitterly harped at himself as if trying to alleviate some feeling of responsibility that slowly seeped in every time he was defenseless, their greatest vice was their rapaciousness and the consequences of obsession were well known even in ancient times but still they persisted and could not just have land but empires, could not have craft but industry, could not hunt but create extinction, could not develop without depleting resources... It was the human flaw that stood over every other flaw. The craving for wealth. Its black heart had withered the land and the sky and the seas until what else could men do than to escape from the place where all grace and beauty had been stolen by earlier generations. He had arrived and praised Allah that he had the great fortune to have been born in this time in this place. It was the will of Allah. Now he had been chosen and by his hand with his instrument would he turn the people toward righteousness again and nothing would stand in his way, not the government, the terrorists, the competition...the doctors still told him it was trouble with his inner ear and he laughed to himself at their pathetic weakness. A few of the men overhearing it took furtive sidelong looks at the strange man who held more power than any other living person ever had on earth. The power alone engendered fear in them as if no man should have such an awesome weapon to control other men, yet they were addicted with an insatiable need to serve him.

"Seems like CWVT was their main target in the West." somebody said.

Suddenly aware of danger Hisham Al-Razio looked fiercely at the table. "There is no vendetta." he pronounced solemnly and with finality across the room unable to stand even the thought of anything coming between himself and the realization of his goals. "It was always random violence." Then added, "They are sociopaths." Images of Roxanne and what he imagined Yzak must look like filled his space as he fumed at the thought of anyone targeting his instrument, especially now that the power was finally strong enough to reach millions. He looked at his watch and mentally began to count the minutes until the most powerful message ever would be transmitted. It was no accident the meeting of the Trust was being held now, here, in the Eastern Metropolis, out of harms way where the consequences could not be predicted and where he could at least claim exoneration by reason of absence.

Charles Iverson had been in meetings for so many days that the darkness and light blurred and became indistinguishable. He managed to pull two hours sleep in the time it took his flight to span half the globe and deliver him to the East for the impromptu meeting of the Trust. Somehow word had gotten out and for the ten days prior to his leaving he had been besieged by lobbyists from every political conviction deluging him with all possible variations on communications, control and public access. He was badgered by the conservatives to redistribute the bandwidth existing on the networks because each particular provider subdivided his government allotment and still had excess space to transmit private communications and corporate programming. And most importantly to sell for folding money. Each Network had additional bandwidth as well, which they sold space on to business for their wide area intranets reaping pure profit having no money invested. Business interests wanted more government subsidized access... *good for the economy*. The government wanted money and the pressure now was to rescind the allotments given in the days when they were needed incentives for the massive private funding of the optical infrastructure. Special interest groups represented every other variation on the theme. Senior officials, long before he'd been appointed to the post, had given up trying to understand the complexities of internetwork communications that had become a maze of protocols, programming languages and representative companies each with their niche in the market and a perceived value thereof, so had left the task of management to the Global Communications Commission, which was supposed to be a bilateral agency though in truth it was a dictatorial coup d'etat. Up until now his bosses were more concerned with income from taxes and other government sources with which to grapple with the ever increasing social cancers that seemed proliferate deep in mans unconscious fervor to move forward and make his civilizations the mightiest powers in the universe, as if nature was an instrument of retribution for the inhumanity suffered by all in the name of progress.

He closed the door on the last person to want something from him nearly bruising the man's outstretched hand and locked it with the remote given to him by Chaing, the General Manager, which controlled nearly everything particular to his suite of rooms and most of the other general conveniences of the hotel as well. He had stayed at the *Zhejiang Peiching* before and Chaing Li-jen Monlin always outdid himself with his intuitive anticipation of what might make the stay a more memorable experience. In return he had scheduled meetings and important conferences there, not out of any perceived obligation, but rather out of a sense of balance they say native peoples once had returning something to the forest that sustained them so that it never became depleted.

His suite of rooms was dimly lit with an incandescent glow, which was difficult to see the source of, and small pools of light in corners or high up recessed and subdued coming from nowhere. The walls were shimmering and through the gossamer blanket of light that lie on their surfaces scenes of the imperial household could be witnessed as holographic avatars that came and went without regard as to who was watching them. His depth perception was altered and it gave him the feeling of being slightly intoxicated possibly because he had not had sufficient sleep for several nights running. Lacquered chairs upholstered with fine silk tapestries surrounded him in luxury and wall hangings portrayed fabulous panoramas of a China centuries earlier awash in mists and intrigue when the culture was at its zenith and no one walked inside the Forbidden City unless he had been summoned. They say the ghosts of the many Emperors' concubines inhabited the vacant chambers long after the dynasties were finally decimated and kept the memories for those who were banished from their home and their legacy. Perhaps, thought Charles Iverson, he was himself a broken piece of what might have been a great world empire ruled in an iron clasp by brilliant tyrants and now even this fragment was facing extinction. He walked with trepidation and inhaled the ambiance of the ancients who, despite their lack of science and technical advantages, always appeared wiser and more able to view lucidly the truth through the voices and devious acts of depraved men who then as now filled the social hierarchies.

Through the long entrance hallway he walked and as he entered larger chambers they were illuminated with a pass of his hand across the rheostat on his remote setting the lighting to where he desired. The avatars made him feel self conscious though he knew they were not sentient and could not see him and were only preprogrammed diversions a part of what the hotel was known for, but he could not shake the feeling none the less. They were not turned off though he had the power to extinguish their lives and blot them out of the cosmic order as if a god with his remote, but preferred to keep them wandering about unexpectedly and to continue hearing the sound of the dialects that had been dormant for three hundred years and observe their behavior as an uninvolved participant, a silent guest humbled by his own lack of decorum. He poured himself a drink of a strong clear liquor at the small bar that was constructed entirely of jade whose lights flickered through it and the anomalies of each particular surface gave off distinctly different hues of green and reflected on the walls in a honeycomb of soft shades. It burned his throat and he liked it. The sensation made him remember he was alive. After so many days of talk and discussions of business he was drawn taut and dry of any semblance of human sensitivity and so he savored the torch of the liquor. It was a local drink only found in this section of the Eastern Metropolis and had strong narcotic properties that kept it off the commercial market, but General Manager Chaing saw to it that the hotel was always stocked with the finest selections of it that could be had on the black market.

He collapsed on the great round bed that lie in the center of a room that was dark at one end and graduated to the color of eggshells at the other. The spread covering it was exquisite silk and he ran his hand across it in wonder certain it was one used by the royal family far back in the forgotten histories. There were porcelain vases, carved jade and ivory and a dark, rich wood he did not know the name of from which intricate screens were fashioned that he imagined ethereal Chinese women discreetly undressed behind mysteriously extinguishing the light before they emerged.

Trying with all his concentration to let down and allow the knot in his stomach to resolve he could not extinguish the fury inside him. His whole life he had walked the bureaucratic ladder placing one foot in front of the other so that its heel was just touching the toe and because of that it took a very long time for him to get anywhere. He did however finally arrive subscribing to the philosophy that forward progress no matter how tediously slow was forward progress. To others he knew the trials he had faced were nearly invisible and he had carefully nurtured the PR image of the bright young man with the brutal honesty who was fueled by righteous indignation and a passion to serve. Money was not an object for him and because of family wealth he had the wherewithal and the time to approach public service with a sweepingly idealistic platform that had attracted the power centers and prompted them to place this cyclone in an area they would rather not confront, or more exactly one that was not producing an income and had little prospect of doing so. The Global Communications Commission. It was, after all, a bilateral organization bowing equally to the East as to the West. The pleasures his fortune bought him soothed the frustrations. Charles Iverson was aware of his gifts and as in all such cases where ability is mirrored in the self concept he had a great contempt for most people though he rarely betrayed it, and then only in times of severe stress such as the Phan elicited in him with their insidious fanaticism and petty bombings that did nothing more than infuriate him and help cement his already strong resolve to annihilate them. What he was after was a pinnacle of power he knew he would never reach. That made it twice as sweet. He did have power, but when he was surrounded by the other parties of the trust who had followed the commercial route and had amassed not only fortunes much greater than his but systems to generate fortunes guaranteed by government monopoly...it touched off an insatiable fury in him, an emotional explosion that originated deep in the well of his soul and would not abate even with the most rational and logical reasoning but fumed to the surface like the massive eruption of a latent volcano.

The bilateral agency had been transformed from within to the most powerful world bureaucracy. It had earned him universal respect from the private sector and a certain disdain from government workers because he had usurped his power from the conduit of the people. He didn't care. The people were followers and needed leaders as vitally as they needed religion. What he did care about was the fact that he had leverage with the Providers, they respected his position and would do nearly anything to comply with GCC regulations on the theoretical basis that the agency could pull the plug, could redistribute the bandwidths and even withdraw all network rights from any Provider who refused to come into the fold. It was a game he played. A highly dangerous game. For he knew that when push came to shove any one of the three Providers was more powerful than...some nights he had lain awake in a sweat fearing they would truly send someone to kill him. He had taken it to the limit before, played close to the chest, but then threats were his only defense and the fury he felt drove him to do irrational acts. Perhaps this time he would restructure the networks. It may be time for a fourth Provider, and as luck would have it he was past retirement age and would need something to keep him busy soon, something worthy of his talents.

He poured another drink and aimlessly wandered around the suite with his shoes off and shirt undone. Thirst for power was stronger than a need to rest and though he had not slept well in a week his body was charged and electrified by events and he was wide awake and bristling with energy. And then there was the ire. It lie coiled up in his belly and made his muscles tight and his stomach tense, he felt strong, superhumanly strong, as if the shell of the body was an encumbrance to the real purposes he was born to. He suddenly saw himself below as if he were looking down from the ceiling.

From the dark end of the bed chamber an elegant Chinese woman with huge, cryptic eyes walked with long deliberate steps. She wore open flowing robes with gold and fuchsia thrushes exploding off cream colored gardenias on a black silk field beneath which she was nude. Her raven hair was pulled straight back off her forehead and hung three feet down her back. She was barefoot. The room abruptly smelled of saffron. A wave of emotion coursed through him. Once again he was struck by the longings of the body.

She hovered in radiance her beauty was so exquisite appearing not even to be touching the ground. Charles Iverson watched without moving his eyes becoming hooded, then took one more drink of the clear, strong liquor and threw down the glass, which shattered against the wall. The robe was not removed, but rustled aside as the woman reclined in the exact center of the circular bed so weightless and restless there was hardly a wrinkle on the silk spread beneath her and curled and cradled the naked body as giant petals do the pestle and stamen. He wondered at her translucence and was amazed that he could not see through her skin to the inner workings of the body with its organs pulsing and churning sending chemical signals automatically from one end to the other. She looked directly into his eyes and did not for an instant let her attention waiver making him forget all else around him so enrapturing was the gaze and so strong was the flow of affinity as if there was nothing else. The lightness of her being lifted him. He studied the form of her, the shadows and highlights, the incomprehensible glow of her flesh that made his hands tremble. In a moment he was perched over her and inhaled the aroma of saffron and Gardenias and a peculiar sweet female humanness that sank deep into his chest and was absorbed like a drug making his body more on edge than it already was. He gasped in huge breaths of air trying to merge with the feminine qualities that were so opposite to his middle age, muscular gruffness, but could not satiate his desire to possess not just the physical but the quality of her beingness as well subconsciously feeling that it was an unguent of youth and vigor and hope that he had lost somewhere on the long road of his life and now would pay a dear sum to regain its command. His eyes wandered on their own across her skin exposed as the robe had fallen open; small breasts with dark Tuscan red nipples that were firm and pointed, the flow of her navel running down from the chest in a softness beneath her ribs that was indescribable within the context of the languages he knew but could only be thought of as many partially opaque layers creating a ghostly ethereal appearance moving like a river caught by the sea. Her thighs were extraordinarily long and rounded and slightly apart revealing the dusky skin of her sex enflamed by a tiny tuft of long ebony hair. He was afraid to touch her.

Bending down he let his lips brush across her abdomen and breathed in her scent. He thought he knew then how an animal felt, a base creature that had not the presence or cognitive capabilities of a man yet was subject to the same tests of survival, a coarse, strong organism who had the wild instinct to do whatever was needed without a thought of appearance if it was necessary...he could not withhold himself though even he possessed some semblance of moral turpitude that had its roots far within the concept of religion he had. Perhaps it was the liquor, he would have liked to think it was the liquor, but more actually it was age that gave him a sense of grossness and a feeling of loss mixed together with a driving physical passion that was almost beyond him unlike that of a younger man who, though weaker, was more one with the body. It could not be recaptured. He tasted her. With his lips he kissed her sex. With his tongue he felt her sweetness. Her legs welcomed him and he could feel the warmth of her inner thighs sliding against his rough cheeks as they moved invitingly. She gasped silently when his tongue touched a certain part, and exhaled with a long, sweet breath. He was driven with a curious exterior view while his body was stirred against his will. The overwhelming urge was to devour her as an animal with his prey and to tear at her flesh with his teeth until it ripped from the bones and he could taste the blood and so he ravaged her without shame. Would she sacrifice herself to him? Her eyes did not leave his and whenever he looked there she'd be and he felt truly profane yet the smell and taste of her filled his chest and brought all the tension and strength he had felt for the past week to the absolute wild pinnacle. The fury demanded release. He raced before the wind. He did not know what the woman thought and could not bear what may have been a truth and so imagined scenarios some of which were fleeting and others dogged him and made him rapacious, but for whatever reason she may have had for offering herself to him he was

341

drawn into her as into a maelstrom without any logic or rationale just purely as a rampaging genetic urge.

He raised himself up on his knees before her and stripped the rest of his clothes away swaying slightly from the drink and paused like the hurricane before the onslaught aware of his worn body before her sparkling grace, conscious of his callused and brutal appearance before her loveliness. He frowned as perspiration formed on his brow and shoulders shaking with anticipation his breathing coming in a frantic staccato. She lie in motion before him, not still for an instant her eyes constant with his, her exposed body like the tides and currents and eddies awash with such immaculate beauty that he could not face her directly. The smell of the shore and distant sea birds came to him. The elegant woman faced him with comfort as if taunting him, a slight mischievous but serious gleam in the huge almond eye baiting him, daring him to touch, to caress, to even attempt...unexpected strength welled up inside and blurred his vision and drove him on. He fell heavily on her as an assault making her suck in her breath and jerk upward tossing her hair as he impaled her viciously his pale yet stocky, muscular middle aged frame convulsing with an energy welling up from the genetic source, moving with a driving, tribal rhythm pouring out the last of its life from all the lifetimes until now for this one chance, this one opportunity to procreate before death. It gave him an immense headache yet he mindlessly pummeled the exquisitely fine porcelain skinned woman whose legs wrapped around him to lock into death's embrace, her arms flaying out of control, her hair flying in all directions, her lips mouthing silent screams, her eyes watching his eyes. He held himself above her with his arms planted one on each side like pillars, the sinews on his shining back rippled, the backs of his thighs and buttocks grew taut and knotted his strong belly moving against the light bird-like woman's alabaster softness like a piston, a dynamo wound too tight that was unraveling with complete abandon. Her breath came in sharp bursts. In the back of his mind he wondered how he would repay general manager Chaing Li-jen Monlin.

The aged woman's name was Genjii Hideyoshi. She was born in the ancient city of Edo on the island of Honshu. She was the only woman ever called Kensei, sword-saint, because of her masterful business acumen. Chaing had accompanied her to the suite of rooms that had been reserved walking behind and slightly to the side as was the custom with the woman who, he considered, had fallen from grace. The general manager had an ominous view of Genjii Hideyoshi despite her high position as head of one of the three Providers and a prominent force in the Trust and could not think of her as Kensei and though that was regarded by him as another unrefined Japanese custom he still would not let it be associated with her. In his mind there was a sacred sense of order about which the universe revolved, there were things to be kept in balance such as good and evil too much of either would send the world tumbling on its catastrophic demise no matter what the intentions were. There was a higher call, a more sublime way which men were not privileged to except in rare moments of catharsis. Life was not as it appeared. So she had let herself into the rooms with Chaing accompanying as he felt his presence was important even if his role had been usurped. A woman belonged where a woman belonged, he thought, certainly not in command of global power.

Long after the general manager had left, whom she had hardly noticed and any glimpse of him lingering around the periphery had been dismissed as those of any other servant in her employ, she worked. It was a solvent for all the unfulfilled dreams of her youth that seemed unfairly to have been vanquished one by one as she grew from child to woman until as she reached maturity there were no illusions left to capture her imagination, to drive her forward with hope, to set her heart racing with anticipation or to enrapture her with the mystical quality inherent in the act of living. There was one performance in which she found contrition for the things of life that were stolen by circumstance and could never be regained and that was the planning of an action and then the fulfilling of it through others. She was a sword-saint of management, a Kensei born with a gift.

It was seldom that she retired before 3 AM and even more rare that she did not appear in her office before 8:30 AM. Sleep she believed was a waste of time and her only use for it was to let an idea fully germinate through the night so that it could assume its full power and force the following morning if it had the Spirit in it that is, only then. Otherwise it would fade with the sun. The Spirit was something she could not define though it was brutally abused as a truncheon when she was trying to get compliance from her subordinates, but she knew it as an ethereal quality that imbued life to an idea and recognized its source as coming from a state of grace. The first thing she did was to close down all of the holographic virtual reality simulations in her suite so that the walls were silent and then to engage all available vidtels for the incessant surveys of each provider's networks so that she maintained a continuously updated concept in her mind of all their content. At any given moment in the day she could recite what was available on-line, who the key audience was and their demographics, what its most current rating and share was and if it had an option for syndication outside the network that developed it and owned the copyrights. The overriding concern was her own network of backbone and trunk lines and what streamed over them to the multimillions of viewers she cherished and thought of as willing constituents who absorbed her ideas on sociopolitical issues as gospel by reason of her acute ability to target programming from each network to reach the key demos for the geographical area it served. She commanded a legion of script editors who analyzed the immense volume of material according to strict guidelines and passed along all new projects for her personal approval. It was rumored she could read 500 pages a day, still keep her busy schedule and still remember almost every word. She was an awesome business machine with grit.

The finger of her right hand reached out and lightly touched the burnished, rosewood finish of a high backed chest that stood against the wall a sentry from centuries earlier that perhaps mused at the train of events paraded before it, the quiet observer whose witnessed adventures were reflected in the brass hinges and fittings that held their luster even after all this time. In her mind images of the red Imperial city ran up against the blue flare of light that was a metaphor for the present and she figured on how to reconcile the two. Extinction was the one thing that she was obsessed with and the fundamental challenge to her intellect was as basic as the concepts that had been known to man since the creation of the Rig Veda Samhita and the *Hymn To The Dawn Child* nearly ten thousand years distant. All things end, nothing lasts forever, every man must die. The Imperial dynasties had fallen and she saw no specific reasons yet and was determined that her power would be infinite and live through her successors as stand-in progeny by reason of her barren womb.

Dusk fell. Finally she was alone with the flickering images on the screens of the Vidtels surrounding her. She had become hoarse with talking in the past two days and now wished to speak to no one until the next morning. Yet there were onlookers. There was normally a VT for every room in the suite, but general manager Chaing had more installed in anticipation of her stay knowing intimately her preferences and habits and despite the fallen woman's indifference to him fulfilling his duty. Faces enveloped her. Images circled her. Eyes watched from the virtual void.

The hold on power that was so tenuous in some others' hands she maintained with a smooth, firm assurance and felt no anxiety at all one way or the other about the threat to revenues from the rumored redistribution of bandwidth or the loss of market share to the one that was so driven. There was no threat of loss because she did not possess anything living merely as an apparition wafting through the business environments having all her needs anticipated and fulfilled before she had to voice any of them and taking advantage of the things of others as a sojourner. Power was Spirit, it was intangible. The accouterments that came and went with fortunes did not interest her and so she allowed the passion play unfolding around her to sustain all her material desires. With bare feet she padded from room to room in the low light her short, muscular legs giving her an extremely symmetrical and forceful stance like a bulldog despite the luxuriously deep plush carpet that absorbed every movement on its surface so that one had the sensation of floating. *Kensei* admired all the antiques that filled the spaces and exuded the aura of royalty breathing in the ambiance and then out again not willing to become too comfortable with the sensations of richness lest she become complacent. From VT to VT she wandered sometimes taking notes on her small computer that was shamed by her constant intellectual activity only interrupted by the calls she made out of necessity to her juniors ensuring compliance was obtained to some action or another according to the plans and programs she meticulously kept in her head. Soon the night waned into early morning.

The critical point in her life occurred when she was only fourteen years old. She was reading a history of Japan that had survived the Kaeien and had not been collected by the rememberers and so, by reason of her family's wealth and influence, had found its way into her possession. It told of Kublai Kahn and of the Divine Wind. It was when the Mongols ruled Asia from the Yellow Sea to Vienna. In 1274 they sailed out one morning on Japan to make its shore their eastern tip. A storm forced them back. Again in 1281 they sailed with a great armada this time of thousands of ships and an undefeated army whose morale was at its zenith. The Spirit arose against them and the typhoon drew such force and fury and pounded with such savage sounding that 4000 of the Kahn's ships were lost and over 100,000 of the fiercest fighting men the world had seen to that point vanished into the brine. Kamikaze they called it, Divine Wind.

The soldiers on the shore who waited, who had already given up their ghosts to the coming battle and even though they had learned to fight as a team like the enemy, it was a daunting, relentless and unyielding foe that approached and they had chosen death as was the warriors way. The wind was so powerful it confirmed the cosmic order. Were they too lost then? She had wondered about the soldiers on the shore who witnessed the annihilation of the fleet yet had already chosen death, how did they go on then? Where did they go? Not back to their wives or to the communities who had ceremoniously severed their spiritual ties as consecration of their vows to defend to the death. She imagined they wandered, and many indeed had become *Ronin*, masterless Samurai. And others, she thought, roamed the centuries looking for resolution and then it came to her. She, herself, was a Ronin who had chosen death for Japan on that day in 1281. The pictures were as clear as the windy day she had first set foot on the pebble strewn beach where the hoards were bound. From that point on she thought not just within the context of the short span of time that encompassed her memories of this one life, but of many lifetimes all in one linear moment from then until now. It gave her perspective and made her see the futility of owning material goods. From that moment on she had owned nothing and owned everything.

At the prescribed hour the servant arrived with the tea. She had slipped into an antique Kimono, one of many that she used and were spread across the territory of the Provider so that they would be there whenever she needed them. They were gifts. She left them where they were and used them at will. When the servant had left she fastidiously turned off the sound on all the VTs, though the faces still watched with muted voices, and knelt down before a low lacquered table, which even if it was Chinese drew no complaints. It was then she performed the ceremony. Alone in the huge suite of rooms haunted by lingering phantoms with low light and shadows the only company and hollow video images as witnesses she executed the tea ceremony exactly as she remembered it from the year 1290 when she had learned it. She placed cups for her companions who were not there.

The burn of the brandy touched his lips and then his throat. It was a luxury he relished, but was always reserved for a stay at the *Zhejiang Peiching* for he never drank anything stronger than wine otherwise. This though was truly special. An ancient Napoleon brandy. His bony fingers carefully held a delicate porcelain vessel painted with a miniature panorama of a river valley where a monumental battle was taking place. It was a creation of the Qing state, hand painted by a Jürchen or as they later became known a Manchu. The whole ritual was laced with symbolism and it was that he cherished for his fiber called out for ceremony it being the bed of life through which the river flows. Hong Taiji was eighty-six years old and bore the name of the founder of the Qing dynasty and he too had struggled his way to the pinnacle of power in order to channel the clear, infinite wavelengths direct to the soul. It gave him a tremendous feeling of command touching so many lives with so little effort and at the same time gave him an insatiable greed for the capabilities to touch more. He was not necessarily a moral man though one might have called him a spiritualist as he was given to calling upon ancestors, which was another reason he so looked forward to his stay at the hotel because it was the Imperial furniture that gave him a sense of belonging, a sense of home and a cultural identity that had eluded him for each of his eighty six years for he was royalty within China and even after the succession of many revolutions social, economic and technical he knew and the people knew that Empire could never be without an Emperor. The territory of his Providership was the largest of them all. He was by far the richest of the rich and held the most power in his hands and of the three leaders of the Providers was the most genuinely humble and for this reason was surrounded by his entourage both day and night.

Hong Taiji left the virtual holographic phantoms to wander through vignettes of royal life as it had been though there were many others occupying his floor with him. Of course they had sleeping arrangements elsewhere, but for now they blended in with the electronic apparitions and pandered to him just as they would have to the Emperor's court. With a gesture he had dismissed the rumors of redistributing existing bandwidth and could find his way to easily understand the frustrations of Charles Iverson that had fueled those rumors. After all, he was not likely to attain the heights he dreamt of as a younger man and now that he was in the middle years he would find what little climb lay before him twice as difficult contrary to the belief that life became easier with age. He knew better. It was his experience that the difficulties became more insurmountable and what small irritations had festered throughout the years were likely to explode into major traumas and only the strong survived and it was their face that gave the apparancy of life becoming easier. Strength was the virtue. However, he was not a man to allow the petty failings of others to color his opinion of them rather he took each occurrence as an opportunity, a challenge and leapt at the chance to advance his goals and ingratiate others. Moral decline was a sign to him that a man was folding up inside, cashing in his chips, calling all notes and was the surest indicator of someone not to trust and therefore someone to seduce. He attacked weakness, fed it and clawed at it in efforts to engender strength or at the very least the will to fight. Sometimes it worked and sometimes it didn't and he knew it was the animal still in humans that drove him to do it and the fact that he lacked any other method for rehabilitating a fallen spirit. It was something he had learned a long time ago from watching caged lions cope with their captivity.

Under these circumstances he called upon the General Manager. Chaing Li-jen Monlin had made elaborate preparations for the arrival of Hong Taiji even going to the extreme of reserving the whole floor for him on his own volition when a grand suite would have done just as well, but it was good joss to back a winner he had rationalized. Later though he had rare second thoughts for when the Arab had received word of the Chinese man's accommodations he demanded the same not to be outdone during this council of the Trust that was seemingly a show of force. So it passed that he was without two whole floors for the term of the meetings and would have to donate a portion of his hard earned graft to the hotel coffers in order to balance the books. Chaing was in his bed and dreaming of distant constellations when he got word that the old man wanted to see him.

He bowed deeply in the Japanese manner as a sign of reverence to the one he believed to be the Emperor reincarnate and out of the corner of his eye his gesture was vindicated by the complete indifference of the elderly man who turned on his heel and began to pace from side to side while he spoke as only one born to the purple could.

"It has come to my attention," the elderly man spoke in a confident and practiced voice, "that you are a man of exceptional qualities." He ceased pacing momentarily and waited peering down his small weathered nose at the young man. "You have given me a taste for brandy."

General manager Chaing smiled graciously and bowed again though not as deeply his head beginning to feel light at the close proximity to power.

"I think perhaps it is because you are so intimately involved with anticipating what is required by your guests that you may have developed an understanding of the more essential motivations." Hong Taiji watched Chaing carefully as he talked and gave the younger man the impression of a hooded cobra swaying to and fro to the rhythm of some Fakir's hand. "It is with this hope that I have asked you here."

"If there is anything..." the younger man stuttered knowing that surely this was a step in the right direction, "you just need to ask it of me."

"Sometimes a man does something that is not wholly..." he searched the air, "...sane. Out of anxieties and frustrations comes an irrational act that he later may regret very deeply, but then it's too late isn't it?"

"Yes..." he replied half heartedly not just sure of what the old man was getting at.

"You must have acted rashly at some time or another? Am I right?"

"Yes."

"Well then, you see... we live in a closely woven fabric where the joss of one man is not immune from that of another and so the conflict both cannot have the very same luck. We are inhumane at times aren't we? It strikes me that we should all just stop and reexamine the premises upon which... but being human," he shrugged, "I have asked you here to speak to you about someone, a very dear friend of mine."

"I see." Chaing replied in complete mystery and feeling dull that he had not grasped the meaning of the request by now and blamed it on the fact he had been dragged out of bed in the middle of the night and was not as sharp as usual. He hoped Hong Taiji wouldn't notice.

"He's not balanced...right now, he's under severe pressure...the fact is I think he's frightened by getting older. I myself, of course have ceased my fear of the specter as you can plainly see and have embraced it."

A faint light of understanding began to glow on the general manager and it was at once obvious to him that whatever was wanted was something that could not be asked for directly and from his experience that narrowed the target considerably. "If you explain it to me a little more..."

"We go through seasons," the old man interrupted not wishing too much communications in response to his. "When a man begins to get older he suddenly becomes aware that he has passed through certain intervals of time and they have vanished and will never come again, you understand? To some it's quite a shock, devastating even. Sometimes you can trace a man's moral decline to such a catharsis."

"I understand."

"I knew you would." He considered the General Manager with a cold gleam in his eye. "My friend for instance, I think he's had such realizations. Of course in time one finds compensation in growing older, other pleasures, more sublime even...but in the passing a man's moral fiber is in jeopardy. He looks in the mirror and sees unrealized hopes."

"May I ask your friend's name?"

"Of course. Iverson, Charles Iverson."

Chaing Li-jen Monlin was charged with a political assignment. He was as certain of this as he was of the color of the sky and so he assumed it very seriously because it had taken years to set up this brush with dominion and he had worked and waited and pandered to all those unreasonable whims just on the chance that he might be called upon some day to perform a delicate task vital to the maintenance of power. It didn't matter that he was asked, not in so many words, but implied, to be the hotel pimp, a role he had mastered to such a degree that he had elevated it to an art form, and once again found himself delivering up lotus blossoms to bolster some aging man's vanity. It didn't matter. They were only pawns. Out of small acts empires are built, and besides he knew the rewards would far outweigh the trouble.

The cold polar wind penetrated the darkness. Its inhospitable temperatures were deeper than the arctic night during which even sprits slept leaving no one to witness the shot spray of the universe glittering incandescently far away in the heavens that the nocturne gave window to as if there was no distance between it and us. The breath of the ether touched down. The earth froze.

The stars of winter danced above the horizon line; Taurus the bull, Aries the ram, Auriga the charioteer, Gemini the twins and Cassiopeia the Queen along with billions upon billions of others. The Crab Nebulae was still blooming from its supernova in 1054 AD and the Pleiades cluster rained the seven lights of Elysium. The firmament was filled to overflowing with wonder and the celestial plasma cradled the planet whose inhabitants lived in two worlds, one of day and one of night. Men scattered anonymously across the earth where the vapor of industrial clouds blotted out the heavens in both shadow and light causing a lapse in memory as to where people really lived, and what was the nature of their home. The sky watched them through the haze because they could not look back and it had been that way for so many generations that the memory of a bejeweled star laden universe which Earth rode through as a huge ship had been lost in time. Here, though, over the pole where the ozone layer had worn away and the winds wrath was uncontrolled and wild the universe poured through the opening and filled the space between earth and sky, which was all that most men knew and perhaps it was this dusting of cosmic air that kept hope alive. Or was it something greater, something each person carried within him that knew no confines of space, no obscured horizons?

They were caught in the slipstream created by the cosmic wind that seeped in through the hole in the ozone layer and encircled the planet invading the homes of men and touching them when they least expected it. A shaft of cream colored light gently fell from the window's opening through the indigo of the dark room and drifted to the floor dissipating as it went so that it cast no shadows. Nash witnessed the night.

Fionica whispered. "When I was a child I remember a family who owned two goats. They were gray. A male and a female. I used to watch them on the hillside in the winter. I can smell the wood smoke." While in her mind she weighed the data flooding her senses for consequences and moral inequities at the same time keeping mental notations of the physical reactions that were happening carrying her along as if she were just a sailor on a genetic sea. "They were clones, offspring of an experiment from before the Kaeien, but I thought they were real."

"You wouldn't like it here," he said as she looked him in the eye. "This is nowhere you should be." And he kissed her so hard he drew blood.

Nash balked at the fury of the storm. For years he had roamed the fringes as an interloper descending for those who may have needed his aid purposely avoiding complications, emotional ties, attachments. It had made him tough in the way a fisherman became inured of the elements driving through them with the one terrible purpose of his life as a beacon. A force beyond him too impelled Nash.

"Why are you afraid?" she asked swimming through confusions of her own. So many times she had felt the life flow out of bodies while her hands sought the magic, the elixir that could restore them to vigor and the future. The mystery lay between what she knew and what she did not know and the failure to grasp onto the answers when they were needed as the will slipped away without any method of saving it. Could she elicit life? The biology was something she was intimate with, knew of as family not like the stranger she was to the house of the spirit. There must be a middle ground, though she did not know it.

He clasped both hands at the small of her back and pulled her to him. "I am lost in this world."

"You'll have to carry me," she looked into his eyes and saw swirling constellations, "I can't walk here." Then she said to herself so quietly no one could hear, *Does love exist?* ...and kissed him ever so sweetly on the mouth.

No words passed from that moment. There seemed to be a well that opened and swallowed them, a refuge, where neither harsh wind nor currents nor predators could follow and suddenly within them all was silent. Both felt safe. Two incomplete souls who had placed themselves in the path of destruction out of some inner need that could never be voiced or described fumbled with the fundamentals of being human. Their hands awkwardly caressed yet not really perceiving the skin beneath which hearts heavily beat. It was a ballet to which neither knew the steps. For hours they sat with each other in Fionica's small deserted office saying little holding each other's hand.

On the day of the last meeting of the Trust general manager Chaing had the perfect conference rooms waiting in full regalia and had not slept all the preceding night so that nothing would go unnoticed and every plan would unfold smoothly. He greased the hotel's support staff with barked orders as he was greased with folding cash. All other things came to a stand still and even the surrounding neighborhoods were unnaturally quiet as if everyone knew the weighty agendas that would be butting heads were far more important than any of their own lives and affairs. The kitchens also had been running all night. Hotel chefs, some of the finest in the world, were at odds with the private chefs imported with each Provider's retinue and their bickering and shallow foibles goaded each of them to outdo themselves perhaps as penance for the swollen egos that masked them all beyond recognition. The delicious aromas wafted through the lobby and the first few floors causing the majority of guests to eat unusually large breakfasts.

The first speakers were minor executives and they surveyed the strategically placed occupants of the huge conference room with the boldness and aplomb expected from managers of the ranks of the Providers. They were, after all, the aristocracy of business, all else depended upon them and the structure that had been so venemously guided by private capitol and then tacitly supported and enfranchised by governments now ruled the earth. It was no small matter that all interlinking computers, voice phone, video image transmissions for government, industry and the private sector were exclusively the domain of the Providers and their optical networks when it could have just as easily gone with satellite technology or digital broadcasting like it was in the beginning, when there was competition. As with all competitive endeavors there can only be one winner. The land lease possibilities of greedy owners to the cable laying companies and the opportunities for immediate gain from taxation and continental hosting sites were overwhelming incentives and so over time the opting for short term profit eclipsed any long range planning. However nobody foresaw the eventual outcome of a small, tightly knit cartel evolving that would dominate it all, but it was simply money in the end. The three providers had managed to amass so much wealth that they bought out all competition and then intimidated the government so thoroughly that it became an adjunct to their community, just another node on the network.

The one who grasped it all sat silently watching the proceedings through dark, brooding eyes. Mostafa 'Ali Fayed Al-Razio listened intently as each Provider's layer of management presented detailed visions of their networks, programming and missions for the future. Little was done to mask the specter of proprietary gain and the ubiquitous thrust for excellence in seducing markets and then bleeding them for profit as even prior to the ascendancy of the Providers that philosophy had become the moral chord, the anthem of youth and the point of all socially useful living. They were among friends. Al-Razio, however, believed in the deeper meaning, he alone felt he held knowledge of the reason for the dedication of the masses to the Vidtel and the incredible consumption of entertainment. It had not been a difficult ride for the people had fueled it, they had demanded it and the providers had supplied the infrastructure and the economic environment that supported the mass dissemination of a vicarious life. As each executive extolled the benefits of his skills summed up in the hourly viewing times of sectors, classes and subcultures it was abundantly clear that a child was born into the womb of the Vidtel and did not leave it until death spending nearly one half of his waking hours in its presence absorbing its messages and living its life in the mind. He did not understand this part and so summed it up as the will of Allah in the gathering of the flocks from the dispersed fields of the earth so that they may all be as one pair of eyes and one pair of ears. He would do the rest. The others were nihilistic barbarians lost in their soulless, goalless pursuit of profit and power that was as ephemeral as the life of one body.

"The rights of men have no place if they interfere with the common good!" Mostafa 'Ali Fayed Al-Razio spoke out over the crowd with a deeply clear, strong bell-like voice that was tinged with an accent giving him a slightly exotic sound. "If there's anything we should have learned from the past, that is it." His face was red and his blood was up now that his time to speak had come and he confronted his peers, but not equals. The right to rule raged in him and he could hardly contain the power now that it was coming full circle and within a few days the world would testify to his genius, and his ascendance as a prophet. The utter brilliance was not entirely in the new technology, but in his use of it and there lie the reason naked in the sun though he could not speak of it and could not explain what had transpired during these many months that had resulted in an explosion of market share for CommNet even though that was why the council of the Trust had been called and though an explanation was not really expected, the equilibrium of the three Provider triad depended on it. Instead he extolled the philosophy of a market based religion.

"It is not, as you all know, ourselves who determine the content of our networks, but the dynamics of the market. We provide what is needed and wanted. If the profit's there the programming will continue to be a part of our social landscape. At CommNet our success has derived not only from delivering programming that is desired more intuitively than our competition, but providing guidance in a socially responsible manner. Clearly we are being called on with a social mandate." He paused looking out over the unresponsive faces and added because he couldn't resist it, "Perhaps even a divine mandate!"

There was no feedback from the crowd. Polite applause and curious looks all around with more than one person wondering what he was talking about. It did not bother Mostafa 'Ali Fayed Al-Razio as he detested public speaking and besides knowing the petty reason for the meeting of the Trust and certain the intention was one of curtailing CommNet's expansion he was distinctly cold. So he retired to his floor of rooms and continued planning secretly for the transmission that was to occur the following week and that was to be the culminating blow in the conversion of the Western Metropolis. He had been working closely with Roxanne and her programmer Yzak to guide the project and under his auspices the firm sFx Technos had developed new effects to even heighten the power. He was wildly pleased and excited feeling the excess of his own power and the pressure of the project at the same time. So it did not worry him that he had spells when he completely lost the feeling in his arms and heard ringing in his ears assuming it was a prelude to another message from God.

- XIV -

Nexus

For the first time since he had committed himself, Nash felt fear. His cheek lie pressed up against the cool, smooth dampness of the concrete wall and its permanence gave body to emotions that washed over him in uncontrollable races and waves and threatened to disperse his resolve. This was not who he was. They had just crawled down the tunnel opening discovered last time. Moonlight spilled in from the night above where the winds still swept across a nocturnal landscape scouring the unprotected surfaces to carry off keepsakes never to be seen again. The Northerns brought cold that only visited once every decade. From darkness ahead came sounds. Something mechanical was moving inexorably toward them. The smell of panic invaded with its acrid taste. He peered motionless as the glow from the moon was reflected off the man's jaw who stood glued to the wall before him, it was damp from perspiration and tiny pulses ran through it bathed in cerulean blue shadows as he clenched his teeth nervously. He was being swept away.

The whirl of events had escalated like a firestorm since the discovery of the single *Golden XiOma* and flitted through his consciousness as flashes of light revealing each step in context to the next all woven together as inevitable consequences. The insatiable human urge to outrun technology was the catalyst as the mysterious disk was deciphered and finally had brought him to where he stood again in the tunnel above the Archives. He knew that despite the complete sublimation of men's will to virtual systems and devices there was an inextinguishable spark of living defiance that sailed their harbors somewhere.

McGilvery held his hand suspended over the touchscreen and did not breathe as code images spewed across it. He peered as into an abyss whose radiance washed his face with cobalt and amber light drawing shadows around his mouth at the corners where it was turned down in concentration. Fionica stood hovering at his shoulder trying to decipher events from the monitor. He could feel the heat of her in the cool computer strewn rooms of VOX.

"Has he reached the target?" She asked.

"The GPS images have him located there, but I don't have any confirmation yet." The rarefied air was taut with anticipation throughout the four adjoining rooms separated by thin, glass walls that reflected a myriad of monitors crammed in among all the other equipment and peripherals each with distinctive protocols arrayed on their screens. They changed and refreshed in syncopated rhythms as computers spoke to each other in their private languages once envisioned by a living being then lost in the cyber world where men cannot follow, where thoughts are made real with numbers, where things occur at the speed of light.

"Will you connect before or after he reaches the inside?"

"We're connecting now, matching protocols, making sure it's stable and ..." McGilvery looked over his shoulder, "...we don't want alarms going off."

She did not take her eyes away from the information flowing across the screen. "You sure this will work?"

"No." He replied thoughtfully.

A long moment passed then she uttered with quiet resignation. "We bought the ticket."

"...whaaat?"

"Surgery." Fionica said bluntly. "The last ditch effort...an operation with almost zero chance of success...where the patient is gone anyway so you..."

He gazed up. "Yea... bought the ticket."

"...I don't mean to say...!"

"I know."

"I'm not used to this."

"I am."

"Why did he go with *them*?" she asked in an anxious chatter suddenly frowning letting the pressure come to the surface unlike her own element where chaos did not phase her. "Why not a VOX team?"

"It's illegal."

"Hmmm, I forgot..." Fionica frowned and suppressed the antagonism she felt, "you're the cops."

"Listen," he said, "we're stretching it here," McGilvery reached up and turned a small monitor on and immediately numbers began streaming across its face that spoke to him in shorthand, his mind translating, "hooking up to that old network and patching into CommNet... Christ! Violates at least fifteen GCC regulations not to mention that it's prison for unauthorized theft of bandwidth, and using government facilities for private business, and..."

"I get it."

"...plus the fact I got my best guys working on it..."

Fionica placed her hand on his shoulder and gently squeezed. "Thanks."

There was silence. "Yea...love to catch those God dammed sons of bitch criminals!" He cast glances in both directions and gestured with his hands. "That's what we do after hours when were not chasing some red herring we've been ordered to follow up on so we won't get too close."

"To what?"

"The plutocracy. The money machine."

Breathing could be heard above the staccato of keystrokes and the hum of electronics, but Fionica was holding her breath automatically as she did during an operation just to steady her hand. She was divided between what was happening at VOX where the clandestine group worked in the cool, cloistered rooms during the early hours when all else was closed down and only the sysops were around and what was happening far away. Nash was out there. She had unfamiliar feelings about him, feelings she couldn't put her finger on and was not sure she liked it. Before him she had felt so distinctly ordered she could envision her entire life all the way down the line until...suddenly everything was uncertain. Fusing was the catalyst. It was something she had never expected, could never have anticipated and even when the undeniable slammed into her she never dreamed they would uncover so bizarre a scene. Who would believe it? Indeed, she knew that was its protection. Fionica had always been able to feel the rhythm that flowed through living things with her hands and it was partially why she had become a healer. Now the pulse was getting away from her. Ever since the first inkling that *Electrically Induced Neurosynapse Failure* was actual and not just theoretical she felt a frantic urgency and her nerves were becoming frayed yet still she screamed out for an act of consequence that would stamp an indelible, moral viewpoint across the course of events. Her viewpoint. She needed no one's permission. How often in her life had unconfronted evil terrorized people because someone had been too comfortable, too complacent, too sure of their own rightness pouring out rhetorical platitudes and criticisms without taking any effective action. In truth, she was expendable. They all were.

McGilvery had been the first. He had through some digital sorcery deciphered the *Golden XiOma* that Nash had stolen out of the Archives of the Old Religion, only rumored until that moment. It was a feat of technological fortune that on the first or second guess it worked, but the full description of the language took the complete power of the combined main frame servers and was never understood by Derek or any of the others who assisted him. It was later the real magic occurred. The team was challenged by technology that eluded their under-standing, they were affronted by it and secretly none of them wanted any technology to be greater than the capability of men and so became determined to crack it, to subdue and bring it under control. Gradually the task took possession of their collective wills and by sheer circumstance brought them together with a singular purpose. While Nash was experimenting with the unlocked information from the disk and marveling at the results, the team worked far into the night hours where the silence enhanced their concentration and they could let imagination run without the hindrance of more mundane realities. Sleep became something they did only when nature would not let them grasp the next thought, and then just for a few hours to refuel–because the essence of code writing and deciphering required long periods of uninterrupted focus. McGilvery monitored the progress while he handled his regular duties and the team itself became a group within a group each person obsessed with cracking the technology and at the same time working for something inherently human. People, they innately knew, must be free to choose, must not be subservient to technology of any kind no matter what its benefit because that would put it their master and man the creator simply as a peripheral. There was a great paradox that lay within all of them, each was obsessed with the development and use of technology yet driven to balance it with humanity.

The syntax of the medium came in fits and then floods. It had happened one night starting at 3:43 AM and lasted until noon the following day amid the excited flurry of work by the team who by then were elated at the breakthrough. One small algorithmic translation led to others and then it blossomed reproducing geometrically as a sort of an intellectual fission resulting in the full revelation of the language and the media. The task then was how to transmit the disk while automatically translating the antiquated technology and language into the modern on the fly. McGilvery solved that by creating a miniaturized read-only-memory peripheral device that processed the data through an optical chip embedded with the language code and then spewed out the raw digital data as light pulses ready for any optical network to read.

To what end all of this was meant, none of them were certain except that there was an incompleteness to it all made more acute by McGilvery's discoveries the following week monitoring activity on the WEB by Yzak, the savant programmer. Precursors of more ominous discoveries.

They had arrived weeks ago at the luxurious penthouse restaurant that lurked on the edge of the entertainment district where the studios and network executives all had lunch and was the highest point in the Western Metropolis. It was just as the sun completely disappeared below the horizon line and half the sky was dark with faint hints of swelling constellations behind the oblivion of smog and the other half ablaze with magenta, crimson, olive and indigo silently fading into the twilight of night. The winds had returned and could be heard whistling outside the double polarized floor to ceiling arched windows where they buffeted against metal moldings. The view went on in all directions for a hundred miles on rare occasions when it was clear, but tonight the city fell off in the distance part way disappearing into the murky darkness. Up until that point it was a grand and magnificent glittering carpet composed of millions of cross thread fabric lives that intersected in layer upon layer as a parfait society–where most individuals never knew one another or even suspected others existed in their myopic attempt to cope with the unbelievably of the megalopolis. It was far beyond what anyone had ever dreamed of in numbers from people to automobiles to buildings to businesses–it had always been assumed in the past that a city was a self-limiting organism that could never reach the megalithic sizes that the modern metropolis had without some form of self destruction whether it came from crime, disease, economic disaster or simply implosion. However, each had occurred in its turn and had only hardened the city and increased its collective resolve. The city was inured and autonomous of the people who lived in it now rising to heights and sizes on its own that defied statisticians and economists and political scientists. It was the beast that swallowed the best and the worst of all men and spat it back out.

They were seated at a round table near the windows. Nash, Fionica and McGilvery, who was extremely uncomfortable in the environment and began drinking as soon as he sat down. The final arrival was Sabiha who made her entrance like the illuminati who frequented the restaurant drawing all eyes as she gracefully sailed through the crowded room wearing a thin, tight black dress whose fabric stretched around her body and breathed as one with her and a long scarf that flew behind. Men turned from their wives and others turned away knowing the temptation was too far out of reach and so had gone into apathy years ago.

"I've got news!" she said breathlessly as if she had raced from the United Nations translations office afoot without stopping and landed in a chair poised, leaning forward still in motion. "Something is happening."

It had been her idea to all meet at the restaurant reasoning that there was no more unlikely place to be observed than the most obvious one, and also because the entertainment crowd congregated there and, Sabiha being a windblown creature, was drawn into the vacuum all their money and life on the edge created.

"I was translating delivery contracts between CommNet's regional buying officers and reps from the Eastern Metropolis suppliers. Big orders. Huge orders. Most are new monitors for the public vidtel stations, but there's a lot of other electronics being shipped in as well. Signal amplifiers and repeaters, optical hardware...there's a major expansion going on."

"CommNet's market share had exploded." McGilvery said dryly. "It's just support."

"More than that! Listen, there's going to be a major transmission that will tax existing lines, that's why the back up."

Nash interjected. "Major transmission?"

"Something new," Sabiha replied excitedly, "something that would overload their existing lines."

They all looked at each other with unspoken horror. "We've been monitoring Yzak," McGilvery sat forward placing his elbows on the table and spoke in hushed tones, "traced the Mark everywhere it appeared the last two weeks. He's hacked into some of the most divergent sites imaginable."

"What do you mean?" Fionica asked.

"...banks, travel agencies, hospitals, including CenMed VAN where I've brought in Rosemund to monitor the activity...airports, and, this is really out there, key economic statistical databases."

Nash scowled and considered the hodgepodge. "Doesn't make much sense."

"Maybe..." McGivlery replied thoughtfully, "Let me ask you this..." he directed the question to Fionica, "if you wanted to monitor responses from a patient, all responses to a series of tests what do you do?"

"Wire him."

Sabiha lowered her head and twirled her hand as if wishing to raise the volume. "Translation?"

Fionica shrugged. "We hook him up with electrodes. Key him to the gene bank database and feed all data through there where it's processed and the complete diagnosis, treatment and gene therapy regimen is laid out in probability factors as low as .00041."

"Exactly." McGilvery pronounced.

Nash was startled. "You think he's plugging in to monitor social reactions?"

"Looks like it."

"To what?"

"Sounds to me," Fionica interjected with a muted, monotonous tone, "like mass induced trauma."

"That's right," Sabiha added, "something out of the ordinary is happening."

"I don't get it. Why now?" Nash wondered out loud.

McGilvery answered confidently. "It's just good economics. When you get a rise in market share you pour it on. Feed it."

"Yea," Sabiha jibbed, "kick it while it's down and not looking."

McGilvery ordered another drink. The prospect was unsettling. Out over the city lights flared in the haze except for certain areas where the winds were especially strong and there they burned with a crisp intensity that was a throw back to earlier eras when the world was more pure. In the background the clink of glasses and china and the din of voices ebbed and flowed as a symphony and everywhere the aromas of food–exquisite food of the fabled good life. The unlikely group ordered and the conversation turned to scenarios in the aftermath, the what-ifs and the in-the-event-thats...the one overriding element that had escaped all their efforts was the greed, which drew men to do nearly anything.

"Before gene therapy we were much less adventurous." Fionica suddenly uttered as if they had caught her mid conversation with someone else. "Now," she focused her eyes inward viewing the realization, "we are able to act more boldly, to take chances medicine could not have in earlier periods. In fact it would have violated ethics."

"Technology." Said McGilvery.

"Maybe... I think it's more a certainty, an ability to take responsibility for consequences. You can destroy if you can create as well."

Nash nodded intently. "You can do harm if you can eradicate harm."

"Yes."

"Why do we fear things?" Sabiha broke in, "Because they affect the future, they cause disaster, death, things we have no control over. For instance you could kill somebody if you could also bring them back to life..."

"And," Nash interjected, "make the spiritual trauma disappear."

McGilvery cracked, "I'm really trying to follow all this..."

"If someone does send out a massive transmission that creates *EINF* in thousands, maybe millions what can we do? One thing only!" They all looked at him. "We can give people the ability to understand and undo what is being done to them. The truth. We can only help them help themselves."

"If what you say about the technology on the *Golden XiOma* is accurate, then there's possibly one way to accomplish that." Fionica concluded.

"We've got to get the rest of the disks!" Nash said. "I knew it was coming..."

"There's no time, whatever's happening it's soon...!"

"I can't see it...not again...we can't..." McGilvery complained, "It's..."

"You don't have to. I know some people. They've have been waiting for an opportunity just like this."

"You don't mean what I think you mean?"

"The Phan? You're going into the Archives with terrorists?"

"Idealists...we have to cut some slack at this point don't we?"

"C'mon!"

"...I've got to meet with them somehow. I think it'll work."

"We've got data readers, and they're fast too! What if..." McGilvery clasped his chin with thumb and forefinger suddenly intense, "What if..."

"What?"

"...Yzak did it, he plugged into that old network that the Archivists are using, so..."

"So...what?"

"...what if we do our own broadcast?" He sat back smugly, intent, strong.

"You mean...?"

"I think we can patch that old network into CommNet's optical system through VOX and there's certainly a jacking station we can rig on site so you can send out the data from those disks simultaneously as their transmission goes on air!"

"Yes!" Nash said dramatically feeling for the first time a sense of strength against overwhelming odds. "Dead agent them. Through public access channels...we just need the exact time schedule!"

McGilvery smiled, "I got no problem with VT schedules, no secrets there my team can't get to." Then he paused, "There is one problem, I can contact the Phan, but they won't talk to me."

"Everybody can talk to a minister."

In a high rent district, down an alley from the World Financial building there was a line of trucks circling the open doors at the rear of the Convention Center where yellow light streamed out into the blue night and mingled with the beams of headlights, klieg lights, street lights and all the other glittering incandescent glows that crowded the bustle of activity. An orchestra was unloading instruments while caterers hurried in trays of prepared food and case after case of wine and spirits. The marquee out front read: *Special Convocation of the*

Church of the Old Religion, Fri-Sat-Sun. Spotlights tore through the sky like a blaze of angels.

Behind the scenes were a hundred acolytes who had gone without sleep for the preceding three days in order to set up the splendor within the halls. A thousand tasks were taken care of from the raising of chairs and tables to the state-of-the art staging, lighting and sound systems. There were bands and orchestras, laser light shows and huge holographic vidtel transmissions that were produced at great expense especially for the event. No detail was too small to pull off the star-studded entertainment extravaganza dotted with speeches and requests for donations for various worthy programs, not the least of which was the Church itself. Religion cost money these days and was hit with inflation like everything else the chief fundraisers were quick to rejoin to criticism. Caterers vied for the prime positions on the floor that would put them in the light and also make the set-ups easier and perhaps land them the contract as prime supplier next time, which was worth twice as much as the regular caterers. The church personnel were dedicated, hard working people whose intentions were fine and whose labor elevated every activity of the Church into one of truly professional standards. Besides they worked for free, unless one could call room and board payment for a lifetime of devoted toil, but it gave the congregation the ability to put on frequent world-class fundraisers. It was a well-oiled, well-rehearsed show that usually came off without a snag and more importantly, was a moneymaker.

The High Advocator sat in a back room parlay. In his bony fingers he held a long, black, hand rolled cigar from which blue smoke shift-lessly curled adding to the azure haze that had formed close to the ceiling from all the smoking going on. Like cigarettes they were illegal, but men of means gravitated towards them and they gave an excuse to talk alone in the well appointed VIP rooms set up off the convention floor. He sipped at the large glass that was blessed with a half an inch of cognac. Commander Rybin sat at his elbow with the sour look that was a permanent fixture on his face and of which some parishioners said he carried the burdens of the world. Those that knew him better were certain he was just harboring a grudge. Each VIP room was decorated in the mode of a different period and the one the High Advocator liked most emulated 15th century Borgia Italy with a statue of a nude Madonna he had brought up especially from the archives for the occasion because he liked to look at perfection.

Across the small table littered with glasses, ash trays, papers, hand held computers and various other personal items sat an overweight and worried man who nervously puffed on a cigar in brief little bursts each one causing the tip to light up and glow bright red and the hot smoke to burn his lips and mouth. He was an inexperienced smoker, but liked the crass shock of the heat against his somnolent body that craved feelings he could never quite get enough of. He compulsively rubbed the top of his thigh with his pudgy hand. "I don't see how we can do that!" he blurted out.

"Come now," The High Advocator droned patronizingly as music and muffled noise from the convention floor seeped into the room, "we've been working on this for a long time."

"I know..." The man replied sympathetically, "but you just can't go too far."

Commander Rybin, who stood up near the door and held a cigar to his lips without taking in any smoke because he was reticent about its impurities, but continuously rolled it in his fingers satisfied by the taste of the tobacco, carped, "Your election wasn't going too far." He gritted his teeth watching closely for the man's reaction while he plotted his offensive.

"I think what the Commander is trying to say is that we kept you from straying on path to nowhere." The High Advocator added comfortingly.

"Yes... I know," the man replied with stoic resignation.

The Commander was impatient and could not understand the High Advocator's long, drawn out manner in dealing with others. "Well I don't suppose just anyone can get a bond issue through these days as confused as the City is with its finances." He was continuously involved in petty communications that Rybin had zero tolerance for, but mysteriously seemed to work. If he had his way people would just comply, as his subordinates always had in the service, after all they were devoted to the Canon as anyone could see and it was a universally accepted religion even by non-believers. It was full of practical wisdom so why would anyone buck command? He had long ago concluded religion like anything else should be run on a hierarchy of orders for the good of all. Individuals be dammed.

The man glanced up at Rybin from under hooded eyes. "I don't think you..." he replied venomously then abruptly changed his tone and shrugged, "things are coming along, you're just impatient. Perhaps you should practice being more composed, it's a characteristic politicians and clergymen should have in common."

"Humph!" The Commander muffled affronted by such defeatist concepts. "Battles are lost through vacillation."

Gentleman," The old man watched the two become flushed with unexpressed resentment and then, smiling, spoke. "...we are not fighting a battle. This is simply a business deal."

"It's an act of faith." Rybin added unable to feel wrong in any way. "The Canon says purpose is the strongest measure of a man and by his acts...!"

"As you well know this issue could mean a lot of money for all of us." Interjected the High Advocator cutting right to the chase anxious at the possible loss of income and refusing to accept it. "Our programs must have funding from somewhere, and I'm sure your... well, suffice to say it will bring your bills up to date."

Annoyed by the pressure, "It seems to me," he frowned through the cigar smoke, "the Church has more than enough for operating expenses if the stories of the Archives have any truth in them at all."

"Rumors," the High Advocator intoned waved his old hand knocking a cigar ash to the floor, "simply unsubstantiated claims by those wishing to discredit the Church. Look at us, we're not rich, we are servants of God." Rybin nodded quietly looking down pleased to have his position confirmed and with it the expectation of unqualified respect and reverence for the sacrifice he was making for the good of all. His crown of thorns was heavy on his gray haired stubble.

The man peered at the High Advocator through beady eyes and was perspiring in the warm room. He had much to atone for, but, he rationalized, the nature of politics was granting concessions and if he'd had to moderate some of his more idealistic feelings throughout his career it had served him. After all here he was a councilman and chief financial officer for the City, a position envied by many, and he had based all his success on the maxim that in order to succeed one must always compromise and it was that formula that gave him the distinct confidence that he always made the right decisions in the end. It was easy for those who did nothing commercially, had no competition to contend, no marketing or sales just the garnering of support and the soliciting of donations all under the specter of God. He could not quite bring himself to disbelieve though as much as he tried to be an atheist when life was at its most difficult he found himself prostrate and subconsciously asking for help from some higher power. The subject threw him into a moral dilemma. On the one hand he wished it was so simple that he could shuttle off his more consequential responsibilities in life to an omnipresent invisible being whose benign qualities could always be called upon by the faithful, on the other he resented the power that loomed over him as a result and took destiny from his own guidance placing it into the void and under the sway of the Church. That and the god damned prying into his personal life... He didn't trust people who were always after money, though that described him exactly he was not self aware enough to make the connection. The bond issue frightened him. It was pushing it.

They had come to him sixteen months ago with the full plan worked out in military detail, which he attributed to Commander Rybin, and asked, no, expected him to railroad it through the council as one of the faithful and get it approved. Even though it was a thinly disguised scheme that even he could not obfuscate–though he'd tried by making it so complex that nobody completely understood it. The issue was presented in a 1200-page, cross-referenced document The bonds would apparently finance a sprawling public park on Church land and at face value was attractive because of the scarcity of open parcel real estate, but the financing was excessive and through a devious and elaborate wording provided an annuity to the Church that lasted well into the next century ostensibly as a trust for the parklands. It was a free ride pure and simple. There were tens of millions involved, his cut was substantial and why not? His risk was the highest. What he didn't know was the proposed park land was situated directly over the Archive tunnels and was strategically planned to preclude any real building and development that would include subterranean digging and the uncovering and disruption of the Archives and adjacent tunnels with the old forgotten Metrorail network they had appropriated.

The High Advocator knew what was going on in the man's mind. He was an old confessor and had learned what to expect and what could be gotten out of people with a concentration of effort and a little prodding. Everybody was malleable. It was such divine inspiration in his great success at just such ventures that brought him to the exalted position he was in. His brilliance was in getting others to get done what he envisioned. He considered it the highest faculty. Why others couldn't do it equally as well mystified him, but they could not and the proof of it was in their ability to make things go. He had finally concluded that it was the intangible qualities of which some have reserves and others paucity that give specific individuals the ability to excel at particular things. It fostered his abiding belief that providence was on his side and the Church was right in all things simply by the mandate of God–or at least by association. Talent was a heady thing that complimented his greed perfectly and the possibility of losing a masterstroke deal such as this one, of which he was the architect, was an intellectual challenge he could not resist. *God,* he exclaimed to himself in exuberance, *how I love the religious life!*

On the Convention center floor was a huge audience filling the rows of theater seats and additional folding chairs with enthusiastic spectators. On stage was a full scale review with the latest in a line of singers, dancers and brassy, electronic music that was being pumped out of an incredible variety of synthesized orchestration. The theme was off-world travel and the upper reaches of the auditorium were filled with holographic laser images of local planetary systems, star scenes and various space port resorts, (to which several all expense paid vacations were being given away through just one of the fund raising activities going on simultaneously), alternately hung suspended above the crowds and flew over the room seemingly right through the walls, making the crowd go wild each time it happened. A great entertainment value. World-class. People loved it. They came with the expectations of being enveloped in a virtual multimedia environment where every sense would be fulfilled with screaming sounds, flashing images and most of all the deep inner satisfaction that they were contributing to the spiritual foundations of society and were helping the Old Religion that had endured since before the Kaiein.

But what they were really waiting for and what the whole event was centered around was a climactic special transmission arranged with the designated permission of CWVT and their network affiliates who patched in all the other congregations in the Western Hemisphere. Extraordinary new equipment had been installed courtesy of CommNet who explained they were testing these huge, nanoflat panel systems that were based on the same new technology as the home units that were causing such a sensation. Sounds were computer timed by engineers who placed speakers at different locations and programmed in delayed signals to give the apparancy of echoes, reverberations and other real life representations. The effect was reported as absolute, virtual reality. If it worked as planned, and there wasn't the slightest reason why it shouldn't as CommNet had dedicated their top scientists to it for months, they had promised to install identical systems free of charge in key locations for the public good. Naturally the Public Information Agency was ecstatic over this prospect and unconditionally backed the whole project–and the Church got an additional draw to gather converts and funding. The fact that it just happened to coincide with the broadcast of the latest programming recently developed through a partnership of CWVT with Roxanne, the savant Yzak and sFx Technos was unknown to even the industry experts who had not gotten wind of anything out of the ordinary thanks to herculean efforts of senior management at CommNet. It was the biggest thing that had ever happened and Church officials were looking forward to great returns.

A young woman entered the room delivering a message to the High Advocator. He snatched it up without looking and read it quickly. Then he whispered something to which she had an opinion. Immediately he squinted up his eyes and said, "Look at the Canon chapter thirty-six, section thirteen and I think you'll see what I mean. I don't expect backflash!" Her eyes suddenly grew wide, but instead of the fear he was hoping to inspire they were wild, churning inside with repressed conflict the way an animal looks when he must do as commanded even though it goes against his nature. She withdrew to his bidding resigned with the hope of future advancement. Careers were made out of following such orders.

"Have you ever considered the idea that free and equal are non-compatible social concepts?" The High Advocator turned pleasantly back to the man in the chair with the cigar stub nearly burning his fingers at this point and gave him his full attention fighting hard to hold back his acerbic tongue, which had free reign when amongst his staff.

"I have never given it any thought at all." The man looked up at Commander Rybin who scowled unflinchingly conveying the impression that he understood completely the implications of the statement, which of course he didn't. "Of course both ideas are essential to modern society."

"People are not born the same. There are some who exhibit from birth a certain level of skill–we call it talent, aptitude, a gift…it's undeniable. Wouldn't you say?"

"I suppose."

"Then let me ask you, how can they be equal?"

"Well…" he fumbled thinking quickly unwilling to the be the dupe, "It's more of a legal concept, an equanimity before the law. I think it's more to keep the able in line than the criminal."

"Really? You're full of surprises."

"Nothing but observation." The man took it as a compliment. "Take for instance my career."

"Yes, you've been fortunate…"

"Maybe fortune… I've had to scramble plenty. Now Joe Velosto-vitch, he's charmed, talent I guess like you were saying. He just seems to be in the right place at the right time and for some reason he can't help but succeed. Makes lots of money… I could never figure out how one person could make so much money, there's nothing that one person can do that's valuable enough so I've always figured there's hundreds of people working beneath him in the economic structure just to support him–that he gets a piece of in some way. Rent seeking. At any rate, it's easy for him...'

Commander Rybin spotted a weakness, "Are you getting a little hot there?"

"Aruugh...well, I just have forceful ideas, that's how I got where I am."

"You're a power broker...that's why we talk to you and not someone else." The High Advocator drawled happy with the turn of the conversation.

The man continued encouraged by the interest and besides he just naturally loved to talk and bring people around to his way of looking at things. After all, to succeed you always have to compromise. "He's a man without a moral compass. Without the law he could and probably would do whatever he wanted to increase his wealth regardless of others, like me... I worked hard to get where I am, he just charmed his way into it. So it's the law. Criminals we can spot, it's the able who historically have taken advantage of situations. So you can see how important 'free' and 'equal' are before the law.

"Then you of course can see where this is a moral issue, it's part of our crusade." The High Advocator sat forward intently and spoke in an official, hushed confidential manner that immediately drew the man to the inner circle and made him feel privileged. "Some in the government even feel we should be completely subsidized to remove the economic burden that we can just work for the public good. A society is as strong as its spiritual base, wouldn't you agree?"

"Yes of course, but..."

"We need to bring this bond issue to fruition." He pronounced with the aloof finality that rang with the evangelical tone once heard echoing from pulpits warning of the fires of damnation. "Are you with us on this? We're looking for a player, we thought you were one."

The man was swept into the inner circle of the Church and was deeply impressed by its inner power and structure. Besides, he knew he had reached a limit to his career advancement in the real world, the world of everyday politics, and others like Joe Velostovitch blocked his path with their devious machinations. Here, in the bosom of his Church, surrounded by his confessors, men who liked and appreciated his talents… "You can count on me."

"Then when can we expect to see tangible results?"

Just then another young woman burst into the room as politely as she could and rushed over to the High Advocator and leaning down urgently whispered something into his ear.

He knew as soon as he had seen her that something was wrong. She was not just one of the administrative drones that hovered close by him, but the chief sysops for the Archive network and so was a senior executive ultimately trusted with the security and confidentiality of the proprietary system they had resurrected in the hills and purloined after millions were spent to get it operational and to effectively cut it off from any outside access. But now all that was in jeopardy… He could not quite believe what she was saying to him as it was so completely unexpected and so alarming had her repeat it. "We're not alone anymore!" She said determinedly. "Someone has hacked into the system!"

In the nexus of night amid the swirling web of dreams spun from millions of impassioned cries set loose of their mortal confines was where Roxanne felt most at home—when there was as much darkness passed as there was to come. Inspiration came to her in solitary moments out on the fringe when civilization slept. Power loomed above her as if the rise of an immense celestial body out on the paths of ether poised fantastic and luminous with impossibly infinite distances defying comprehension by mere human beings. She could not yet touch it completely, but its closeness imbued her with magic and the energy coursed through her reckless and wild as the consummation between her and it was nearly complete.

Sitting in the back of the limousine in a skimpy, black evening dress that barely covered her enough for a public appearance, bejeweled and intensely radiant from the constant sensation she felt all the time now that the power was within reach, she knew she shouldn't have left the studios. Tonight of all nights! She cursed the men that drew her away under her breath placing all blame on them because knowing she had needed release did not make the fact easier that something had gone wrong while she was away and now she found herself racing through the streets hoping to reach the station in time for the broadcast window. During the past seven weeks there had been nothing but concentrated effort bringing together all the disjointed elements into one contiguous whole that would roll out sweetly into the public domain with perfectly timed military precision as an optical broadcast of unprecedented virtual power. It was the creation of a new reality. It was profound history. She had assumed everything was alright or she would never have left; was moving along on schedule with each system fully supervised and regularly gone over with a checklist of every conceivable point that could possibly make trouble. The sFx Technos had a special team on-line and an entire back-up digital studio was built just for this first time. It was an event, a catharsis of imagination and reality, an experience that could only happen once, at this point in time when the technology was new and the virtual world had been so completely absorbed into the routine of life that no one viewed it as separate from the real. Each person in the Western Metropolis was as if a blank slate upon which new realities were to be written by her, and of course Hisham Mostafa 'Ali Fayed Al-Razio. The thought of him opened a cold pit in her stomach and she shuddered at what might happen if she were to fail at this juncture and he were to find out. Roxanne screamed at the chauffeur to go faster and threw her shoe at the glass that separated her from him as the long, sleek limousine barreled through the streets a vengeful god to anyone who got in its way.

Earlier in the evening her mood had been much different. She had attended a dinner at a palatial estate perched in the dry hills up the coast and had been stunned by the glimpse of the moon peering from under clouds across the pall of the city and reflecting off the ocean like hundreds of thousands of footprints darting across the water. It had taken her breath away and reminded her that they indeed lived upon a planet whose wild embrace had been forsaken by the overbearing populations in return for progress and technology. Roxanne herself was a disciple of the new age and now viewed this glimmer of the old as a quaint but lovely reminder of what once had been and was now irretrievable so it did not affect her in any other way than to make her sense more detachment from the effects she created and drive her to more excesses in her quest to feel alive.

With the worn remote control attached to a bold, silver bracelet that was set with precious stones, (accidentally found in a molybdenum mine she had controlling interest in,) it was nearly certain now the device would never leave her side again as it did one day the week before when under excessive pressure it was left behind. She clicked the channels over on three vidtels as she entered the house and passed through three rooms taking note of exactly what programming was in progress, noting the time of day and if anything new had been squeezed into the schedule since the preceding day. The heels of her shoes made light clicking noises across the cool marble floor as she walked in a graceful, stately manner to the long dinner table and unceremoniously slid into a chair with the fluid movement of a cat. She felt luxurious and sexual and was so confident and obviously stimulated she could easily have been in the privacy of her own bedroom and settled back in the chair her short dress languidly revealing her thighs. It was of no concern to her what anyone thought as she greeted people effusively pleased to be embraced by adoration once more as even the short ride in the limo had left her feeling void, but here she was at the height of her sublime ascension and all in the crowded room had noticed her. Even those who did not stop talking unconsciously followed with their eyes because power was a drug and just the slightest hint of it was enough to attract an entourage who would not have any access otherwise. Roxanne wielded her hammer with abandon and carelessness having neither the wisdom nor the purpose that gave such things direction.

The aroma of different foods was a perfume to her. Her golden lipped goblet was filled instantly with a pale, clear white wine that was so cold that it frosted the glass by a Negro butler dressed entirely in black. She brazenly looked him up and down and he did not flinch or pay the slightest attention to her so she concluded he must be mentally deficient or a eunuch. The delicate wine and seafood with saffron and garlic sauce only whetted her appetites.

They fell on her from all sides; elegantly dressed women with adoring eyes and men vying to get close, touching her or casually placing an arm around her waist and as the evening wore on through the talk and the flirting she began to feel driven for real sensation not the frail, social fru-fru that was a mask for true human desires. Recently the needs had grown and she had become much bolder in seeking them out because, as the power crept nearer, Roxanne discovered there were experiences that held no feeling anymore, simple things lost their significance and she drank excessively, slept less and ripped through a flurry of one night stands in rapid succession, male and female, in a desperate effort to keep herself in a high state of volatility. She needed the stimulation in order to create at the level where disbelief could be completely suspended was the justification and when Yzak had expired under her demands she sought release elsewhere, but each encounter left her more unfulfilled. So she focused on the power and it had finally become the grail for which there could be no substitute and only death would keep it from her. All the rest was of no consequence and she took it or left it alone at her leisure.

The butler though had never even looked at her, his nostrils had not even flared at her scent as she had seen men do before, it was as if she were common. All that evening through the constant ring of admirers Roxanne watched the black man and tried to get the measure of his movements seeing that the suit he wore hid a powerful body, which she could judge from his step. The fawning hands continued to touch her and the cacophony of voices lost all meaning as she drank glass after glass of chilled white wine mostly just to get the man to serve her and to taste his presence covertly. Each time was the same. A pall of indifference clouded his face and he did not even make eye contact. She became infuriated and it showed in the cruel, hostile comments she inflicted on the sycophants surrounding her. Suddenly she became aware that she had lost track of him. Perhaps, she thought, he had just gone to get more of something, to the kitchen, but he did not reappear and so, being drawn into the center of the vortex where her thoughts took her on the quest for more and more sensation she was compelled to seek him out even though he was obviously some sort of employee and she, well she was…celestial.

Down the long hallway she caught a glimpse of the black coat slipping through a door. There were no other people. She turned on her heel in a huff incensed at herself for looking after the man and angrily clicked a few station changes into a nearby vidtel without paying the slightest attention to the result and fended off several drooling social climbers who were trying to get too close. Over her shoulder she glanced down the hall. It was dark with only a dim light glowing. The circumstance was too much and her feet took over and on their own accord lead her where curiosity and her bruised pride wanted her to go, but in her mind she was still detached, as if she watched herself moving along the corridor with complete anonymity knowing that Roxanne would never do that. Her hand fumbled with the door knob, it was cold and slick and in a breath, a flash too quickly passing for any second thoughts she found herself on the inside of the room, a bathroom in the house, back up against the door staring at the Negro man who stood before the sink straightening his clothes. He did not move, but raised his head slightly and looked directly at her in the mirror. She felt a wild fluttering sensation in her stomach and liked it.

Many long moments passed and neither one of them spoke a word. The man continued to look sternly in the mirror and she saw reproach in the chisel of his features, the look of indignation in his eye and the set of his jaw that she recognized as the thin line of propriety which encircled all that comprised the remains of society and any vestiges of future hopes. The obsession to destroy those boundaries flared up inside her and burned and she felt a deluge of sexual heat surge through her body like a flood of tears from the eye of a blue bird over water unable to land and destined to die on the wing. She shuddered yet she could not move. Her legs grew weak. With her fingers Roxanne wanted to violate him, to sear her brand into him, to tear at his resentment and degrade him and in hot flashes of imaginings sensed what it would be like to drop to her knees and violently shred the cloth hiding his skin, feel the warm smoothness of his flesh, the hardness of his muscle and then to take him against his will forcing him into depraved acts for the pure, unadulterated pleasure it would give her to be completely sexually satisfied by this brutal stranger, before a mirror in a public room where someone might walk in any second catching her lying vulnerably beneath him. She clasped her wine glass against her bosom with both hands spilling one cool drop that ran down beneath her dress sending a chill right through her. A gasp escaped her lips that gave the man the impression she was embarrassed, shy, and overwhelmed at the awkward situation she had found herself in, but he still he did not move or speak. Roxanne's eyes began to flutter and her face flushed when at precisely that moment her tiny cellular phone emitted its harsh, disturbing tones.

"Hello," she spoke into it suddenly all business while the man just watched incredulously her face contorting into a frowning mass of fury as she listened to whoever was on the other end. "What!!" She screeched at the top of her voice. What followed next the man still can not relate accurately to anyone because the woman he looked at defiantly held out the phone with one hand while she violently tossed the glass shattering to the floor with the other scowling in rage at him all the time. Then she hurled the phone so close to his ear he could hear the person on the other end of the line talking as it passed and it crashed into the mirror sending a million pieces showering to the ground in a glittering fusillade.

Roxanne stormed into the studios at CWVT disregarding all the security people that accosted her trying to verify identity and force her through procedures she had absolutely no intention of putting up with. After several violent encounters, where both male guards wound up on the losing end, the night director finally came to her aid and smoothly escorted the whirlwind trailing in fury to the on-line bay where trouble in the optical connection was soon to be dwarfed in comparison with Roxanne's outrage.

The door slammed into the wall so hard both small windows in it burst and the automatic sensing devices that usually opened and closed it automatically were broken beyond repair. "I *hate* incompetence!!" She wailed in the harsh blast a jet engine makes when reversing its thrust after landing. "Somebody's gonna' to pay for this! Somebody! And it's *not* gonna' be me!!"

Crayton rushed white faced across the room towards her flanked by Ghina and other sFx Technos personnel with his hands flared out in supplications for pity. "We were just testing out...something just... must have overloaded the optical circuits...I can't understand why we can't reconnect!"

"Get out of my way you sniveling little shit you're not even old enough to shave, you haven't even learned how to sweat yet and those god dammed two thousand dollar suits you wear don't help a bit! Harold! Where's Harold?" she yelled, "Harold!"

"Oh...I bet it's nothing...really, just a small..." Ghina began to try to smooth things over in her most accommodating salesman-like manner, but did not get a chance to finish because Roxanne took two steps toward her and slapped her across the face with a resounding crack that was heard all the way up into the engineering booth.

"Harold!" she screamed as if calling a recalcitrant lost dog who had gaily pranced down the street despite the sweetest of begging not to.

From out of the dark of the studio an aging man walked with a worn and cynical expression on his face that no one, not even Roxanne could intimidate out of him. His legs were slightly bowed and he walked with a rolling gait that was balanced and sturdy notwithstanding the lack of symmetry, his sleeves were rolled up over massive forearms one of which had a faded tattoo of a woman's name from some long forgotten affair and his left front tooth was missing. His hairline, too, had gone somewhere over the years and so he had given up on caring for it in any way explaining the messy tangle on the back of his head. "I hear ya," he said disgustingly and resigned at the same time, and added just loud enough for Crayton, who stood indignant and fuming, to hear as he passed, "Never send a kid to do a man's job."

Nash squeezed into the recess with four other men and a woman along the side of the dark, cold tunnel that was meant as an escape for just two workers as the automated robot maintenance machine clattered by leaving three or four inches clearance between it and them. The astringent odor of the others' fear and perspiration shocked him as he was pressed up against their bodies surprised to think they were afraid unlike he who wasn't used to such dealings. It was, he mused, their stock and trade. Thankfully, they had hours to go having allowed too much time so he could pull himself together.

A draft of wintry December air flushed through the shaft as it ebbed and flowed with the changes in pressure from the rush above where night took on a fury as if it knew momentous events of men were about to change the course of peoples' lives. Nash tread upon the fulcrum to the path of history and knew these breaks in the seamless fabric of life were rare, freakish moments where individuals were thrust unprepared for the choices they needed to make. He had made his decision. He tended to see things in black and white while others perceived them with infinite shades of gray. Clarity was an attribute he had always aspired to and was one of the characteristics that put him on the fringe out of the mainstream where all ideas and actions were mediated down to the most common denominator. If there was any weakness in him at all now was when it would show.

"Shhi...ht! Hate tight spaces!" exclaimed the short, wiry woman as she pushed back out mid-corridor again once the machine had passed. Her age was impossible for Nash to determine because the face had that drawn, androgynous look of someone who had worked too long in the sun or whose selflessness had erased the stamp of individuality.

Four other men lofted their heavy backpacks and awkwardly, but energetically stumbled after her. He wondered what they held that made them so heavy as they were not large or cumbersome and they had agreed this was not to be a mission of explosive sabotage, as much as that was desired from his first meeting with the Phan. Once explained, however, the leader had accepted the fact that just the tangently opposed transmission was destructive enough, at lease theoretically, for now he promised, but would not guarantee no return with the real goods. They ranged erratically through the tunnel with the wild lack of direction of feral dogs they way he had seen them frantically dashing through the streets in certain sections of the metropolis as if desperately searching for a door leading back into nature which had been irretrievably lost a century or so earlier. Every few hundred yards they would stop because one of them had discovered something needing inspection and would aimlessly give it the once over, animals scent marking defining the boundaries–Nash felt that way now, behind these men who many had considered were over the edge, beyond the borderline where sanity and chaos blended in a razor thin band.

"It's an old tunnel!" one of them barked under his breath dropping back to talk to Nash. "Pre-Kaiein."

"Yea. We figured it was first generation optical."

"I can tell. The terminal tech, back there," he gestured roughly with the shrug of one shoulder, "it was remedial."

Nash suddenly understood that the Phan would be highly skilled in certain disciplines, especially electro-optical and photonics as that was the main conduit of communications and the main proponent of the technological oblivion they believed men were destined to if not for them. He also gleaned something else, that they had a grasp on the sciences for a completely different purpose and that their understandings were based on a deconstruction of the whole machinery upon which lives were based instead of the creation of it. He wondered if the fundamental principles were the same, if axioms still held true as they did for the materialists with their utopian dreams of life without effort which had been their goal, the aims of legions of scientists and technological demigods who had lead successive generations to their view of high-tech enlightenment. The act of living, in their vision, was that of master where the material world was subservient by reason of superior machines and technical wonders that removed all the force from living, that caused the vanishment of all the barriers to immediate gratification, which was, in their view, the prerogative of humans. Man the spirit, the ephemeral, the vital force behind all natural phenomenon was old, antiquated thinking and was relegated to the lore of the past, or the dim mumblings of ministers of the Old Religion, such as himself, or to the ravings of lunatics much like the ones he found himself running with now. Nash felt a renegade kinship with the technophobic anarchists whose simple minded hate of all things industrial, automated and technological was perhaps the word of God kept alive through the only metaphor a modern, virtual world could understand.

"I wouldn't know," he replied, "they all look the same to me."

"Naw. It's all bandwidth, you can tell if you look close." He glanced over at Nash and revealed a strong yet bland appearing face that was void of any comfort and taut with what he imagined was years of anxiety. "This was built before they figured out how to break the bottleneck."

"It was...?"

"Yea." He replied matter-of-factly keeping his gaze straight ahead and lumbering through the darkness with long strides Nash had to struggle to keep up with. "That's when it really got bad. With the new equipment they could shove so much content down the lines that full sized, live action, holographic video with quadraphonic sound and complete interactive, real-time creative feedback became reality overnight. Animators could create avatars who were photo-real, flesh and blood dimensional and could modify their personality traits at a moment's notice according to the feedback from the audience. Each market was mirrored back to itself only in the basest terms because those were the points everyone agreed on. That was the hook, the drug... people were mirrored back to themselves and of course they ate it up. There was a market revolution, that was what brought us out of the Kaiein; new hardware, new programming, new forms of entertainment to absorb all available attention so no one had the chance to realize what a prison they were really in."

"Sort of a drug to mask the pain."

"That's right. People need technology to know they're alive, they've forgotten who they really are. Networks like this were obsolete overnight...just abandoned."

Someone whispered hoarsely, "Mark one!" They had found the short corridor and all slipped into its shelter.

"You really think this'll work?" The man questioned Nash, "'Cause I'd just as soon blow hell out of it as leave here empty..."

"Can't stop a river with a storm," he replied, "it's our best chance."

"Right…" The woman said about twenty feet up ahead, "here's the network connection your friend reported."

"Found it," a voice called from out of the dimness of the ten foot chamber. "Help me with this hatch."

Nash hurried along to the point where he had entered the huge space before and was pleased to see that the massive iron lid with the imprint from the old Metrorail was exactly as they had left it, slightly off center. Back in the main corridor the woman silently flipped off the metal cover of the network repeater terminal and caught it with one hand on the fly while the other tools were readied for the furious work of making a secure connection without causing any fluctuations in the system that some sysops would notice. Although VOX was already on-line, they needed to string an optical feed to connect the remote devices they had brought. It took her just 37 seconds and when it was complete she smiled confidently in the dark, returned the tools to their pouch on her hip and reeled out a filament of industrial optical cable as she carefully moved in to join the others.

The heavy hatch was cracked open and the deep ultramarine light streaked past their fingers catching faces peering down inside for the first time each one frozen with a peculiar wonder painted across it. They must have felt the same eeriness that Nash had when he first gazed into the unearthly environment and at the same instant were slightly awe struck by the sheer scale of the room and its constructed archival containers with glass fronts reflecting azure hues lined up in row after row looking like a miniature Atlantis swimming in the blue light. A low hiss rose from below. Noiselessly the lid was slid to the side and all of them stood around the portal to the other world and looked down weighing if it was worth the cost, or in Nash's worst scenario they were having second thoughts and would just opt to detonate the site and escape ruining the intricate plans he had made and all hopes as well. In a fit of senseless abandon he flipped himself over the edge with such force he nearly missed grabbing onto the first steel rung and as it was only just caught himself from falling headlong onto the concrete floor one hundred and fifty feet below. He had wanted to inspire confidence.

It was cold and the dry, dehumidified air bit into his throat. Quickly recovering his composure he was elated and pleased with his daring lunge as he continued to scramble down afraid to look up, afraid the vacillating Phan may have left or worse were just about to shower him with explosives their radical nature incited beyond reason. Just then he heard a whooshing from overhead and he shuddered when a body hurled past him on the left. Then another whoosh and a body flew by to the right. Each landed sprightly against the wall like two-legged spiders on a single thread in absolute silence grappling down the sheer wall with a speed and grace he could never match locked to the ladder. He climbed down a few more rungs as the two who had passed him nearly disappeared into the twilight of the murky, blue light when the other three came hurtling by in rapid succession and though he was startled, his heart beating so loudly it drowned out the constant hiss of air from below he swore he could not hear a sound as they hit the wall and lowered themselves in huge, plunging leaps slowing their descent only at the last minute gently gliding to earth. He felt foolish as they hurried him down the last few rungs as if he was holding up the operation.

Soon as they were all solidly on the floor and they were still. Each listened intently and breathed in slight breaths barely making a sound if any at all. It was hushed. It was quiescent. Nash moved out across the open toward the nearest cluster of chambers where he remembered the disks being fully aware of how quickly the guards had come upon him last time so careful not to make a sound he ran. All five of the Phan followed without hesitation until they reached the final container where they sat down close to the edge as it met the floor and took bearings and it was then, for the first time, that Nash saw each one was armed, heavily, with automatic weapons and other paraphernalia he assumed were armaments for fighting in close quarters and realized what had been so heavy in their packs.

"How far is it?" one of them whispered.

"Here," Nash stuttered preoccupied not liking the guns, "on the end."

"How's the line?" Someone asked.

"OK...it's OK." The insulated optical cable was being fed off a reel to its destination in the Archive.

Nash could see they were nervous, even in the dim blue light could perceive the glistening sweat on their faces despite the cold and dryness. The floor suddenly felt hard to him and he skimmed his fingertips across its porous, clammy surface connecting solidly with the reality of the moment, feeling his heart beat wildly beneath the turned up shirt collar hoping it would not shake the earth and breathing in measured cadence to keep from gasping for air and panting from the hysteria that was boiling just below the surface. *Every moment in life should be like this one,* he thought and almost started laughing uncontrollably, managing to suppress the urge, but he was still grinning madly in his dark corner. He felt every slight waft of air as it came imperceptibly by him and thrilled at the heightened perceptics; the acute hearing, the clarity of sight and the presence of mind that gave him the complete confidence he could deliver a dissertation, an oratory, a sales pitch on the material aspects of theology to these terrorists right on the spot possibly converting one or another of them in the process. He could not tell if it was glee or the impending event that would have a momentous impact on lives in the future that was affecting him so profoundly, but he nurtured the feeling and drew from its crazed insouciance a kind of courage he had never had the opportunity or necessity to display. In an instant the mystery of the Phan was swept away and he saw that for a cause it would be easy to let one's life become a vehicle. The sacrifice would be a pleasure. The man at the end looked down the line and Nash recognized himself in the expression.

He finally found the entrance of the huge archival chamber he'd remembered followed by the woman with the optical line and one of the men brandishing an automatic rifle. The others stood guard with their weapons poised and their senses on the burning edge. With his hand Nash gripped the door jerking hard as if he half expected it to be secured, locked against his transgression. It swung open unexpectedly throwing Nash off balance and he stumbled back a few feet surprised there was no resistance and that his earlier break-in remained undiscovered. He paused then looking around as if not even the spirits of the air should see him enter and slowly stepped inside hesitating impercep-tibly at the threshold wishing he could retreat to the way it used to be, like a child, into unknowness where everything held an aura of hope. There were clues in life, clues to the final outcome when one was young, but now where he had taken the step, had the knowledge and no matter what justified him he could not deny his actions. Here, now, he knew he was approaching a lair in which lie, if he was right in his assumptions from the first disk, the synthesis of human wisdom. The fabled answers, distilled truths. What would people do with such things? Where they might have come from he couldn't even guess and who in the past had the foresight to discover and organize them remained a mystery, but he was certain that they had been meticulously collected and cataloged by the Rememberers for a reason, and for that same reason they had decided to spirit them away, the golden disks he had first read about in the Canon. It violated his creed, went against his grain and no matter that his alliance to the Old Religion had been firmed up through years of hard and thankless work...the truth belonged to those who would use it, not like a commodity, a service to be marketed or wealth to be hoarded by the elite...it was bread and mortar and sweat and blood. An incredible lightness overcame his senses and he felt faint and dizzy for a moment and then everything was even more clear than before except that there were no doubts lingering, no hesitations left and he continued to the third door, which he opened and entered his two anarchists following him carrying the remote transmitters that McGilvery had developed and stringing optical cable that was securely connected to the old network up in the tunnel. If the virtual technology was meant to entrap men within their minds, make them slaves to a virtual, vicarious existence and subjects of suggestion then the sacred lore contained in the *Golden XiOmas* was the resolution. It was freedom and it was his destiny to deliver it.

The High Advocator was an imposing figure when he was really angry. Despite his age he could wither the spirit of stronger men than himself and send weak spirits into fits of introspective groveling. "You convinced me!" He thundered as he strode on long spindly legs into the network hub of the Church that had been set up in the penthouse of a modern building a short distance from the Old Cathedral. "It was safe! The whole damn thing was supposed to be safe! Perfectly safe!! Convinced me!! God I hate computers!!" Young archivists scrambled left and right.

He stood as a frail yet towering icon of strength amid a technological whirlwind of computers, monitors, optical cables, peripheral equipment of every variety and the latest, state-of-the-art optical repeaters cooled by liquid nitrogen. The whole floor had been torn up and instead of walls cavernous bulkheads of digital equipment loomed. He thrust a fist up into the air unable to find the words to express himself the range of his emotions completely outside the scope of language. The Church had spent millions in acquisitions and constructing this computer center that was the hub of its worldwide information system, but more importantly it tapped into the Archives, which were not supposed to even exist. "Can you imagine the government getting hold of this information?!!" The old man finally screamed. He had been against it from the outset. The data center had been set up under the guise of a private enterprise so that it could maintain its anonymity and all the latest equipment had been brought in except for the one thing they could never afford, the optical network itself. Luckily the old abandoned first generation network was discovered on Church property and through a stroke of fortune directly above the archives. The work of the Archivists for decades had been to transcribe all the collected manuscripts and other riches to digital records the theory being that they would then have the most valuable proprietary system on the planet and could furnish salvation to anyone for a nominal subscription fee. It was to be the Church of the future.

"Somebody tell me what's happening!"

He was immediately surrounded by several young people, all fair skinned and clear eyed looking as if they were the progeny of a lost Aryan tribe.

"We thought it was a power surge."

"A what."

"Fluctuations."

"I see!" the old man said hotly. "Does everyone here know all about this except me?" He pronounced looking around as if there was breach of security.

"Well..."

"I see...!" he scowled.

"Everyone's online here–it's democratic...out of necessity. It's all about the exchange of information."

"Yes I know...! It seems that somebody else feels that way too. Isn't that the problem?"

"We don't know."

"What!?"

"It's not that simple."

"Well...?"

"We think somebody hacked into the network, but until they access something or download something we can't tell for sure. It's only the nodes. Slight power fluctuations."

"The nodes...?" the High Advocator sighed in exasperation. "Fine. Will somebody give me a straight answer around here?"

"We're trying." Was the exasperated reply.

"Try harder!" he boomed causing a general shudder in all personnel within earshot.

"Maybe you should come over here." He lead the High Advocator to a cloister of monitors that were displaying stacked screens of horizontally running readouts on the status of all the network systems. "See this bar here?"

"Yes."

"That's what's wrong."

The old man looked at the fluctuating figures on the screen for a moment and then leaned closer scrutinizing them. "Tell me, what the hell am I looking for?"

"If it was a true break-in it would be flashing and displaying horizontal magenta lines through it. But see, it's not, it's just exhibiting fluctuations."

He looked up unimpressed. "Why then was I informed that there was a break-in?"

"It's almost certain someone's on the other end of those figures, a hacker most likely. You can see his footprint. I don't think it's anything to get too alarmed about actually..."

"You don't...?"

" No... there's bound to be hackers...but it doesn't mean they can get in. We have impenetrable firewalls," he finally stated with great fanfare, "custom programmed."

"Hummm..." the High Advocator mused considering the young man as next to worthless except for the fact that he could talk the talk, not that it made much sense, and sat down in front of the monitor putting his face up to it and watching the tumult of digital figures race by his eyes. "What, then, am I looking at?"

Across the city where the aspirations of millions mingled into a single crying voice that answered to the name of Tempest were other eyes from other windows looking at the same thing yet seeing it differently. Who knows what burdens sleep with a man regardless of the face he shows the world, what cyclones torment him or drive him or hold him down destined to the futility of reaching for something he can never have. The Tempest knows, but isn't saying because into the cauldron everything must come tumbling and it's the process of living that shakes it out, determines who will live and who will not, what is profane and what is sacred, and what is right and what is wrong. The only thing the Tempest doesn't know for certain is what choice a person will make, for that alone defines a man. Nash told her once that to really know someone, to understand him and his motivations...watch him, observe him for a very long time and he will eventually reveal himself. Sabiha observed the screen motionless. The exquisite curve of her neck tapered up into the mass of tangled, black hair that circled her face in violent esthetic flames. She did not betray her emotions yet had come out of a need to shepherd their plot to a resolution. She placed her hand with its long, brown fingers against McGilvery's back just to connect to a virtual world where everything was represented by something else.

Fionica sat close. Her eyes too were fixed on the streaming data flow that hurled itself across the screen in defiance of human understanding. It was quiet except for the hum of electronics, the hiss of air conditioning. The atmosphere was intense. "It just seems like we've all gone too far," she uttered with a strange concentration that drew out each word singularly and in its own unit of time.

Sabiha looked over to her.

"Barriers, just barriers...one after another we've placed them around us and given them power and relied on them for so long that ..." She continued looking at the monitor, "The virtual world has a life of its own, don't you think?"

"Everyone still has their signature, if they're good enough," said McGilvery. "I can see whoever's on the other end of this line and I know they can see me."

"You mean..."

"You bet...someone knows were on."

A hush fell over the room. "What now?!" Sabiha said in alarm.

"Nothing."

"Nothing?"

"That's it...we're modulating the flow to cover our tracks. They'll never pick up the connection to the CommNet network until its too late because all they can tell is that there's a connection somewhere, don't even know where...sort of like creating a back flow of water to compensate for what's being drained out. You can tell something's going on, but can't be certain...unless they..."

"What?"

"...guess."

"Then what?"

They can jam us by scrambling the signals and we wouldn't have time to decode them during the broadcast window."

"Will they?"

"Never happen."

"Why?"

"I'm the best there is. We're already in and they don't even know it...probably think we're hackers still trying to crack the firewalls."

"I hope you're right." Fionica was riveted to the screen. "I hope so." *We have gone too far,* she mused and considered the complex of digital equipment that enveloped and comprised the medical profession. The gene data bank that was the core of all treatment and where each living being was automatically logged into at birth adding their unique combinations of chromosomes as a unique password to the already infinitely incomprehensible complexity that was the crutch upon which everyone relied. She had often wondered as a young doctor what would happen if it were erased, if suddenly all that data ceased to exist and men were thrust into the scenario of having to depend on their wits. How long would it take to remaster the fundamental skills of survival again and what would be the cost? A third of the population she had once figured, maybe half–like the Black Death in 14th century Europe. The basics were slipping away. Communication had even been digitized and automated–few people retained the skills to stand up one against the other and exchange ideas on the spur of the moment, where rhetoric was once a major field of university study now it was just considered an evil of politics. Everyone was secure hidden behind their own personal firewall consisting of electronic hardware, social media, virtual interfaces, email, voicemail, personal digital assistants now ubiquitous tablets hyperconnected to all networks and all beings all the time...and most of all the virtual vicarious nature of life experiences which left people as spiritual zombies, weak and entirely unprepared for any onslaught of the real. It was bound to happen, the temptation was too great and all it took was one significant technological advance for the snowball effect to occur. People were ripe for it, plugged in their whole lives from birth and vulnerable...perhaps subconsciously they had all been part of a movement towards human annihilation and with each scientific advance they moved further and further from the spiritual source. Suddenly she thought of Nash and as she watched the digits flash by on the flat screen imagined his face as if a mirror into his soul. She was pleased; imagination was a quality of life.

The rows of small drawers were just as he'd remembered and no one had disturbed them since the last visit. He had been so frantic then it wasn't certain he would recognize the same place again, but he did. He walked down to the end of the row to the first register where etched onto the metal tab was the inscription *XiOma - 01940 - 01950*. Looking over his shoulder he saw the woman was crouched down setting up the transmission device, testing its connection with the optic filament attached to the old network and making sure VOX could receive and read the data. This was done, once the other tests were complete, with a simple protocol handshake that she initiated manually with the entry of the digit zero. Almost instantaneously a confirmation code appeared on the small illuminated active matrix screen.

What they didn't know was that off in the infinite cyber distances the signal was perceived by hundreds of omnipresent eyes. VOX was only one of them and McGilvery, Fionica, Sabiha and the team thrilled with the anticipation of success. But they were only one.

The sad, wrinkled yet icy blue and vindictive eyes of The High Advocator had also caught it as a glimmer of a flash and a fleeting glimpse of the magenta lines he had been warned about. "You see that?!" *Didja* see that?!" He demanded the young man begin a trace and the Firewall System Crawler software was unleashed to find the source of the break-in and instantly when that occurred all data would be scrambled and corrupted.

But as it sped on its mindless and amoral errand there were others alerted, the digerati all over the city who roamed the networks' systems day and night seeking out anomalies, the quirks and the glitches that would allow them inside to disassemble proprietary systems and wreak mischief. It was human nature and had paralleled the rise of computers in the human mind. They too tracked the course of the game, plotted the progress of the Archivist's Crawler robot and knew far better than any sysops the network lines and which were corporate, which were public access and which were not supposed to be there at all according to available network maps. One after another they logged on alerted by all manner of contrived digital alarms, vidtel calls from friends and fellow enthusiasts, emails, automatic alerts posted on news feeders, blogs, social networks and the like bringing all eyes to life. They were the conscience of the global information system.

"We're online," she said and held open the cartridge port for Nash to insert the first disk.

He looked at his watch and saw that all the extra time he imagined before had now evaporated. The broadcast window was almost upon them. Inching the drawer out effortlessly as it rested on the reverse polarity system he was still afraid it was bugged and listened with all his essence for an alarm. What he heard was worse than he could have ever imagined. It sounded far away and echoed in the reaches outside the doors they had passed through. At first he wasn't quite sure he heard anything, and then thought it sounded like a rhythmic, muted pounding a hammer might make against boards. Then he suddenly placed the staccato sound in memory with what he had seen earlier. It was automatic weapon fire. And it was close. He lifted the first disk from its cradle and held it hovering over the transmission device waiting for exactly the right instant to hit the broadcast window exactly as they had planned. His breath hung in the air somewhere between life and death.

Harold had been tinkering for hours with the network connection hardware and reinstalling systems that had mysteriously been corrupted only emerging from his labors long enough to toss off another pessimistic opinion... "I think you guys got a virus in your software!"...making hearts skip beats and passions run from hot to cold as recriminations and blame shifting became epidemic.

"No virus." Crayton answered coolly inured to the insults he had to endure.

"How can you be so sure?" Roxanne latched onto him vehemently. "If you...!"

"It's not a virus..." Harold stuck his head into the engineering bay once again, "I think the program's corrupted. Must'a been the digital recorder." He smiled in his laconic way.

The whole studio was dark. There was little activity because little had to be done in a virtual world. That was the whole point, experience without the liabilities, incident without responsibility. The irony of it was not lost on Roxanne who sat in the center chair of the bay surrounded by her assistants and the crew from sFx Technos. Down slightly below her were the three technicians manning the board. Across the high front of the darkened room were a dozen monitors all the same size with time codes racing across them in real and network moments. Connection status was displayed in each monitor at the upper left corner, which was a black square at the moment owing to the fact the connection had been lost. Over to one side was a wall devoted to all the other networks and affiliates, one monitor for each, displaying the current program along with all pertinent demographic data for the show accumulated in real time from the interactive nature of the vidtel operating system. It could report who each consumer was down to the way he or she combed their hair. That was essential for the creation of the animated, holographic avatars. It calmed Roxanne to see all the programming up and live reassuring her that the networks were still all OK and the optical lines had not been disrupted by a natural or man-made catastrophe.

She became quiet, sullen and elusive for some reason becoming tired of the constant figuring that went on in her head over the infinite details of the programming and the pressure of comparing them to the details of all the other programming on all the other networks and then sifting it through the moral wasteland her criterion for good work had become–judging everything by its rating and share and of course by the resultant power it generated for her. Her hands gripped the padded arms of the chair as if she were about to depart and was afraid of lift off. It was an historical occasion she knew. Never had there been a moment like this and she considered it, apart from any entertainment value, the apex of technology and therefore of science so far that century. Roxanne was suddenly humble and flushed with a dizzy, spinning reeling that made her slightly nauseous and she had to fight in order to maintain her physical equilibrium. *A drink,* she thought, *need a drink.* The window was approaching through which they had the opportunity to transmit their new art form. Mostafa 'Ali Fayed Al-Razio had blessed it and secretly worked with the sFx Technos team to "fine tune" the subliminal input. That was of no consequence to her, she could not bear to think in any detailed form now, only in the most broad, sweeping generalities because it eased her anxiety.

Roxanne knew it would come off on schedule. There had been no doubt as soon as she had Harold working on it, but enjoyed making

Crayton squirm. It was part of her flawed character and as she grew more silent waiting in the darkened bay looking out past the technicians through the windows into the lightless studios below that were a throwback to when live action actually took place she began to ponder those missing elements. It would have been easy at that moment to change the course of events, to alter history and to deny the equinox of power that lay within a hair's breath of her. Roxanne considered that in a rare moment of self-doubt. Perhaps, she thought, if she could replace her flaws with what was missing, what had always been missing in her existence and what she had longingly, rapaciously and viciously tried to make up for in all other ways...love, it had always been absent and she doubted if she ever even experienced it let alone understood the concept of it. There were times however when the memory of its loss overwhelmed her and she, for brief instants, would have traded her immortality for its compassion. Times like this, but then Harold appeared and the little black square in the corner of the screens again chalked up the digital network connection status and he announced, "We're online again...thanks to me."

The moment had arrived and in the bay all were silent, breathless and forging ahead into the country where none of them had ever been, where no one had been. The images began to flicker on the screen and Roxanne imagined her work going out over all the cables and all the satellite feeds across her virtual dominion where at this instant millions of faces were just turning up to become lost in the virtual. She felt exalted with the power that flooded over her and shuddered visibly in ecstasy.

"Now!!" the woman commanded holding open the device and looking at the digital readout on her wristwatch in the same instant.

Nash, who was listening to the approaching gunfire, had shoved the first disk into its slot and they confirmed it was reading, translating and sending. *Amazing*, he thought and watched the progress indicator as it swept across the small LCD screen indicating how fast the information was uploading. The first one was through. So he thought.

"Wait a minute!" The woman fiddled with the small device and read the message scrawled across its screen. "It's from VOX, the data is being scrambled!"

"Try again!" he yelled, "Try again!"

At VOX they were frantic. The transmission from CWVT had just begun and already they could judge the force of the new virtual technology. On the new-style monitors people could not even watch it without becoming dizzy and disorientated with almost immediate lapses in consciousness. The input from Nash with all the information from the *Golden XiOmas* they had hoped would be transmitted at the same time was garbled and scrambled.

"What is it?" Fionica demanded.

"I think they found us..." McGilvery said angrily, "no, wait its translating now..."

"You sure?"

"Yes!" he said loudly and then punching in some code added, "Look!"

Immediately all the monitors in the room clearly displayed the transmission and the whole team cheered crowding around to watch. It was funneled to VOX from jacking into the old Archives network, then rebroadcast across the patch to the CommNet network and all their affiliates. In certain sectors it was even preempting Roxanne's transmission. It was disruptive as planned. Nash had added an introductory line he hoped would attract some attention. It swept over interrupted screens everywhere.

"YOU ARE BEING PROGRAMMED!"

Across the city other eyes had followed the whole drama unfold and immediately understood what was happening. Social media networks were ablaze as people interacted with people instantaneously messages flying through the ether and flash-solutions were evolved on the fly. Many pairs of eyes witnessed the drama all separate yet in unison. The Archivist's system Crawler had discovered the VOX connection too and had begun to scramble the data just as Nash began to send it, but the phantoms on the system were quicker first one then another then a flurry of them patched in routing transfers until the signal was routed randomly and almost instantly confounding the robot firewall software. Nash's transmission was bypassing the danger and coming through clear and strong via a hundred different routes no one could hope to track down and block. No single person knew what was going on—it was a convocation of amateur hackers.

"Will people get it?" Sabiha asked.

"Well, the truth is out there." McGilvery replied.

Nash frantically fed in the disks one at a time until the job was complete. His shoulders ached from leaning over so long, sweat stung his eyes and he was shaken from the specter of violence just outside, but they had done it. The woman swept up what equipment she could and Nash helped her set charges along all the drawers. He could not leave the *Golden XiOmas* in the wrong hands, so he loaded all the original disks into one of the packs and prepared to destroy the empty files.

They crept cautiously into the deep, murky blue light of the outer chamber. It was absolutely silent. The gunfire had ceased some time past. Nash couldn't see anyone. They stole out the door and slithered along the wall of the huge container back to where they had left the others and both of them nearly jumped out of their skin when four men appeared suddenly in the low light.

"Shooting?" Nash whispered.

"Guards..." one answered, "They couldn't see us any better that we could see them. I don't know why they haven't turned the lights on us! Probably don't want to be seen either—makes 'em better targets. Let's just hope they haven't guessed how we got in here."

"They walked right under me last time." Nash offered up hopefully as the rag-tag group scurried across the vast open floor to the steel rung ladder that waited for them. Lights finally gathered in the distance, individual beams shooting randomly out in a crazed and ominous dance as the security force prepared for an open assault. The woman who held the equipment in her pack scrambled up the ladder first followed by Nash with the disks and the others. At the top Nash could just make out the moving figure of a guard below lifting his weapon. Some had come without lights in hope of surprise. It was then he detonated the files and there was an incredibly huge, deafening explosion. The immense container jumped three feet off the ground with the blast, but that was dwarfed by the massive slam of the structure as it came back down upon the concrete floor again. Guards were knocked off their feet by the repercussion and as the last man crawled through the opening the cover was slid in place and tightly secured.

Nash stood at the open window and watched the traffic below. He had been up most of the night with a man who could no longer bear the force of living and had ministered to him with what new knowledge he had learned until the man felt better and then left. It was nearly morning and he could just see the thin line of light that glowed in the East as a precursor to the dawn. Cold permeated his latest apartment where he had neglected to keep the heat on. Wind stirred outside in brief gusts, breaths of the coming day awakening. An overcoat drooped down from his shoulders and he had not yet removed his scarf.

It had been a long time since his discovery of the *Golden XiOmas* and though they were being studied thoroughly by scholars and scientists alike, both lay and clerical, none could agree on where they had come from. It was clear they had originated in the late twentieth century long before the Kaiein and were a remarkably detailed, completely unprecedented system of codified knowledge about life, the human spirit and the mind. They and their author had been lost in time.

The effects on society were striking, but not immediate, or as Nash had hoped. The information they had broadcast was gradually absorbed into the culture and soon it became known what the networks were doing to people, but much of it was too arcane or complex to be absorbed easily by the masses and so it passed over them. Many did not care seeking personal oblivion out of self-abnegation or a simple addition to the virtual drug that already had a vise grip on their souls. The network launched high-velocity PR campaigns funded by deep pockets as damage control to discredit the information and any implied allegations of wrongdoing. The disks were duplicated and shared with educational institutions and research centers that dissected them interminably providing endless grist for scientific journals across the globe helping many academics to gain institutional tenure. Almost immediately there was a conservative backlash questioning the validity of the information and the authenticity of the disks judging them an affront to belief in God. Legislative hearings were held to determine if any of this information should be allowed in the public schools. Government agencies all had ongoing investigations to find out if any laws had been broken or the public defrauded in any way and all had preconceived agendas that things were not as transparent as they should be. Stories circulated that the disks were a hoax perpetrated by the Phan in some anarchistic scheme to subvert technology authored by those who lived in hidden terror that anyone anywhere might get help, become better than them and crush them just as they would do to others if they had the opportunity. Journalists had a field day linking every sex scandal and seedy innuendo to the new discovery obfuscating the truth in favor of those coveted yearly awards that so inflated their resumes. The popular media took jibes with covert witty stories and exposés that made anyone seeking truth look foolish and gullible and ran up viewership of their scandal-fueled channels. Few observed that the information revealed on the disks when used produced remarkable changes for the better in people's lives...and the wars raged on just as they had for millennia unchanged by the Fates–though in the end gods and men alike had to submit to them,.

Nash had already found this out. He was on the run now. A fugitive. People were after him. He had betrayed his Church by invading their Archive and releasing highly sensitive information, which the clergy vehemently denied had come from them as the "Archive" was just a rumor–it didn't really exist. They could not press charges by reason of the denial, but he could never have returned even to his office to collect personal things. An encyclical was issued indicting him as an apostate and fair game for any misfortunes that might befall him, the latter ambiguous enough to be a veiled threat. Mustofa Hisham Mostafa 'Ali Fayed Al-Razio was so enraged he had resurrected an ancient Islamic tradition and invoked a fatwa on Nash personally judging him to be unholy–rumor had it he even put out a contact on his life. Roxanne, struggling through disgrace and penance before Hisham Al-Razio, was spearheading the search for the most qualified personnel to do the job just as she had when finding the right team for her programming production. As a consequence Nash moved frequently and lived in the shadowlands. He confided in no one, not even Sabiha in order to distance himself from those he cared about to keep them safe. He had not seen Fionica since the break-in, and had spoken to her only once. He communicated through his social media channels, which were somewhat anonymous and enigmatic and through which no one could trace his whereabouts. He had been an outsider all his life perhaps, he now thought, as preparation for this.

Though many copies of the disks had been distributed, Nash had kept the originals. He held them out of some intrinsic understanding that they needed to be safeguarded by someone who could comprehend their immeasurable value. In that sense, he was not much different than the Archivists of the Old Religion and in fact had taken on a lifetime vow just as they. In so doing he kept his purpose alive and was still, in his own world, an active member of the Church of the Old Religion. When McGilvery asked him where they were, he only replied, "They're safe." Much of his time was now spent in their study so he could utilize the knowledge gained to help others and in hope of a future. The truth, he knew, belonged to those who used it.

He loved the old buildings and as he placed his hand on the wooden windowsill and lamented the loss of the forests that had made them possible. There were not many left. All things change. He remembered how he had felt approaching the future before as if something was missing and had always attributed it to a rift in his own character, but now he knew that somehow he had become different. *Man cannot live without hope*, he spoke out loud to himself quietly as light began to fill the indigo shadows of night and he gazed out over the magnificent sweep of the city stretching its sinewy arms, bending its strong back and rearing up on its legs ready for anything, coming to life for one more day.